MARGARET TRUMAN'S

DEADLY MEDICINE

A CAPITAL CRIMES NOVEL

▸ DONALD BAIN ◂

A TOM DOHERTY ASSOCIATES BOOK | NEW YORK

MARGARET TRUMAN'S DEADLY MEDICINE: A CAPITAL CRIMES NOVEL

Copyright © 2016 by Estate of Margaret Truman

A Forge Book
Published by Tom Doherty Associates
175 Fifth Avenue
New York, NY 10010

www.tor-forge.com

Forge® is a registered trademark of Macmillan Publishing Group, LLC.

ISBN 978-0-7653-7989-4

Our books may be purchased in bulk for promotional, educational, or business use. Please contact your local bookseller or the Macmillan Corporate and Premium Sales Department at 1-800-221-7945, extension 5442, or by e-mail at MacmillanSpecialMarkets@macmillan.com.

First Edition: June 2016
First Mass Market Edition: December 2017

Printed in the United States of America

0 9 8 7 6 5 4 3 2 1

Praise for the Novels of Margaret Truman

For my mother, father, and sister.

*Thank you for a loving upbringing that
I wouldn't trade with anyone.*

ACKNOWLEDGMENTS

For Margaret Truman, friend and collaborator.

Clifton Daniel Truman, who has kept the Truman spirit alive.

Editor Bob Gleason and agent Bob Diforio, true professionals and friends.

MARGARET TRUMAN'S

DEADLY
MEDICINE

1

Flo's fashions was located on upper Wisconsin Avenue, at the tail end of Georgetown's main commercial drag. Flo Combes, lady friend of Robert "Don't Call Me Bobby" Brixton, had opened the women's clothing boutique six months ago and all signs pointed to it becoming a success. Word had gotten around that the lines of American-made clothing she featured combined casualness with a touch of flair, and business had been brisk. She'd owned a similar shop in Savannah, Georgia, when she and Brixton had lived together in that genteel southern city and before they ended up in Washington, D.C.— after a brief detour to their native Brooklyn—and it was in a retail setting that Flo felt most comfortable.

Although Brixton was proud of Flo and her determination to open the shop, he had mixed emotions, which he managed to keep to himself—for the most part. Since returning to D.C. and establishing his private detective agency in a small suite adjacent to the law offices of Mackensie Smith, Brixton's patron saint in the nation's capital, Flo had been his decorator, confidante, painter, booster, lover, and receptionist/secretary. Her decision to strike out on her own and open the boutique had sent Brixton into a funk that negatively impacted the investigative work he did, and it had taken pep talks from Smith and his wife, Annabel, as well as some gentle soothing of his ruffled feathers by Flo, before he snapped out of it and accepted the fact that she was no longer in his outer office greeting clients with her infectious smile. Flo had personally chosen her replacement, Eloise Warden, aptly named as far as Brixton was concerned, a stern, no-nonsense middle-aged woman with a headful of tight graying curls who was every bit as efficient as Flo had been, but who lacked her beauty and outgoing personality. Had Flo deliberately picked Ms. Warden from the roster of women who had applied for the job, most of them young and sexy, to head off competition for Brixton's affection? Flo had flared when he'd raised that possibility and he'd wisely not brought it up again.

On this lovely spring day Brixton stood across the street from the boutique and admired a new green-and-white awning that had been installed above the large window and door. He'd just returned to the city from time spent following a young Department of Agriculture bureaucrat whose wife was convinced that he spent his lunch hours visiting a lover. Brixton followed the guy from the Department of Agriculture building to a Virginia town where he entered a one-story building in which customers raced miniature cars around a large, elaborate track using a joystick to control the cars' speed. Brixton figured that as long as he was there he might as well sign up for a session, too, rather than sit outside in a hot car waiting for his target to emerge. He ended up racing the man he'd been following, a pleasant way to spend the afternoon although he lost every race.

"You come here often?" Brixton asked casually, realizing that he sounding like a guy using the oldest icebreaker in the world to chat up a woman at a bar.

"Every chance I get," the man said. He was short, chubby, prematurely balding, and wore thick glasses that rendered his eyes twice their normal size. Hardly the lothario type.

"I really enjoy this place," the man said after winning their fourth race. "My wife won't let me race real cars so I come here. It's an addiction I suppose."

"Like sex?" Brixton asked as he positioned his small yellow race car at the starting line in preparation for the fifth race.

"Sex? Addiction? I wouldn't know. You have that problem?"

"Me? No. But I can see how this can get in your blood. It's my first time."

"You'll get the hang of it. Ready, set, go!"

They shook hands as they left the racing hobbyists' emporium.

"A pleasure meeting you Harold," the alleged cheater said, using the name Brixton had assumed. "What do you do for a living?"

"Ah, I'm self-employed. Finance."

"Well, hope to see you here again. Have a nice night."

Brixton surreptitiously followed the guy home until he pulled into his driveway. On his way back to the District Brixton could only laugh at what he would consider writing in his report to the suspicious wife: "Husband skipped out of work and spent the afternoon being aroused while playing with his joystick." *Nah. Don't be a wise guy Robert. Make the wife happy by reporting that her husband's passion wasn't another woman, just little model cars going around in circles.*

He dodged traffic as he crossed Wisconsin Avenue and stepped into the shop where Flo was busy with a customer. She waved and flashed him a smile. "Robert," she called, "I want you to meet someone."

Brixton circumnavigated clothing racks and went to where Flo stood with a strikingly beautiful woman who was admiring her image in a full-length mirror.

"Jayla," Flo said, "this is the Robert I've been telling you about."

The woman with the unusual name smiled at Brixton. That she had African American blood in her genetic makeup was obvious from the rich cinnamon sheen of her face and hands. Her features were what writers termed "classic," a thin nose in perfect proportion to her facial architecture, somewhat angular, a lovely set of lips above a proud chin, all of it framed by ebony hair that glistened in the shop's overhead lighting. Brixton recognized the tan fitted dress she wore. Flo had shown that model to him when the shipment had arrived two months ago from the San Francisco designer with whom she'd forged a close working relationship.

"Hi," Jayla said, extending long, slender hands tipped in red to match her lipstick. "Flo is always talking about you."

"Probably better that I not know what she says about me," Brixton said through a grin.

"Would I ever say anything bad about you, Robert?" Flo asked, feigning hurt.

"Probably, but then I suppose I deserve it." He kissed Flo on the cheek and said to the customer, "I see you're wearing one of Flo's creations, Ms. . . ."

"King, but please call me Jayla."

"I don't create it," Flo protested. "Jason in San Francisco creates it. I just sell it."

"But you have a very good eye for what looks good," Jayla said.

"I'll accept that," Flo said.

"I second it," Brixton threw in. "Nice name, Jayla King."

"I obviously didn't choose it," Jayla said. She turned to Flo. "I really like this dress."

She disappeared into one of three fitting rooms at the rear of the boutique.

"A knockout of a woman," Brixton commented.

"Isn't she beautiful? She's a scientist."

"A beautiful scientist," Brixton said reverentially.

"She does medical research for a company in Bethesda."

"Maybe she can give me something for my bald spot," Brixton said. "It's getting bigger."

"It's supposed to. You're a man. Get a testosterone shot."

"Bad for the prostate."

"I wouldn't know about that."

Jayla emerged from the dressing room wearing the new dress. "I love it," she announced, doing a pirouette in front of the mirror. As she did, her cell phone, which rested on a small table next to her purse, sounded. She picked it up and said, "Hello? . . . Yes, this is Jayla . . . Eugene? . . . Is something wrong? . . . Oh, no . . ."

She sat heavily in one of two tan barrel chairs near the dressing rooms.

"How, Eugene? . . . When? . . . Oh, my God . . . Yes, of course I'll come . . . As soon as I can . . . What? . . . The lab? . . . Why? . . . I know, I know, I'll know soon enough . . . Thank you for calling, Eugene . . . Yes, good-bye."

"Something wrong?" Flo asked her.

She slumped in the chair, her face a portrait of despair. "That was my father's lab assistant. He's been killed."

"The lab assistant?" Brixton asked.

"No, my father. He's been murdered." Her fingers trembled as she brushed a hand through her hair.

Brixton and Flo expressed their dismay at the news and asked if they could do anything.

"Thank you, no," Jayla said. "I have to get home and pack, book a flight." She realized that she was wearing a dress that she hadn't purchased. "I love it but—"

"I'll put it aside for you," Flo said. "Please, Jayla, let us know if there's anything we can do."

Jayla changed back into her own clothes, gave Flo a brief hug, and shook Brixton's hand. "It was good to meet you," she said. "I have to run."

"Travel safe," Brixton said. "Sorry for the reason for your trip."

After Jayla had left, and the shop was empty aside from Brixton and Flo, Brixton took a bag of trash to a dumpster in the alley behind the shop. He returned, made sure that the back door was securely locked, and rejoined Flo. "Her father was murdered, huh?" he said. "Where's she from?"

"New Guinea. Papua New Guinea."

"Where's that? In Africa?"

"Somewhere near Australia. I feel terrible for her. She's a terrific person and a good customer. Let's turn out the lights and go home. It's been a busy day."

2

PAPUA NEW GUINEA

Jayla King caught the last flight that evening from Washington to Los Angeles where she would connect with a Qantas flight to Sydney, Australia. It had been a mad scramble to make the flight. She'd raced home to haphazardly pack a carry-on bag, and called Renewal Pharmaceuticals' CEO and president, Walt Milkin, to tell him that she wouldn't be at work the following day due to a family emergency.

"Your father was *murdered*?" he said, his voice mirroring his shock. "You take all the time you need, Jayla."

She called a car service to rush her to Dulles Airport where she boarded the United flight a little after nine. It was fourteen hours earlier in Papua New Guinea, seven o'clock in the morning. It had been three A.M. there when her father's assistant, Eugene Waksit, had called her cell to deliver the devastating news.

Because she'd booked the flight at the last minute she ended up in a middle seat, between a middle-aged woman with a seemingly endless supply of chocolate-covered fruit candies and who obviously wanted to engage in conversation, and a heavyset man with a perpetual scowl who opened his laptop computer immediately upon sitting and made a show of angling it away from Jayla, who wasn't the least bit interested in what was on his screen. As she tried to get comfortable in the hard, narrow coach seat she wished that she'd been born shorter. The back of the seat belonging to the passenger in front almost touched her knees; with any luck he wouldn't decide to recline once they'd taken off.

Jayla King stood three inches shorter than six feet thanks to her father, a lanky man who seemed always to be leaning slightly forward. "You have a socialite's slouch," a colleague used to say, which amused her father. His untamable shock of white hair also elicited the comment, "You have the look of a mad scientist," which also brought forth a hearty laugh. Dr. Preston King's laugh was always at the ready, and Jayla heard his laugh as though he was there with her as the flight attendants closed the aircraft's doors and the recorded preflight instructions came through the speakers.

There hadn't been time to cry between the moment she'd received the bad news and boarded the 767 to Los Angeles. Now strapped in the metal tube that would wing her on the first leg of her trip, the tears came softly, quietly. She did her best to keep her sorrow to herself, not wanting others to be aware of her sadness. It was hers alone to suffer.

Once the plane was airborne, the passenger in the seat in front of her reclined his seatback as far as it would go, and Jayla wished that she was wealthy enough to have booked a first-class seat, assuming one had been available. While well paid at her job at the Renewal Pharmaceutical Company in Bethesda, whose financing came mostly from venture capitalists, she knew that she would never be rich. Not that she aspired to riches, aside from when forced to squeeze into a torturous airline seat.

She'd achieved her lifelong dream in 2010 of earning her PhD in molecular biology from the Australian National University in Canberra. Landing a job as a researcher in the United States with Renewal Pharmaceuticals added to her joy and sense of accomplishment. The memory of her father beaming at the ceremony when she was awarded her doctorate brought more silent tears as she maneuvered her body to shield her emotions from her seatmates. She'd managed politely to fend off attempts at conversation by the woman next to her, who eventually fell asleep. Jayla wanted to sleep, too, but each time she closed her eyes her father's smiling face roused her: "Just remember, Jayla," he'd often said, "medical research is controlled by those with money, big money. Never let their money corrupt you. Always be true to yourself."

Her sudden audible burst of tears captured the attention of her male seatmate, who looked up quizzically. "Just relax," he said. "These planes don't go down." He went back to his laptop, and Jayla managed a grim smile. He'd thought she was afraid of flying. At least he hadn't grabbed her hand to offer comfort. Her only concern about flying was whether she would arrive in Los Angeles in time to catch the Qantas flight that left a few minutes before midnight. On other trips to Sydney she'd broken up the long, tiring trip with a layover in L.A, but this time was different, of course. Her only thought was to get to her hometown of Port Moresby, Papua New Guinea, as quickly as possible.

He's dead? Murdered?

How could it be?

Headwinds from west to east had thankfully been light, and the flight arrived at LAX a few minutes early. She raced through the terminal with her small carry-on bag, made it through the second layer of Security without incident, and was the last passenger to board the Qantas 747 before its doors closed. This time she had a row to herself and managed to doze off, awakening when the cabin crew served meals, and when the captain announced that they were approaching Sydney where, he happily reported, the weather was sunny and pleasant.

Her nap on the flight had served only to contribute to her grogginess as she deplaned at Terminal One in Sydney's Kingsford Smith International Airport. She passed through Customs and headed in the direction of the Air Niugini desk where she was told that the next flight to Port Moresby would depart in two hours. She purchased a ticket, found the nearest restaurant, and took a chair in an exterior section that jutted out into the terminal, affording a view of the multitude of passengers scurrying to and from their flights. She'd sat in that same outdoor café with her father during a previous trip home.

He'd flown to Sydney from Port Moresby to meet his daughter and only child and they'd spent a glorious four days together, taking in shows, dining in good restaurants, and catching up on their respective lives. She hadn't accompanied him back to Port Moresby that time—her vacation days were few—and now wished that she had. While her father was unfailingly pleasant and at times even gregarious, it was in Papua New Guinea (PNG) that his good nature and belief in his work truly emerged.

Dr. Preston King had trained to become a physician in Sydney and had begun his medical practice at the Royal North Shore Hospital in that city, where he advanced through the ranks to become the youngest doctor in the hospital's history to be named head of a department, in this case the bustling emergency room. He was revered by staff and patients alike, although he could be harsh on those who didn't live up to his high standards. Medicine was his life; he hadn't married by the age of forty although he'd had affairs and was considered a prize catch by the many single women with whom he interacted, professionally and otherwise.

But Preston King had another passion besides medicine, and that was anthropology, particularly the indigenous tribes of New Guinea, the world's second largest island, trailing only Greenland. He devoured books by anthropologists, and began making trips to the island to learn firsthand about its myriad tribes. It was during one of those trips in 1982 that he developed a powerful sense of mission to bring an improved health system to the island's people. Upon his return he made a shocking announcement to his superiors at the Sydney hospital: "I am resigning and moving to Papua New Guinea."

A year after settling in Port Moresby and opening his clinic, King fell in love with Lanisha, one of his nurses, a stately, sensuous black woman whose Melanesian heritage traced back thousands of years to one of hundreds of primitive tribes. Eyes were invariably raised over the marriage between the fair-skinned Australian physician and his ebony wife, which cut into their social life. It meant little to King. He'd become immersed in his work, both as a clinician, and in the laboratory he'd built as an addition to their modest house.

A year later Lanisha gave birth to a daughter, Jayla, whose arrival filled them with unimaginable pride and joy. For Lanisha that ecstasy was short-lived. She died of pneumonia when Jayla was three, leaving Dr. King with the task of being both mother and father to the child.

When Jayla was sixteen, her father left her at home in Port Moresby while he traveled to the jungles of the Sepik River where he was privileged to witness the coming of manhood in native boys. They were initiated by having their backs, chests, and thighs sliced open with a bamboo razor, one cut after another until, despite having ingested a drink made from coconut leaves to dull the pain, they passed out. Ash was then worked into the gaping wounds to create what resembled the backs of crocodiles, and the wounds were rubbed with clay. The young men then waited together for days in a special hut until they were told by tribal elders that they were now men and could rejoin the world, having been "ingested" by the mighty crocodile and emerging with the power of those powerful, mystic reptiles that ply the waters of Papua New Guinea. Those with the most grievous wounds were considered especially attractive to the tribe's females.

"A brutal rite of manhood," Dr. King told Jayla after he'd returned and had recounted his firsthand look at the practice, "but with important meaning for the tribes. Despite the cruel nature of the initiation, they are peaceful, kind people, and treated me with respect."

By the time King's wife had died he'd purchased acreage in the Sepik River region, a remote area of the island on its northwest corner named after the winding river, where many of Papua New Guinea's primitive tribes still lived. He didn't buy the tract as a land speculator. He'd become infatuated with the need to develop more effective pain medications after treating patients with intractable suffering, and it was in his lab that he'd begun experimenting with natural herbs and plants grown in his four-acre plot in search of a more potent medicine without the addictive qualities of the day's popular prescribed painkillers. To say that he was dedicated to that goal was not an overstatement.

Jayla was so consumed with memories of her father and of growing up in Port Moresby that she almost failed to hear the boarding call for her Air Niugini flight and had to run to the gate.

She was going to what had been her home, but it would not be the same without him. She handed her ticket to the gate agent and prepared for the final four-hour leg of her sorrowful journey to Papua New Guinea, seventeen hundred miles away—a million miles away in her heart.

3

PORT MORESBY, PAPUA NEW GUINEA

Jayla had called Eugene Waksit from the Sydney airport restaurant to give him her arrival time at Port Moresby's Jacksons International Airport, and her father's assistant had assured her that he'd be there to meet her flight.

She'd had mixed emotions about Waksit since the day her father hired him. A Papuan by birth, he'd moved from his remote village to Sydney to complete his advance degrees and had answered an ad that Dr. King had placed in an Australian medical journal, more a monthly newspaper that reported on the latest medical news and listed job openings. King had arranged a day of interviews at a Sydney hotel, and had chosen Waksit from among the seven young men and women who'd responded. Handsome and self-assured, and surprisingly fair-skinned considering his background, Waksit had won King over by waxing poetic about his ambition to work alongside a man like him in his quest to bring quality health care to the indigenous people, and to develop a more effective pain reliever. He'd previously attended a medical conference in Sydney at which King had presented a paper on his work with native medicinal plants, and told King that his presentation had been inspiring.

"I'd give anything to work alongside you," he'd said.

To which King replied, "Then pack your bags and get to Port Moresby. You're hired."

Jayla's conflicting reactions to Waksit couldn't be neatly packaged. He'd always been unfailingly courteous and pleasant with her. He'd also made romantic overtures, which she'd deftly sidestepped. Not that she didn't find him attractive. She did. He was tall and physically fit, with eyes the color of jade, and a wide smile. She was aware that he had been involved with a number of women in Papua New Guinea, and in Australia when vacationing there. But there was something about him that put Jayla on edge.

Disingenuous? Smug? She'd conjured many adjectives to describe her feelings about him, none of which adequately nailed it down. Maybe it was his use of cheap cologne called Cuba Black with which he liberally doused himself that contributed to her avoiding spending too much time with him. She'd once asked her father how he could stand being in the lab or clinic with Eugene and his piquant cologne. Her father replied, "I never notice it," which was typical of Dr. Preston King. His focus on whatever he was doing at the moment was intense, so much so that nothing around him ever seemed to register. Besides, he seemed to have unbridled faith in the young man, which Jayla never questioned. But she knew that for all his education and worldliness Dr. Preston King could be too trusting of people at times, too willing to accept the image they presented and unwilling to question their motives. Of course those qualities contributed to her father's openness and charm, but also, in her estimation, posed a potential weakness.

Waksit was at the gate when Jayla arrived. Seeing the first person from her father's life since receiving words of his murder activated a switch in her. She let her tears flow freely as he wrapped his arms around her and said repeatedly, "I know, I know, Jalya. Let it out. Don't bottle it up."

Jayla pulled herself out of his arms and brought herself

under control. She accepted his handkerchief. "Murdered!" she said. "Who would do such a thing?"

"That's what the police are trying to determine," Waksit replied, his pessimistic tone not lost on her. Port Moresby was one of the world's most crime-ridden cities, and too many of the local constabulary's officers were known to be corrupt. The city was particularly dangerous for women; rape was commonplace, including sexual assaults by police officers. Another reason for Jayla to be grateful Waksit had come to meet her.

"Luggage?" he asked.

"Only what I'm carrying."

"I'm parked right outside."

He took her arm and they headed for the airport's exit.

"It's hot," Jayla commented when they reached the outdoors.

"Unusually so," Waksit agreed.

Waksit's Range Rover was parked in a restricted area, and a uniformed member of the airport's security force eyed it suspiciously.

"I've only been here for a few minutes," Waksit said pleasantly. "Picking up a passenger."

"You are in the wrong place," the officer said. "No parking zone."

Waksit reached in his pocket and pulled out a five-kina banknote with the Port Moresby parliament building prominently displayed on its face. He handed it to the officer, who shoved it in his pocket and walked away without saying a word.

"Nothing's changed," Waksit said to Jayla through a sardonic laugh.

"*Everything* has changed for me," she responded sadly as he opened the door for her.

Waksit negotiated a construction zone that held up traffic. Once clear of it he gunned the engine and sped down a narrow street leading from the airport to the center of town, causing pedestrians to scatter.

"Slow down," Jayla said brusquely.

"Sorry," he said, decreasing his speed. "Bad habit." He stole a glance at her. "I'm sorry to have been the one to break the sad news to you, Jayla."

"I'm sure it wasn't easy for you," she said. "How did it happen? When?"

"The night before I called."

"How? I mean, how did he die?"

"It was—well, it wasn't pleasant, Jayla. Someone used a knife. He was in his lab working late."

"How is Tabitha?"

"She's a wreck."

Tabitha had been hired by Jayla's father shortly after Jayla's mother had died. She'd been with the family ever since, becoming Dr. Preston's trusted and beloved housekeeper once her services as Jayla's nanny were no longer needed.

"She must have been devastated," Jayla said.

"She hasn't stopped crying," he said as he turned a corner and pulled up in front of the house that had been Jayla's childhood home. "I cried, too, once the shock had worn off. I couldn't believe that it happened."

He turned off the ignition and watched Jayla's face as she stared at the modest house that her father had maintained in pristine condition. The yellow paint was fresh, the green shutters immaculate, a small patch of lawn and flower beds in front carefully tended.

"Where are the police?" she asked.

"They finished up their investigation."

"And left the property unattended?"

"They knew that Tabitha is here a lot, and that I spend most of my time in the lab. They're stretched thin. An investigator from the Australian Federal Police is in charge. He works with two locals from the constabulary."

"It happened in the lab?"

"Yes."

"How did someone get in?"

Waksit shrugged. "You know how lax your father was. The house had been broken into a few times over the years. I used to get on him all the time about becoming more security conscious, locking up when he went out, having an alarm system installed, at least in the lab. He always agreed to appease me, but he never followed through. Too late for alarm systems now."

Waksit was right; her father had been blasé about his personal safety. At the same time she resented criticism of him, as accurate as it might be.

She opened her door and stepped onto the sidewalk. Waksit came around the tan-and-black Range Rover and stood next to her. "Want me to go in with you?" he asked.

"Please."

There were two entrances to the house. One led into the living quarters, the other to the clinic where Dr. King treated the city's underclass. "The only way to judge a society," he often said, "was how it treats its less fortunate and most vulnerable." That message was deeply instilled in his only child and she often cited it to friends, and to colleagues at work.

The laboratory was to the rear of the building, accessible from both the living quarters and the clinic.

Jayla took tentative steps into the house's small vestibule. Hanging on the wall to her left was a rendering of the King family coat of arms. A portrait of her mother posed in front of a huge wild begonia bush dominated the opposite wall. She saw herself in the handsome woman in the painting, staunch and proud, a hint of a knowing smile on her face.

"You okay?" Waksit asked.

"Yes, I'm fine."

The living room was dark; the drapes had been pulled tightly shut, allowing only tiny slivers of light to penetrate the gloom where the fabric didn't meet. Waksit switched on a table lamp. Jayla stood in the center of the room and slowly turned to take in the familiar setting.

A folding wooden game table captured her attention. On it was a chessboard; she and her father had spent many pleasant hours opposing each other, with him winning a majority of the time while Jayla managed to salvage an occasional match. Had he let her win on those occasions? He'd denied it the few times she accused him of it but she still had her doubts. He would feign exasperation when she declared "Checkmate." "Is the clinic closed down?" she asked.

"Pretty much," Waksit said, "but I've been seeing certain patients." He laughed. "I've been practicing medicine without a license, I suppose, but no one has complained."

"Had the clinic been busy before?" she asked.

"It was always busy. Want to go there?"

"I'd like to see where . . ."

He waited for her to finish her thought.

"I'd like to see the lab."

They passed through the living and dining rooms until reaching the kitchen where the door to the lab was located.

"You don't have to, you know," Waksit said.

Jayla seemed unsure whether to proceed. She'd spent many hours in the lab with her father, and it was this exposure to the world of research that had determined her career path. Visions flashed through her mind of her father wearing a white lab coat and heavy apron, hunched over whatever he was examining at the time, his total attention directed at what was displayed before him. She knew, of course, that he would die one day, and could accept that reality. But to have been savagely murdered by someone wielding a knife was beyond any reality.

Who? Why? To what end?

She stepped into the lab, turned on the overhead fluorescent lights, and stood silently, allowing the moment to wash over her. Everything seemed in perfect order, the two long tables that held the paraphernalia of a laboratory—two microscopes, Bunsen burners, an operant conditioning chamber, a row of glass beakers in their racks, reagent bottles, Petri dishes, test tubes, and an expensive Glen mixer that mixed ingredients from native plants and herbs while expelling air from the mixture—and against a wall a large commercial microwave oven as well as a full-size refrigerator and freezer.

"He loved working in here," Waksit said.

"This was his real home," Jayla said, skirting one of the tables until her eyes went to the floor where a faint brown stain had created an irregular pattern on the white stones.

"He was found here?" Jayla asked, pointing.

"Yes. The police did a cursory cleanup, and Tabitha worked for an hour after they left. The stone is porous. The blood—"

"I know, Eugene. His blood seeped into the stone."

"They'll have to remove those stones and replace them."

She turned to take in more of the gleaming white space. "Did the police come up with any clues as to who did this?"

"They didn't mention any when I spoke with them."

"Did my father have enemies that you know of?"

Waksit sighed and shook his head. "I suppose we all develop enemies as we go through life, but I didn't know of anyone in particular. It was probably a thug, a drug addict looking for money. Your father must have encountered him and—"

"Was anything taken?"

"I checked. The police asked the same question. His notebooks are gone."

"*His notebooks?* Where he kept his findings, the results of his experiments?"

Waksit nodded. "They're not where he usually kept them. The sealed packets of herbs and medicinal plants he'd been experimenting with are also missing."

"A drug addict might take the herbs, but wouldn't bother to take notebooks," Jayla said sternly.

"Of course not."

"Then—?"

"I can't imagine why they were taken, Jayla. I haven't the slightest idea. It was the first thing I noticed when the police allowed me into the lab."

"Did you inform them about the missing items?"

"Yes. They questioned me, of course, but they quickly realized that I admired, even loved your father, and could hardly be considered a suspect."

Jayla ignored his comment and continued her slow, deliberate path around the tables, taking mental inventory of everything she saw. "Where is Tabitha?" she asked.

"At her daughter's place in Koki. She visits her occasionally."

"I'd like to see her. You say that she was the one who found him."

"Yes, poor thing. She's getting old, Jayla. She has health problems. Cancer. Your dad had been treating her for pain."

"You said you spoke with the police. I would like to do that, too."

"I have the name of the Australian who's in charge. I can call and set up an appointment for tomorrow. They'll want you to identify the body."

"I assumed that they would. I dread it."

Jayla excused herself and climbed the stairs to the tiny bedroom that was hers while growing up. She sat on the bed and let the tears roll, heaving against the spasms that knotted her stomach and caused her to lose her breath. She knew that she had to pull herself together. Her father's death was fact, and what mattered now was the aftermath, the resolution of what he'd left behind and answers to why he'd been killed, and who killed him.

Drained, she returned downstairs where Waksit waited.

"You'll stay here tonight?" he asked.

"No, I'd rather not," she said. "I'll go to a hotel."

"The Grand Papua on Mary Street? It was your father's favorite when he had visitors."

"That will be fine. Have burial plans been set?"

"The police will know more about that. Come on. We'll get you settled into your room and have dinner together."

Two hours later, after checking in, unpacking what little she'd brought with her, and freshening up, Jayla met Waksit on the terrace of the Grand Bar where he'd ordered two bottles of Australian red wheat beer and an appetizer platter of cold seafood.

"I called Dad's attorney from my room," she told him as they looked out over the city, and the Coral Sea in the distance. "I'm seeing him tomorrow at three. Dad had a will. The lawyer will go over it with me when we meet. Mr. Taylor and my father go back a long way. They were good friends. I know that I can trust him to handle everything that has to be done."

"I called the detective while I was waiting for you. You have an appointment at ten."

Waksit took a drink from the bottle—Jayla preferred a glass—and his expression told her that he had something else, something difficult to say.

"Eugene?" she said. "What is it?"

"More bad news, I'm afraid. Your father's acreage in the Sepik region."

"What about it?"

"It's been vandalized."

"*Vandalized*? How do you vandalize four acres of crops?"

"I really don't know all the particulars. All I know is that during the night someone set the field on fire and bulldozed what was left."

Jayla had been about to take a sip of her beer. Instead, she brought the glass down on the table with such force that its contents spilled over the rim. Waksit was surprised the glass hadn't shattered.

"That's more than vandalism, Eugene," she said.

"*Bulldozed*? Set fire to four acres? Who did it? It's all gone, the medicinal plants, the special hybrid herbs Dad had cultivated, *everything*?"

"Evidently."

Jayla fell silent and leaned back in her chair, her glass cupped in both hands, her eyes focused on it. Finally she said, "I want to go there and see for myself."

"I don't know why you'd need to go," he said. "There's nothing left to look at."

"I still want to see it firsthand," she said. "I'll book a flight for the day after tomorrow. Will you come with me?"

"I don't think I can, Jayla. There's too much to wrap up at the clinic and lab. I assume you'll want possession of your dad's lab equipment, and that the house will be sold. If I can help with this, contact realtors, anything, just name it."

"I want Tabitha cared for, money left to her."

"I'm sure that your dad took care of her in his will."

"If he didn't I'll see to it," she said. "Eugene, would you mind if I begged off having dinner? It's been a long, tiring trip and I'm exhausted. I'm afraid I might fall asleep here at the table."

"Of course not. Want to take what's left of the seafood to your room?"

"No, I don't think so. You stay and enjoy the rest of it."

"All right. Get yourself a good night's sleep. I'll be back at nine thirty to drop you off at the constabulary for your appointment with the detective."

Jayla's fatigue had drained every ounce of energy from her. When she reached the room she locked the door, used the bathroom, stripped down to her underwear, and crawled into bed. The next thing she knew it was seven in the morning and rain pounded heavily against the windowpanes, perfect weather for what she was feeling.

The meeting with the Australian detective, Angus Norbis, a pleasant fellow with an old-fashioned walrus mustache, provided Jayla with little useful information about the murder, just a series of assurances that he and others were working on the case and would keep her informed of their progress. As she anticipated, he told her that she would have to identify her father's body. "Are you up to it?" he asked.

"I don't think I'll ever be up to it," she replied. "Now is as good a time as any."

The detective escorted her to the police morgue where an attendant pulled back the sheet covering her father's remains, revealing only his face. Jayla gasped; the detective put his arm about her.

"It's him," she managed, "my father, Dr. Preston King." Although seeing his lifeless form was startling, she was surprised at the serene expression on his face. She'd expected a look of horror considering the brutal way he'd died, and that final glimpse of him was comforting in its own way.

The sheet was quickly replaced and the attendant wheeled away the body.

"Sorry you had to go through this," the detective said as they returned to his office.

"When will his body be released?" Jayla asked.

"In a day or two," he said. "There's no question of the cause of death, or the means. As soon as we're satisfied that there's nothing more to be learned from him about his assailant, he'll be released for burial. We took hair samples from the lab where he was found and are running DNA on them, but I don't expect anything useful will come from it. Have you made plans?"

Jayla shook her head. "I'm meeting with his attorney this afternoon. I'll speak with him about it."

"I don't suppose that you'll want to see any of the crime scene photos," Norbis said.

"Photos?" Jayla said. "I hadn't even thought that there might be photos."

"All part of the case file," said the detective.

"I would like to see them," she said.

Norbis cocked his head as though asking for assurance.

"Please," Jayla said. "I've been through the worst of it identifying my father's body."

Norbis pulled a file folder close to him and opened it. He removed the first 8×10 color photo and handed it to Jayla. Her father, wearing his usual white lab coat, was facedown on the alabaster white stone floor of his lab. An irregular pool of his blood had seeped from his body in many directions, creating a macabre form of pop art. The pale floor provided a perfect background for the vivid red pool that had seeped from him and into the stones' pores.

Jayla extended her hand to Norbis, who passed the next photo to her, and the next. He hesitated before delivering another. Jayla raised her eyebrows. He passed it and three others to her. They'd been taken after the body had been turned faceup. Because he'd been stabbed in the chest there hadn't been a bloody entry wound on the back of his lab coat. Now, where the knife had been jammed into his chest, the wet crimson circle surrounding the wound covered much of his coat. But Jayla's attention was focused on his face. He looked at peace as though the brutal way he'd died hadn't registered with him.

She closed her eyes and envisioned her father smiling, laughing, telling a corny joke.

"That's all of them," Norbis said.

"I'd like a set," Jayla said, now in the present, her eyes wide open.

"You would?"

"If it wouldn't be too much trouble."

"That shouldn't be a problem. I'll have the lab print copies for you. Shouldn't take more than a few hours."

"I won't be able to wait that long," she said.

"Then I'll have them delivered to your hotel."

"That would be fine. I very much appreciate it. Thank you for all your courtesies, Detective Norbis."

The afternoon appointment with her father's attorney, Elgin Taylor, also a displaced Australian, was more fruitful, and less traumatic. She felt supremely comfortable being in his presence, and basked in the warm words her father had injected into his will about her and what she meant to him. He'd left everything to her with the exception of $15,000 to Tabitha, and $5,000 to Eugene "for his service." Jayla wished there had been more for Tabitha, and silently pledged that she would add to the amount. Leaving money to Eugene bothered her, although she knew that it was an irrational response. He'd evidently served her father well and was entitled to whatever he wished to leave him. Still . . .

"I'll deal with the insurance company," the attorney said, "and see that all monies are properly distributed."

"I didn't know that he'd wanted to be cremated," she said.

"Hardly a surprise, Jayla. Your father was a pragmatic man, as well as lacking pretension. As you can see in the will he wanted his ashes placed in your custody, to be dispersed as you see fit."

"He'd want his ashes spread here, on PNG, perhaps in the gulf, or in the Sepik River."

"If you want I'll arrange for his ashes to be stored here until you have a chance to fulfill his wishes. How long will you be staying?"

"Not long. I have to be back at work. I'm in the midst of an important project and can't stay away long."

"Well," the attorney said, "there's certainly no rush. The ashes will be here whenever you return, or when you tell me where to scatter them." He smiled. "Your father wasn't a rich man," he said, "but he was rich in satisfaction with the way he'd lived his life, giving back to society through his work in the clinic."

"Did he talk with you about his efforts in the lab?" she asked.

"Not very much, although I was aware that he was determined to develop a new class of pain relievers using plants the natives have relied on for centuries." The corpulent attorney sat back, his hands clasped on his chest.

"I remember a few times when we attended local football matches together. He felt that he was close to achieving that goal. He had tried out some concoctions on patients at the clinic who were in pain, and he said they seemed to work. Shame he didn't live long enough to reap the rewards of whatever success he had. I would think that if his work ended up being patented and sold commercially he might have become a wealthy man."

"Eugene, Dad's assistant, told me that all my father's notes and packets of medicinal plants he was working with are gone from the lab."

The attorney came forward and a serious expression replaced his smile. "That seems odd," he said. "The police assume that whoever killed your father was a street thug after drugs or money. Such a person wouldn't have any interest in those items."

"I know," Jayla said. "There's something else."

"What's that?"

"Dad's four-acre plot that he cultivated in the Sepik region has been 'vandalized.' At least that's the way Eugene characterized it. He said the acres were burned and bulldozed."

"Do the police know that? It might be tied in with your father's murder."

"I met with the lead detective this morning and told him about it. He said that he'd look into it, although he basically dismissed the notion that the two events were related. I don't agree. I've booked a flight to Wewak tomorrow."

The attorney's expression was now one of concern. "Sure you should?" he asked.

"I have to," Jayla said. "I can't help but think that what's happened to Dad's plot of land is somehow linked to his murder."

"If it is," he said, "that's all the more reason for you to reconsider traveling there."

"I don't feel that I have any choice."

He came around his desk and placed large hands on

her arms. "You take care of yourself, Jayla," he said. "You were the most important thing in your father's life."

"I will, and thank you for everything."

"When you get back from Wewak I'll have papers for you to sign. Or I can send them to you if that's more convenient. Don't worry about any of the legal issues. I'll take care of everything, including selling the house and—you do want it sold, I assume."

"Yes, of course. I'm so pleased that Tabitha will be provided for."

"I hear that she's been worried about you," he said, as he handed her some of his business cards with all his contact information on them.

"She's worried about me since I was a baby," Jayla said through a smile. "She's staying with her daughter. I'll make a point of seeing her before I go back to the States."

4

Jayla had declined dinner with Waksit that evening. Room service delivered soup and a salad to her room and she read the second half of a paperback novel that she'd started at home and had tossed into her carry-on bag before leaving D.C. The book had been a blessed distraction from her father's death and the trip she would take to the Sepik River. She was sorry to see the story end and wished she'd brought a second book with her. Maybe it was just as well. She was physically and mentally exhausted and needed a deep sleep, if that were possible.

The following morning, her body rested—but mentally fatigued—she took a taxi to the airport where she joined nineteen other passengers on an Airlines PNG DeHavilland Twin Otter turbojet aircraft for the two-hour flight to the town of Wewak, in the Sepik region. It had been years since she'd set foot there and the anticipation was both exciting and anxiety-provoking.

She was going to see firsthand the destruction of her father's four acres. Would it provide an answer to why he'd been brutally slain? She hoped so. She'd second-guessed her decision to travel to the Sepik more than once since making her reservation. But it had to be done.

The emotional upheaval that his murder had created in her, and the mystery of why someone had ravaged the patch of land on which he grew and cultivated his plants, had now been replaced by a more cognitive determination to understand *who* was responsible.

The plane encountered turbulence from the moment it lifted off from the Port Moresby airport, and Jayla, who'd never been afraid of flying, gripped the armrests of her seat for almost the entire flight. Looking out the plane's window she could see the mysterious Sepik River curling through the dense jungle like a writhing snake, its myriad indigenous tribes the keepers of PNG's deepest, darkest secrets. Although she had been born and raised in the more urban atmosphere of Port Moresby, Jayla felt a link to the remote region, home to her mother's ancestors.

A windy rainstorm caused the pilot to abandon his first attempt at a landing and to go around again, slamming the plane down on the runway on his second try. Jayla stood on shaky legs as she joined other deplaning passengers. The rain had suddenly stopped, and a hot sun replaced it, the humidity causing perspiration to instantly soak through her blouse and run freely down her face as she walked to the small building that served as a terminal.

She hadn't made plans beyond booking the flight, and knew that she would have to hire a driver to take her to the village of Pagwi, where her father's land was located. But she first checked on return flights to Port Moresby. The last flight of the day departed at six that evening. She reserved a seat, left the terminal, and approached a young man standing next to a battered maroon sedan with white hand-lettered "Taxi" on its doors. After some haggling they reached an agreement on the fare to Pagwi, and Jayla settled in the rear seat for the bumpy ride over a deeply rutted road, during which the driver sang unfamiliar songs in a loud voice, blissfully unaware of people crossing in his way who had to hurry to safety. When they pulled into the center of the village the driver asked if she wanted him to wait to take her back to Wewak. "No taxis here," he said in his Melanesian Pidgin language, or Tok Pisin as it was known throughout Papua New Guinea. "No ride back."

"How much will it cost for you to wait for, say, two hours?"

He gave her a price, to which she agreed.

"Your English is pretty good," she said. "How much for you to come with me to translate?"

She accepted the sum he requested.

She was glad that she'd reconsidered staying overnight in Wewak. She was used to heat and humidity in Washington's summers, but the air in Pagwi felt as though the small town was engulfed in a steam room. Mosquitoes, called *natnats* by the natives, buzzed about her head and bit her ankles, causing her to silently curse her decision to wear a dress. Slacks and socks would have been a more prudent choice.

The man who'd watched over her father's property was Walter Tagobe. Using the taxi driver's services, she asked villagers where Tagobe could be found, aware that she was being scrutinized by everyone she passed, especially by some of the tribesmen who were nearly naked except for their loincloths. A few directed comments to her which she was sure were suggestive, and her discomfort level increased as she sought someone who could direct her to Tagobe's home. She stopped a woman whose breasts were barely covered by some sort of fur and repeated Tagobe's name. The woman pointed to a hut on stilts above a stream on the fringe of the village, just beyond an outdoor market in which women wove skirts and baskets known as *bilum* bags, and men hawked vividly colored ceremonial masks and even a few head hunter's skulls. One woman pounded the pulp of the sago palms to make *sak-sak*, a popular dish. Others sold crude necklaces and bracelets made of pig tusks and shells, or headdresses fashioned from bird-of-paradise feathers. Young men, their groins and buttocks barely concealed, pressed close; one played a bamboo mouth harp, hoping that Jayla would reward him with money. Some of the young men's backs testified to their initiation into the crocodile legend. The sight caused Jayla to wince as she imagined the pain they must have suffered.

She reached the house and looked up the rickety set of steps made of irregular-shaped pieces of wood tied together by heavy lengths of rope. As she was about to ascend to the open door ten steps above, a woman appeared in the doorway.

"I'm looking for Walter Tagobe," Jayla said.

"Not here," the woman said.

"Does he live here?"

"Not here."

"Where did he go?" Jayla asked, aware that a circle of villagers had formed around her. Consumed with curiosity, their garishly painted faces and near-nakedness increased her discomfort.

"Far away. You go now," the woman said, disappearing inside the home.

Jayla had never seen the acreage that her father had purchased and cultivated, but knew from his description of it that it was close to Pagwi. She turned to the people who surrounded her and asked a young man whose mouth was blood-red, "Do you know where Dr. King grew his crops?"

The man answered with a grin exposing blackened teeth, the result of chewing betel nuts from the areca palm, a popular narcotic enjoyed by tribesmen.

"Dr. King?" Jayla repeated. "Big, tall man, medical doctor?"

The native nodded, his grin becoming wider.

"Do you know where Walter Tagobe is?" the taxi driver asked.

"He go away," was the answer.

"Where?"

The man shrugged. "Walter, he's long-long."

"Long-long?"

He used his index finger to make circles at the side of his head.

"Oh, he's—he's loco," Jayla said. "Can you take me to where the big doctor grew crops? Plants? Plants for medicine?" She pointed to plants growing at her feet.

His face lit up with recognition of what she was saying. He nodded enthusiastically and beckoned her and the taxi driver to follow him.

They walked into the jungle, following a narrow overgrown path that ran alongside a stream on which women fished from dugouts. Other villagers had fallen in behind them. They passed wild sugarcane, breadfruit trees, and myriad palms. At one point her guide stopped and pointed at a crocodile, its huge head and glistening white teeth barely above water. "*Puk-puk,*" he said, the local term for croc.

They eventually reached her father's acreage. She knew they were close because of the acrid smell of recently burned plant life; an occasional wisp of smoke still wafted into the oppressive air. Although she had never visited the site before she felt as though she knew it intimately based upon her father's frequent descriptions of it, and photographs of the plants and herbs growing strong and tall in the jungle heat. Now it was all gone, wiped out by someone.

"Who did this?" she asked her companion.

"Blue eyes," he said. "Many blue eyes."

Jayla was surprised. She'd assumed it might have been a neighboring tribe that had destroyed the acreage.

"White men?" she asked.

"Yes," he said, flashing his vampirelike smile.

"Who were they?"

"Big men," he said, indicating their height with his hand.

She stepped into the field and picked up pieces of charred plants. *Why?* She asked herself. *Who would benefit from destroying the field?*

A machine with large tires had gouged deep, wide troughs in the earth.

She stared at the destroyed field for what seemed a long time before turning and starting back along the path leading to the village, the taxi driver and the young man with the red mouth falling in behind. A dozen native men joined them. As she walked she wondered where Walter Tagobe had gone. Her father had often spoke of him with fondness: "He's a good man, Jayla, slightly better educated than most of the men in the village. He understands enough English that I can communicate with him."

Had Tagobe fled because of the field's ruination, embarrassed that he hadn't protected it? Or had he been told to leave by those who had destroyed the field, perhaps paid to disappear?

She handed the young man some kina banknotes, and stopped to purchase from an old woman a beautiful necklace made from shells and colorful cassowary feathers, a gift for her nanny, Tabitha. She climbed into the car and her driver delivered her back to the Wewak airport. Her flight back to Port Moresby was considerably less bumpy than the earlier flight had been, and she filled the time consumed with questions, each delivered to her brain only to be replaced by the next, and the next, a jumble of jarring mysteries.

She took a taxi directly to her father's house where to her surprise Tabitha was in the kitchen preparing herself a late dinner. The old woman immediately broke into tears upon seeing Jayla, and wrapped her pencil-thin arms about the child she had helped to raise.

"I am so sorry about your father."

"I know how much he meant to you," Jayla said, disengaging. "He's left you money in his will."

"I know, I know. The lawyer, he called me. Dr. Preston was such a good man, a saint. He wanted me to call him by just his first name but I could not do that."

"He loved you very much," Jayla said.

She guffawed. "Loved me? Perhaps. But his great love was you. How proud he was of you, your education, your big important job in America."

"How are you, Tabitha? You're feeling well?"

She lowered her eyes, as well as her voice. "No, I am not well," she said. "I have the cancer."

"Oh, I'm so sorry. Are you being treated?"

"Yes, by a fine doctor, a friend of your father. But your father, he helps me with the pain." Her face brightened. "No pain when I take his medicine. Your father makes special medicine for me. When I take it, the pain is gone." She clicked her fingers. "Like magic," she said. "Like that." Another click of her fingers.

"The medicine takes away your pain but doesn't make you sick in other ways?"

"No, no, it is good medicine. Your father, he makes it himself in his laboratory."

Jayla sat at the kitchen table and processed what the sickly old woman had said. As far as she knew her father's quest to create a more effective pain reliever was still in the formative stage. But here was anecdotal evidence that he'd progressed beyond theory and had succeeded.

"Tabitha," she said, "do you know whether my father also used the medicine with other people?"

"Oh, yes," she said. "My friend has terrible pain in the arms and legs. She comes to the clinic and your father gives her the medicine. No pain when she has the medicine. Others, too."

"I was in the laboratory yesterday with Eugene," Jayla said.

Tabitha's expression turned sour. "Mr. Eugene," she said disparagingly.

"You don't like him, do you?"

"I should not say that," she said. "It is none of my business."

"Eugene told me that my father's notes, and packages of his medicine that you and your friend took, are missing from the laboratory."

"I don't know about that," she said quickly. "I didn't take anything."

"Oh, no, Tabitha," Jayla said, patting the older woman's hand. "I know that you didn't. But someone did. Did father have any visitors recently, men you hadn't seen before?"

Tabitha thought before saying, "No, no one. But your father, he was—well, he was different lately."

"How was he different?"

"He was worried. I could see it in his eyes and on his face. I knew that he was worried when he gave me the package for you."

"A package for me? What package?"

Her answer was to walk from the kitchen, returning minutes later carrying an 8×10 manila envelope sealed with tape. She handed it to Jayla. "Your father, he told me that if anything happened to him I should give this envelope to you, only you and no one else."

Jayla weighed it in her hands. "Do you know what's in it?" she asked.

Tabitha shook her head.

Jayla removed the tape and withdrew the envelope's contents, a letter addressed to her from her father. She fanned through the nine single-spaced pages handwritten in her father's recognizable tight, small script, and looked at the four small plastic packets of seeds that accompanied the letter.

"You say that my father told you to give this to me in case something happened to him. He must have been fearful that something would. Do you know why he felt this way?"

She shook her head again. "No," she said, "but he had that worried look on his face, so worried."

Tabitha offered to make tea or coffee, but Jayla insisted on doing it. When she'd served them tea, and had broken open a package of sugar cookies, she asked what the old woman intended to do. "The house will have to be sold, I'm afraid," Jayla said.

"I have already arranged to live with my daughter in Koki. She is a good girl."

"I remember her well," Jayla said. I'm glad that you spoke with the attorney. He will take care of everything."

"He is a good man, like your father. You take care, my lovely Jayla. Be well, and find your happiness."

Jayla and Tabitha rode together in a taxi to Tabitha's daughter's house, where Jayla gave Tabitha the necklace she'd bought for her and spent a few minutes catching up with the daughter's family.

"You can't stay longer?" the daughter asked when Jayla said that she had to leave.

"No, but thank you. The taxi is waiting for me, and I leave tomorrow for the States. I'm glad that your mother will have a good home with you."

"She is very sick," the daughter said as she walked Jayla to the waiting cab.

"Yes, she told me. I wish there was something I could do for her."

"The medicine your father gave her for the pain is so good. There is no pain when she takes it."

"Maybe I'll be able to make that medicine myself one day," Jayla said.

They embraced, and Jayla rode back to the Grand Papua Hotel where she had dinner in her room and pored over the contents of the envelope Tabitha had given her. The letter was long, and filled with terms of endearment. Professionally, he was ebullient about the advances he'd made in the lab to concoct an effective painkiller. Unlike his missing documentation that traced every aspect of his research in scientific terms, the letter provided a more informal narrative about the progress he'd made and what it might mean to millions of men and women suffering pain.

But there was also an undercurrent of concern about what the future held for him personally. He wrote that in the event something were to happen to him she was to take his notebooks in which he chronicled every step of his research, as well as the myriad packages containing the medicine he'd formulated, and carry on his work. "You know where to find my notebooks in the lab," he wrote.

"But the notes are gone," she said aloud, as though speaking to him. *"They're gone!"*

Eugene Waksit had insisted on driving Jayla to the airport the following morning for her flight to Sydney, and then on to Washington.

"What will you do now that the clinic and lab are closed?" Jayla asked as they sat in his Range Rover in front of the terminal.

"I haven't figured that out yet," he said. "I'll be leaving here, of course, maybe go back to Australia. No definite plans yet. Maybe I'll take a trip to Washington someday. If I do I'll call and you can show me the sights."

"I'll be happy to do that, Eugene."

"It was good seeing you again, Jayla, even though you had to come home under such sad circumstances," he said as he opened the door for her. As she stepped from the vehicle he kissed her cheek. "Travel safe, Jayla."

She turned and strode into the terminal without looking back.

WASHINGTON, D.C.
A FEW DAYS LATER

U.S. senator Ronald Gillespie was in a foul mood when he left his home in Falls Church, Virginia. He and his wife, Rebecca, had fought bitterly the night before, the genesis of the argument lost in the flurry of harsh words. The senator had little patience—no, make that *no* patience—with his wife. Of course he was all sweetness and light with the voters back in Georgia. For them, he was a savvy, caring, wise, gentlemanly politician who had their backs, a man with principles and moral values bucking those in the nation's capital who were responsible for the Congress's dismal approval rating. That he was divorced and remarried to a much younger woman mattered to only to a zealous few.

He'd stayed up late after Rebecca had gone to bed, sipping bourbon and reading memos prepared for him by his staff in preparation for the next day's meeting. At times like this he found himself questioning his decision to have married Rebecca following his divorce. He was sixty-four; Rebecca was thirty-three. He'd come to the conclusion that her only bankable attributes were her stunning figure, long red hair, and ability in bed. Other than that she was an intellectual embarrassment and he kept her away from gatherings at which she might be asked a question about—well, about anything aside from choosing drapes.

He peeled out of the driveway in one of a matching pair of red Mercedes convertibles and drove down I-295 for five miles until reaching the exit for the National Harbor Marina in Snoots Bay on the Potomac River, where the lobbyist Eric Morrison docked his thirty-three-foot Aquariva yacht. Morrison was on the boat with a hired hand and preparing to cast off when the senator arrived.

"Sorry I'm late," Gillespie said as he climbed aboard.

"Late night?" Morrison said.

"Unfortunately."

Morrison refrained from asking whether the senator's lack of sleep had to do with Rebecca. He was well aware of the ongoing tension in the Gillespie marriage because the senator frequently used him as a sounding board, bemoaning the state of the relationship in a quest for understanding and approval. Male bonding it was called. While Morrison found those confessional moments painful to sit through, he was a willing listener. Gillespie was, after all, chairman of the Senate Health, Education, Labor and Pensions Committee (HELP), in whose hands legislation impacting the pharmaceutical industry rested. Morrison had been cultivating the relationship with the powerful senator for years. Lending a sympathetic ear to his marital woes was a small price to pay for his support, a much smaller price than the millions of dollars Morrison's client, the Pharmaceutical Association of America, the PAA, funneled into the crusty senator's campaigns.

"You need your sleep, Ron," Morrison said. "You're not a kid anymore."

Gillespie laughed. "You don't need to remind me. My brain tells me I'm still a twenty-year-old stud but the bones tell a different story." He looked up. "Good weather for a day on the water."

"Any day on the water is a good one," Morrison said as he took the helm and guided the sleek craft away from the dock and headed up the Potomac.

To the casual observer it was an idyllic scene, an invigorating breeze off the water, the bright sunlight, the engine's muffled drone. Senator Ronald Gillespie was, however, anything but relaxed. He'd been summoned to this last-minute cruise because Eric Morrison, one of the premier lobbyists in Washington, D.C., was not happy. Morrison appeared to be in good spirits while at the wheel, but when he turned it over to his helper and joined Gillespie on the rear deck in the yellow-and-white webbed deck chairs his smile had evaporated.

"I know what's on your mind, Eric, but I don't have news for you, good or bad," Gillespie said.

"I suppose I should believe that no news is good news," Morrison said, sipping from a container of coffee provided by his deck mate.

"Not a bad way to view things," said Gillespie in his southern drawl that became more pronounced when under pressure. "The legislation isn't dead yet."

"You've been saying that for a long time."

Gillespie shifted in his chair and looked out over the water, avoiding the lobbyist's hard gaze. Lately Morrison had been ratcheting up the pressure concerning a pending bill in the Senate to tighten the rules on the importation of cheaper prescription drugs from Canada and Mexico. Gillespie had explained more than once that the Department of Homeland Security, charged with matters pertaining to the country's borders, was the lead agency in that effort and had been dragging its feet.

"Look," Morrison said, "I understand that you've been doing what you can to get legislation passed to tighten up the borders, but my people are getting tired of the excuses. The way it stands now any U.S. citizen can import medicine from Canada and—"

"Provided certain conditions are met," Gillespie said gruffly, defensively.

"Yeah, some conditions," Morrison said. "As long as it's for personal use, there's a prescription from a U.S. doctor, no more than a three-month supply, yada yada yada. Look, Ron, my clients pay me and my firm big bucks to protect their interests. They're the top pharmaceutical companies in the world. They pay for action, and all they hear is how the border with Mexico is broken. Everything is pouring in. They want to hear about congressional action to keep prescription drugs from being brought in over the borders, and they're entitled to some positive results."

Gillespie said, "Don't forget that there's a law on the books that prohibits drugs manufactured here in the States from being sold to Canada and resold back here. That's something. In case you hadn't noticed the Senate is fractured. You can't get bipartisan support for anything these days other than a new post office opening."

Morrison snickered. "When was the last time anybody was prosecuted for reimporting drugs from U.S. manufacturers—thirty, forty years ago?" he asked snidely. "There's no teeth to that law."

Gillespie changed the subject. "By the way," he said, "your clients will be happy with the legislation my staff is drawing up to prohibit the importation of drugs from Third World countries, and from Canada when the drugs they're selling are actually manufactured elsewhere. I'm moving ahead on that front, too."

"Good to hear it, Ron," said Morrison. He changed his tone, something he was adept at doing. "Look," he said, "you've been a champion of Big Pharma ever since you won your seat in the upper house. Your work on their behalf has always been appreciated. But they're putting pressure on me to get some bang for their bucks where Canada and Mexico are concerned. You can't blame them."

"No, no, no, Eric, I understand. My staff has also drawn up new legislation to tighten rules on Canadian manufacturing. It's not easy getting support from my colleagues. Restricting the importation of cheaper drugs from Canada and Mexico means higher prices for our citizens, hardly popular with constituents. But I'll do everything I can to garner support on both sides of the aisle. You can count on it, and so can your people."

Gillespie knew it was empty talk. He was running for reelection and he counted on Morrison's clients to fill his coffers. But it seemed to have appeased the lobbyist.

Morrison stood and slapped the senator on the back. "Glad we've cleared the air," Morrison said. "I'm meeting with representatives of my client firms this afternoon and I'll assure them that you're on the case and doing everything you can."

They spent the next hour anchored in a cove where Morrison's deck mate broke out booze and a cold lobster lunch. Conversation was no longer contentious. They swapped racy stories about government and media people they knew in common, most of the stories coming from Morrison, who made it his business to know as many people in Washington and their dark secrets as possible. Scandalous stories about lawmakers were capital for the lobbyist, and no one had a bigger file of them than Eric Morrison.

They returned to the dock at two.

"Where are you headed?" Morrison asked.

"The Hill. Committee meetings, a fund-raiser tonight."

"How's your campaign shaping up?"

"Fine, just fine. My opponent is playing dirty, no surprise. Every time a new poll is released showing him falling further behind he pulls another dirty trick out of his sleeve."

"Takes a tough hide to be in politics," Morrison said.

"And a willingness to go for the jugular," Gillespie said. "I get better at it every election. Thanks for the pleasant day, Eric. The lunch was excellent."

"Always a pleasure to spend some relaxing time with you, Ron. You need anything, you just have to holler."

Morrison watched the senator walk to his red convertible, get in, and drive from the parking lot. As confident as Gillespie was about retaining his Senate seat, Morrison had become aware lately that the senator had lost some of his swagger. "Damn fool," the lobbyist muttered under his breath as he prepared to leave the dock and get into his car. Gillespie's marriage to the much younger, sexy Rebecca Prewell had been a huge mistake, a classic case of a man getting older and needing to prove that he wasn't. Morrison had attended the small wedding and remembered thinking during the ceremony that the esteemed senator had made a bad decision, one that would sap his energy and in all likelihood send him on a downhill spiral.

"Damn fool," he repeated.

Morrison hadn't been entirely truthful when he said he had a client meeting to attend that afternoon. There was a meeting, but not with representatives of the Pharmaceutical Association of America, which comprised a huge chunk of his client base. He was meeting with a man he knew as George Alard.

Morrison had been introduced to Alard by a friend who had used Alard's services a few times. "He's sort of a soldier of fortune," Morrison's friend had said, "willing to take on assignments that are—well, let's just say that he doesn't mind getting his hands dirty, for a hefty fee, of course."

Morrison's initial visit to Alard's office in a nondescript one-story office building in Washington's southeast quadrant had occurred two weeks ago. He'd been wary of the neighborhood and the building itself, and had considered calling Alard and canceling the meeting. But he felt he had an obligation to go through with it on behalf of the largest member of PAA, a giant pharmaceutical company with billions in sales each year, much of it from the sale of a popular, and expensive, pain medication.

That first meeting with Alard had lasted an hour. Morrison's initial impression was that Alard was nothing like how he'd pictured a soldier of fortune, big, hefty, probably with tattoos up and down beefy arms. Instead, Alard was a small, slender man with slicked-down black hair and a pencil mustache. Morrison thought he resembled a rodent. He was dressed in a blue collared shirt, khaki pants, and black tasseled loafers that looked expensive. Furniture in the small office consisted of a desk, a chair behind it, and one additional chair on the other side. Blank gray walls were brightened somewhat by travel posters. There was no phone on the desk; Morrison's call to him had reached a cell phone. The office didn't contain any of the usual business equipment—copy machine, fax, computer. The desktop was bare except for a ruled legal pad and a pen that rested on it. Alard had been seated behind the desk when he buzzed Morrison through the front door.

"Mr. Alard?" Morrison said.

"Yes, and you are Mr. Morrison," Alard said with a trace of an accent. French? "Please, sit down."

Morrison hesitated and looked at the chair as though it might contain foreign matter.

Alard eyed him impassively, a hint of a smile on his pinched face. Once Morrison was seated, Alard said, "I understand from our mutual friend that you might be in need of my services."

"Possibly," Morrison said.

"Perhaps if you tell me what services are needed I'll be able to decide whether I'm able to provide them."

Morrison, who seldom felt intimated by anyone, shifted in his chair and mentally went over what he'd intended to say. He cleared his throat. "I have a client who might need something accomplished in a foreign country, something—well, it's the sort of thing that requires . . ."

* * *

Morrison wasn't sure how to put it. What he was looking for was undoubtedly illegal. It wouldn't result in physical harm to anyone, although it did involve stealing secrets from another person. But that was done all the time in industry, wasn't it? Industrial espionage was a necessity in the dog-eat-dog world of big business, particularly in the highly competitive pharmaceutical industry.

The client who'd raised the issue that brought Morrison to this drab office hadn't requested any specific action, certainly not an illegal one. Their chat had come out of getting together for a drink at Bobby Van's Steakhouse.

Morrison's companion at the small corner table was the vice president of operations for a giant pharmaceutical company, the leading force behind and the largest contributor to PAA. The VP had casually mentioned a concern they had about experiments being conducted in quest of a cheaper form of pain medication. He'd made light of it at first, but as the conversation progressed Morrison realized that the VP was hardly amused by the situation. He needed an answer to his dilemma, and Morrison, the lobbyist for PAA, was expected to provide it.

"There's a rogue doctor in Papua New Guinea, of all places, who's been trying to develop a painkiller from locally grown plants and herbs. He was a hotshot doctor in Australia before moving to New Guinea to open a clinic and do research in a lab he set up. He's a bit of a crackpot from what I'm told, but he claims that he's been having success with plants he's mixing together. Whether that's true or not is conjecture. It's not like he's conducting double-blind clinical trials, just uses the stuff on natives who come into his clinic. Our sources tell us that whatever he's come up with does seem to work pretty well, and without side effects."

The VP didn't have to elaborate for Morrison why this

doctor and his primitive painkilling concoction threatened the veep's company. It produced many popular prescription drugs, but its biggest seller was a pain medication that worked relatively well, produced myriad possible side effects including addiction, and generated huge yearly profits. Having another company latch on to a competing medicine made of herbs and plants, whose price would be minuscule compared to Morrison's client's company, certainly justified the VP's concern.

"Are you looking to buy him out?" Morrison asked.

"Hell, no. What we're looking to do is put him out of business before a competitor decides to make a deal with him." The VP snorted. "Although I can't imagine that happening. This doctor is one of these do-gooders, wants his painkiller to be available cheap, nickels-and-dimes, according to our sources. Not good for our business, Eric."

"No, it wouldn't be. What's his name?"

"I wrote it down for you." He slid a slip of paper across the table.

"Enough of this," the VP said, downing what was left of his drink. "I just thought that you might have some ideas how to solve this."

As pleasantly as it was put, Morrison sensed the steel behind the VP's words. There had been rumors that another large K Street lobbying group was using its own considerable clout with Congress as the basis for stealing the lucrative PAA account away from Morrison, and he'd been looking for ways to enhance his value to the pharmaceutical trade association. Solving this problem would put him in good stead. That realization was very much on his mind when he said, "I'll think about it."

"Whatever you do leave me out of it," the VP said. "Strictly off the record."

"Of course."

As Morrison was paying the tab the VP said, "This is also off the record, but there's a hefty bonus if you come up with a way to get rid of this problem. They're putting the pressure on me."

* * *

Morrison prefaced what he said to Alard during that first meeting with, "Before I get into the specifics, Mr. Alard, it's important that whatever we decide to do remain highly confidential."

Alard nodded.

"The stakes are large," Morrison continued.

"They usually are, Mr. Morrison. Now that we've established that discretion is of paramount importance, please tell me what it is you want me and my organization to do."

Morrison told Alard about Dr. King and his experiments. "I assume that you and your organization does business in New Guinea?"

Alard smiled. "We do business in every corner of the world," he said. "Please continue."

Morrison had learned during a follow-up conversation with the pharmaceutical company's VP that Dr. King owned an experimental farm in the Sepik region of PNG.

"This doctor has a patch of land, four acres I believe, in Papua New Guinea. He's cultivating some of the wild plants on it."

Alard said nothing.

"Some of these plants are used for medicine," Morrison continued. "You know, it's like a superstition with the natives there. Anyway, my client would like to see that field disappear."

"That shouldn't be a problem," Alard said in his tinny voice. "What else does this person you represent wish done about this Dr. King?"

Morrison stiffened. There was something ominous in what Alard had asked. He quickly said, "Obviously we don't wish to see Dr. King harmed in any way. We would like, of course, to have access to his files about his experiments, and would appreciate having that material delivered to me *provided* it can be retrieved without—well, without running afoul of the law."

"I understand what you're asking for, Mr. Morrison, and I can assure you that my people will be able to accomplish what you wish. I have a few more questions, and there's the matter of our fee."

While making arrangements with Alard had been easier than he'd anticipated, Morrison drove away with a knot in his stomach. He'd done many favors for clients over the years, including some that bordered on illegality or immorality. But he knew that arranging for this shadowy group to destroy a man's crops and steal his research had crossed over the line.

Now, weeks later, he was back with Alard to deliver the second half of the agreed-upon payment for services rendered, and to learn how the project went.

"The field is no longer there."

"What did you do?"

"Me? Nothing. The native man who oversees that plot of land was persuaded to leave the village for an extended period of time. While he was away there was a fire and the plants burned. Naturally, he was compensated for his decision to vacate the area."

"I'm pleased to hear it," Morrison said.

"But I'm afraid that I do not have such good news about Dr. King's research findings."

"Oh?"

"It seems that the operative I assigned to visit his lab and remove what you requested was thwarted before he was able to accomplish that mission."

Morrison's heart skipped a beat and he came forward in his chair. "What do you mean 'thwarted'?"

"It's been reported to me that when he'd gained entry into Dr. King's laboratory he was faced with an unpleasant situation."

Morrison drew heavy breaths. "Jesus," he said. "Get to the point. What happened? What was this 'unpleasant situation'?"

Alard's smile was meant to be reassuring. "It seems that Dr. King had other enemies. My operative found him dead in his laboratory, the victim of a knife attack. Naturally it was prudent for my operative to flee the premises without taking the time to search for the materials you were seeking. A project like this always involves some hazards, as I'm sure you can appreciate. My apologies for not having files to deliver to you, but the field is now rubble, as instructed."

"I assume your fee will be lower," Morrison said, summoning the courage to suggest it.

"Why?" Alard said.

"Along with destroying the field you were to deliver the pertinent files found in the doctor's laboratory. That was understood."

"Mr. Morrison, you insult me," Alard said. "What you required was an illegal act, which you specified you'd prefer to avoid. Nevertheless we attempted it on your behalf. I must ask you for the full balance owed despite the unfortunate outcome with the doctor. As I said, a mission like this always involves some risk of discovery, and things don't always go as planned. As it stands nothing about this incident can be traced back to you but . . ."

The threat behind Alard's words weren't lost on Morrison. The friend who'd introduced Morrison to Alard had alluded to Alard's organization being involved in myriad illegal activities around the globe, including some that involved physical violence. He was not someone to be trifled with.

"You needn't worry about anything being traced back to you—or to me, for that matter, Mr. Morrison," Alard said to calm his client. "My people are the best at what they do. They never leave tracks. The balance of the agreed-upon fee, please." He held out his hand.

Morrison turned over the money and quickly left, relieved to be out of the little man's presence. He got into his car, closed his eyes, and banged his head against the headrest. He waited until he'd calmed down sufficiently to start the engine and drive back to his office. By the time he arrived he'd formulated a different view about what had happened to Dr. King, at least as far as what he would tell his client.

Dr. King and his tract of medicinal plants no longer posed a threat to his client's pharmaceutical company. He, Eric Morrison, powerful Washington lobbyist, had gone out on a limb to get it done. It was a shame that the doctor had been killed, but he, Morrison, certainly hadn't played a part in that. He'd specifically told Alard that he didn't want anyone hurt.

Had Alard been telling the truth about the doctor's death? Had one of his own operatives, as he was fond of calling them, been confronted by the doctor and stabbed him in self-defense? Morison decided that it didn't matter. What *did* matter was that he was owed the bonus the VP had promised, as well as undying loyalty to his lobbying firm. He was just relieved that it was over, and looked forward to getting home and enjoying a drink with his wife on the patio.

6

Jayla took a few days to recover from jet lag before returning to work at Renewal Pharmaceuticals and to fall back into the pattern of everyday life. She remembered that Flo Combes had put aside a dress for her, and went to the store where she was welcomed warmly. "What an ordeal you've had to go through," Flo said after hugging Jayla and making her a cup of tea in the small kitchenette she'd had installed during the shop's renovation.

"I'm not sure I'll ever get over the shock of that phone call I received the last time I was here. It all seems surreal, although I know it's real, *very* real. I'm lucky to have one of my father's best friends, a lawyer, handling all the legal issues, selling the house, executing his will, dealing with the police."

"They haven't caught the person who did it?"

"No, and I wonder if they ever will. The police there aren't exactly models of efficiency. There are so many questions to answer. My father's research notes were missing, and someone burned and bulldozed a four-acre plot of land he owned where he grew plants used in his research."

"That's odd," Flo said.

"More than odd, I think. I visited where his land had been razed. It's in a remote part of the island known as the Sepik, very primitive. I thought that by going there I could make sense of his murder, find some link between what had happened to the land and his death."

"A wasted trip?"

"It turned out that way."

The small bell over the door announced that customers had entered the shop.

"Go try that dress on again," Flo said, getting up to greet her new customers.

"I've lost weight," Jayla said.

"Not a problem," Flo said over her shoulder. "I work with a terrific tailor."

Jayla's weight loss had worked in her favor where the new dress was concerned. It fit perfectly. Pleased with the way she looked, she changed back into the clothes that she'd worn to the shop and was preparing to leave when Flo rejoined her, blowing an errant strand of hair from her forehead. "There are some people you simply cannot please," she said, nodding toward two women leaving the shop. "They want clothes to make them look like super-thin models but their bodies say something else."

Jayla laughed.

"It's different with you. You could easily be a model," Flo said.

Another laugh from Jayla to brush away the compliment.

"It's good to see you laugh," Flo said. "I know it's difficult, but a good laugh cures lots of the blues. Are you holding up okay?"

"I guess so, only my father's murder is always in my thoughts. Who could have done such a thing to a gentle, loving man who only wanted to help other people?"

"I suppose there's some sort of wise saying to answer that, but I don't know what it is."

"People have been telling me that time heals all

wounds," Jayla said. "I wonder if that will ever be true for me."

"It does help," Flo said while knowing that it hadn't seemed to help Robert Brixton get over the daughter he'd lost two years earlier in a terrorist bombing attack in a D.C. outdoor café.

"It comes to me at the strangest times," Jayla said. "I'll be thinking about something else and there it is, someone's voice that sounds like my father, seeing people I work with at the lab in their white coats. It's always there."

"Mind a suggestion?"

"Of course not."

"Robert and I are having dinner tonight with dear friends, Mac and Annabel Smith, at their Watergate apartment. You'll love them. Mac's an attorney. Annabel gave up law to open a pre-Columbian shop in Georgetown. Mac has been a mentor to Robert, set him up in an office next to his and gives him all his private investigation work. A federal court judge and his wife will also be there, and a dear friend of Robert's, Will Sayers, a real character. He's the Washington editor of the *Savannah Morning News*. Please say you'll come. A night out would do you tons of good."

"You're sure I wouldn't be imposing?"

"Absolutely not. Want us to pick you up?"

"No, thank you, I'll find my way. I know where the Watergate is. Doesn't everyone?"

Flo said, "The infamous Watergate, Richard Nixon's downfall."

Flo wrote down the Smiths' apartment address and phone numbers for Jayla. "Be there at seven. It's informal. The Smiths are down-to-earth people despite being lawyers, and Will Sayers defines informal. Maybe sloppy is more apt."

Jayla left Flo's Fashions with mixed emotions.

On the one hand Flo was right: an evening of good food and conversation could be therapeutic. On the other hand she didn't know if she was up to making pleasant chitchat, especially with a judge, lawyers, a private investigator, and a journalist.

Too late now to back out. She'd force herself to shed the shell she'd developed since returning from the other side of the world, at least for one evening.

Jayla arrived at the Smiths' apartment at seven and was welcomed by Mac Smith, who'd donned an apron with an abstract drawing of jazz great Duke Ellington on it. "Pardon my appearance," he said, "but Annabel has pressed me into kitchen duty."

"I think it looks nice," Jayla said. "That's Duke Ellington, isn't it?"

"Ah, you know your jazz, I see," said Mac. "I've been a jazz lover my whole life. The Duke was one of my favorites. He was from Washington, you know. Come in. Most of the other guests have arrived."

He led her into the kitchen and introduced her to Annabel.

"It's a pleasure meeting you," Annabel said. "We're pleased that you could make it."

"It was good of Flo to invite me," Jayla said.

"Any friend of Flo's is always welcome."

"This is a lovely apartment."

"Thank you. We enjoy it. We gave up a house in Foggy Bottom to move here."

"That's where I live," Jayla said. "Foggy Bottom. It's a nice area."

"Drink?" Mac asked. "The bar is pretty well stocked, and I make a mean mojito."

Jayla opted for a club soda with lime. Mac escorted her to the terrace overlooking the Potomac River where Brixton and Flo conversed with the federal judge, Karl Wilson, and his wife, Emily. Introductions made, Emily Wilson complimented Jayla on her dress.

"Thank Flo," Jayla said. "I bought it at her shop."

"Flo tells me that you're a scientist," the judge said.

"I work for Renewal Pharmaceuticals in medical research," Jayla said. "It's a smaller but up-and-coming firm in Bethesda."

"Exciting work, huh?" Brixton said. "Finding a cure for some weird disease."

"I'm not sure that 'exciting' is the right word," Jayla said. "Developing a new drug that ends up with FDA approval can take years of experimentation, clinical trials, thousands of hours running experiments, and testing different compounds."

"Sounds exciting compared to what I do most of the time," Brixton said. "I spend my days following errant husbands cheating on their wives, or vice versa."

"That's not what I hear, Mr. Brixton," Judge Wilson said. "You were involved in solving the murder of that congressional intern, as I recall."

"Robert likes to play down what he does," Flo said. "He was also stabbed by a psychopath, and ended up in Maui breaking up an illegal arms dealer's operation. Hardly a dull way to make a living."

"All in a day's work," Brixton said, laughing to indicate that he didn't mean it. "The truth is that as long as there are yahoos out there doing dumb things, I'll always have an income."

Mac, who'd retreated to the kitchen, reappeared with Annabel, drinks in hand.

"We were talking about Robert's escapades," Flo said.

"I'd rather hear about Ms. King here and how she's conquering rare diseases," said Brixton.

Jayla was in the process of disabusing them of that notion when the doorbell rang.

"That must be Will," Annabel said, leaving the terrace to greet the final guest of the evening, journalist Will Sayers, Brixton's close friend from his days as a cop in Savannah. While Annabel made a detour to the kitchen to pour their latest visitor his usual bourbon on the rocks, Mac introduced him to the other guests.

Sayers was dressed in what was almost a uniform:

baggy chino pants, vividly colored red-and-white striped button-down shirt, wide red suspenders, and a red-and-white railroad handkerchief hanging out of his rear pants pocket. He navigated the group in search of a chair that would accommodate his three hundred pounds, accepted his drink from Annabel, and eased down next to Jayla.

"Robert tells me you're from Papua New Guinea," Sayers said.

"I was born there," she said. "My father was from Australia and moved to Port Moresby to open a clinic and laboratory."

"I know Port Moresby," Sayers said. "I wrote a series of articles years ago about World War II and how the natives of New Guinea fought the Japanese. I got to spend a few days there."

"I'd enjoy reading your articles," she said. "Are they online?"

"Isn't everything these days? I'm sure I have a print-out I can give you, save your having to look it up."

Conversation turned to many topics on the terrace until it was time for dinner. Mac and Annabel had whipped up veal martini as an entrée, accompanied by a salad, freshly baked bread from the Watergate bakery, and Mac's favorite vegetable, broccoli cooked in his special garlic and pepper sauce. Drinks had been replenished and spirits were high at the table. Jayla had abandoned her nonalcoholic drink for a glass of Chablis, and Sayers was on his third bourbon; his ability to consume alcohol without showing the effects always amazed Brixton and the Smiths.

"What's the latest in drug research?" the judge asked Jayla during dinner. "It seems that someone is always coming up with a promising new cure for one disease or another."

"Or one that'll kill you if you take it," Sayers said. "I see those ads on TV for medicines. They spend most of the time telling you all the serious side effects you'll suffer if you take any of them."

This brought a round of laughter from the guests.

Sayers adopted his best TV announcer voice: "If you take this drug for your hemorrhoids you might get dizzy, throw up, lose weight, have heart palpitations, develop ulcers, rashes, muscle weakness—and *die*." He drew out the last word for emphasis.

"The FDA requires that advertisements include mention of side effects that occur above a certain threshold, even if it's only a fraction of a percent," Jayla informed him.

"What drug are *you* working on?" Brixton asked Jayla.

"My company's involved in a few things," she answered, "trying to develop a drug for hepatitis, a skin cream for eczema, and a new painkiller. I'm on the team looking for a better pain med."

"You mentioned your father," Emily Wilson said. "Is he involved in medical research, too?"

"He was," Jayla said, "until his recent death."

"Oh, I didn't know," Emily said. "I'm so sorry."

"That's all right," Jayla said. "But yes, besides running his clinic in Port Moresby he was also involved in trying to develop a more effective pain reliever, one with greater potency and fewer side effects." She looked at Sayers. "Side effects like the ones you mentioned."

"Addiction to prescription painkillers is a growing problem," the judge said. "OxyContin, Percocet, other opioids. Highly addictive."

"Me, I take an aspirin every day," Sayers said, "one of those little ones they say help stave off heart attacks and strokes."

"Eighty-one milligram," Jayla said. "Aspirin is a wonderful drug, but it only goes so far in alleviating pain."

"Aspirin must make Bayer filthy rich," the judge said. "They own it, don't they?"

"Bayer owned the rights to aspirin until a German company bought them out years ago, after the First World War," Jayla said.

"I was reading the other day that Americans consume something like eighty million aspirin pills a year," Sayers said.

"And you're working on the next aspirin?" the judge's wife asked Jayla.

"Wouldn't that be wonderful?" Jayla said. "Actually we're trying to synthesize an aspirin-like compound. My father was working differently. He was convinced that a powerful painkiller could be created using only native plants."

"It's hard to imagine that effective medicines can be made from simple plants that grow wild in the ground," Annabel said.

"Many of our drugs come from chemicals derived from plants," Jayla said. "They always have. Aspirin was originally made from salicylic acid that's found in the bark of willow trees, and a possible cure for ebola looks like it could come from tobacco leaves."

"Wouldn't you know it?" Sayers proclaimed. "Every couple of years the medical profession changes its mind. Cholesterol is bad for you, then it's good for you. Drinking is bad for you, then it's good for you. Smoking is bad for you but maybe tobacco will cure ebola."

"Drinking in moderation," Annabel said.

"Tobacco *leaves,* not smoking," Mac added.

"Sounds like what you're doing is a noble undertaking," Emily Wilson said. "You say your father was involved in the same sort of research to develop a better aspirin?"

"He was experimenting with plants native to PNG. The country has thousands of them. The trick is to come up with the right combination. That's what he was working on when he died."

"Had he gotten very far?" Mac asked.

"I think he was well on his way to succeeding," Jayla

said, thinking of the long letter and packets of seeds that he'd left for her with the housekeeper, Tabitha, that Jayla had secured in a safe deposit box at her bank. "He used what he'd developed on some of his patients at the clinic. He said it alleviated their pain without side effects."

"Maybe you could carry on his work," Emily Wilson said.

"I might," Jayla said.

Mac sensed her discomfort with the subject and changed it. He asked Will Sayers, "What's the latest scandal in D.C.?"

"I thought you'd never ask," the corpulent journalist said. "Let's see. The VP opened his mouth again and said something stupid about Russia, breaking the rule that he's never to say anything in public unless he's reading what somebody else wrote for him. That congressman who is accused of having plagiarized the thesis he wrote to get his advanced degree is in the news again. Seems he not only plagiarized his thesis, he stole what somebody else wrote for the op-ed piece he supposedly penned for the *New York Times*. Oh, and our esteemed senator from Georgia, the honorable Ronald Gillespie, might have gone too far in accepting money and other favors from his favorite lobbying group, Big Pharma. Everybody knows that he's on their payroll—he's never seen a piece of legislation favoring them that he doesn't love— but looks like he's gone overboard this time. That's the story I'm in the process of running down."

"Business as usual in the nation's capital," Brixton commented.

"Robert's not a fan of our nation's capital," Mac said.

"What's to be a fan of?" Brixton said. "Lawmakers don't make decisions that are good for the country. They're for sale to the highest bidder." He turned to Sayers. "Like your Georgia senator Gillespie. Pay me and I'll vote for anything that's good for you and the hell with what it might do for the citizens."

Mac and Annabel could see what was coming, a rant

from their jaded friend about politics and the political system.

"Dessert?" Annabel asked. "Key lime pie."

"Key lime pie, my favorite," Sayers said. "And is there any of that good bourbon left?"

Brixton and Flo offered to drive Jayla home, but she'd taken her car to the Watergate and didn't need a lift.

"It was a pleasure meeting you," Mac said.

"Please don't be a stranger," said Annabel.

"If I need a lawyer I know who to call," Jayla said.

"Anytime you need legal advice," Mac said, "just yell."

"You look great in that dress," Flo said, hugging Jayla.

"Thanks to you, Flo. Good night everyone. And thanks again."

Karl and Emily Wilson left right after Jayla, and the remaining guests repaired to the terrace for after-dinner drinks.

"She's a knockout," Sayers commented.

"As nice as she is beautiful," Flo said.

"Tragic what happened to her father," Mac said.

"How did he die?" Sayers asked.

"He was murdered," Mac said. "Stabbed to death. Do you know much about it, Flo?"

"No, just that he was a physician and ran a clinic and lab in Papua New Guinea."

"Maybe some druggie looking for a fix," Sayers offered. "The doctor confronts him and the druggie pulls a knife. Not unheard of, even here in our nation's capital."

"But Jayla said that someone bulldozed the land where her father grew his plants. Could that possibly be just a coincidence?" Flo asked.

"It could be," Mac said. "If you believe in coincidences."

"There has to be some connection," said Annabel. "It sounds like his murder and the destruction of his property happened at about the same time. What do you think, Will?"

"Papua New Guinea is a strange place," the large newspaper editor and reporter replied.

Brixton had retreated to a corner of the terrace. As Mac passed, the attorney said, "You're unusually quiet this evening, Robert, although we did enjoy your view of government and politics."

"I've got stuff on my mind," Brixton said.

As Annabel carried dishes from the terrace to the kitchen she stopped to talk with Brixton. "Emily Wilson suggested that Jayla carry on her father's work," Annabel said. "Maybe that's what she's doing at the pharmaceutical company she works for."

"I'm not a fan of Big Pharma," Brixton said. "They gouge people who need their medicines and can't afford to pay for them. These pharmaceutical companies own Congress with their lobbying and the big bucks they throw at the politicians to keep medicines from other countries getting here."

Neither Mac nor Annabel were in the mood for another pontification from their friend, and simply nodded and disappeared into the kitchen. Mac's final words to Brixton were, aside from a pleasant good night, "I'm thinking that if Jayla's father did succeed in inventing a better pain reliever without side effects and addictive qualities, there would be a lot of pharmaceutical companies shaking in their boots."

7

Jayla was glad that she'd accepted the invitation to the Smiths' Watergate apartment. Aside from the brief conversation about her father's work, the other trains of lively conversation had distracted and amused her, a welcome respite.

But now, as she walked through the door of her Foggy Bottom apartment, it was as though darkness had followed her inside, like the black cloud that always hovered over a cartoon character in the *L'l Abner* comic strip.

She responded to the flashing red light on her answering machine.

"Jayla, it's Nate Cousins. I thought that you might be up for dinner tonight but I see that you've already gone out. Hope it's a pleasant evening. Please call me at home if it isn't too late, or at my office tomorrow." He left both numbers.

Nathan Cousins had been vice president of public affairs at Renewal Pharmaceuticals when Jayla went to work for the company, but resigned a little over a year ago to open his own PR agency servicing the pharmaceutical industry. Some people, Jayla included, wondered why he made that move considering the generous salary, stock option plan, and package of perks he received as an executive at Renewal. But his motive became clear once it was learned that before leaving he'd cut a sweet deal with the company paying him four times what his salary had been.

Cousins had brought to Renewal an eclectic background. Like Jayla he'd been born into a mixed marriage. A native of Oakland, California, mother white, father black, he had excelled in sports while attending high school. Upon graduating he'd been signed to a minor league baseball contract by the San Francisco Giants, and played a year for the San Jose Giants, the Giants' A-level team. He'd performed well enough to be elevated the next season to the AA-level team, the Richmond Flying Squirrels, but that step up proved too much of a hurdle for the slick-fielding, light-hitting prospect.

Upon his release he enrolled as a marketing major at the University of California, San Francisco, with an eye toward applying his education to an administrative position in professional sports. But the university was particularly known for its graduate-level health sciences curriculum, and a professor who'd become a mentor persuaded him that the pharmaceutical industry offered greater opportunity. Cousins took several elective science courses, and upon graduating applied to a number of pharmaceutical firms around the country. He landed an entry-level job with one in California, moved from there to a better paying one in Chicago, and eventually ended up with Renewal Pharmaceuticals in Bethesda, Maryland.

His rise up the corporate ladder was swift. Tall and slender, clothes draped on him as though he was a runway model. An easy laugh, and the useful attribute of making everyone feel as though he or she was the most important person in the room, served him well. He was universally liked by everyone at Renewal, and when he was tapped as the replacement for the departing VP of public affairs the congratulations from co-workers were numerous and heartfelt.

Cousins had never married, which spawned some snide comments about whether he was gay. He attended company functions on the arms of an assortment of attractive ladies, and office scuttlebutt had it that one of them represented a serious relationship. But she faded from the picture as he continued to play the field. He'd made it known to certain colleagues at Renewal that he considered Jayla King one of the most beautiful women he'd ever met—certainly the most beautiful PhD medical researcher—and he'd made overtures to her about going out. She'd refused his advances, not because she didn't find him appealing but because she wasn't interested in dating anyone at that juncture. She threw herself into her work and had a bare-bones social life, something she questioned at times when in a reflective mood. She and Cousins had their mixed parentage in common, although his complexion was fairer than Jayla's. He was often assumed to be Hispanic. Her darker looks suggested that less cream had been added to the coffee than his. He was successful, engaging, and intelligent—"What a catch," a friend often told her. But she continued to turn down his requests that they get together socially, and he eventually shelved the pursuit.

He bumped into Jayla at Renewal's headquarters while there for a meeting.

"I heard about your dad," he said. "I'm so sorry."

"Thanks," she replied.

"No word on who killed him?"

She shook her head and swallowed a tear.

"From what you've said about him he was quite a guy."

He sensed that she wasn't in the mood for further conversation about her father's untimely demise and quickly said, "Up for lunch? My meeting will wrap up before noon. My treat. I'm in the mood for something French, like Mon Ami Gabi. Best onion soup and steak frites in the area."

"I don't think so, Nate, but thanks anyway. I brought something from home."

"How about lunch tomorrow? Or dinner tonight? Same place."

She was about to decline his offer but thought of Flo's advice to get out more. The pleasant evening she'd spent with the Smiths and their friends influenced her decision making. "All right," she said, "dinner would be nice."

He picked her up at seven and they drove to the restaurant on Woodmont Avenue where a valet took the car. The popular French bistro was bustling, and while they waited at the bar for their table to be vacated, Cousins ordered a perfect Manhattan, and a white wine for Jayla.

"I'd never been here before," she said, "but some of my friends have. It has a wonderful reputation."

"Yes, it's great. I come here often to entertain media people. I have a house account. How does it feel to be back in the grind?"

"It feels good," she said. "It takes my mind off—well, off other things."

"Walt Milkin is really high on you, Jayla. He told me that you have a very bright future in medical research."

She wasn't prepared for the compliment and uttered a weak, "That's nice to hear."

He offered his glass, and they touched rims.

"I suppose that medical research is in your genes," he said.

"I guess it is, although I don't think I could ever be as devoted to it as my father was."

"What sort of research was he involved with?" Cousins asked casually.

"He was trying to develop a pain reliever using indigenous plants grown on Papua New Guinea. There are thousands of them, and the natives use many to cure all sorts of ailments—asthma, antiseptic for wounds, orthopedic pain, hypertension, even cancer at a small hospital on one of the islands. You name it."

He laughed. "They really work on all those problems?"

"They do as far as the natives are concerned," she said, sipping her wine.

"Maybe a placebo effect?"

"Maybe," she said, "but my father believed that there were legitimate physical medicinal values to those plants. The trick was to find the right combination, and the proper processing of them."

"Your table is ready, Mr. Cousins," someone from the restaurant staff said. "I'll bring your drinks to you."

Cousins ordered another drink; Jayla nursed her wine. Upon his recommendation they ordered onion soup and the chilled seafood platter for two—lobster, jumbo shrimp, oysters, and salmon tartare. Jayla took in the handsome dining room, tables covered with pristine white tablecloths, the glassware glimmering in the flattering light. The man across the table from her sat quietly, his attention directed at her.

"How is your new agency doing?" she asked.

"Fine, couldn't be better. I just hired my fourth person. The pharmaceutical industry is under a lot of scrutiny these days, pressure from the government. It's never needed smart PR as much as it does now. The whole health care industry is in chaos, especially prescription painkillers. The Centers for Disease Control and Prevention is underwriting programs to prevent prescription drug overdoses. It's reached epidemic proportions." He sipped. "So tell me more about your father's research, Jayla. That is, if you don't mind talking about it."

She had no reason to hold back on details, yet she did. Nor did she talk about the letter and plastic sleeves containing seeds that her father had left for her that rested securely at the bank. She didn't have a tangible reason to withhold the information from Cousins, or from anyone for that matter. It wasn't that she intended to do anything with the envelope's contents—at least not at the moment. It was more a matter of the highly personal nature of those items, a love letter from her dear father combined with his narrative of what strides he'd made with his research. Since returning to Washington she hadn't told anyone what he'd left her.

"Did he have others working with him?" Cousins asked.

"Just one assistant," she said.

She hadn't thought of Eugene Waksit in a while and wondered what he was doing.

"Maybe *he* can carry on your father's work," Cousins said.

"Oh, I don't think so, Nate. He's a bright guy, but I assume he'll move on to another lab, another clinic, maybe go to work for a hospital in Australia. He was educated there. So was my father."

She thought of Waksit again, and of her father's detailed scientific notes and packets of medicinal plants that had gone missing from the laboratory. She'd wondered initially whether Waksit had removed those notes and plants, but had quickly dismissed the notion. Among many things her father had instilled in her was to avoid thinking the worst of people—unless they gave you a tangible reason for it. Her father had placed his faith in Eugene, and that should have been good enough for her. Still . . .

"So," Cousins said as they awaited the arrival of their dinner, "tell me about Jayla King."

She laughed. "What is there to know? I work for Renewal Pharmaceuticals the way you did until you resigned."

It was his turn to laugh. "No one can be *that* modest," he said. "I mean Jayla King the person. You were born and raised in Papua New Guinea. That's a part of the world I know nothing about, absolutely nothing."

"Well, let's see," she said. "It's off the northern coast

of Australia, a series of islands with Port Moresby as its capital. That's where I was born and brought up. Most parts of the mainland can be very primitive. My mother was descended from the Chambri tribe. They live in the Sepik region named after the Sepik River, a village called Pagwi. It's a fascinating, poorly explored place. It has thousands of plant and animal species that have never even been examined and named. It's not an easy place to navigate. The last I knew there were more than eight hundred separate languages spoken."

"Whew!" he said. "How can people communicate with each other?"

"There's an accepted general language, sort of a Pidgin English. It's called Tok Pisin."

"I'll take your word for it," he said.

Their dinner was served and they dug into the sumptuous platter, and a basket of warm bread.

"Enjoy it?" Cousins asked when they were finished eating.

"Very much."

"Let's get back to my knowing Jayla King a little better," he said. "I take it that your ending up working at a pharmaceutical company was not a coincidence. Did you work with your father in his lab?"

"A little, not much. He spent most of his day in his clinic treating people. He was such a warm and sympathetic man. He considered it a personal failure when a patient died."

"Sounds like he was a missionary as well as a physician."

"In a way he was."

"What was he working on when he died?"

She sighed and sat back. "He was convinced that he could create a new pain reliever from the local plants that didn't have all the serious side effects of our modern drugs."

"Like what Renewal is working on," Cousins offered.

"It's different," Jayla said. "We're trying to synthesize

a new pain reliever from existing chemical compounds. My father's goal was to accomplish the same end using naturally grown products."

"And?" Cousins said, eyebrows raised.

"And?"

"Had he succeeded?"

She realized that she'd said more about her father's work than she'd intended, and simply answered, "He thought that he was making progress."

"Maybe you can build upon his work, Jayla."

"I don't think so," she said, folding her napkin and placing it on the table. "Dinner was delicious."

"Dessert?"

"Thank you, no."

"After-dinner drink? I think this dinner deserves their best Cognac."

"Please, go ahead," she said, "but I'll pass."

He walked her to the door of her apartment building in Foggy Bottom.

"I'm glad I had the chance to learn more about Jayla King," Cousins said.

"There isn't much to learn," she said. "See you at work tomorrow? Oh, that's right, you don't work at Renewal anymore."

"But I might as well. I spend most of my time there. Can we do this again sometime soon?"

"Only if we talk more about you than about me," she said.

The moment when he might have attempted to kiss her good night passed. He squeezed her hand, wished her a good night's sleep, and walked away.

She turned on the TV in her apartment, the talking heads on a cable news channel providing background noise as she changed into pajamas and a robe. She settled at a desk in the living room to catch up on some bill paying, which she'd fallen behind on while away. Meticulous in the way she structured her approach to her finances, she used a spreadsheet on which she entered each bill and the date it was due. It was a system that she'd developed for herself and she was pleased with the way it worked. When she'd leased the Honda CRV she currently drove, the manager at the dealership had complimented her on her high credit score.

As she prepared to pull an invoice from its folder in the "Bills To Be Paid" section of the file drawer, she suddenly sat back and surveyed her desktop. Something was different. Her father had always stressed the importance of paying attention to detail. As a result her approach to keeping the desktop neat and organized bordered upon an obsessive-compulsive disorder, although she knew she didn't suffer from that. She simply enjoyed order in every aspect of her life, including the externals. She wouldn't leave the apartment for work unless items on the desk were square to each other, pens and pencils lined up, nothing askew and out of alignment. To leave for the day without having made her bed, or ensuring that every item of clothing wasn't where it was supposed to be, was unthinkable to her.

But something on the desk was wrong. She was convinced that she hadn't left the pads and pencils where they were now. But could she be certain? She mused. It had been a hectic period in her life, racing to make the flight to Papua New Guinea, the turmoil surrounding her father's murder, returning to Washington and catching up on what she'd missed, including paying the bills, going back to work, and always the letter her father had left her occupying her thoughts.

She forced a laugh and shook her head. "You're getting messy," she said aloud, and after squaring the items on the desk got back to paying her bills.

That chore completed, and envelopes ready to mail the next morning, she settled back to watch two guests debating a decision the president had made regarding another hot spot in the world that had potential ramifications for the country's national security. Eventually she turned off the TV and headed for the bedroom, pleasant memories of the evening at the Smiths', and the dinner with Nate Cousins accompanying her. But before climbing into bed she returned to the living room, switched on the lights, and surveyed the desktop where everything was now the way she wanted it to be. She turned off the lights, smiled, climbed into bed, and was asleep in minutes.

8

WEWAK, PAPUA NEW GUINEA

Walter Tagobe was drunk. He'd been drunk since arriving in Wewak.

He sat at the bar in a shabby, fragrant waterfront pub next to a small house that had been converted to a hotel of sorts, more a rooming house, and stared vacantly at the glass of amber whiskey in front of him.

His first day away from his native village of Pagwi in the Sepik River basin had been exhilarating for the forty-year-old Tagobe. Aside from six years spent as a youngster in a Catholic missionary school for the "slow-witted" he'd never left Pagwi and had lived in the makeshift home on stilts he shared with his wife and two young boys his entire adult life. Walter may have been slow-witted, the label the nuns had assigned him—feeble-minded others termed it—but he wasn't stupid. In some ways he was intellectually superior to the other men in his family, although admittedly that was a low bar to vault. Walter had sold wooden bowls he fashioned from fallen trees to tourists until Dr. Preston King had arrived one day to examine a four-acre parcel of land he'd purchased, and on which he intended to grow native plants. Walter thought it was strange to farm plants that were easily collected in the jungle, but he was delighted when the doctor said that he needed someone in Pagwi to oversee the acreage. He hired Tagobe on the spot.

It was a gift from the heavens as far as Walter was concerned. He would be paid a small monthly stipend, which elevated him to almost regal status among the tribe, and despite the frequent expressions of resentment and envy from others he threw himself into the work, hiring local men to plant the species of plants that the doctor wanted, and making sure that the tract was well watered and that local youths didn't use it for play. He took to wearing a used blue suit jacket and a pair of pants he'd bought from a traveling merchant to better identify himself in his new executive role, despite the oppressive heat and humidity of the river basin, and boasted to his wife that he would eventually be called to Port Moresby to work at Dr. King's side. His wife scoffed at his pretentions and called him "long-long," crazy in local parlance, which didn't quash Walter's unrealistic dreams of becoming an even more important man.

When the two big white men with blue eyes arrived with a tractor fitted with a large blade, Walter was at the small farm tending to the plants.

"Hello," one of the men said, smiling. "Name's Paul. This is my pal Joey. We're here to bury the crops. Dr. King who owns this plot of land wants the plants overturned and burned to make way for new ones."

Walter's only contact with the doctor was when King came to the area and gave him instructions.

Joey handed him an envelope.

"Open it," Paul said. "The doctor wants you to have it."

Tagobe did as instructed. In the envelope was money, more money than Walter had ever seen before.

"The doctor says that he wants you to go to Wewak and wait for him there. That's what the money is for, to take a taxi to Wewak, check into a hotel and—" Paul grinned. "Find yourself a woman and enjoy yourself." He laughed and slapped Walter on the back of his blue suit jacket. "You know, pal, go and have a good time, lots of pretty girls there." He pulled a slip of paper from his pocket and wrote on it. "You go to this hotel. Nice place. The doctor will meet up with you there. Right Joey?"

Walter smiled. The doctor wanted to meet him in Wewak. That was good. Important men went to hotels to meet with other important men. And so Walter Tagobe wrapped a few belongings in a woven *bilum* bag, told his wife that he would be gone for a few days "on business," and took his first ever taxi ride to Wewak where he found the seedy hotel and secured a room. Despite the soiled sheets and single chair with a broken leg repaired with duct tape, it was palatial compared to the bamboo hut in which he and his family lived in Pagwi. Life was good for Walter Tagobe.

After checking in and paying four days in advance, he shoved the remaining cash into a pouch under the waistband of his pants and went to the adjoining bar where he ordered a meal of turtle in *sago,* a wrap for the meat, and a glass of rye whiskey, and waited for the arrival of Dr. Preston King.

The bartender, who was also the owner, eyed Tagobe suspiciously, his hand never far from the wooden club secreted behind the bar. His clientele certainly weren't upscale, but he seldom served illiterate natives straight from the jungle.

Tagobe stayed at the bar into the evening, becoming more inebriated with each refill of his glass. The bar began to fill up, mostly waterfront workers, many of them Australians. A group of them began talking with Tagobe, who was pleased to have the attention. In his drunkenness he didn't realize that they found him amusing and were deliberately getting him drunk.

"You say you're a big man, mate?" one of the men said.

"Very big," Tagobe managed in his Pidgin English, smiling broadly as he tried to keep up the conversation with his newfound friends. "I work for a doctor, Dr. King."

"Who is this doctor? What does he do?"

Tagobe tried to explain but wasn't getting through. He reached into the pocket of his blue suit jacket and withdrew the slip of paper on which the man had written the name of the hotel. "See? Doctor comes here to see me soon."

One of the Australians noticed the name printed in red at the top of the paper, "Alard Associates." He pointed it out to one of his buddies. "Paul Underwood works for them, doesn't he?"

"I think so. Where is Paul these days, Port Moresby?"

His drinking pal said, "I saw him here in Wewak yesterday, him and his buddy Joey drinking it up at the Lizard Lounge. He'd just come from Port Moresby."

"What's this Alard company do?"

"Beats me. Odd jobs. Paul never says much but he always has money in his pocket."

They returned their attention to Tagobe, who by now had to struggle not to fall off the barstool.

"You work for Alard?" Walter was asked.

"What?"

"Never mind."

Tagobe suddenly lurched from the stool, grabbed one of the men to keep from hitting the floor, stumbled outside, and vomited before bouncing off walls on his way to his room where he collapsed on the bed, still wearing his treasured blue suit jacket. When the other men realized that he wasn't coming back, they laughed, paid their tab, and left to continue their barhopping into the hot, humid night, heading for the Lizard Lounge, a popular Wewak bar with more upscale patronage.

"Look who's here," one of them said when they walked in and spotted Paul Underwood with two friends at the Lizard's bar. "Just talking about you, mate." They joined Underwood, a bear of a man with a buzz cut and wearing a T-shirt, jeans, and leather sandals, and his friends, including someone they knew only as Joey. One of the men who'd been with Walter Tagobe pulled out the note that Tagobe had shown him, and that he'd kept. "What's with this Alard company you work for?"

Underwood took the note and squinted at it through bloodshot eyes. "Where the hell did you get this?"

The man explained about meeting "this ignorant native in a bar."

"He gave you this?"

The man said through a laugh, "He says he's some big shot waiting for a doctor to meet up with him. He's a moron."

Laughter all around.

"He say who this doctor is?" Underwood asked.

The late arrivals looked at each other.

"King, I think," one said.

"I'll be back," Underwood said, leaving the bar and going outside where he made a call on his cell phone. When he returned Joey asked, "A problem?"

"No," Underwood said, grabbing his glass from the bar and downing its contents. "Let's go."

Underwood and Joey headed across town to the hotel in which Walter Tagobe slept.

"What room is the native in?" Underwood asked the owner, who sat at the makeshift desk.

"Who?"

"The native." Underwood turned to Joey. "What's his name?"

"Toboggin, something like that."

"Yeah, Taboge," Underwood said. "That's it."

"He's expecting you?"

"Yeah, he's expecting us."

The owner gave him the room number, which was on the ground floor at the rear of the building. The men went to it and Underwood opened the unlocked door. "Hey," he said, "wake up. Come on, get up." They stood over Walter on opposite sides of the bed.

Tagobe looked up through his haze, fear in his black eyes.

"Hey pal, it's me," Underwood said. "Remember? I gave you the money to come here."

Tagobe managed to sit up. He rubbed his eyes and moaned against the throbbing in his head.

Underwood and Joey reached down, grabbed Walter under his arms, and yanked him to his feet, holding him upright as he threatened to slip from their grasp and slide to the floor.

"You've been going around talking, huh?" Underwood said.

Walter didn't understand and said nothing.

"Come on, we'll take a walk."

Tagobe pulled loose from Joey's grip and stumbled back toward the bed. "The doctor," he said. "Where is the doctor?"

Underwood looked at Joey and grinned, said to Tagobe, "Right, the doctor. He's here, wants to see you."

"Where?"

"In the bar next door. He sent us to get you."

"The doctor is here?" Tagobe said.

"That's right," Underwood said as Joey regained his hold on Tagobe. "The doctor is here."

Tagobe's mouth felt as though it was stuffed with cotton, and the incessant pounding in his head hadn't abated. But he nodded, and a small smile came to his face. "I go to see the doctor. Big man, important man."

With Underwood and Joey holding him up, they left the room, passed through the lobby where the owner pretended not to be interested, and went out to the street. Underwood nodded toward an alley that separated the hotel from the bar, and they escorted Walter into it, rats scurrying out of their path. Underwood slammed Tagobe against a wall and snarled in his face, "You don't talk about nothing, damn it!"

"The doctor," Walter said.

"The doctor doesn't give a damn about you," Underwood said. "You keep your black mouth shut, you hear me?"

Walter tried to shake loose but the two big men had him securely pinned to the wall.

"You don't get it, do you?" Joey said, and slapped Tagobe's face, hard. He slapped him again, and Underwood rammed his fist into his belly, causing Walter to double over. He retched, his vomit spewing from his mouth; some of it landed on Underwood's toes that protruded from his sandals.

Underwood kneed Tagobe in the face, breaking his nose and neck. He slowly slid down, blood dripping from his broken nose and split lip.

Underwood swore again. "Look what he did to my foot," he growled.

"Let's get out of here," Joey said.

"Yeah," Underwood agreed. "He got the message."

Walter Tagobe's lifeless body was discovered the following morning by the owner of the bar in which the Sepik River tribesman had done his drinking. Before calling the police he went to Tagobe's room and removed the primitive bag in which Walter's few possessions were wrapped. He then called the police, who dispatched a unit including a small white panel truck into which Tagobe's body was loaded for a trip to the city morgue. He was stripped naked upon arrival, which revealed to the technician not only the raised welts on the back and torso of a man who'd undergone the ritual of the crocodile in his youth, but also a wad of kina banknotes that had been stuffed into his loincloth. The tech shoved the bills into the pocket of the lab coat he wore and continued readying the body for insertion into a vault.

"Any ID on him?" one of the cops who'd responded asked.

"Just this." He handed the cop a wrinkled, smeared one-page letter from a nun at the Catholic school where Walter had studied as a boy. On it she had written that he was a good boy and did his schoolwork. Walter had carried that letter with him ever since, seldom leaving home without it, and it had been taken from the blood-spattered blue suit jacket he'd been wearing.

"Walter Tagobe," the cop muttered.

"Must be from one of the tribes, maybe in Sepik," the tech said.

"Anything else on him?"

"No."

"He got beat up? A mugging?"

"Looks like it. Back of his head bashed in. Here." He handed the cop half of the money he'd taken from the body.

"*Ta*," the cop said, slipping the bills into his pants pocket. He shook his head. "That'll teach him to stay with his own. What's a Sepik native doing here in the city? Serves him right. G'day, mate."

9

WASHINGTON, D.C.

Private investigator Robert Brixton wasn't anxious to start the day.

The desire to remain in bed and pull the covers up over his head had been present ever since his youngest daughter, Janet, had been slaughtered by a terrorist bomber in an outdoor D.C. café two years earlier. Although he'd managed to help bring the brains and money behind the terrorist attack to justice—which was supposed to bring "closure" according to those who enjoy bandying about that word—he awoke each morning with vivid visions of Janet being blown up along with a dozen others in the name of God knew what, some warped religious fervor or sense of geopolitical justice? While those visions had been with him every morning since, they'd become more prevalent of late and lasted longer.

Flo Combes, the love of his life—he considered himself too old to use the term "girlfriend," live-in or otherwise—had tried a variety of ways to help mitigate these painful episodes, but had come to the conclusion that she was losing the battle. She'd sought mental counseling to help her formulate approaches to Brixton, and had put some of the professional advice into play, but ultimately she was told that the only hope for him to ever come to grips with his sorrow, and occasional bouts of rage, was to work with a psychologist or psychiatrist and hopefully banish the demons that lived within. She'd finally come to the point where she urged him—no, begged him—to see a psychotherapist, her pleas falling on deaf ears.

Not that she was surprised by his reticence to seek the help of a professional.

Brixton had been a cop, a good one, and had a cop's mentality that tended to dismiss "shrinks," who he claimed ended up in that business only because they were nuts themselves.

He'd put in a short tenure on the D.C. police force before heading for Savannah, Georgia, where he retired after twenty years on that southern city's MPD, and became a private eye. Savannah was also where he'd fallen in love with the feisty, attractive Flo, like him a transplant from Brooklyn, and who gave as good as she got to the crusty, cynical Robert "Don't Call Me Bobby" Brixton. Flo told friends that while Brixton could be difficult, he could also be "adorable"—her word for him—and they'd been together ever since, aside from occasions when Flo decided she needed a break from his jaded view of the world and the people who populate it. Those separations never lasted long. The fact was that they loved and needed each other.

Getting up this day was no different from the others since Janet's murder except that there was one added reason to dread it. He'd finally agreed with Flo that a session or two with a psychotherapist might be helpful, or, as she'd couched it, couldn't hurt. She'd made an appointment for Brixton with one of the professionals she'd consulted, John Bradford Fowler, whose office was in his Capitol Hill apartment.

"I don't trust somebody with a name like Bradford," Brixton groused as he joined Flo at the small table in their kitchen after showering and dressing.

"His name is *John* Bradford Fowler," Flo countered. "What's wrong with his name?"

"What is he, some nerdy little guy with a beard and big glasses?" Brixton said.

"He happens to be a very handsome man, and a very smart one, too."

"What's he want me to say, that I'm crazy?"

"Robert, stop it!" she said. "All he wants is for you to talk about what's bothering you. By discussing it you can hopefully put it to rest."

"Put it to rest? How do I put to rest the fact that some whack job blows herself up and takes my daughter with her?"

"That's why you're seeing him. You can work out those feelings so that they don't dominate your thinking all day, every day."

He guffawed. "Fat chance of that," he said as he slathered an English muffin with cherry preserves.

The conversation continued in that vein until Flo put a stop to it. "Robert," she said with finality, "you go see Dr. Fowler and see whether he can help you. If he can't, that's fine, but you at least have to try. You can't continue living this way, and neither can I."

He knew that she was right and didn't argue the point any further. They left the apartment together, she on her way to open Flo's Fashions, he to keep his appointment with Dr. John Bradford Fowler. As he headed for Fowler's office he felt as though he was about to face the guillotine. "John Bradford Fowler," he muttered to himself as he searched for a parking space within walking distance of the psychologist's apartment and office. He'd faced many tense situations as a cop and private investigator but had never felt the anxiety he suffered as he stood in front of the townhouse and summoned the courage to climb the short set of steps and ring the bell.

Lobbyist Eric Morrison also had reason not to want to get out of bed that morning.

He and his wife, Peggy Sue, had entertained sixteen people at their expansive home in Chevy Chase the previous night, and Eric was hungover. Eric and Peggy Sue were known for their parties—or "soirees" as she preferred to term them. While their gatherings always included friends, Eric also used them to cement relationships with those who could do him and his lobbying group some good, congressmen, congressional staffers with clout, and media types.

It had been a pleasant evening. Drinks flowed freely, a sumptuous array of hors d'oeuvres were passed by two uniformed servers from the caterer, and a young musician played popular tunes on the living room's black grand piano. But halfway through the party Morrison received a call from the VP of the Pharmaceutical Association of America's biggest and most powerful member.

"Can you talk?" the VP asked, cued by the sounds of music and cocktail party chatter in the background.

"Not at the moment," Morrison said. "We're entertaining guests and—"

"This is important, Eric."

"Can't it wait until morning?"

"Yes, it can, but no later than the morning. Meet me at eight at Hains Point at the eastern end of Potomac Park."

"What's this in reference to?" Morrison asked, put off by the VP's tone.

"I'll tell you in the morning, Eric. Get back to your guests."

"Who called?" Peggy Sue Morrison asked.

"Oh, just a client. Get the piano player to play more up-tempo songs. The party's dragging."

The VP was waiting when Morrison arrived. Tourists had already begun to show up; a family posed two children for photos.

Morrison and the VP shook hands and walked to a bench away from the gathering crowd.

"What's this all about?" Morrison asked.

"That doctor in Papua New Guinea."

"What about him?" Morrison asked, twisting on the bench against a knot forming in his gut. He hadn't told the VP about Dr. King's murder.

"He was murdered," the VP said.

"Murdered? Who? How do you know?"

"We have a source in Papua New Guinea who reported to me, but who told us is irrelevant. The question is who did you make arrangements with to burn and plow that plot of land?"

"Who did I—?" Morrison shook his head. "I can't tell you that. But if you're suggesting that whoever I hired killed the doctor, you're wrong." He didn't sound convincing.

"Who did you hire?" the VP repeated. "Whoever it was failed to get ahold of the doctor's research results."

"Please, I can't reveal who it was. It's a very reputable group. All I know is that the acreage was destroyed, per your instructions. As far as the research results, something must have kept it from happening. Maybe the doctor's murder had something to do with it. Maybe whoever killed him took the results. Yes, that must be it. Look, the doctor's murder is news to me. Sorry to hear it but it has nothing to do with what I did on your behalf."

Did the VP buy his lie? Did it matter? Did the murder of some crackpot doctor in a far-off place like Papua New Guinea matter? Had Alard and his people not only uprooted the plants but also killed the doctor? If so, so what? He, Eric Morrison, had made it clear to Alard that no one was to be hurt. Besides, Alard's people had nothing to do with the doctor's death. He believed that. Probably some drug addict. *Why question me about it?*

The VP answered his unasked question.

"I just hope that you didn't do anything to put the company in an awkward position, Eric."

"Of course not. Look, I accomplished what you

wanted by getting rid of this doctor's field. His murder had nothing to do with us. Relax. Everything is cool."

"That's what I want to hear," said the VP. "We'll just forget about the whole thing."

"Exactly," Morrison said, feeling the tension ebb.

"Before we go," the VP said, "what's new with Senator Gillespie?"

"He's in our pocket," Morrison assured him. "He's working both sides of the aisle to get the legislation you want passed. No concern on that front."

"Are you making any progress in helping defeat that goddamn bill that Senator Barnes has been pushing to reward pharmaceutical companies who develop drugs that can immediately be marketed as generic instead of waiting twenty years?"

"That doesn't have any chance of even coming up for a vote," Morrison said. "Gillespie is fighting it tooth-and-nail. The bill will fail big-time."

"Good."

The VP got up, shook Morrison's hand, and walked to where he'd parked his car. Morrison waited a few minutes before doing the same. The meeting had gone okay. The VP seemed to buy his denial of knowing anything about the murder of the doctor. Hopefully this conversation marked the end of it, for which Morrison was grateful. He'd never imagined that arranging for a four-acre plot of useless land to be bulldozed would also involve a murder. Did one thing have to do with the other?

It didn't matter.

He drove to his office feeling considerably lighter than when he'd gotten up that morning.

Jayla King wore her new dress with the "Flo's Fashions" label to work that morning.

While getting ready to leave the apartment she'd reflected on her dinner with Nate Cousins, and was glad that she'd accepted his invitation. She knew that it was important for her to try and live as normal a life as possible while simultaneously mourning the death of her father. She also thought back to the evening spent with Flo Combes, Robert Brixton, and the others at the Smiths' Watergate apartment. The journalist Will Sayers had been entertaining with his stories of political figures in the news, and the judge and his wife and the Smiths had been welcoming and intelligent dinner companions. She'd wondered at times about Brixton, Flo's boyfriend. Aside from his iconoclastic view of the world, she sensed a pervasive despondency and wondered what was at the root of it. She didn't know, of course, about his having lost a daughter in a terrorist bombing. Had she known, her having recently lost her father would have given her a sense of kinship with the brooding private investigator. Before leaving the apartment she took a final glance at her desk. Everything was in place, papers neatly aligned with each other, two pencils and a pen lined up like soldiers.

After arriving at Renewal Pharmaceuticals she slipped a white lab coat over her dress and entered the lab where two male scientists were already busy. They'd worked as a team for more than a year in search of a more effective, less expensive painkiller without the addictive qualities of such current popular prescription drugs as oxymorphone, oxycodone, hydromorphone, and morphine.

"Anything new?" she asked as she settled at her station.

"No. Those tests we ran while you were away came up a cropper. The blends of the synthetic compounds never produced anything useful."

"Does Walt know?" she asked.

One of the men laughed. "No. We figured we'd let you deliver the bad news."

"Me? Why me?"

"Because he likes you," was the response. "He's got a thing for you."

"Oh, stop it," she said. "He does not."

"Hey, I may not be the sharpest knife in the drawer but I can see when a guy has the hots for a woman."

"He's a happily married man," she said.

"Which doesn't mean he doesn't have an eye for an attractive woman. Hell, I'm happily married, too, but I still look."

She ignored them and started perusing the written results of their failed test.

"What's this I hear about your father?" one of them asked. He received a stern look from his colleague. "I mean about the research he was into. Word around here has it that he was after the same thing we're after, a better mousetrap, aka a better pain med."

"That's right," she said, not looking up from her reading.

"Using what, medicinal plants?"

"Uh, huh," she said.

"How far did he get before—?"

"He was making progress," Jayla said. "He used what he'd developed on his patients at the clinic he ran. It seemed to be working."

"So why don't we pick up on what he was doing? Do you have his lab results?"

"No. I mean, I know some of what he'd accomplished but not enough to carry on with it."

"That's a shame. Make you a fortune."

"My father was never after making a fortune, and neither am I."

The phone rang.

"It's Walt Milkin's office," the tech who'd answered said. "He wants to see you, Jayla."

"See what I mean?" the other lab worker said, chuckling.

She smiled and went to the executive floor where the company's president and CEO, Walter Milkin, had his office. Milkin possessed both a PhD in cell biology from Johns Hopkins, and a law degree from George

Washington. He'd founded Renewal Pharmaceuticals fifteen years ago, and had guided it to some minor successes, enough to sustain its constant quest into the development of the next "wonder drug" that would vault it into the sphere of Big Pharma. He was a charming man, nicknamed "the Silver Fox" thanks to his thick head of snow-white hair that was always meticulously groomed. He was a popular guest at pharmaceutical company gatherings, and had testified before numerous congressional committees and the FDA. He'd just returned from a conference in Geneva. But beneath his hail-fellow-well-met exterior was a steel trap of a mind and a commitment to succeed no matter what the cost.

His secretary ushered Jayla into his handsomely furnished office where he got up from behind his desk.

"Glad to see you," he said as he grasped her hand in both of his and indicated a chair. "Sit down, Jayla," he said. "Coffee, tea? Midge whips up a decent cup of coffee."

"Nothing, thank you, Dr. Milkin."

"I'm coffee'd out myself this morning," he said, taking a chair across from her. "So, you've been through the mill lately with what happened to your father."

"Yes."

"Murdered! We never think that something that terrible can happen to us and our families. Any word on— well, on who did it?"

"No, I'm afraid not."

"And how are you holding up?"

"Pretty well. The horror of it is never far from me, but I'm managing. It's what my father would have wanted. He didn't have a lot of patience for people who cave in to sorrow. He was a very philosophical man—and a wonderful one."

"I'm sure he was that, and more. His work had piqued some interest in the industry."

Jayla's face reflected her surprise. "I wasn't aware of that," she said.

"He'd been mentioned at a few conferences I've attended." He laughed. "Not that anyone knew precisely what he was up to in his lab. He was sort of a loner."

Jayla wasn't sure that "loner" was an apt description of her father. He'd been deeply involved in the health issues of patients in his clinic, and was known as a pleasant, sometimes gregarious neighbor. But she said nothing.

"Of course you, more than anyone, would know what successes he had in his experiments."

She thought once more of the long letter he'd left her, along with the packets of selected seeds. And then the bloody photos of the crime scene came and went.

"I'm afraid I'm more immersed in the experiments we're conducting here at Renewal than in dwelling on my father's work. His research notes were stolen at the time he was murdered."

"Adding insult to injury."

"Just another piece of the puzzle," she said.

"Lucky for us that you're immersed in your work here."

Should she use that moment to break the news that the latest round of lab work hadn't paid off? She decided not to. He'd find out soon enough. Besides, that particular failure only meant that they would go on to another attempt. That's the way pharmaceutical research went. Win some, lose many.

Milkin continued, "I suppose what I'm saying is that I'd like to know more about your father's work. After all, breakthroughs sometimes come from unexpected sources. Who was it that said all the advances of society are carried on the backs of its neurotics?"

"Are you saying that my father was—?"

"No, no, no," he quickly said, reaching and patting her hand. "What I mean is that those of us in the business of discovering and developing new medicines sometimes overlook the fact that it doesn't necessarily take a fancy laboratory and dozens of smart people to succeed in that goal. Your father worked alone, far from where we're sitting, and from what I've heard he might have latched on to something important."

"I know how pleased he would be to know that," she said, eager to leave. His kind words to her about her job at Renewal were welcome, but the shift of focus to her father's work was unsettling.

"Was anyone else involved in his research?" Milkin asked.

"No. Well, he had an assistant, Eugene Waksit, but I don't know to what extent he was directly involved."

"Interesting name," Milkin said.

"Not an uncommon name in PNG."

"PNG?"

"Papua New Guinea."

"Yes, of course. Are you in touch with this fellow?"

"No. I saw him when I returned home following my father's death, but I haven't heard from him since."

"He's from PNG?"

"Originally. I suspect that he's gone to Australia."

"I'd enjoy meeting this fellow."

"If he ever decides to visit me here in Washington I'll make a point of introducing you. I really should get back to the lab."

"I understand. Thanks for spending time with me, Jayla. As I said, we're extremely pleased to have you working here at Renewal."

He stood and offered his hand, and she left the office. Rather than return directly to the lab she stopped at an employee kitchen where she made herself a cup of tea and sat at a window reflecting on the meeting.

That her father's work was known to others really wasn't a surprise, although she seldom thought of him as someone who would be talked about in larger medical circles. She knew that he'd maintained contact with some of his physician colleagues during trips back home to Australia, and it was likely, even expected that he would discuss his work with them. But Milkin's interest in her father was off-putting for reasons she couldn't identify. Interesting, she thought, that Milkin asked whether anyone else had shared in her father's research. That question had resurrected Eugene Waksit to her thinking, and she wondered whether he was still in Port Moresby or had moved on. Would he ever show up in Washington as he said he might? Despite her mixed feelings about him, she would be glad to see him again, glad to see anyone with a direct connection to her father.

Psychologist John Bradford Fowler glanced at the wall clock above Robert Brixton's head. The session was almost over, ten minutes to go. Brixton had taken note when first meeting the shrink that he wasn't anything like Brixton had imagined he would be. Fowler was a big, rawboned man with a ruddy complexion and steel gray hair. If he didn't know that he was a psychologist Brixton would have pegged him as a retired drill sergeant.

They'd spent most of the appointment talking about the loss of Brixton's daughter. It hadn't been an easy conversation. Fowler had initially asked how Brixton preferred to be addressed, Mr. Brixton, or Robert.

"Your choice," Brixton replied. "Just don't call me Bobby."

Fowler had laughed, said, "Fair enough, provided you don't call me Johnny."

"Dr. Fowler?"

"Whatever you wish."

Fowler was not out of the Freudian psychoanalytical school of therapy, sitting passively while the patient talks. He engaged Brixton numerous times, asking questions to clarify statements Brixton had made. Toward the end Brixton said, "I really don't know why I'm here."

"You're here I assume because Ms. Combes asked for my assistance in helping you put the tragic death of your daughter in perspective. She encouraged you to see me, and here you are."

"Flo means well," Brixton said.

"That's a left-handed compliment, Robert. She obviously loves you and wants you to feel better about yourself."

At that moment Brixton feared that he might tear up and gave himself a harsh, silent reminder to not allow that to happen.

"What does she think, that I'll go out and jump off some building?"

"Have you thought of doing that?"

Brixton laughed. "Here in D.C.? They have height limits for buildings. The worst that would happen if I jumped off one is a broken leg."

Fowler smiled. Brixton's MO seemed to be to make a joke out of something he didn't wish to confront in a serious manner.

"I'm afraid our time is up," Fowler said. "I've really enjoyed our conversation."

Although Brixton didn't admit it, he'd enjoyed it, too.

"Will I see you again?" Fowler asked.

Brixton gave him his best Robert De Niro shrug. "Yeah, okay," he said.

"I'll look forward to it," Fowler said. "Make an appointment with my receptionist on your way out."

Brixton made the appointment for three days later, stepped out onto the street, and drew a deep breath. He'd dreaded walking into the shrink's office, but now that what he'd anticipated would be a waste of time and money was over, he felt lighter in spirit than when he'd arrived.

Of course, the forty-five minutes spent with Dr. John Bradford Fowler had had nothing to do with it. While he told himself that, he looked forward to seeing the shrink again.

10

Later that afternoon Nate Cousins left his public relations agency and drove to Renewal Pharmaceuticals in Bethesda where he met with the firm's president and CEO, Walter Milkin. He'd sensed urgency in Milkin's tone when the CEO called to request the meeting, and wondered what was on the man's mind. He found out soon after settling in Milkin's office.

"Glad you could make it," Milkin said as he poured himself two ounces of single-malt scotch from a small bar he maintained in one of the closets. Cousins declined a drink.

"It sounded important," Cousins said.

"I don't know whether it is or not," Milkin said, "but it could be. What I need to know is whether it *will* be."

"Another government intrusion?" Cousins asked.

"No, nothing like that. You know Jayla King?"

"Sure I know her," Cousins said, adding, "As a matter of fact we had dinner together last night."

"Yes, I'm aware of that."

Cousins laughed. "Word gets around fast, doesn't it?"

Milkin joined in the laughter. "If we had a water cooler I'd say that's where the rumors take life, Nate. Pleasant evening?"

"Very. She's charming as well as beautiful."

"And damn smart. Did you and she talk about her father and his work?"

"A little."

"I met with her this morning. I asked about her father's work. She seems—well, she seems reluctant to discuss it."

"Understandable considering how recently he died."

"Yes, of course, but I'd like to know more about the work he was doing using natural ingredients."

"I got the feeling in talking with her that she wasn't especially involved in his work."

"But that doesn't make sense, does it?"

"In what way?"

Milkin shrugged. "Well, here she is a PhD working in medical research. It seems to me that father and daughter would have a lot to discuss. At least she'd be aware of what he'd discovered."

Cousins wasn't eager to further the debate and simply said, "You're probably right."

Milkin picked up a piece of paper on which he'd written "Eugene Waksit" and handed it to Cousins. "She ever mention this name?"

"Waksit? No, I don't think so. I think I'd remember a name like that. Who is he?"

"According to Jayla he worked as her father's lab assistant."

"Doesn't ring any bells for me."

"I'd like to know more about this Waksit fellow," Milkin said.

"Shouldn't be hard to trace."

"I thought maybe that you could do it for me."

"I can certainly try but—"

"Now that you're seeing Jayla socially it might make the task easier, you know, find out from her about him, make a few casual inquiries while you're enjoying dinner and a glass of wine together." He was about to add "pillow talk" but thought better of it.

"All right," Cousins said, not sure he was comfortable with the request.

"I think that 'casual' is the operative word here, Nate. I wouldn't want Jayla to know that I'm going around her. Understood?"

"I believe so," Cousins said.

"And while you're using your sizable charm to find out from the talented Dr. King what you can, you might also use your considerable network of friends to add to your knowledge of this Eugene Waksit. Waksit! Shouldn't be too many people in the world with that name. I'll see what I can scout up, too. By the way, Nate, the PR work you're doing for Renewal is splendid, much appreciated."

"Thank you, Walt. Is there anything else?"

"Not at the moment. You have my private and home numbers. Stay in touch."

Cousins took a detour on his way out of the building to stop by the lab in which Jayla and her two colleagues were at work. She spotted him through the door's window and joined him in the hallway.

"Here for a meeting?" she asked.

"Just wrapped up," he said. "I just wanted to say how much I enjoyed last night."

"I did, too. Thank you."

"We have to do it again soon."

"I'd like that."

"What are you doing tonight?"

"Tonight? I—"

"I'm in the mood for steak," he said. "I have a house account at Morton's and especially like the one in Georgetown. Game?"

"A rain check? I need a night alone with a good book."

"Sure." He looked at his watch. "Almost quitting time. How about a quick drink after work? I promise to get you home for that good book in an hour."

She smiled. "All right," she said. "But just an hour."

"It's a deal. It's a little after four. How about I pick you up at five?"

"I have my car."

"Okay, then meet me at five thirty at the 1905 roof bar. It's on top of 1905 Bistro & Bar, on Ninth Street, in the Shaw District between U and Florida Avenue. Not as noisy as most after-hours watering holes. If you change your mind about dinner we can pop downstairs to the restaurant."

"I'll meet you there," Jayla said, her emotions mixed.

Cousins was at the bar when she arrived. He'd commandeered two stools. A perfect Manhattan sat in front of him, along with a platter of truffled deviled eggs.

"Hope you like deviled eggs," he said. "I could live on them."

"I like them, too," she said. She looked out over the city at the Washington Monument in the distance. "Lovely view," she said.

"That's what's nice about height restrictions on buildings here in D.C.," he said. "Roof bars are a thriving industry."

Her white wine arrived and Cousins touched the rim of his glass to hers. "Here's to you," he said, then laughed and added, "I sound like Bogart in *Casablanca*. Here's to you, kid."

"Are you a movie buff?" she asked.

"Love the oldies. What about you, Jayla? What's your taste in movies and books?"

They spent the next fifteen minutes in easy conversation about their preferences in literature and films. As they talked Jayla realized how impressed she was with the handsome man seated next to her. There was a gentleness to him that was appealing, and his focus never left her and what she was saying.

The conversation shifted when he asked, "What about your father, Jayla? Did he work alone or with a team?"

"He worked pretty much alone. Actually his work in the lab was limited because of the clinic. He was in the lab mostly at night and on Sundays."

"Did you ever work with him?"

"No. Oh, sometimes, but never to the extent that I was involved in any experiments. As much as he loved me I think he preferred to work by himself."

"What was growing up in Papua New Guinea like? I'm sure it's nothing like Oakland where I was born and raised."

"Different in some ways, of course, but with the same sort of problems as most places I suppose. I was raised in the capital, Port Moresby, more urban than most of the country. My father was white."

"A mixed marriage. My parents were a mixed race couple, too. It posed problems for me every once in a while."

"Someone told me that you used to be a professional baseball player."

His laugh was self-effacing. "I had a minor league contract and played a couple of years. Good field, no hit. That was me." He grunted and shook his head. "I was just thinking," he said, "about your father and his work. If he worked alone as you say, whatever advances he'd made in his research died with him. What a shame."

She started to respond but held herself in check.

"I really should be going," she said.

"Another wine?"

"Thank you, no."

"How about dinner downstairs?" he asked. "The food is good and they have live jazz on Thursdays, only this isn't Thursday. Bad timing."

"I'd like that, Nate, but I really need to get home."

"I understand, and I promised I'd see that you got there."

He paid the check and walked her to her car.

"I enjoyed it," she said. "It's a nice place."

"Being with you was what was nice about it," he said.

She smiled demurely. He placed fingertips on her cheek and brushed his lips against hers. To his surprise she intensified the pressure.

"We'll do this again soon, right?" he said.

"Yes, we will," she said, pleased that he hadn't pressed to extend the evening.

"Enjoy your book," he said, "and careful driving home."

11

At a few minutes before midnight Jayla turned off the television and headed for the bedroom when the phone rang.

"Jayla, it's Elgin Taylor. Please tell me that I didn't wake you."

"You came close," she said. "I'm usually asleep at this hour but I became engrossed in an old movie. How are things with you?"

"Things are good with me," said the Port Moresby attorney, "but a few complications have set in regarding your father's estate."

"Oh? Anything serious?"

"Not yet, but it could develop into something nettlesome. I don't suppose that you've heard what happened to the fellow who took care of your dad's plot of land in Pagwi, Walter Tagobe."

"No, I haven't heard anything."

"He was found dead in an alley in Wewak."

"Oh, my goodness, how dreadful. In an alley you say? Had he been attacked?"

"Yes. The police are labeling it a mugging and robbery that went wrong. I only know about it because I received a phone call from the acting police commissioner in Wewak, a fellow named Rauba. The police traced Tagobe back to Pagwi and were told that he oversaw your father's land there. He'd received a monthly stipend from your dad for his services, and the police wanted to inform your father of his death. I told Mr. Rauba, of course, about your father's demise, which should have put an end to their inquiry. But Rauba has turned the case over to an Australian detective."

"Why?"

"It seems that the possible connection between Walter Tagobe's murder, your father's murder, and the razing of your father's land, has piqued their interest, which when you think about it makes sense."

"Yes, it certainly does. What had Walter been doing in Wewak?" Jayla asked. "According to my father Walter Tagobe never left Pagwi. He used to say that Walter would benefit from seeing a bit of the larger world."

"I don't know why he was in Wewak, Jayla. Actually, the Tagobe murder is only one of a few issues that I need to raise with you. Your father had written and executed a codicil to his will that I was unaware of. I found it among numerous papers he left. It was hand-written, signed by him, and witnessed by a nurse your father hired from time to time. In that codicil he left this Walter Taboge chap what amounts to a thousand U.S. dollars."

"I wasn't aware of that either, but I'm not surprised. My father was kind to those who worked for him. What will happen to the money now that Walter is dead?"

"I'll have to sort that out with his family. But there's more to the story, Jayla."

"I'm listening, Mr. Taylor."

"I received a call from the young man who worked as your father's assistant in the laboratory, Eugene Waksit."

"You heard from Eugene? How is he?"

"I'm sure he's fine, although the reason for his call was unsettling. He told me that your father had vowed to him that should he die, all the results of his experiments would belong to him in return for his years of service."

Jayla thought for a moment before saying, "That doesn't make any sense. My father would never do such a thing."

"My reaction exactly."

"Dad willed everything to me, aside from specified amounts of money for his housekeeper, Tabitha, and for Eugene."

"Precisely."

"Does his unsubstantiated claim hold any water?" Jayla asked.

"It could, Jayla. Obviously, having something in writing to bolster his claim would help his cause, but a verbal agreement, especially since he worked for your father for a number of years and was thought of highly enough to be left five thousand dollars for his service, adds a certain gravitas to what he says."

"I can't believe this," Jayla said through a burst of exhaled air.

"I suggested that Mr. Waksit meet with me to further discuss this, which he agreed to. He said that he would call again. He hasn't."

"He lives in Port Moresby," Jayla said.

"Or did," Taylor said. "I have his address from your father's papers, as well as his phone number. I called it but was informed that it was no longer in service, which leads me to believe that he's now living elsewhere. Of course he'll have to make contact with me if he wants to receive the money your father left him in his will, but that's months off. The probate system grinds slowly here in PNG. Do you have a more recent address for him?"

"I don't. I mean, I assume that the address I have is the same one that you have, the apartment he lived in since he came to work for my father." She gave him the phone number, which matched the one that Taylor had called.

"I'll let you know if I hear from him," Jayla said.

"I'd appreciate that. I suspect that this will all blow over, but better to nip it in the bud. A suggestion?"

"Please."

"Do you have an attorney there in the States?"

"No. Do I need one?"

She heard him sigh. "Probably not. I doubt whether this will develop into a legal issue, and if it does it will have to be adjudicated here. My suspicion is that this Waksit fellow will realize how weak his claim is and will simply disappear. But you might want to have an attorney on tap in the event you need legal advice closer to home."

"All right," she said. "I can't believe that Eugene would do such a thing."

Taylor's laugh was deep and throaty. "The older I get," he said, "the less I know what seemingly rational people are capable of doing."

"I'm sorry to hear about Walter Tagobe," Jayla said.

"I'll also keep you informed of what happens on that front. Go to bed. It's late where you are."

She did as he suggested, but her sleepiness prior to the call had abated and she was now wide awake and dealing with her anger at Eugene Waksit.

The following morning, fuzzy from a fitful sleep, she padded into the kitchen and turned on the Keurig coffeemaker. The anger at Waksit reemerged as she waited for the water in the reservoir to heat. How dare he make such an outlandish claim? Her father had no obligation to leave him anything in his will, yet had left him $5,000. Waksit's lack of gratitude was offensive to her, but confirmed the vague, negative feelings she had about him. She glanced at the time. Seven o'clock. Three the previous afternoon in Port Moresby. She retrieved Waksit's phone number from the desk and dialed, but received the same recorded message that the attorney had: "The number you have called is no longer in service."

Waksit had obviously moved. To another apartment in

Port Moresby? To Australia? Would Tabitha know? Probably not. Maybe the attorney could trace Waksit's whereabouts.

Showered and dressed, she left the apartment at eight thirty and had breakfast in a neighborhood coffee shop. While there she decided to call the phone number Flo Combes had given her for Mackensie and Annabel Smith. Annabel answered.

"Hi, it's Jayla King."

"Hello, Jayla. How nice to hear from you."

"I hope I'm not calling too early."

"Not at all. Mac is in the shower, and I just came in from filling the bird feeder on the terrace."

"I so much enjoyed the dinner with you and your friends."

"And we enjoyed having you. Something we can do for you?"

"I hope so. I received a call from my father's attorney in PNG about possible legal problems that may arise with my father's estate, and he suggested I confer with an attorney here in the States. I was wondering whether I could arrange a time to speak with your husband."

"I'm sure he'd be delighted to, although I doubt whether he knows anything about the law in Papua New Guinea."

"I wouldn't expect him to," Jayla said. "I probably don't even need legal advice but thought it wouldn't hurt to run a few things by him, you know, some questions in general."

"I'll tell him that you called and . . . oops, my clean old man has just emerged. Here he is."

"Good morning, Jayla. What can I do for you?" Mac asked.

She repeated what she'd told Annabel, and Mac replied that he'd make himself available whenever it was convenient for her. They made an appointment for five that afternoon at his office.

"I can't imagine what help I can be to her," Mac told

Annabel after ending the conversation. "Her father's death is a matter for the authorities overseas."

"She didn't specify what she wanted to discuss?"

"No, but I'll find out soon enough."

"Oh, Mac, I almost forgot. Robert called. He wanted me to tell you that he'd be late coming in this morning. He's having breakfast with Will Sayers." Annabel laughed. "Ever since Flo quit as his receptionist and opened her shop, Robert has been in a foul mood, especially with Ms. Warden. He seems to want to spend as much time as possible *away* from the office."

"Maybe I can get him an assignment in Papua New Guinea," Mac quipped.

Robert Brixton sat in Will Sayers's apartment. The heavyset journalist had made his guest a cup of instant coffee, which Brixton abandoned after a few sips. Sayers struggled with a nauseatingly yellow breakfast shake he'd concocted in a blender.

"Since when are you drinking that stuff?" Brixton asked.

"Since my doctor told me that either I lose weight or reserve a casket with my name on it."

"That bad, huh?"

"I'll give it a try," Sayers said. "Probably last a week. It tastes like—well, it tastes like what it looks like." He pushed the half-empty glass away and belched.

"Try moderation," Brixton said, "you know, only one piece of key lime pie after dinner, skip the fries at lunch."

"Wise words from a man who doesn't practice moderation. You busy these days?"

"No. Things have slowed down, although I'm up for a job tracing where the funds went from a nonprofit. Into the treasurer's pocketbook, I figure, but what I figure doesn't stand up in court. You said you might have something for me."

"Yeah, I might, and if you're nice to me I'll consider telling you about it."

"Anybody ever tell you that you're the spitting image of George Clooney?"

Sayers laughed. "Okay, enough phony niceness. I mentioned to you at the Smiths' dinner that I'm digging into the finances of Georgia's esteemed senator, Ronald Gillespie."

"Despite having had a couple of martinis, I seem to remember that."

"Ever hear of a lobbyist named Eric Morrison?"

Brixton grunted. "I think I've seen his name in the papers, got a hotshot agency on K Street."

"One and the same. He and his agency represent a number of clients, every one of them with open checkbooks to buy congressional votes. His biggest client is PAA, the Pharmaceutical Association of America. Senator Gillespie has always been a major recipient of their largesse."

"That's old news," Brixton said.

"Very astute, Robert."

"So what's up with the lobbyist, Morrison?"

"He's a strange cat," Sayers said from where he stood at the kitchen counter cutting a large piece of crumb cake. "Want some?" he asked.

"Moderation. Remember? Yeah, give me a piece, and something to wash it down with other than what you call coffee."

Sayers resumed his seat at the small kitchen island with two plates of cake and an orange juice for Brixton. "Where was I?" he said. "Oh, right, Eric Morrison. Morrison is nothing more than a conduit for the money his clients put up to influence legislation."

"I've heard this before."

"But as they say on TV infomercials, 'Wait! There's more!' Mr. Morrison, whore that he is, has also been rumored to provide certain services to his clients above and beyond simply passing their millions on to our greedy politicians."

"What kind of services?" Brixton asked.

"Oh, little favors, like arranging for a professional lady now and then—"

"Hookers?"

"If you insist on being crude."

"Pardon me."

"You're pardoned, Robert. Let's see. Ah, yes, hookers. Certainly not scandalous in this day and age. But I've come into information from a source I will not name that Mr. Morrison has gone beyond simply providing female companionship for a price. His prize member of Congress is Senator Ronald Gillespie. What do you know about Gillespie?"

"I feel like I'm on a quiz show," Brixton said. "Gillespie. Aging senior Georgia senator married to a woman who could be his daughter. There used to be a comic here in D.C. who would say from the stage that he thought it was sweet that so many older men in the audience were treating their daughters to a night out."

Sayers laughed. "I'm sure that Senator Gillespie was in that audience. At any rate, the senator's wife, whose name is Rebecca, isn't the only young woman who has attracted his roving eye. There was, I'm told, a teenager—granted an older one—who succumbed to his charm, if you can call it that. And . . ." Sayers paused for effect. "And, I'm also told that a pregnancy was the result of their exchanging precious bodily fluids, as Sterling Hayden so aptly put it in *Dr. Strangelove*."

"Senator Gillespie knocked up a teenage girl?"

Sayers's exaggerated sigh was accompanied by a slow shaking of his head and a pained expression on his face.

Brixton ignored him. "What happened to the kid?" he asked.

"My best sources back in Georgia say that the senator, generous fellow that he is, paid the girl to cancel the birth."

"She had an abortion."

"Again according to my sources, the senator not only paid for it, he bestowed a generous financial bonus on her for her silence, which pleased her family who, I'm told, were dirt-poor."

"That's quite a scoop you're working on," Brixton said.

"Yes, working on, but still without sufficient proof to run with it."

"What does this have to do with the lobbyist Morrison?" Brixton asked.

"It has a great deal to do with Morrison. If my sources are correct, it was Morrison who arranged for the abortion, and paid off the girl's family on Senator Gillespie's behalf."

"If you think I'd be shocked, you're wrong. You said when you asked to get together this morning that you might have something for me. I'm between assignments, as they say. Does this story have a place for me?"

"It does, Robert. I need someone to apply his investigative skills to come up with the proof I need."

Brixton sat back and processed what he'd just heard. Sayers was a skilled and tenacious journalist who'd broken many stories over the course of his career. Why now seek the help of someone else? More important, as far as Brixton knew, Sayers didn't have money to pay for help.

He bluntly brought up the questions.

"First," Sayers said, "the people who might be able to provide the proof I need will undoubtedly head in the opposite direction if approached by a journalist, especially one whose reputation for digging up dirt is well known. Second, I happen to have funding to continue my query into the senator's life."

"Who's providing the funding?"

"I'm not at liberty to divulge that. Let's just say that it comes from people who would be delighted to see Senator Ronald Gillespie go down in flames. Satisfied?"

"I'm shocked," Brixton said, holding his hand to his heart.

"At what?"

"At a journalist of your standing accepting payment from a source."

"Strictly to pay expenses, not a cent into my pocket. Gillespie is scum, Robert. I'll be doing everyone a favor by ushering him out of the Senate."

"Okay, okay, what do you want me to do?"

Sayers handed him a sheet of paper with a name, address, and phone number on it.

"Who's this Paula Silver?"

"She was on Morrison's payroll, only she really didn't do anything except service her boss. She was his mistress."

"Past tense?"

"Yeah."

"What's she do now?"

"She lives in an apartment in Adams Morgan stewing in her anger at being unceremoniously dumped by Mr. Morrison. She's originally from California, had a few small roles in B movies but never made it in Tinseltown. Google her. Two movies she was in are mentioned. She's supposedly writing a book chronicling her affair with Morrison and dishing the dirt about his lobbying group. If she tells it like it is, she'll need a good libel lawyer."

"Does Morrison support her?"

"If so, not in the grand style to which she's been accustomed. She works as a receptionist in a restaurant in Adams Morgan, Char Bar. Nice place. I stopped in once to grab a look. By the way she's a knockout of the blond bombshell variety. Better not tell Flo what you're up to. Ms. Silver won't talk to me for good reason, but if you were to make her acquaintance she might open up. You're good at getting people to do that. I can pay you two grand out of my fund."

"Okay. I hate politics, but like I said things are slow."

"Here's a down payment, a thousand. One condition, Robert. This is strictly between you and me, and that means nobody—n-o-b-o-d-y—knows."

"Got it," said Brixton. "I'll get back to you if I come up with anything. One condition on my end though."

"What's that?"

"You buy a coffeemaker and pour that instant crap down the drain."

Sayers laughed heartily. "You drive a tough bargain—Bobby!"

12

Nate Cousins stopped in at Jayla's lab at Renewal Pharmaceuticals and asked whether she had dinner plans that night.

"I have a date," she said, referring to her five o'clock meeting with Mac Smith. She didn't have plans after that but wanted to leave the evening open. While Cousins's attention was flattering, she didn't like to be pressured. Plus, she looked forward to a leisurely evening at home.

CEO Walt Milkin also popped in that afternoon.

"Just wanted you to know," he told Jayla and her two colleagues, "that although your efforts with the previous experiment didn't bear fruit, I have every confidence that your future endeavors will tell a different story."

They were appreciative of this vote of confidence from the top dog and told him so.

"Got a moment, Jayla?" Milkin asked as he prepared to leave.

She accompanied him into the hallway.

"I was just wondering whether you'd heard from the fellow who worked with your father in his laboratory. Waksit is it?"

"Yes, Eugene Waksit. But no, I haven't heard from him."

She thought of the call from the attorney in PNG, Elgin Taylor, and the call that he'd received from Waksit.

"Damn shame that your father's notes were stolen. You did tell me that."

"Yes."

"Do you think that Waksit might have taken them?"

"I'd like to think that he didn't," she said.

"Well," Milkin said, "if you do hear from him I'd like to know."

Why? she wondered.

He noted the puzzled expression on her face and added, "As I said before, if he ever gets to Washington I'd enjoy meeting the man who worked side by side with your enigmatic father."

"I don't expect he'll ever come here," she said, "but I'll keep in mind what you said."

"Can't ask for more than that," he said, sporting a large smile. "Keep up the good work, Jayla. Renewal is counting on you—and your colleagues in there." He pointed to the lab door, placed a large hand on her shoulder, and walked away.

Enigmatic father.

She showed up at Smith's office precisely at five and told his receptionist that she had an appointment. Mac emerged a few second later.

"Hello there," he said. "Good to see you again."

"I appreciate the time."

"Come in, come in. Robert Brixton, Flo's lesser half, is with me." He lowered his voice. "Don't tell him I said that. He's armed."

Brixton was reading a magazine as Jayla entered. He got up and shook her hand, said to Smith, "Want me to leave?"

"Not unless Jayla wants you to."

"No, please stay," she said.

They settled in chairs and on a couch around a glass coffee table.

"So," Smith said, "what sage legal advice can I give you?"

Jayla repositioned herself in her chair and said, "I received a call from my father's attorney, Elgin Taylor, in Port Moresby. He had a variety of issues to discuss about events following my father's death." She related the news about Walter Tagobe's mugging and murder, and the codicil her father had handwritten leaving a small amount of money to Tagobe.

"You say that Mr. Tagobe oversaw a plot of land that your father cultivated to grow plants used in his research?" Mac said.

"Yes. He was a tribesman in the Sepik River region."

"A tribesman?" Brixton said.

"Much of PNG is extremely primitive," Jayla explained.

"And his death came on the heels of your father's death," Mac said.

"Yes. That plot of land that my father cultivated was burned and bulldozed, also at the time of my father's murder."

"If I believed in coincidences," Brixton said, "I'd say that this is definitely one."

"But you don't believe in coincidences, Robert," Mac said, "and neither do I." He said to Jayla, "This is the same land that the tribesman, Tagobe, was responsible for."

"That's right," she said.

"Where was he when the field was destroyed?"

"I don't know," she said, "but since he was killed in Wewak—that's a town in the Sepik River area—it's possible that he'd gone there before the men burned the field."

"Or maybe after. Any more bad news this attorney delivered to you?"

"Yes. My father had an assistant who worked for him in the lab for about five years, Eugene Waksit. Mr. Taylor said that he'd received a phone call from Eugene claiming that my father had promised to leave his lab results to him."

"Did your father have a will?" Brixton asked.

"Yes," Jayla said. "In it he left five thousand dollars to Eugene 'for his service.'"

"But no mention of your father's research?"

"No. Mr. Taylor learned of the money left to Walter Tagobe when going through Dad's papers. He'd hand-written a codicil to his will stipulating that."

"Maybe he wrote another codicil leaving his research to this Waksit guy," Brixton said.

"No," Jayla said, shaking her head for emphasis. "I believe he would have told me if he had."

"Was that why he was killed, somebody after his notes?" Brixton asked.

"I don't know."

"What about this Waksit guy?" Brixton asked. "If he claims your father willed him the results of his research, maybe he helped himself to the notes." Mac and Jayla looked at him anticipating his next supposition. "And maybe this Waksit guy killed your father."

Jayla wrapped her arms about her, closed her eyes, and slowly shook her head. When she opened them she said, "I've never been especially fond of Eugene but I can't believe that he's a killer."

The finality with which she said it prompted both men to drop the subject. Smith said, "So, Jayla, what can I do for you?"

"I'm afraid that I'm not making a lot of sense, Mac, paraphrasing what Mr. Taylor told me, and I'm not sure why he suggested that I consult with a lawyer. Would you be willing to talk to him?"

"Of course."

She handed Mac one of Taylor's business cards.

"There's a big time difference between here and Port Moresby," she said. "It's fourteen hours earlier."

"I'll keep that in mind," said Smith, "and make sure I don't wake him in the middle of the night."

"It was good seeing you again," Brixton said, standing and stretching against a sudden back spasm, and flexing the knee that had stiffened, the one that had taken a bullet in Savannah when he was a cop there.

"Same here," Jayla said. "Please give my best to Flo."

After Jayla had left Mac asked Brixton for his take on what she had told them.

The private investigator hunched his shoulders and continued to exercise his knee. "If I was a writer and writing a book about it," he said between grunts, "I'd have this Waksit guy—weird name, huh?—kill her father and grab the notes. Then he has somebody burn down the plants the father cultivated as part of his research."

"And you'd have him kill this tribesman, Tagobe? Why? To keep him quiet?"

"Or hire somebody to do it."

"But her father left Waksit five thousand dollars in his will."

Brixton guffawed. "Five grand? If the father came up with an improved painkiller, five grand is chump change. Of course, why would Waksit call the attorney and claim that the father left him the research if he's already got the notes?"

"Because if he tries to sell the research results to a major pharmaceutical company, they'll want proof that he owns it."

"I hadn't thought of that."

"That's why I'm a lawyer," Smith said.

"And good thing that you are. I have to run."

"Dinner with Flo?"

"No. Her shop's open late tonight. I'm running down a lead I was given."

"Oh?"

"Give Annabel a kiss for me. See you in the morning."

Brixton went to his car and reviewed a page he'd printed after Googling Paula Silver. There wasn't much about her, only that she'd appeared as a sexy vamp in two soon forgotten B-grade films, and hadn't been heard from since. The films in which she appeared were *Burn Baby* and *Depravity,* neither likely to be nominated for an Oscar. She was thirty-seven years old. Her last known address was Washington, D.C.

He drove to Adams Morgan, Washington's vibrant multicultural neighborhood, and found a parking space across from Char Bar. While driving there he'd gone over in his mind how he would approach Paula Silver, the role he would assume, and the extent to which he'd lie. He'd gone undercover before; his recent interplay with the model car racing husband from the Department of Agriculture had been his latest venture playing someone other than himself. He'd dressed nicely that morning, suit and tie and shined shoes. He took a deep breath and walked into Char Bar.

Paula Silver stood behind a podium at the front of the restaurant. Although she'd obviously aged, there was no mistaking her from the one photograph that Brixton had run across online, obviously taken when she was in her early twenties. She had a mane of nicely coiffed blond hair that framed a beautiful face. She was visible to Brixton from the waist up, and he could see that she was amply endowed where aspiring movie actresses are supposed to be, nicely filling out a blood-red blouse. Eric Morrison might be a jerk—that's how Will Sayers characterized him—but he had good taste in women, at least the mistress variety. She glanced up at him as he approached.

"A table?" she asked.

"I think so," he answered. "Could I see a menu?"

"Of course. The specials for tonight are on the insert." Her voice was husky, sexy.

Brixton took the menu from her and pretended to peruse its offerings.

"Lots of choices," he said.

She smiled, a nice smile, red lips and perfect white teeth.

"I'll take a table," he said.

"For one?"

He gave her a friendly laugh. "Unless you'd like to join me."

Her smile disappeared. *Bad line,* he thought.

He recouped. "Please don't think that this is a come-on," he said, "but you look familiar."

"Really?"

"Yeah. I know I've seen you somewhere before. It'll come to me. I'll take that table now."

She came from behind the podium and he followed her to a vacant spot toward the rear of the restaurant; the bottom half of her was equally as impressive. He stopped her. "How about that table over there?" he said pointing to one that afforded him a view of the podium.

"If you prefer," she said, and placed a menu on it. "Enjoy your dinner."

Brixton ordered a martini—with gin, not vodka, straight up, with a twist—from the waiter who walked as though his feet hurt. Brixton had carried that day's *Washington Post* in with him and pretended to read it while sipping his favorite drink, occasionally glancing over at Paula Silver as she welcomed new customers. He decided to put his plan into action whenever there was a lull, which happened minutes later. He'd given the waiter his dinner order—a shrimp cocktail and a strip steak cooked "Pittsburgh style," rare on the inside and charred on the outside—before going to the podium.

"Excuse me," he said.

"Is something wrong?" she asked.

"It just hit me where I know you from."

She stared at him blankly.

"You're an actress," he said.

Her expression didn't change, but he could see the wheels spinning in her pretty head.

"I'm a movie buff," he said, "especially older ones, movies that don't have a lot of car chases and things blowing up, movies with good characters." Because it was true he could say it with authority. He clicked his fingers a few times to indicate he was in deep thought. "Let me see, let me see, I remember you from . . ." A few more clicks of his fingers before saying, "Something with 'burn' in it. Yeah, *Burn* something."

"*Burn Baby?*" she said.

"That's it! *Burn Baby!* You were in that."

"You saw it?"

"Yeah, on TV, you know, the channel that shows old movies, interesting ones that weren't big at the box office. You were terrific."

"Thank you," she said, obviously flattered.

"You were in other movies, too, right?"

"A few. I had a big role in another. It was called '*Depravity.*' Stupid title, huh?"

She excused herself to seat a couple. When she returned to the podium Brixton said, "My dinner's on the table. Better eat it before it gets cold. The steak I mean, not the shrimp cocktail."

She nodded.

"Hey," he said, "any chance of getting together to talk about old movies?"

"They weren't *that* old," she said.

"You know what I mean. Buy you a drink when you get off?"

She thought before saying, "Okay."

"Great. I'm Robert Brixton."

"I'm—"

"I know who you are. Paula. Right?"

"Paula Silver."

"Right, Paula Silver. What time do you get off?"

"We're slow tonight. About an hour."

"Great. I'll have my dinner and hang around until then."

An hour later he came to the podium and asked, "Got a favorite place nearby?"

"Bourbon, on Eighteenth Street?"

"Sounds good to me, Ms. Silver. I assume bourbon is on the drink menu."

"Hundreds of them. At least it seems that way."

They walked a few blocks to the busy night spot and found a small table in the bar area. She didn't hesitate to order a single-barrel bourbon, and Brixton did the same. As they made small talk he couldn't help but wonder at how Hollywood worked. She was as beautiful as any famed movie star, a little shopworn around the edges but time has a habit of doing that to beautiful women. Of course he didn't know whether she could act, nor whether the few roles she'd landed had been based solely on her platinum good looks.

"So, what do you do for a living?" she asked.

He'd expected that question.

"I'm a researcher," he said.

"That's interesting. What do you research?"

"At the moment I'm looking into the influence that lobbyists have on our elected officials."

Her widened eyes mirrored her interest.

"Yeah," Brixton continued, "it's gotten pretty bad. There are lobbyists who own certain pols." He laughed. "I don't know if you know it but lobbying used to be legit. The lobbyists helped the elected officials understand things about their clients—but they didn't buy them the way they do now. But I'm sure you're not interested in stuff like that. Let's talk movies."

He hoped that she would disagree; he knew little about motion pictures and would have trouble keeping up.

"No" she said, "I am interested in lobbyists." She paused, and he wondered whether she would bring up her affair with Eric Morrison.

"I used to go with a lobbyist here in D.C., a big one."

Bingo!

"No kidding. That's a coincidence. Anybody I'd know?"

"Sure. Eric Morrison."

"That's an even bigger coincidence," Brixton said.

"He's scum," she said. "I'm writing a book about him."

"Whew!" came from Brixton. "A book? You have a publisher and all?"

"Not yet. Actually, I'm *thinking* about writing a book about him."

"I guess you have to be careful, you know, libel and stuff like that."

She sneered. "I know plenty about Eric Morrison, plenty about his dirty dealings with politicians."

"I can't believe this," Brixton said. "Wow! Maybe I could help you with your book. I know plenty, too, about Morrison and other lobbyists like him."

"Maybe," she said.

"This might be the best coincidence you and I will ever have," he said. "Here's to your book." He raised his glass.

"Thanks," she said, raising hers.

They chatted for almost an hour until she announced that she had to leave.

"Are you married?" she asked as he slapped a credit card on the bill.

"No, but I live with somebody. It's not working out too great."

"Sorry to hear that," she said.

"How about dinner some night?" he suggested.

"I'm off on Tuesdays," she said.

"I'll call you," he said.

She wrote her number on a cocktail napkin.

When he walked in the door of his apartment he asked Flo how her evening at the shop had gone.

"It was busy," she said gleefully. "How was your evening?"

"Okay."

"Did you have dinner with someone?"

"Yeah. Look, I'm following up on a lead that Will gave me, and had a drink with her tonight. Name's Paula Silver. If she should call and you see her name on the phone, don't answer, okay?"

Flo cocked her head at him. "Robert," she said.

"What?"

"Who is she?"

"I'll pour us a drink and tell you all about it."

13

Angus Norbis, the detective with the Australian Federal Police (AFP) assigned to Port Moresby, stood at the blackboard in his office at the PNG Constabulary headquarters in the suburb of Konedobu. Meeting with him that sweltering morning were two senior members of the Royal Papua New Guinea Constabulary (RPNGC). Norbis, one of fifty Australian police officers assigned to aid the PNG force of 4,800, ran his fingers between his neck and shirt collar, and wiped beads of perspiration from his prized rust-and-gray walrus mustache. The office's air-conditioning, never especially efficient under the best of circumstances, had stopped working completely. Repairmen would try to get there by day's end but no promises.

"So, Angus, what is this all about?" one of the constables asked.

"The King case," Angus said, pointing to a crude chalk chart on the blackboard. He addressed one of the constables. "No sign of Waksit?"

"No, nothing. The landlady let us into Waksit's apartment and we looked around. She says that the place came furnished, which explains why he would leave the furniture behind. The only thing missing as far as we could tell were suitcases, and clothing from his closet. At least we assume he had luggage to carry the clothing."

"Did you check the bathroom for toilet articles?"

"Yeah. Gone."

Norbis grunted and looked at the blackboard. There were four items contained in boxes outlined by yellow chalk lines. The first was the name Dr. Preston King. In the box next to it was the name Walter Tagobe. To its right was "Razed Land." Eugene Waksit's name occupied the fourth box.

"A question," the second constable said. "I thought Waksit was cleared of any suspicion in the doctor's murder."

"That's right, he was. I personally questioned him. He had a partial alibi for the night of the murder, a woman with whom he spent time. It took us a few days to locate her. She says that they were together but not for the entire night, leaving him plenty of time unaccounted for."

"A quickie, huh?" the first constable said, laughing.

Norbis ignored him. "It was also my judgment at the time that Mr. Waksit had no reason to kill the good doctor. He spoke highly of him and was treated fairly and with a generous salary."

"So, Angus, what has changed?"

"I spoke with Dr. King's daughter, Jayla King, when she came here from the States. Not only had her father been murdered, whoever did it stole the results of his years of research." He waited for a response until saying, "We've been going on the assumption all along that Dr. King was killed by a druggie looking for a quick fix and money." Norbis smiled knowingly. "Unfortunately we come to such conclusions all too quickly and frequently."

"That's because it's usually the case. I still think it was an intruder, a lowlife," said one of the constables. "We have plenty of them here in Port Moresby."

"Except," Norbis said, forefinger in the air for emphasis, "somebody like that wouldn't know to steal the doctor's research results."

"So what are you saying, Angus, that maybe it was this Waksit fella?"

"I'm not saying that at all," Norbis said. "But I got a call from the attorney who's handling Dr. King's estate. You've heard of him, Elgin Taylor, very respected here in PNG. He'd received a call from Waksit during which he claimed that Dr. King had promised that if he died Waksit would inherit all his research results."

"Ah," a constable said, "a motive."

"That's assuming that the doctor actually did say that to Waksit, of which I'm not at all confident. Elgin Taylor is not the sort of man who would fabricate such a thing, but maybe Waksit is." He paused before continuing. "Dr. King also bequeathed Waksit five thousand U.S. dollars in his will. The attorney told Waksit when he called that he would have to be able to get ahold of him once the estate was settled. Waksit said he would call again. He hasn't."

"Five thousand," a constable said. "Seems he would stay around to collect it."

"Unless what he took from the doctor's laboratory is worth more—a lot more! I've contacted AFP in Sydney to keep an eye out for Mr. Waksit. But let's not have any misunderstanding. Waksit is not considered a suspect, at least not at this time. But his leaving Port Moresby so suddenly, and his claim that Dr. King had left him the fruits of his research, make it prudent to have another talk with him. Check the airlines to see if he's taken a flight recently, but keep up the investigation on the street in case anything new turns up." Norbis consulted a sheet of paper. "All right then, enough of the King case. Let's move on to the next item on the agenda."

Before heading out for the evening, Eugene Waksit arranged for the Sydney, Australia, hotel in which he was staying to place his black leather briefcase in its safe. He debated doing it. Since leaving Port Moresby the satchel had never been out of his view. He trusted no one, and kept it close to his person.

But after two days in the upscale hotel, and taking three meals a day in its restaurant, he felt the urge to get out, if only for a few hours.

After walking aimlessly he found himself in Kings Cross, Sydney's red-light district, an area of the city in which prostitution was legal, and where adult clubs lined both sides of the street. He ignored the pitches made by young streetwalkers and settled at the bar of one of the clubs where he sipped drinks and watched the nude dancers perform. He was approached a number of times by prostitutes working out of the club but shunned their advances. While some of them appealed, he was afraid to allow anyone to get close.

Leaving Port Moresby had been a last-minute decision. The police investigating Dr. King's murder hadn't said anything to him about staying for further questioning, and he saw no need to tell them of his plans. As far as he was concerned he was not even remotely considered a suspect. He was free to do what he pleased and to travel where he wished.

His call to the attorney Elgin Taylor had been, in retrospect, a foolish, impetuous decision. What he'd said to the attorney hadn't been an outright lie in his mind, although he had wildly stretched what Dr. King had said: "Maybe one day you and my daughter can carry on this work." Or, "I appreciate the work you've done, Eugene, and value what you've contributed to the research." Taylor had been courteous and pleasant on the phone, but Waksit picked up on his underlying message—that they'd have to have further talks and that Waksit would need to provide more tangible proof of what he was alleging.

His mind kept going back to the briefcase at the hotel and he left the club; he'd be more comfortable back at the hotel with the briefcase in his physical possession.

He drew a sigh of relief when he'd entered the hotel lobby, went to the desk, and presented his chit for the satchel. Alone in his room now, the briefcase on his lap, he watched a TV show until hunger set in. He ordered room service and ate while watching a movie. When it ended he clicked off the set and opened his laptop on which he'd been researching pharmaceutical companies around the world. There were a number of them in Australia, including that country's largest, CSL, and he'd considered approaching one of them with the results of Dr. King's work. But he'd decided to eliminate them from the list, reasoning that it would be better to deal with companies in another country, particularly the United States. Without written, certified proof that he'd legally been given the rights to King's research, the Australian legal system might step in and challenge his claim. He rationalized that his status as an outsider might hold him in better stead in America.

His online research of American pharmaceutical firms resulted in a number of possibilities, too many to make an informed judgment. He knew little about the American pharmaceutical industry, didn't have a clue as to which companies would be the most likely to respond favorably. He needed advice from someone with a broad overview of the industry and who could point him in the right direction. He spent another hour peering at the screen, and making notes on a legal pad.

Finally, he sat back and exhaled. He'd made his decision. He would fly to the States and contact someone named Eric Morrison, who was listed as a lobbyist for the Pharmaceutical Association of America, which put him in the position of knowing which of its members would be most likely to be amenable to an approach.

He called his old college roommate, who'd settled in Los Angeles, and arranged to spend a few days with him before continuing his trip to Washington where PAA and Morrison were located. He was fond of American movies and looked forward to seeing where most of them had been made. His next call was to book a flight for tomorrow evening to L.A. He'd wait to reserve a flight to Washington after he'd outlived his welcome with his college chum.

As he mentally prepared for the trip, thoughts of Jayla King came with regularity. She'd worked with her father in the lab and likely was familiar with his successes. Too, she worked for a pharmaceutical firm and lived in Washington, D.C. Would she offer what she knew to her employer? That could seriously get in the way of what he intended to do.

14

"Why do you blame yourself for what happened to your daughter, Robert?"

"I didn't act fast enough and get her out of that place."

"But you say that your instincts kicked in and that you tried to get her to leave."

"I didn't try hard enough."

Visions of that horrific day when the crazed young Arab woman detonated the bomb and blew away Brixton's daughter along with a dozen others flooded him. He sat across from Dr. John Bradford Fowler in the psychologist's client room, rigid in the tan leather armchair, determined not to go on a rant about terrorists and how he'd like to personally kill them all.

"Your friend Flo is concerned about you," Fowler said.

"Yeah, I know, but she doesn't have to be."

"She cares."

"Flo's good people."

"Have you ever discussed getting married?"

This shift in topic brought Brixton up short.

"I only ask," Fowler said, "because she's someone you can lean on while you work out your feelings about your daughter. As you say, she's 'good people.'"

"I'll never work out my feelings," Brixton said.

"You can if you want to and work at it."

"Easy for you to say."

"True, but the reason you're here is to accomplish just that, to work out your feelings so that they don't paralyze you. How is your work going? The last time you sat here you said that the tragedy with your daughter got in the way of it."

Brixton shrugged. "I've got a few assignments."

"I'm glad to hear that, Robert. Work is therapeutic."

"That's what Flo says."

Fowler continued to probe Brixton's inner feelings for the duration of the forty-five-minute session. Toward the end he said, "It might be helpful if you wrote down your feelings, committed them to paper."

Brixton guffawed. "Why? I'm no writer."

"Just a suggestion. Putting our feelings on paper sometimes helps clarify them. Think about it. I'd also like you to consider how your daughter would feel if she knew that her death was negatively impacting your life. I think she'd want you to go forward as a tribute to her."

What Fowler had said made sense, and Brixton had thought the same thing on many occasions. He left after making another appointment. As he walked down the street to where he'd parked his car he had the same sensation as the last time he'd come from a session. He felt better and walked with a lighter step.

What was going on here?

15

Eugene Waksit stayed for three days in Los Angeles with his college friend, which gave his former roommate a reminder of how annoying Waksit could be—and cheap. His friend paid for everything, figuring that Waksit eventually had to make a gesture, which he finally did, picking up a small tab in a Chinese restaurant during his last night in L.A. He hadn't changed much from his undergraduate days in Australia, filling his conversation with delusions of grandeur, saying that he was on the cusp of great wealth. He was never specific beyond mentioning that his former employer in Port Moresby had willed him the results of experiments that would "stand the pharmaceutical industry on its ear." His friend pressed him but never managed to elicit more specifics. He was aware, however, of the black briefcase that Waksit seemed to always be cradling, and that he slid beneath the bed whenever they went out.

"What's in that briefcase?" he asked when driving Waksit to the airport.

"My future," Waksit replied.

He didn't ask any follow-up questions. He bid Waksit a safe and pleasant flight and drove home, thankful that the visit was over.

Waksit arrived at Dulles International Airport in suburban Washington with a sour stomach from drinks and a barely edible airline meal on the six-hour flight. He climbed into a waiting taxi and gave the turbaned driver an address in the District of Columbia, near Rock Creek Park. He settled back in the cab, his carry-on suitcase on the seat next to him, the leather satchel containing Dr. Preston King's research results on his lap, his fingers intertwined with its handles.

The driver pulled to a stop in front of a small, modest two-story apartment building. Waksit paid the fare, added a small tip, and stood looking at the building as the taxi sped away.

There were myriad times during the journey when he'd second-guessed his decision to pick up and leave on the spur of the moment. His invalid mother still lived in Australia, and he felt a modicum of filial guilt for not having told her of his plans. Waksit's father had succumbed to cancer when Eugene was ten years old, his father's battle with the disease responsible in part for his son's decision to pursue a career in medicine and medical research. His one year as a premed student had gone badly, and he'd switched his major to biology, graduating with an undergraduate degree in that discipline, although his academic results were anemic.

As he prepared to climb the short flight of stairs to the front door it opened and Nikki Dorence, a pretty young redhead wearing jeans and a T-shirt, stepped out.

"Hello," she said.

"Hey, hello, Nikki," Waksit said, going up the stairs, dropping his suitcase, and using his free arm to embrace her. "Great seeing you."

"I wondered whether I would ever see you again," she said pleasantly. "Good trip?"

"Tough trip. I thought I'd never get here."

"Well, here you are. I bet you wouldn't turn down a drink."

He grinned. "Sounds like a plan," he said.

Her apartment was on the ground floor of the building. He dropped his suitcase just inside the door but held on to the briefcase.

"Nice place," he said, taking in the sunlit living room.

"Thanks. It's at the top end of my budget but I love living here. A drink? I have wine, and some vodka."

"Make it wine," he said, going to a couch near the window and falling heavily onto it. "Whew!" he said. "I'm beat."

"I bet you are," she said, returning from the kitchen with his drink. She held up the glass of iced tea she'd been drinking and said, "Salud!"

"To seeing you again," he said.

"Yes," she said with less enthusiasm than he'd exhibited.

Nikki's mother and father, both Australian, had worked in Australia's High Commission in PNG's capital city, and had given birth to Nikki while stationed there. She'd been attending college in Australia when she met Waksit during a visit home, and they'd fallen into an affair that ended when she returned to school. But they'd stayed in touch, even after she'd graduated with a degree in public administration and had left Australia for a job in New York with the Papua New Guinea Permanent Mission to the U.N. She'd worked there a year until landing a position in Washington with PNG's embassy on Massachusetts Avenue, D.C.'s Embassy Row.

"So," she said, "here you are in Washington, D.C. When you called you said that you were on a business trip."

"That's right."

"What sort of business? You were working for that doctor."

"King. He died."

"Oh. He was involved in some sort of medical research, wasn't he?"

Waksit changed position on the couch and winced at pain in his lower back. "Yeah, he was researching a new painkiller using plants and herbs. I could use one."

She laughed. "Sounds like voodoo."

"It does, only it isn't voodoo. It works. I've seen it firsthand with patients in the clinic Dr. King and I ran."

"You ran a clinic, Eugene? I didn't know you were a doctor."

"I'm not, but I knew enough to treat patients. King wasn't much of a doctor. I knew more than he did."

His boast reminded Nikki of some of the conversations they'd had when dating. She'd decided that while Waksit was a bright young man, he tended to overstate his knowledge and accomplishments, an overactive ego at play.

He sat forward as he said, "King left all his research to me when he died."

Now she sat forward in her chair. "That's impressive," she said. "He must have really liked you."

"Yeah, he liked me, but more important he knew how much I contributed to the research. I came here to talk with some big pharmaceutical companies about selling them the results of our work. It's worth millions, could be billions."

"And you know that it's effective?"

"Of course I do. Look, this is a painkiller made from simple plants, it's cheap, and doesn't have any of the usual side effects—and it's *not* addictive!"

"Wow!" was all she could think of saying.

"I just have to be careful about protecting my interests. You know how these Big Pharma companies rip people off."

"Do they? I mean, I'm sure you're right. What did this doctor do, leave everything to you in his will?"

"It was more of an understanding that we had."

His explanations didn't ring true to her but she didn't pursue it. Instead she asked, "How did the doctor die?"

"Somebody broke into our lab and killed him."

She groaned. "How awful. And the police have never caught the killer?"

"No, and they never will. Hey, you know how incompetent and corrupt the police are in Port Moresby. They can't find their left hand with their right."

Nikki offered to refill his glass, which he accepted. When she returned from the kitchen she asked about Dr. King's family.

"Just one daughter," he said.

"Where is she?"

He shrugged. "I don't know. She's a flaky character, probably thinks that because he was her father she should be the one to benefit from his research. King knew that I was the right person to carry on his work. But I'll take care of the daughter after the deal is made."

It occurred to him as he said it that there was the possibility that Nikki might know Jayla King. After all, how many young women from Papua New Guinea could there be in Washington? Did they have an expat club of PNGers in D.C.? Did women from PNG get together for girl talk over drinks one night a month? Of course, Jayla and Nikki traveled in different circles. Jayla worked in medical research for a firm in Bethesda; Nikki was with the embassy. He gave himself a mental reminder to not bring up Jayla again.

"So," Nikki said, "what are your plans while you're here? Where are you staying?"

Waksit grimaced and shook his head. "I have a cash flow problem," he said. "I have a ton of money waiting for me back in Port Moresby, money the doctor left me. But you know how slow the government is in settling an estate. The truth is I got here on my credit card but it's almost maxed out, and I don't have a lot of cash, at least not enough to check into a hotel. I hear that hotels here in Washington are bloody expensive."

Nikki said nothing.

"I suppose I can find some sort of hostel, you know, a place where students stay on the cheap."

"I don't know about them," she said.

"Any chance of my crashing here with you for a few nights? I'm sure that when I make contact with the right pharmaceutical company the money will be rolling in."

"I don't know, Eugene, that might be—"

He flashed his most engaging grin. "Hey, Nikki, I'm not suggesting that we pick up where we left off back in PNG. I'm just talking as a friend." He patted the couch. "If I could sleep here for a few nights I'd really be grateful. I'll stay out of your hair. I know you have an important job at the embassy and I promise I won't get in your way." Another wide smile. "Hey, I may be short of cash but I'm not *that* broke. I'll treat you to a nice dinner, your choice of where. I just need a few days to get my bearings in this city. Man, it makes Port Moresby look like some native village in Sepik, huh? I have an important contact I have to see in the next few days, a man with big connections in the pharmaceutical industry. I'm sure he'll give me an advance and I'll pay you for any time I'm here." He paused. "What do you say, Nikki, for old times' sake?"

"I suppose it would be all right for a few days," she said. "I'm leaving to attend a conference the day after tomorrow, but you can stay until then. I have small room I use as a home office. It has a pull-out sleeper couch. I'm sure you'll be comfortable there."

"That's great, Nikki. I'll leave when you do. Want me to make us breakfast? I make terrific scrambled eggs."

"I don't eat much breakfast," she said.

"Whatever you say. How about dinner tonight? You have a favorite local place?"

They went to a neighborhood Thai restaurant where Waksit spent much of the evening extolling the plans he had for the research that Dr. Preston King had bequeathed him. Nikki listened patiently and kept to herself her doubts about his grandiose ideas and claims of being on the cusp of a fortune. They returned to the apartment, drank wine, and she went to bed—she had an early morning meeting at the embassy. Waksit fell asleep on the couch in her office/guest room wearing his boxer shorts and a T-shirt. Nikki lay awake for a time in her darkened bedroom and thought over what had occurred since his arrival. She second-guessed her decision to allow him to stay, but kept justifying it based upon their former, albeit brief relationship, and the need to be gracious to a visiting person from her home country. But while explaining away her decision to give him a place to sleep for a few days made sense, she was uneasy having him in the next room.

Sleep finally put an end to these doubts—at least for that night.

16

As promised, Mac Smith contacted Elgin Taylor, the attorney in PNG handling Jayla's father's estate, calculating the time difference before placing the call. Taylor's secretary answered, and the lawyer came on the line seconds later. After the initial introductions were out of the way and they'd settled into a comfortable lawyerly conversation, Mac said, "Ms. King is quite an impressive young lady."

"Yes, sir, she certainly is that," Taylor agreed. "She was Preston King's little princess, even after she'd become an adult." He laughed. "Her dad was so proud that she'd followed in his footsteps and was forging a career in medical research."

"How did Dr. King spend most of his time?" Smith asked, "practicing medicine, or doing laboratory research?"

"Quite a bit of both actually. He was passionate about healing his patients, most of them from the poorer echelons of our society. But he was also passionate about his research, became more so toward the end when it seemed to be bearing fruit."

"Yes, Jayla told us quite a bit about him and his work when she was our dinner guest one evening. You say his work developing a better pain medication was beginning to bear fruit. Had he documented his findings in the papers that Jayla said were missing?"

"I'm sure he did. Preston was a complicated man. As his best friend I saw the many sides of him. He wore his heart on his sleeve, but was at the same time extremely protective of his research. I suggested to him more than once that he share it with others, but that was unthinkable to him. He was also meticulous about keeping records."

"But he did have an assistant, didn't he, someone named Waskit?"

"Waksit," Taylor corrected. "That's one of the things I'd like to discuss with you, Mac."

He recounted for Smith the call he'd received from Waksit in which he claimed that Dr. King had given him ownership of his research.

"Jayla mentioned that," Mac said, "and claimed that her father would never have done such a thing."

"I've been trying to make sense of it the past few days. Waksit said that he would call again but hasn't. I've been in touch with the officer in charge of the King case, a delightful fellow, Angus Norbis. He's one of a number of officers assigned to Port Moresby by the Australian Federal Police. Our local police don't have the best reputation, Mac, but Norbis is a bright gentleman with a sterling record. I was afraid that the local boys would chalk Preston King's murder up to a drug addict and not bother to pursue it, but Norbis is keeping the case open and is in the process of trying to locate Mr. Waksit. He's had some success on that score. His people checked airline records and it seems that Mr. Waksit took a flight from Sydney to Los Angeles."

"What would bring him to the States?"

"I don't have an answer to that, but I do have some additional news about the murder of Walter Tagobe."

"Jayla told us about him."

"Walter was a tribesman from Pagwi. That's a village in the Sepik River region of Papua New Guinea. Very primitive. He'd been found beaten to death in Wewak, one of the larger towns in the region."

"So she said. According to her, this tribesman had been hired by King to oversee his four acres outside Pagwi where he grew and cultivated native plants used in his pain medicine." Smith paused. "I see where this is heading," he said. "First King is murdered, and then this fellow he hired to watch over his acreage is killed. Add those two deaths to the fact that the doctor's research results went missing from his lab—and on top of that his acreage is destroyed—and any possibility of coincidence falls apart."

"It seems that way. Allow me to pass along one additional bit of information. The authorities in Wewak have arrested someone in the Tagobe murder."

"You *are* full of news," Smith said.

"According to Detective Norbis, the Wewak police have taken in a man they claim beat poor Tagobe to death. This fellow—his name is Paul Underwood—was evidently drunk at some bar bragging about having beaten up a native from Pagwi. He claims it was an accident and was acting in self-defense. The cops continue to question him."

"Any connection to Dr. King?" Smith asked.

"None that I know of. He's a roustabout, works for an international firm, Alard Associates. Ring a bell?"

"No. What sort of firm is it?"

"All I was told is that it hires out people to do contract work for governments, security, that sort of thing, Afghanistan, Iraq, other places I'm sure."

"What does the accused do for this Alard Associates?"

"I don't know. Underwood is Australian if I'm not mistaken."

"Anything else?" Mac asked.

"Just wondering how Jayla is doing," said Taylor. "It's somewhat difficult handling her affairs with so much distance between us."

"She seems fine," Smith said. "Considering."

"Please give her my best," Taylor said.

"I certainly will."

"And stay in touch," Taylor said. "If you become confused about the time difference and wake me in the wee hours, I'll understand."

"We'd be better served exchanging e-mail information," Smith suggested. "I prefer voice communication, but considering the time difference and—"

"A splendid idea," said Taylor.

They swapped e-mail addresses and promised to stay in touch.

Smith hung up and ran through his mind what he'd learned from the Port Moresby attorney.

There was obviously a connection between the doctor's death and that of the man who oversaw his acreage. Taylor had mentioned during the call that the missing documents from King's lab probably ruled out the murder having been done by a drifter, a drug addict. That scenario just didn't play. Jayla had mentioned that her father's plot of land had been bulldozed and torched at the same time her father had been killed. What connection did that have with the theft of his research results? It sounded to Smith that whoever killed Preston King and taken his documents had also arranged for the destruction of the land, possibly to erase any evidence that King had made progress in his search for a better painkiller.

Who would benefit from that?

The obvious answer was a pharmaceutical company with much to lose if an inexpensive, nonaddicting painkiller came on the market in competition with its own pain medication. Smith knew that the pharmaceutical industry was a cutthroat business with billions at stake.

Big enough to motivate someone to commit murder in pursuit of profits?

Brixton had been out of the office for much of the day. While having lunch he reflected upon his most recent appointment with the shrink and tried to talk himself out of believing that the two sessions had been beneficial. But he had to admit, if only to himself, that he was now thinking about aspects of his life that he'd kept secluded in a dark corner of his often befuddled mind. His receptionist/secretary, Mrs. Warden, was a good example. He'd resented her from the moment she'd started working for him. But as he pondered the situation while eating the final wedge of his BLT and washing it down with a draft beer, he realized that he'd been unfair. Mrs. Warden was a nice woman, efficient, not unpleasant (although she would never be crowned "Miss Sunshine"), and had told him that she needed the job since her husband passed away. *Be nicer to her* he told himself as he drained what was in the glass and paid the bill.

Later that day, he swung by the apartment to freshen up and change clothes. His "date" with Paula Silver, the former B movie actress, was that evening, and while he didn't have carnal thoughts about what might develop, he did want to look his best. He was glad that Flo was at her clothing shop and not home to further question him about his dinner plans. While she seemed to have bought his explanation why he would be spending time with Ms. Silver, he sensed skepticism on Flo's part that created a certain awkwardness between them, nothing overt but enough to leave discomfort wafting in the air.

When he'd called Paula on Monday to see if she was free for dinner the following evening it took her a moment to remember who he was.

"Robert Brixton," he reminded her. "We had drinks the other night and we talked about the book you're writing."

"Oh, right, sure. Sure."

He wondered if she'd been drinking.

"You said that Tuesday was your night off, and I wondered if we could have dinner tomorrow."

Her long pause told him that she might decline. But then she said, "Yeah, sure, that'd be fine. Brixton?"

"Robert Brixton," he said pleasantly.

"Right, sure."

He offered to pick her up but she seemed reluctant to give him her home address. He suggested instead that they meet at the Jack Rose Dining Saloon on Eighteenth Street, a popular Adams Morgan establishment that boasted almost two thousand bottles of scotch, bourbon, and other whiskeys, and three dining levels. Ordinarily, Brixton would not have chosen such a place. It had become a go-to spot later in the evening for party animals, and friends who'd been there said it was noisy. Brixton preferred smaller, more intimate venues in which to enjoy drinks and dinner. But he thought that its cachet might appeal to her; the goal was to spend time together again no matter where.

"That's a nice place," she said. "I've been there a few times."

"Great. We'll meet at the bar on the roof at six?"

"All right. Sure."

She was twenty minutes late arriving, and Brixton wondered whether she'd be a no-show. But she suddenly appeared and stood at the edge of the terrace looking for him; based upon their phone conversation he wondered whether she'd even recognize him. He left his seat at the bar, approached, and extended his hand. "Hi," he said accompanied by a broad smile.

"Oh, hello," she said.

She was dressed for an evening out, body-clinging red-and-yellow silk dress with a deep neckline that exposed freckled cleavage, gold drop earrings, and heels.

"Come on," he said, taking her elbow, "I saved a seat for you at the bar."

He was aware as they crossed the room that Ms. Silver, former minor-league screen actress, elicited plenty of admiring male glances, and Brixton enjoyed being with the target of their interest. She made a show of settling on the barstool and looked up at the array of bottles in the backbar.

"This place is known for all its whiskeys," Brixton said.

She told the young bartender that she would have a single-barrel bourbon, which she had also ordered the first night they'd been together. Brixton's Beefeater martini sat half consumed before him. He raised the glass. "Here's to seeing you again," he said.

She took a healthy swig of the drink and continued to stare straight ahead.

"So," Brixton said, "have you been thinking about your book?"

"What?" She turned and looked as though she was surprised to see him. "My book? I'm always thinking about it."

"I guess that's true of all writers. They're always thinking about it."

She nodded and drank again.

"I thought we'd have dinner downstairs," he said, "but it's nice having a drink up here outdoors. Beautiful night."

"It's nice. I've been here before."

"Yeah, you said that when I called. Funny that you know Eric Morrison."

"What's funny about it?"

"Not funny ha-ha. It's just that he's one of the lobbyists I'm researching."

"Bastard!" she snorted, waving for the bartender and pointing to her empty glass.

"No love lost, huh?"

"I hate him," she said.

"That bad, huh? He's married, isn't he?"

"Sure he is, but he told me—he tells every woman he cons—that he's about to get a divorce."

"An old line. How did you get involved with him?"

She waited until she'd sampled her refreshed drink before answering. "A friend of his introduced us. His name's Howie. Howie Ebhart."

"He a lobbyist, too?"

"I don't know what he does."

Brixton was tempted to ask whether she'd had an affair with this Howie guy but thought better of it.

"Last time we talked I said that maybe I could help you with the book you're writing. I don't know if you're aware that Morrison has a U.S. senator in his pocket."

"Gillespie," she said matter-of-factly.

"Right. Senator Ronald Gillespie."

"He's a pig. I used to think that guys in Hollywood who played the casting couch game were pigs but Gillespie puts them to shame." Raising Gillespie's name seemed to inject animation into her. She turned to Brixton and said, "Eric—Morrison—plays pimp for the senator. I didn't know that when I got involved with him, but once I put two and two together it made my skin crawl. He even tried to hook me up with Gillespie for a one-night stand. That's when I told him what I thought of him and walked away."

Brixton grimaced. "Morrison is more of a lowlife than I knew," he said.

"You don't know the half of it," she said.

"That's why we should work together," said Brixton. "There's plenty that I know that'd be great material for your book."

"That's okay but . . ."

"But what?"

"It's my book. I don't want to share the money with anybody. That's all I've ever done, shared the money, agents, publicists, everybody with their hand out. What do I have to show for it? Nada. Nothing."

"I'm not looking for money," Brixton said.

"Everybody's looking for money. I had a guy who wanted me to do porn movies."

"Did you?"

"No, I did not." Her tone was defiant. "What do you take me for?"

"You brought it up."

"He offered peanuts for me to do it. I told him where he could get off."

"Good for you. What about this guy Howie something-or-other?"

She laughed and finished her drink, was about to signal for another but Brixton said, "Let's wait until we go downstairs for dinner." She pouted but didn't argue.

"What was his name? Howie . . . ?"

"Ebhart. He and Morrison go way back, college or something. When I was getting ready to bail on Morrison, I did some looking through his things."

"At his office?"

"No, the apartment he kept where we used to get together. I lived there for a while."

"What'd you find?"

"Dirt on Mr. Eric Morrison and his buddy Howie."

"I'm all ears."

She glanced at others at the bar before saying, "Look, Mr. Researcher, I can trust you, right?"

Brixton nodded. "As far as I'm concerned," he said, "we're a team. What you tell me stays with me, like in Las Vegas, and I assume that what I tell you does the same."

She didn't confirm his last statement. She lowered her voice—it became sexy when she did—and placed her hand with long nails tipped in pink polish on his. "Senator Gillespie almost had a love child back in Georgia."

Brixton didn't know what to expect from her, but he didn't expect this. He covered her hand with his other and looked into her eyes, exuding supreme interest coupled with honesty, a look he'd practiced over the years as a cop and private investigator.

"That's right," she said. "The senator got some girl in trouble, and Howie fixed it for Morrison."

"Fixed it?"

"Paid for an abortion and paid off the family."

"Howie did this, not Morrison?"

She looked at Brixton as though he was feeble-minded. "Howie introduced Morrison to somebody who could arrange it."

Brixton glanced surreptitiously at his watch. He couldn't believe how quickly the conversation had gotten to what Will Sayers was looking for. *Play it cool, he cautioned himself.* "Ah," Brixton started, "this is really great stuff, Paula. I mean, if you have some sort of proof that these things took place you'll have a bestseller on your hands, be rolling in dough."

"Proof?"

"Yeah. You said you were looking through some stuff. Was there a note, a letter, maybe an e-mail about setting up this abortion?"

"I'd like another drink," she said.

"Sure," he said. *Maybe a third drink will help her remember tangible evidence, or at least talk about it.*

He ordered a second martini. This was getting good.

Drinks served, he asked again about some tangible piece of evidence.

"Eric told me," She replied.

"Morrison told you?"

"Yup. He bragged about it, how he 'owned' Senator Gillespie. That's what he said. He *owned* him because of what he did for him."

Brixton took a moment to enjoy a sip before asking, "Where is this Howie Ebhart?"

"I don't know, and I don't want to know. He's a creep, makes my skin crawl if you know what I mean."

"I think I do. Ready for dinner?"

"Morrison is no better," she said.

"I'm sure he isn't. He's a lobbyist for the pharmaceutical industry. Right?"

"That's right."

"He ever talk about a doctor named King?"

She screwed up her face in thought. "King? No."

"He's—he was—a doctor in Papua New Guinea."

"Where's that?" She slurred her words now.

"Near Australia. He was doing research into finding a better painkiller."

"Like aspirin?"

"I suppose so. Morrison never mentioned him?"

"No. Why?"

"Just thought I'd ask. Part of my research."

"Oh. Who is he?"

"Was. He was murdered."

She shuddered and drank.

"Tell me more about Howie Ebhart and Morrison."

"I'm hungry."

"Then let's eat."

They settled in a booth in the downstairs where they ordered another round of drinks despite Brixton's reluctance, and a ribeye steak for him, Amish chicken for her.

"You were talking about this Howie Ebhart."

"I was?"

"Yeah. You don't know what he does for a living besides setting up abortions for young girls?"

"He used to—well, I think he worked for some congressman but not anymore."

"Who was the congressman?"

"Jesus, I don't remember. He hung out with Morrison and a few other guys like him. Alard was one."

"Alard? That's his first name?"

"I don't think so." She snuggled up next to him in the booth. The heavy, sweet scent of bourbon reached him as she said, "You know a publisher for my book?"

"Well, I–I'll check it out. I know someone who's writing a book for a big publisher. I bet he can come up with one for you."

"For us," she said, followed by a silly, drunken giggle.

"Right," he said. "For us. Here's our dinner. Eat up. Enjoy!"

He knew that he could have accompanied her into her apartment when they parted in front of the building but nixed the possibility. He'd had to prop her up on the walk from the restaurant, keeping her from falling on a few occasions. He was conflicted as they approached where she lived. He didn't like drunks, especially drunken women. On the other hand she'd given him information that he could share with Will Sayers, and he appreciated it, whether or not she talked through her booze.

"You coming in?" she asked when they reached the building.

"Love to," he said, "but maybe another time."

He'd noticed during dinner that she was quick to pout, and his turndown of her invitation brought on a prolonged one.

"I really enjoyed the evening," he said, thinking of how expensive it had been. He'd have to hit Sayers up for more money. "We'll do it again soon. I'll call."

"Good night," she said.

"Good night," he said, and watched her walk unsteadily through the front door and out of sight.

17

Brixton had intended to go home following his dinner with Paula Silver but was too wound up to call it a night. He was excited that she had confirmed what Will Sayers had said, that Senator Gillespie had gotten a teenage girl pregnant back in Georgia, and that the lobbyist Eric Morrison had played a role in arranging an abortion for her and buying off the girl's impoverished family. He called Sayers on his cell phone, hoping that the journalist hadn't made it an early-to-bed night. He hadn't.

"I just left Ms. Silver," Brixton said, "and she had some fascinating things to say."

"You've made my day," said Sayers. "I've gone up nothing but blind alleys since I got out of bed this morning."

"Pour me a drink and I'll share what she said while it's still fresh in my mind."

"My door is open."

Sayers, barefoot, wore a green silk bathrobe over his nakedness, and a Washington Nationals baseball cap.

"You look like that guy in the Rex Stout novels, Nero Wolfe," Brixton said when Sayers greeted him at the door.

"I consider that a supreme compliment," Sayers said, "although I don't suppose that you meant it that way."

"Take it any way you want."

"I happen to be a fan of Nero Wolfe," Sayers said. "I take it you are, too."

"I've read a few of the books," Brixton said, slumping in a blue director's chair with white flowers on its canvas back and seat.

"So," Sayers said, resuming where he'd been sitting behind his desk that overflowed with papers and books, "you've been out cheating on your Ms. Flo this evening."

Brixton started to respond but Sayers held up a beefy hand. "Only joking, Robert, only joking. Tell me about your evening with the faded Hollywood star."

"She's hardly that. I kind of like her, only she can be difficult at times. She's a drinker. She gets a snootful of booze and alternates between pouting and little girl giggles. I think she's been through the mill, been emotionally beaten up by too many guys including Eric Morrison."

Sayers started to ask something but Brixton continued with his analysis of Paula Silver.

"The way I figure it," he said, "she's one of those women who's born beautiful and is told by somebody, maybe in her family or some dorky boyfriend in high school, that she's a natural for Hollywood. Off she goes, gets passed around by a bunch of lying hustlers who promise her great things provided she sleeps with them. She ends up in a couple of forgettable low-budget flicks and thinks she's on her way to stardom. Instead, the next crop of nubile teenage beauties comes along and she's out on the street, ending up handing out menus to customers at the Char Bar."

"You sound like a shrink," Sayers said.

"Well, I—anyway I feel bad for her."

"Maybe she'll meet a nice unattached member of the House of Representatives, get married, and live happily ever after."

"She's better off greeting customers at Char Bar."

"Maybe so. You said she had some fascinating things to say."

"My drink?"

"You know where the booze is. Help yourself, and make me one, too, while you're at it."

Fortified, Brixton gave Sayers a briefing of what Paula Silver had to say about Morrison and his relationship with Senator Gillespie.

"Anything tangible to back up what she said?"

"I asked her the same thing. If there is she didn't mention it. She talked about one of Morrison's buddies, a guy named Howie Ebhart."

"Doesn't ring a bell."

"He and Morrison go back a long way, according to her. She says that Howie put Morrison in touch with the abortionist who took care of the senator's problem. Oh, she also mentioned somebody named Alard. Ever hear of him?"

Sayer's laugh confirmed that he did. "Hold on." He rummaged through an overflowing file bin on the floor next to him and came up with a folder, which he handed to Brixton. Its tab read "Alard Associates."

"Who are they?" Brixton asked.

"George Alard," Sayers said. "He's a shady frog, born in France, came here years ago and set up his company. They hire out to the government, mostly security assignments. The government is depending upon independent contractors more and more these days. At last count there were more than six hundred contractors supplementing the troops in Iraq and Afghanistan. That's fifty percent more than military troops assigned to those places. Blackwater is the biggest, and you know what happened to them. Four of their soldiers of fortune were convicted of murdering Iraqis. That's always been the bone of contention with these civilian hires. Too many of their guys hired by firms like Alard Associates get in trouble in the countries where they're sent, you know, rape a few local women, break the religious laws, gun down innocent civilians because they think they're above the law, offend some important official. Our government tries to cut deals with the local government to absolve independent contractors of any wrongdoing and not have to face being charged. I've been looking into this whole world of independent contractors, especially those providing security for our troops. Alard Associates always seems to come up close to the top of the list of independent contractors available for any assignment, no matter how shady it is, or even downright illegal."

"Well," said Brixton, "Alard and Morrison are buddies, according to Paula."

"Interesting grouping," Sayers muttered.

"I asked her about the doctor, King, who was murdered."

"Why?"

"Morrison is a lobbyist for the pharmaceutical industry. I just figured that he might know something about King. You met King's daughter, Jayla, at the Smiths' apartment. She's a PhD in biochemistry, and one of Flo's customers."

"A beauty."

"Paula never heard of King."

"No surprise. But I'm not interested in Dr. King," Sayers said. "Gillespie's the one I'm after."

"Yeah, I know, Will, but the King murder interests me. Mac Smith feels the same way. He met with Jayla and me. She was looking for legal advice, only Mac really can't do much about things in a place like Papua New Guinea. But after Jayla left, Mac and I got to talking about her father's murder. He had an assistant named Waksit, Eugene Waksit. Great name, huh? Anyway, Mac asked me for my take on the King murder, and I said that if I was writing a novel based on it, this Waksit guy killed his mentor and boss, Dr. King, stole all his research notes from his lab, paid to have somebody kill the native who watched over the doctor's patch of land where he grew the plants used in his research, and burned down the crops."

"Make a good novel," Sayers said. "Maybe you've missed your calling."

"Maybe I did. Of course it's all supposition on my part. By the way, Ms. Silver thinks I'm a researcher who wants to work with her on the book she intends to write."

"For shame, Robert, misleading a nice young lady like that. Where is this Waksit character?"

"Beats me," said Brixton. "Jayla King says that he called her attorney in PNG and claimed that the doctor had left him all his research results. She says that's impossible, although you never know. Anyway, Waksit was supposed to call the attorney again but never did. Chances are he's flown the coop."

"He's a suspect in the doctor's murder?"

"Evidently not. The cops there haven't read my novel."

"Maybe they'll get around to it. I appreciate what you got out of Ms. Silver, although it couldn't have been an unpleasant duty. She's gorgeous."

"She was, although she's still damned attractive."

"I'll pass along to my contacts in Georgia what you've told me."

"Sure, go ahead, but make sure nobody calls her. If she knows why I was pumping her that'll be the end of seeing her again and getting more information for you."

"Fair enough, Robert. Thanks again."

Brixton went home where Flo was watching TV.

"How did your date go?" she asked.

"Date? It wasn't a date. It was strictly business."

"Uh huh."

"Any popcorn left?"

She handed him the almost empty bowl that had been on her lap.

"You hear any more from Ms. King?" he asked her.

"Jayla. No. Why?"

"I keep thinking about her father's murder and all the other stuff that happened. This guy Waksit she talks about, her father's assistant. I'd like to know more about him."

"Then you should call her," she said. "Good night. I'm tired."

He watched her disappear into their bedroom, a puzzled expression on his face.

Do I detect a hint of jealousy? he asked himself as he changed channels and settled in to watch the Nationals baseball game from San Francisco. *I'll have to mention it the next time I see the shrink.*

18

Waksit had pretended to be asleep when Nikki Dorence left the apartment to go to work. Once confident that she wouldn't return, he got up and went to the kitchen where she had written him a note: "Orange juice and milk in the fridge. Cereal in cabinet above sink. Instant coffee on counter. Back about six." She had also left a copy of that morning's newspaper on the table, which he scanned while the tea kettle heated. He poured the boiling water into a cup with instant coffee, helped himself to orange juice, and went to the window and looked out over the street where men and women hurried to work. It was a sunny morning, which contributed to his feeling of well-being. He'd slept well; the pullout bed was comfortable.

His eyes might have been closed while hearing Nikki get ready to leave but his mind was wide awake.

He was now in Washington, D.C., where the Pharmaceutical Association of America was headquartered, and where its chief lobbyist, Eric Morrison, was also based. He'd spent much of the flight from Los Angeles mentally preparing a script he would use when contacting the lobbyist. He'd decided that he needed to put together a clearcut narrative of how Preston King's pain medication worked, and why just the right mixture of herbs and plants was crucial, something that only he knew.

He wasn't oblivious to the roadblocks he might encounter. The Port Moresby attorney, Elgin Taylor, had asked whether he had any documentation backing up his claim that King had bequeathed his research results to him, which, of course, he didn't. But who was to refute that claim? The doctor was dead. He'd worked at King's side for years, and had become so trusted that he was allowed to see patients in the clinic, enabling him to have hands-on experience with the drug. On top of that King had left him $5,000 in his will. Surely that bequest was an indication of the high regard King held him in.

He'd also decided that the nature of the pain medication, and the natural ingredients used to formulate it, helped his cause. It wasn't as though he was stealing a patented synthetic formula from another pharmaceutical company. He would be bringing to Morrison and the companies he represents a revolutionary pain medication made from indigenous plants grown in Papua New Guinea, a medication that is cheap to produce and produces no known side effects. *What a story! Who could possibly turn down what he had to offer?*

But while his grandiose visions of pharmaceutical companies falling over each other to buy the rights from him ruled his thinking, he also knew that there was one person who stood in his way—Jayla King, Dr. Preston King's daughter, who happened to work in medical research and who could challenge his claim to have been heir to the medicinal formula. He didn't know how to deal with that potential complication, aside from making it clear to Morrison and whoever else was involved that it was never to be offered to Renewal Pharmaceuticals, Jayla's employer.

He helped himself to a bowl of cereal with milk and sugar before taking a shower and dressing. He brought the briefcase from where he'd secluded it behind the pullout couch to the kitchen and opened it on the table.

He removed King's research notes and the packets of seeds and took out another envelope. In it was $9,000 in cash, his American Express credit card, and an Italian stiletto switchblade knife he'd purchased in a specialty shop at Dulles Airport. It reminded him of one that an uncle had given him on his sixteenth birthday and that he'd reluctantly left behind in Port Moresby, knowing that it would be confiscated at the airport.

While Waksit prepared for his first day in Washington, Will Sayers was getting ready to launch his day, too, although their plans differed.

The journalist had been buoyed by what Paula Silver had confided in Brixton during their dinner. He was well aware that without tangible irrefutable proof that Senator Gillespie had gotten a young Georgia woman pregnant and arranged for her abortion, he couldn't run with the story. But Paula's comment that Eric Morrison had bragged about "owning" the senator said to Sayers that the rumor was true. Maybe it was time to ratchet up his inquiry into Morrison's relationship with the silver-haired politician, and that meant making direct contact.

He packed the juicer away in a kitchen cabinet—how anyone could start a day with the vile concoction was inconceivable to him—and stopped in his favorite luncheonette where he consumed a double order of pancakes, link sausages, and orange juice. Back in his apartment he formulated his next move. He'd left for breakfast having decided to call Morrison himself, but thought better of that once relieved of his hunger pangs. He called Brixton at home and caught him as he was leaving for the office.

"Just wanted to say how much I appreciated the information you squeezed out of Paula Silver," he said.

Brixton glanced to see whether Flo was in earshot. She wasn't; he heard the shower running. "It was my pleasure," he said. "How often does a former cop like me get to wine and dine a Hollywood star on your dollar?"

"If you say so. Look, Robert, here's why I'm calling. I think it's time to put some pressure on the lobbyist, Morrison."

"Based on what, a woman scorned?"

"She's not the only source of the story," Sayers said.

"Then do it."

"I was wondering whether it would be better, more effective, for *you* to do it."

"Me? Why me?"

"Because you're so good at getting people to talk."

"It's not my fight, Will. Besides, I've got a few potential clients on the string, clients who pay real money."

"A thousand bucks isn't 'real money'?"

"Not when I'm paying for expensive drinks and dinners."

"I'll reimburse you," Sayers said.

"Good. How do you suggest I put the pressure on Morrison?"

"Call him. Make up a story about who you are and why you're calling."

"You're asking me to *lie*?"

"Oh, sorry to have offended you, Robert."

"No offense taken," Brixton said. He'd lied plenty of times as a cop in Washington and Savannah, as well as in his more recent incarnation as a private investigator. His "courtship" of Paula Silver was but the latest example.

"I'll think about it," he said.

"Fair enough," said Sayers.

"Anything else?" Brixton asked.

"Just that I'm going out and buying a coffeemaker today, one of those fancy ones with little cups filled with coffee."

"I'm pleased to hear it."

"I want you to be happy when you visit."

"I'm touched, Will, truly touched. I'll get back to you."

* * *

Jayla King already had a Keurig and used it that morning to brew a cup. She awoke with a headache and finicky stomach, thanks to having had a third glass of wine the previous night, and considered taking the day off. But she began to feel better after coffee and a bowl of yogurt with blueberries.

She'd gone out to dinner the night before with Nate Cousins, who'd introduced her to a charming French restaurant, Bistro Du Coin, on Connecticut Avenue, which he claimed had the best steamed mussels in town. While experiencing his favorite restaurants—an obvious perk of being in the public relations business—represented part of the enjoyment of going out with him, she'd also found herself becoming increasingly interested in Cousins on a more personal level.

Her dating history, if you could call it that, was not extensive, nor had it resulted in her becoming enamored of the men she'd seen. That thought was on her mind as she exercised on the treadmill in her bedroom.

Another female student in her college had accused her of being stuck-up, feeling superior to other women, a charge that Jayla considered patently untrue. Yes, she would admit—but only to herself—that she had a certain disdain for the young men who asked her out, considering them intellectually shallow and immature. She was a dedicated student who always seemed to be studying while other coeds immersed themselves in an active social life that involved multiple dates with an array of young men, their quest for a suitable lifelong mate seemingly as important as obtaining a degree. Jayla's stunning beauty probably played a role in their reaction to her, although an inborn, honest modesty precluded her from thinking that.

As she ratcheted up the treadmill's speed a familiar question occupied her. She knew that her mixed parentage—her father a white Australian, her mother, Lanisha, a dark-skinned Melanesian—played some role in her view of romantic possibilities. She'd dated both white and black young men and could never shake the feeling that she didn't belong to either race. Was Nate Cousins's mixed parentage why she felt comfortable with him, confident that he would understand her confusion about who she was and where she belonged? If so, that was all right. All she knew was that her feelings for him had grown stronger each time they were together.

Their date the previous night had started out with casual conversation over wine and appetizers, world affairs, the arts (he was a voracious reader, partial to biographies and history; she read historical novels but also enjoyed romance novels, which she didn't mention), and other nonprofessional topics. It was during dinner that he brought up her father's research.

"I know you don't like to talk about it," he said, "and I certainly understand, considering what happened to him, but I can't help but wonder how successful he was. If anyone would know, it's you."

"He claimed to have had success with patients in his clinic," she said, "but that's only anecdotal." The letter her father had left her contained a series of stories involving clinic patients who'd received the painkiller he'd created and who reported significant relief from their pain.

"Mind a suggestion?" he said.

"Of course not."

"Since you and your lab colleagues have been trying to accomplish the same thing that your father was seeking, maybe you should apply what you know about his work to developing it further at Renewal."

"I've thought about that," she said, "but I'm not ready to do anything with his efforts in the lab."

"Sure, and I understand. It was just a suggestion. Maybe the reason I brought it up was the fellow you've mentioned who worked as your dad's assistant."

"Eugene."

"Right, Eugene. Waksit is it?"

She nodded.

"Have you heard anything from him?"

"No. The last time I spoke with him was in Port Moresby when I went home following my father's death."

Cousins's face became grim. "You know, Jayla, it's possible that he'll try to use your father's work for his own benefit."

"I know," she said. "He claims that my father willed him—verbally—the rights to his research."

"Is that possible?"

"Not to me it isn't."

"Your dad left everything to you, right?"

"Yes, but Eugene called the attorney handling Dad's estate and made his claim."

"Did he follow up? Estates have to be settled through a legal process."

"He promised to call the attorney again but never did. I assumed that he was still in Port Moresby—he has an apartment there—but he's gone. The attorney tried his number, and so did I."

"Where is he?"

"I have no idea."

"I don't like the sound of this," Cousins said.

"Neither do I, although I keep trying to ignore the possibilities. To think that Eugene would do something underhanded is—"

"Maybe you didn't know him well enough."

Which was true. Most of Jayla's knowledge of Eugene Waksit came through her father, and even he had never said much about his assistant. Her innate distrust of the young man hadn't been based upon anything tangible. But claiming that he was heir to her father's research? That told a different story.

"You said that your father's research notes were missing from his lab."

"Yes."

"It had to be Waksit."

She drew a deep breath and sat back. "I hate to admit it but it does seem logical, doesn't it?"

"It's also logical that—"

"That Eugene killed my father? I pray that's not true."

"You don't know where he's gone?"

She shook her head.

"There's ways to find out, Jayla."

"I'm not sure I even want to know," she said.

"I'll do it."

"You'll do it? What do you mean?"

"I'll hire someone. There are people who specialize in such things."

"Please don't."

"Why?"

She reached across the table and placed her hand on his. "Nate," she said, "I appreciate how much you care about this—about me—but I really don't want to become involved. I don't think that Eugene will ever follow through on his claim. He's probably gone back to Australia and will find a new job and forget about my father and his research." A smile crossed her face. "Dad left him five thousand dollars in his will. He'll return to collect that money and that will be the end of it."

"If you say so," Cousins said, smiling. "I just want to be helpful, Jayla. To be candid, I'd like to be a bigger part of your life."

She cocked her head and looked at him quizzically.

"This may sound corny, but I think I'm falling in love with Jayla King."

19

Jayla didn't know how to respond so she didn't, at least for what seemed a very long time. When she did she said, "I'm flattered."

"I wasn't flattering you," Cousins said. "I just wanted to express what I'm feeling." He laughed. "Please don't take it as something to be concerned about. I'm not suggesting that you respond in kind. I'm just glad that I got it off my chest. Let's have dessert and talk about less weighty things."

After dinner he walked her to her car.

"I know you probably view me as some impetuous fool," he said.

"No, I don't view you that way, Nate. I view you as—well, as someone I like being with. Let's leave it at that for the moment."

"But only for the moment."

They kissed, and she felt sparks.

"Thank you for another lovely dinner," she said.

"Just one of many more we'll have," he said. "Good night."

She'd turned off her cell phone to avoid an unwanted intrusion at the restaurant, and now turned it on once in her car. There were a few messages, including one from

Mackensie Smith. She checked her watch: a few minutes past nine. Not too late to return the call.

"Hello Jayla," Mac said.

"Hi. I just came from dinner and saw your message."

"Nothing important," he said. "I made contact with Elgin Taylor in PNG. Lovely man. We had a long talk."

"I'm so glad. What did he have to say?"

"Many things. Feel like an after-dinner drink?"

"I don't know, I—yes, I'd like that very much."

"Drop by. Robert Brixton and Flo are here doing the same thing. I'll fill you in on my chat with Mr. Taylor when you arrive."

She said she'd be there in a few minutes. As much as she wanted to dismiss what Nate Cousins had said at dinner, his words professing that he loved her had both touched and energized her. She was wide awake and not ready to go home; a nightcap with the Smiths and Brixton and Flo was appealing.

It had started to rain lightly when she and Cousins left the restaurant, and by the time she reached the Watergate apartment complex it had become a downpour. She held a newspaper over her head as she dashed to the entrance and told the doorman who she was visiting. She was buzzed in and arrived at the Smiths' door where Brixton waited.

"Doing doorman duty," he said. "Making myself useful."

"Good for you," she said.

He took the soggy newspaper from her and they joined Mac, Annabel, and Flo in the living room.

"You need a drink," Mac said, disappearing into the kitchen and returning with a glass into which he'd poured two fingers of Armagnac over ice.

"Thanks," Jayla said and sat on the couch next to Flo, who squeezed her hand.

"Mac was just telling us about his conversation with your attorney back in Papua New Guinea," Flo said.

"Just started to," Mac said. "You haven't missed anything. Mr. Taylor sends his best to you."

"He's such a sweetheart," she replied. "Did he have anything new to report? I feel helpless being this far away."

"I'm sure you do," said Mac, "but you obviously have a top-notch surrogate working on your behalf. I was just saying that the police there are considering your father's murder an open case. And he told me that someone has been arrested in the murder of the native gentleman your father hired to oversee his crops."

"Walter Tagobe," she said.

"That's right," said Mac. "Your attorney has been in touch with a police officer named Norbis, Angus Norbis. He has contacts in the town where Mr. Tagobe was killed."

"Wewak," she provided.

"You've got some funny names in New Guinea," Brixton said.

Jayla laughed. "Guess it does sound funny to someone who isn't used to it. What else did he have to say, Mac?"

"Let's see. He mentioned the fellow who used to be your dad's assistant, Eugene Waksit."

Jayla sat up a little straighter. "What did he have to say about Eugene?"

"You already know that he's claimed to have inherited your father's lab research results."

She sighed. "Yes."

"Looks like he might be visiting you."

"What? He's coming here?"

"I don't know about Washington," Mac said, "but Mr. Taylor says that airline records indicate that Mr. Waksit flew to Los Angeles."

"That certainly is news to me," Jayla said.

Brixton interrupted the conversation. "The local police are checking up on this guy Waksit's travel?"

"According to Jayla's attorney," Mac affirmed.

Brixton looked at Mac. "Maybe what I said is true," he said.

"What was that?" Jayla asked.

Brixton hesitated before answering. "Well," he said,

"after you left the last time I played the what-if game, you know, what would I write if this was a novel."

Jayla's puzzled expression reflected her confusion.

Mac interjected, "Robert was speculating, that's all," he said. "He wondered whether your dad's assistant might have killed your father in order to gain access to his research. You said that the notes were missing."

Jayla shook her head. "No matter what I might think of Eugene, he's not a killer."

"Just doing some blue-sky thinking," Brixton said.

"But he's here in the United States?" Jayla said.

"In Los Angeles at least," Mac said.

"Refresh anyone's drinks?" Annabel asked.

"Love it," said Brixton.

"Please," said Flo.

Jayla declined.

The conversation shifted to other things, but Jayla could not shake loose what Mac had told her about Waksit coming to the United States. Los Angeles was three thousand miles away, but she felt Waksit's presence as though he were sitting next to her.

Brixton and Flo announced that they were leaving.

"Busy day tomorrow?" Annabel asked.

"I hope so," Flo replied. "I hate slow days at the shop."

"You, Robert? You have a full schedule?"

"Yeah, I, ah—just the usual."

He hadn't told anyone that he was seeing a therapist and had an appointment in the morning with Dr. Fowler. Seeing a therapist represented for him weakness, something that he was never comfortable with. He'd learned as a cop that showing weakness could get you killed, and he worked hard at conquering that feeling whenever it injected itself into his life.

Annabel insisted that Jayla take an umbrella with her. "You can drop it back the next time you're here," Annabel said, "which I hope will be soon."

After kisses all around, Jayla left. She was happy to

have the umbrella because the rainfall had increased, and the wind had picked up. She scrambled into her car and drove home, the wipers barely keeping up with the deluge. She flipped on all the lights in her apartment and drew the drapes tightly closed. She turned on the TV after undressing for bed but turned it off after only a few minutes. The movies being played were scary ones, and the news channels reported nothing but bloodshed, including a gang slaying in town that had taken the lives of three young men. She turned off the living room lights and climbed into bed with a book she'd started, a thriller set in Washington that wasn't any more relaxing than TV had been.

She clicked off the bedside lamp and thought about Nate Cousins and the dinner they'd enjoyed together that evening. That reflection was comforting. But a vision of Eugene Waksit kept getting in the way, causing her to toss and turn. Finally, unable to fall asleep, she got up, went to the living room where she checked that the door was securely locked, returned to bed, and opened the book again.

Two hours later sleep finally arrived, the windblown volley of raindrops against the window panes providing white noise.

20

Jayla's kiss stayed with Nate Cousins as he headed toward his apartment on Capitol Hill. But instead of going home he went into Lounge 201, a popular bar with a genteel atmosphere and less noise than other drinking establishments in the area. He ordered a single-malt scotch, neat, and found a secluded corner table where he sipped his drink and put his thoughts in order.

He'd promised Renewal's CEO Walt Milkin a call following his dinner date with Jayla, and worked to summon the motivation to place it.

His initial dates with Jayla for drinks and dinner had been at Milkin's urging, and Cousins suffered guilt over it. The CEO had stressed to Cousins his interest in the work that Jayla's father had been doing, and made it plain to him that he wanted—needed—to learn more about it. Not that spending time with Jayla was a hardship: "Somebody's got to do it" came to mind. She was a stunning woman; had she been from a more advanced country he had no doubt that she could have entered and won every beauty contest available, maybe even going on to a Miss World or Miss Universe title. On top of her physical beauty was a heightened intelligence. Beauty *and* brains. What a combination.

But while those initial dates had been at the urging of the man who wrote the monthly checks for Cousins's PR agency, their time spent together had raised his appreciation of her to a new level. What he'd impetuously said at the end of dinner accurately reflected his feelings.

Milkin had told Cousins to call him at home no matter what the hour. As much as he would have liked to have skipped it, he knew that wouldn't be prudent. He ordered another drink and pulled out his cell phone.

"Hello Nate," Milkin said heartily. "I've been waiting to hear from you."

"Dinner ran later than expected," said Cousins.

"Must have been an especially pleasant one."

"Yes, it was very nice. We went to Bistro Du Coin on Connecticut."

"One of my favorites. So, how is our up-and-coming star, Dr. King?"

"Jayla is fine. I admire how she's dealt with the death of her father."

"Especially considering that it was a brutal murder. Did she talk much about him?"

"About his research?"

"Yes."

"Some."

Milkin filled in the ensuing pause. "And?" he said.

"Nothing specific."

Cousins could *see* Milkin's displeasure with his response during the next gap in the conversation.

"What about the father's assistant, Eugene Waksit? Was he mentioned?"

"Ah, yes he was, Walt. I brought up the possibility that Waksit had been the one to steal her father's research notes. She obviously doesn't want to think badly of Waksit but she did acknowledge the possibility that he was the one who took them."

"Does she know where he is?"

"No. I made the suggestion that we hire someone to locate him."

"Good idea."

"She didn't see it that way," said Cousins, taking a silent sip.

"I want to find him," Milkin said firmly.

"I could hire someone but . . ."

"But what?"

"It seems unnecessary," Cousins said. "Jayla is convinced that Waksit will simply drop his claim to having been the recipient of her father's research and go on with his life."

"Maybe he can be convinced to do otherwise, and if he can't, Jayla owes it to us to carry on at Renewal what her father had been doing."

Cousins wasn't sure how to respond.

Did Jalya owe Renewal Pharmaceuticals the results of her father's work? He didn't think so, but certainly wasn't about to debate it with Milkin. He also questioned Milkin's intense interest in King's lab work. The maverick physician and researcher had concocted a crude painkiller using plants and herbs indigenous to Papua New Guinea, and had tested it on patients who'd visited his clinic. That was hardly a history of a drug's development to cause anyone in the modern pharmaceutical world to salivate. If what King had come up with seemed to have alleviated their pain, it was probably the placebo effect at work. Much ado about nothing was Cousins's unscientific view of it.

"Have you pointed that out to her?" Cousins asked.

"Not in so many words."

"Is the research he did really that important?" Cousins asked.

"How can we know unless we see what he accomplished? As I've told you, there's been talk about King at various conferences I've attended. Some paint him as a crackpot. Others have heard—and it's all secondhand—that he was on to something. All I know, Nate, is that I owe it to Renewal's stockholders to check it out. That's what I'm depending on you for. You've gotten close to her. Use that relationship you've developed to get me the answers I need."

Cousins started to respond but Milkin said angrily, "And find this Eugene Waksit character. Between him and Jayla maybe we can determine just how successful King was in his lab."

"Yes, of course," Cousins said.

"While we're on the phone, Nate, your contract renewal is up for review."

"I'm aware of that."

"We'll need to meet about it."

"Whenever you say, Walt. Anything else?"

"Not at the moment. Enjoy the rest of your evening."

Cousins reclined in his chair and held his glass in both hands, peering into the amber liquid. Milkin's final comment about his contract being up for renewal wasn't lost on him. The CEO was perfectly capable of canceling the contract without batting an eye; there were dozens of other agencies who would love to pick up the Renewal account. Cousins decided while nursing his drink that he would continue to try and learn from Jayla about her father's research because chances were that it would amount to nothing. His developing "crush" on her was premature at best. Whether she would develop similar feelings for him was only conjecture. And if their personal relationship were to advance to something more meaningful, it didn't preclude his meeting his business obligations to Renewal.

Or did it?

21

Waksit spent one additional day and night at Nikki Dorence's apartment. She'd made it plain, in a nice way, that she would be uncomfortable having him remain there when she was away attending the conference.

"Hope you don't mind finding another place," she said over breakfast.

"No, not at all. I called a few hotels while you were at work. A few of them are within my budget. I'll be fine."

"Have you begun your talks with pharmaceutical companies?"

"That's on top of my agenda today," he said. "Once I get settled in a hotel I'll make my appointments. I'm really excited about it."

"You should be, and I'm sure they will be, too."

"Take your time leaving," she said as she cleared plates from the small kitchen table. "Just be sure to close the door firmly behind you. It doesn't always catch."

"Yes, ma'am," he said brightly, tossing her a snappy salute.

She laughed. "It's really good seeing you again, Eugene."

"Same here." He lowered his voice to a conspiratorial level. "I thought about making a move on you when you were in bed but decided not to."

Another laugh from her. "I'm glad you didn't," she said. "It would have spoiled things."

He watched her wheel a small suitcase from the apartment and get into a cab in front of the building. She'd be gone for two days, and he briefly considered staying at least an additional night, but thought better of it. After casually perusing her closet, dresser, and bedside table in search of nothing in particular—he took a pair of pink panties and a pink bra from the dresser which he held up and admired—he settled in front of the living room desk with his briefcase, pulled out notes he'd made on a yellow legal pad, and picked up the phone. The call was answered by the receptionist at Morrison Associates on K Street, N.W.

"Mr. Morrison, please," Waksit said.

"Whom shall I say is calling?"

"Eugene Waksit."

"Will Mr. Morrison know what this is in reference to?"

"No, but he'll want to speak with me." He referred to his notes. "It's regarding the work that I did with Dr. Preston King in Papua New Guinea to develop an advanced pain medication. I'm sure he's heard about it."

"Please hold."

Waksit drew deep breaths as he waited for Morrison to come on the line, and debated what he would do if the lobbyist declined to take the call.

"Hello?" a man's voice said.

"Mr. Morrison?"

"Yes. What can I do for you?"

"My name is Eugene Waksit, Mr. Morrison. I'm here in Washington to meet with pharmaceutical companies regarding the painkiller I developed with Dr. Preston King. I'm sure that you're aware of the work we did."

"I'm afraid you've called the wrong person, Mr. Waksit. I'm a lobbyist for the Pharmaceutical Association of America. I'm not involved in any of the actual work our clients are engaged in."

"Yes, I'm aware of that, Mr. Morrison, but surely you have a good insight into which companies might be interested in the results of the work Dr. King and I did. By the way, as you may know, Dr. King is deceased, the victim of a brutal stabbing in his lab. In appreciation of my contribution to the research he left everything to me. I'm here in Washington with the results of that research and—"

"I'm afraid I have to cut this conversation short, Mr. Waksit. There's a long-distance caller on my other line. If you'll tell me how to reach you, I'll run this by some of my people and get back to you."

"I appreciate that, Mr. Morrison, and I'll wait for your call. I'm staying at the Embassy Inn on Sixteenth Street, Northwest." He gave him the number.

Waksit felt as though a huge weight had been lifted from his shoulders. He'd made his initial contact, and thought the conversation had gone well. At least Morrison hadn't blown him off.

As he contemplated what might ensue next he realized that he'd better get to the hotel, at which he'd reserved an inexpensive room. Careful to fully close the apartment, he took his suitcase and briefcase to the curb, waved down a passing cab, and an hour later sat in his room, the briefcase at his feet, the phone inches away.

Morrison's reaction to the call was different. He'd developed a sweat during it and wiped his brow with a handkerchief. Who was this guy Waksit? He claimed to have worked with Dr. King in PNG. Not only that, he further claimed that King had willed him his research. He'd said that he assumed that he, Morrison, was aware that King was dead. Did he know something about the arrangement through Alard Associates to have the field burned and the notes taken from the lab? Alard had told him that his "operative" couldn't go through with taking the notes because when he'd arrived at King's lab the doctor was dead, murdered. Had his assistant Waksit taken the notes? Had he killed his boss?

Other questions and thoughts assaulted him.

Was this a setup? Had someone become aware that he had arranged for the destruction of King's crops and was now building a case against him? His next thought brought about another burst of perspiration. Was someone trying to implicate him in King's murder?

His secretary entered the office.

"I need you to sign some checks," she said, a daily occurrence.

"What?" he said. "Oh, checks. Later. I'm running late for a meeting."

"Are you okay?" she asked.

"Me? Oh, sure. Just pressed for time. I'll be back after lunch."

He left the K Street building and took a taxi to the apartment he maintained a few blocks from the office, the apartment in which he and Paula Silver had often rendezvoused. He stripped off his suit jacket and dialed a number. After navigating a few voice prompts he reached the person he was calling, the VP of PAA's biggest member and one of the world's largest pharmaceutical companies.

"We have to talk," Morrison said.

"I'm listening," said the VP.

"In person," Morrison said. "Meet me in an hour."

"Hey, I can't just run out because you tell me to. What's this about?"

"My apartment," Morrison said firmly. "An hour. We have a problem, a big problem regarding Dr. King."

Jayla spent the day at Renewal Pharmaceuticals immersed in the latest attempt to combine known chemical substances into a better painkiller. One of her male colleagues commented that she seemed distracted, nervous.

"Me? No. Not at all. I just want to see this attempt reap some rewards."

But his observation had been accurate. She would lose

herself in the task for a few minutes, but knowing that Waksit was in the United States intruded. She went through mental games, reminding herself that there was no reason to be upset at learning that he'd left PNG and was in the States. He'd said when they'd parted at the airport that he might visit her one day in Washington. What was wrong with that? The speculation that he might have been the one to take her father's research notes from his lab was solely that, speculation. And the notion that he possibly was her father's killer was—well, it was pure conjecture of the sort crime novelists conjure. Robert Brixton, Flo's boyfriend, had even admitted that he was playing a novelist's what-if game, creating fiction. He, she, or anyone else had no firm basis for thinking such dreadful thoughts.

But hard as she tried, she couldn't stop thinking of Waksit being closer. Eventually, as the day wore on, her reactions faded, and she became more relaxed. But vestiges of her visceral reactions followed her from Renewal's headquarters in Bethesda and into her Foggy Bottom apartment. After doing a load of laundry and cleaning out a closet that she'd been meaning to get to for some time, she phoned Nate Cousins.

"This is a pleasant surprise," he said.

"Hope I'm not taking you from something."

"Nothing as important as hearing from you. What's up?"

"I thought you might be free for dinner."

"As a matter of fact I am."

"That charming French place again, Bistro Du Coin?"

"You liked it, huh?"

"I loved it. You were right. The steamed mussels were wonderful. But one caveat."

"What's that?"

"This time it's my treat. There's something I need to talk to you about."

"I'll be on my best listening behavior. I'll pick you up in a half hour."

* * *

The VP was fifteen minutes late arriving at Morrison's pied-à-terre. By the time he rang the buzzer Morrison was in a high state of anxiety. He'd continued to imagine scenarios regarding Waksit's call, and none of them was pleasing.

"What's going on?" the VP asked when Morrison greeted him at the door.

"Sit down and I'll tell you about it," Morrison said. "You want a drink, coffee?"

"I want to get back to the office."

"I received a call this morning from a guy named Waksit, Eugene Waksit."

"So? Who's he?"

"He was Dr. Preston King's assistant in Papua New Guinea."

That got the VP's attention.

Morrison went on to replay the gist of Waksit's call. He finished with, "He must know something about me arranging to have the doctor's field burned. As you know, the doctor's murder made getting ahold of his notes impossible. I might add that I still had to pay the total bill. The people I contracted to do the job—"

The VP held up his hand. "I'm not interested in who you hired, Eric, and don't want to know."

His words hit home to Morrison. The meaning was clear. Whatever fallout might occur as a result of him having entered into an agreement with Alard Associates would be his problem, and his alone. Until Waksit's call he'd forgotten about the deal he'd struck with Alard to destroy the crops and get the notes. If he never saw the slick little French con man again it would be too soon. But now his connection with Dr. Preston King, as tangential as it might have been, had come to life, and he could only wonder what it meant.

"Look," the VP said, "I have to get back to headquarters. Why don't you get together with this guy who claims to have the doctor's research and see what he's all about. Hell, maybe he's invented the world's next polio vaccine or morphine and we'll make a fortune."

The VP's laugh didn't make Morrison feel any better. But perhaps he was right. It would be better to see what Waksit was all about than to squander time wondering.

"Yeah, I will," Morrison said, unable to keep his disappointment at the VP's lack of concern out of his voice. "Thanks for coming by. I'll take care of this Waksit character."

"Good," the VP said, slapping Morrison on the back. "Let me know how it comes out."

With the VP gone, Morrison stood by the window and peered into the grayness that had settled over the city. As much as he hated to admit it, the VP had been right. He fished the number Waksit had given him and called the hotel, asking to be connected with Mr. Waksit's room.

"Hello," Waksit said after the first ring.

"Mr. Waksit, this is Eric Morrison."

Waksit contained his glee. This had been easier than he'd anticipated. "Yes, Mr. Morrison, thanks for getting back to me."

"Free for dinner?" Morrison asked.

"Dinner?

"If you have other plans—"

"Oh, no, nothing I can't rearrange. Yes, dinner would be fine."

"Good. Bobby Van's Steakhouse, on Fifteenth Street, N.W. The reservation will be in my name. See you there at six."

22

"So Robert," Dr. Fowler said, "how has your week been going?"

"Not so good. I had a couple of possible clients bail on me."

"Sorry to hear it. How are things with Flo?"

"You really like her, don't you?"

Fowler's expression mirrored his surprise at the comment. "Yes," he said, "she's a very nice person. She came to see me because she's concerned about you and the difficulties you're going through relating to the death of your daughter."

Brixton nodded and smiled. "Yeah, Flo's okay. She can be jealous though."

"Of you?"

A nod from Brixton. "I spent a couple of nights with a knockout blonde, a former movie actress. Flo's not happy that I did."

"Is this former movie actress—?"

"It's strictly business, Doc. I'm involved with something an old friend of mine is into."

"Does Flo know that it's—strictly business?"

"Sure. I told her all about it. You know women. They get jealous fast."

"Have you given her any reason to be jealous, Robert?"

"I don't think so. Can we get on to another subject?"

"Of course, but you brought up it up."

"I just don't want Flo to be jealous. It gets in the way of our relationship."

"A relationship you want."

"Yeah, of course. We've been through a few rough patches but we get along okay. She used to work with me but now she has a dress shop in Georgetown."

"So you've said. Are you pleased that she has her own career?"

"Sure. I wish she was still my receptionist but I suppose she needs her space. I realized recently that I've been unfair to the woman who works for me now, Mrs. Warden. It's just that she and Flo are so different."

"It's good that you recognize that."

"I miss Janet." It was as close as he would come to crying during that session.

"Losing a child is always painful, Robert, especially under the circumstances that took her from you. Do you think that you're coming to grips with it a little better?"

"No, I—yeah, I think I am." He was about to add that it was because he'd been seeing the psychologist but withheld the comment.

"You strike me as someone who keeps his emotions in check," Fowler said.

Brixton shrugged. "I've been a cop all my life," he said. "As a cop, letting your emotions get the best of you can get you killed."

"I can understand that. Better to go by the book."

"That's right."

"Sometimes it's beneficial to *close* the book."

"Meaning what?"

"Oh, doing something impetuous, on the spur of the moment, something that isn't written in whatever book you follow."

"Yeah? I'll think about that."

"Good. I see that our time is up."

The session ended with Fowler telling Brixton that he was pleased with the progress he was making and that he hoped that they could continue seeing each other. Brixton paid the receptionist and made his next appointment four days hence. He walked to his car, leaned against it, fought the urge to resume smoking, and thought about the last forty-five minutes. He felt good, and on his way to the office he stopped in a florist's and bought two bouquets of flowers. He swung by Flo's shop and delivered one of them to her. She was obviously touched by the gesture. He handed the second bouquet to Mrs. Warden when he walked into his office.

"What is this for?" she asked.

"Nothing special," he said. "Just thought you would enjoy them."

"Thank you," she said in her pinched voice. "I'd put them in water if we had a vase."

"Why don't you run out and buy one?" he suggested. "Things are slow."

He gave her cash and smiled as he watched her walk from the reception area.

Buying flowers for other than a special occasion?

A new chapter had been written in Robert Brixton's book.

23

Brixton mentally composed the cover story he would use when calling the lobbyist Eric Morrison. He decided on the straightforward approach. He wouldn't mention Will Sayers as the source of his information, would simply say that he was a private investigator looking into the rumor that Senator Ronald Gillespie had fathered a child out of wedlock in Georgia. Better to rattle Morrison's cage at the outset than try to sweet-talk him into providing information. The direct approach had always worked better for Brixton when he was plying his trade as a detective in Savannah. Make 'em sweat!

"Will Mr. Morrison know what this is in reference to?" the receptionist asked, a question she was accustomed to posing,

"Tell him that I'm a private investigator looking into Senator Gillespie's extracurricular activities in Georgia," Brixton said sternly.

"Please hold."

She returned a minute later. "Mr. Brixton? I'm afraid that Mr. Morrison is tied up at the moment."

Sounds kinky Brixton thought but didn't say. "When *won't* he be tied up?" he asked.

"If you'll give me your number I'll pass it on to Mr. Morrison."

"Sure," Brixton said, rattling it off for her. "You might also tell Mr. Morrison that I'll be talking with his friend, Howie Ebhart." Brixton had researched Ebhart, who billed himself as a political consultant.

"All right," she said. "Thank you for calling Morrison Associates."

Brixton grinned as he sat back in his swivel desk chair. He'd been told that Ebhart was the one who had put Morrison in touch with the abortionist. If true—and he had no reason to doubt it—he could envision Morrison placing a fast call to Ebhart to get their stories straight.

He hadn't felt this charged up in too long a time. He knew a man, now deceased, who'd been in and out of prison multiple times for burglaries and grand theft. The last time he'd been released he was sixty-seven years old and should have enjoyed freedom in his dotage. But within two weeks of his release he'd been arrested again for masterminding a break-in of a manufacturing company's offices in search of payroll cash. Brixton had visited him in prison and asked why he'd done it.

"I missed the action," was the reply.

Brixton understood. Action was good. It was healthy—provided you didn't end up in jail or take a bullet.

Brixton's vision of Morrison calling Howie Ebhart was prescient.

"Howie, it's Eric."

"My man," Ebhart said pleasantly. "How are things?"

"Things are not good."

He told him about Brixton's call.

"That's a problem," Ebhart said.

"A big one. Why the hell is he calling *me*?"

"I don't know, Eric. Somebody in Georgia must have tipped him about you."

"Tipped him about me? What the hell did I do? I didn't do anything illegal in setting up the abortion. It was your contact."

"You laid out the money, Eric."

"That's—what does that have to do with anything?"

"Just stating the obvious."

"That's not important," Morrison said, despite knowing that it was. *If this investigator can implicate Gillespie, the senator's in trouble* was his unstated follow-up.

Ebhart laughed, which annoyed Morrison.

"You're involved in this, too, Howie," the lobbyist said.

"Me? All I did was introduce you to somebody. What you and that person decided to do isn't my problem."

Morrison thought of another introduction Ebhart had made, George Alard.

"Look, Howie, this investigator, Robert Brixton, says that he intends to call you, too."

"Let him. I have nothing to hide."

"Really? You set me up with that abortionist and with Alard."

Another annoying laugh from Ebhart. "I do get around, don't I? And what's Alard got to do with it?" He cut off Morrison's next comment. "Look, Eric, there's nothing to be upset about. It'll pass. Believe me, it'll pass."

"When he calls, stonewall him, Howie. You say that it'll pass. I say that we've got a potential mess on our hands."

"*We've* got a problem?"

"Let me know if he calls you," Morrison said, and ended the conversation.

He summoned a young lobbyist he'd recently hired into his office. "I need you to do something and do it fast," he told him. "Find out what you can about a private investigator here in D.C. named Robert Brixton."

"What's this about, Eric?"

"Just do it, okay? Get back to me by the end of the

day. And while you're at it check out a guy named Eugene Waksit. I need it before I leave for dinner."

Calm down, he told himself when his assistant had left. The fact that some private investigator was looking into Senator Gillespie's love life wasn't necessarily the end of the world. But it could be troublesome—for him. If Gillespie were to lose his seat in Congress, that would mean having to cultivate a new champion in the Senate, someone on the right committees and with the clout that came with that. Too, having Gillespie in his pocket helped ensure that PAA didn't decide to seek another lobbying organization to advance its agenda. No elected official had a greater influence on legislation that benefited the pharmaceutical industry than Senator Ronald Gillespie.

The arrangement he'd made with the abortionist to end the young woman's pregnancy was decidedly sub rosa, money paid under the table, no strings attached. Politicians were forever on the receiving end of scurrilous rumors and politically motivated smears. Gillespie had plenty of political enemies back in Georgia.

Had some political foe come across the nasty episode with the teenage girl and was now trying to use it to smear Gillespie's reputation and reelection chances? Had that same person hired a sleazy private investigator to build a case against Gillespie? *What had politics become?* he mused. Ronald Gillespie was a respected member of the United States Senate. To have some down-and-out gumshoe—that's what private investigators were called in trash fiction, weren't they?—poking his nose into something that was none of his business was intolerable to Morrison. The sob sister talking heads on cable TV denounce the role of lobbyist money in the political system. *What do they know?* Gillespie needs the money provided by lobbyists like me, Morrison often told himself, to retain his pivotal role in the Senate and stand up for pharmaceutical companies that create the medicines that keep people alive. Lobbying is honorable. Lobbying is American. Lobbying is crucial to keeping the nation going forward.

That was his mantra when questioned by those with a jaundiced view of money and its pervasive role in politics.

Privately, he didn't believe a word of it. He was well aware that politics had become a business in which money talked and the only goal was to retain power. That was okay with him. He was in the business of buying politicians, and it had provided him and his family an upscale lifestyle. Nothing else mattered. End of internal debate.

Jayla and Nate Cousins were seated at the same table they'd occupied the last time they were at Bistro Du Coin. Cousins was pleased that Jayla had agreed to be picked up at her apartment. It felt more like a real date than meeting up separately. He thought that she looked especially beautiful that evening, and was aware of the admiring male glances as the maître d' showed them to the table. The lavender dress she wore provided a lovely scrim for her dusky complexion.

"I'm glad that you called and suggested dinner," he said.

"I don't usually initiate a dinner date," she said.

"Why the change?"

"Because I have something to discuss with you."

"So you said when you called. A problem?"

"Probably not, but I need some good advice."

"I'm flattered," he said.

She unfolded her napkin and placed it on her lap.

"Is this about what I said the last time we were here?" She looked at him quizzically.

"When I said that I'd fallen in love with you?"

"Oh. No, it has nothing to do with that."

He masked his disappointment. He would have liked to continue that conversation.

"What is it then?"

"Let's order first," she suggested.

They shared a bottle of Cabernet.

"Nate," she said, "I want to talk with you about my father's research."

While he would have preferred to expand on the more personal topic, he was also quietly pleased that the subject of her father's research had come up. He'd not had a chance to pursue what his boss, Walt Milkin, had requested of him. Maybe Jayla was about to hand him the information without his having to work for it.

They clicked the rims of their wineglasses and sipped.

"Frankly, Nate, I'm in a quandary," she said.

"Tell me."

"I haven't been entirely honest with you."

"Oh? How so?"

"I also haven't been honest with Walt Milkin. I know that you've been interested in my dad's research. So has Mr. Milkin. He asks me about it every time I see him."

Cousins shrugged. "I can understand that," he said. "As for me, my interest in it is because it involves you. As his daughter, his work must have special meaning."

"Of course. I take tremendous pride in what he accomplished. You thought that a placebo effect might be responsible for any anecdotal success he had with his clinic patients. That isn't true. My dad left me a package that our housekeeper, Tabitha, gave me when I was home. According to what he left me—a long letter detailing the work he did, and packets of seeds for plants that he used to compound his pain medication—he conducted his own personal clinical studies with patients." Her smile was reflective. "It bothered him that some of his patients received a placebo. He wanted every one of them to benefit. And don't misunderstand. I know that his small, personal clinical trial won't mean anything to an American pharmaceutical firm because it involved only a few patients. But the results were impressive. Those who received the real thing had a dramatic lessening of their pain, while those receiving the placebo reported only minor relief, if any." She leaned closer to him, her hand on his arm. "Nate," she said, "the medication worked. It really worked."

"I don't doubt it for a minute, Jayla."

"I haven't discussed this with anyone because, frankly, I don't know what to do with the information my father left me. You know that the field where he grew his plants was destroyed at the same time he was murdered."

Cousins nodded.

And he had an assistant named Eugene, Eugene Waksit."

"We talked about him the last time."

"Fortunately, my father left me his long and detailed account of his research, fortunate because his official logs and notes disappeared when he was killed."

"Presumably taken by this fellow Waksit."

"I don't know that for certain. He did inform my father's attorney that he'd been granted my father's results before he died."

"Which you feel is a lie."

"Yes. It must be."

"Does he have anything in writing?"

"Not that I'm aware of. It certainly isn't in his will. I've just learned that Eugene is here in the United States."

Cousins sat up straighter. "He is? How do you know that? Has he contacted you?"

"No. My father's attorney told me."

"Where in the States?"

"Los Angeles, as far as the attorney knew."

"Do you think he's come to the States to try and sell your dad's research findings?"

"That's why I decided to discuss it with you. I—well, I trust you, Nate."

"I'm glad I've earned that trust, Jayla. What would you like me to do?"

She paused before answering. "I'm wondering whether I should take what my father accomplished and have Renewal Pharmaceuticals pick up where he left off."

Cousins, too, paused before replying. When he did he said, "I know that Walt Milkin would be overjoyed if you did. But I hope you're not doing it just because I suggested it the last time we were together. This should be your decision and your decision only. Are you serious about it?"

"I'm not sure, but it's been on my mind a lot lately."

Their dinner arrived. Jayla asked, "So, what do you think of my sharing the research with Renewal?"

"I think you have to do what you're comfortable with," he said. "I mentioned the last time we were together that your father's assistant, Waksit, is likely to try and sell the research to a pharmaceutical company. He obviously won't approach Renewal because he knows that you work there. Besides, there are plenty of other pharmas with more money and clout than Renewal. One thing you might consider . . ."

She waited for him to complete what he was about to say.

"Nothing," he said.

"What, Nate?"

"No, nothing. Let's eat."

They said little during dinner. Cousins was in the grip of a conflict of interest. He owed it to Milkin and Renewal to encourage Jayla to turn over her father's research and allow the Renewal labs to work at refining it. His best interests dictated that he do that.

But his emotional side led him to sincerely want to do the right thing by her. She trusted him, and that meant something. He allowed his emotional side to prevail.

"When you joined Renewal," he said, "you signed an employment contract, didn't you?"

"Yes. Doesn't everyone?"

"As far as I know. I just mention it because your contract might have a clause under which everything you develop at Renewal becomes its intellectual property. It's a boilerplate clause in most contracts."

"I haven't looked at that contract since the day I

signed it. Frankly, I never read it closely. I was just so thrilled to have been hired."

"It probably means nothing," he said offhandedly, "but I just thought I'd mention it before you make your decision."

She frowned. "I can't imagine that it would apply in this case," she said. "I didn't develop the research while working at Renewal. My father did in Papua New Guinea."

"You're probably right, Jayla. More wine?"

The conversation at Bobby Van's Steakhouse also centered on Dr. Preston King's research.

Eric Morrison and Eugene Waksit sat at a table for two. An observer would sense that both men were ill at ease. Waksit had arrived after Morrison, who had already finished half his drink when Waksit approached the table carrying his ever-present briefcase.

"I appreciate you seeing me on such short notice," Waksit said as he took the chair opposite the lobbyist.

"Yeah, well, I figured I should at least hear you out. As I said, I have nothing to do with the actual work that my clients do, you know, developing medicines and things like that. I'm their lobbyist. I work with Congress to make sure that their work doesn't get bogged down by governmental nonsense."

"It must be interesting work," Waksit said shakily.

"Yeah, it is. You say that this Dr. King left you the results of his research?"

"That's right. He was a marvelous man. It was tragic the way somebody murdered him. Do you know much about him?"

Morrison shook his head. "He was some sort of maverick doctor in New Guinea, right?"

"In *Papua* New Guinea," Waksit said, hoping that correcting Morrison wouldn't offend him. "PNG for short."

"Right. PNG. What kind of research did he do?"

"He developed a pain medication using plants and herbs grown in PNG."

Morrison's laugh was forced. "Doesn't sound very scientific to me," he said.

Waksit resented the comment but didn't have a ready response.

"Look," said Morrison, "I don't know anything about this doctor and what you say he developed. If it is as effective as you claim, I'm sure that you'll find a pharmaceutical company that'll be willing to hear you out."

Waksit started to respond but Morrison continued. "You have proof that the research belongs to you?" he asked.

"You mean some sort of document?"

"Right."

"I worked closely with Dr. King for many years," Waksit said, unable to keep the pique from his voice. "He told me many times that when he died he wanted me to continue his work."

"Hey," Morrison said, raising his hand. "I'm not arguing with you. Let's have dinner. I have another appointment."

Morrison mostly listened during dinner as Waksit talked nonstop about King's research and his role in it. As he did Morrison went over in his mind what his assistant had come up with about the young man sitting across from him.

There hadn't been much to report. He'd provided his boss with Waksit's educational background, and had confirmed that he'd worked with Dr. Preston King in Papua New Guinea. He'd also written in his report that Dr. King had a daughter, Jayla King, who was a PhD working as a medical researcher at Renewal Pharmaceuticals. George Alard's "operative" had reported back that when he arrived at King's lab the physician was already dead. If that was true—and he tended to believe that it was—Waksit had to be the logical suspect. Here he was claiming that King had verbally willed him the fruits of his research. Had he murdered the physician in order to obtain it? If so, he was breaking bread with a killer.

They skipped dessert and Morrison called for a check.

"Are you interested in what I'm offering?" Waksit asked.

"As I told you, Mr. Waksit, I'm not involved in the workings of my clients."

"But you could introduce me to the right people at those clients."

"I'm really not comfortable in doing that," Morrison said.

"I'm willing to share the money," Waksit said.

"What about the doctor's daughter, Mr. Waksit?" Morrison asked.

Waksit stiffened. He hadn't expected the lobbyist to know about Jayla, and certainly wasn't prepared to have her brought up in the conversation.

"She has nothing to do with this," Waksit said defensively.

"Seems to me that her father would have left his research to her," Morrison said as he added a tip to the bill.

Waksit repeated his offer to share money with Morrison.

"Sorry, Mr. Waksit, but I'll have to pass on your offer. I wish you all the best."

Morrison left the table, got in his car, and drove home. Waksit had come off to him like a cheap hustler. On top of that he might be a killer. Get involved with him? Not a chance.

Later that night he sat in his home office and reviewed the second report given him at the end of the day by his assistant, a dossier on the private investigator Robert Brixton:

Brixton, Robert . . . 53 yrs old . . . former cop in D.C. (4 yrs) and Savannah, Georgia (retired from there) . . .

Divorced, two daughters, one deceased in terrorist café bombing in D.C. . . . involved in Savannah case, teen girl killed, traced to First Lady and D.C. social type . . . involved in other controversies . . . broke gunrunning plot in D.C. and Hawaii . . . considered a hothead . . . office in lawyer Mackensie Smith suite . . . girlfriend Flo Combes, owns dress shop in Georgetown . . .

There was more, and the further Morrison read the more concerned he became. The dinner with Eugene Waksit was a distant memory, a waste of time and money. But this investigator Brixton posed a *real* cause for concern. Brixton had mentioned Howie Ebhart, who'd introduced Morrison to both the abortionist, and to George Alard. Ebhart was a blowhard in Morrison's estimation, capable of shooting off his mouth.

Morrison didn't need all these complications. He was supposed to spread money around Congress on behalf of his pharmaceutical clients, not be arranging abortions or contracting with a slimy Frenchman to have a physician's plot of land bulldozed in some godforsaken place like Papua New Guinea.

He knew one thing for certain. He wasn't about to let some two-bit private investigator destroy everything he'd worked for. His firm, Morrison Associates, was successful and respected. He'd built it from scratch into one of Washington's top lobbying forces.

He made two decisions.

He would call Robert Brixton in the morning to find out more about what he knew.

And he would call Senator Gillespie to give him a heads-up.

Jayla King also did some reading after returning from her dinner with Nate Cousins. She dragged out the employment contract she'd signed when going to work at Renewal Pharmaceuticals and read it carefully. Cousins had been right; it did contain the standard clause that gave the firm intellectual property rights to any break-through conceived and developed by her as an employee.

But did her father's research fall under that clause? She needed legal advice. A call in the morning to Mack-ensie Smith was very much in order.

24

Jayla took the day off following her dinner date with Nate Cousins, using personal days she'd accrued. She had a number of items on her to-do list beginning with a ten A.M. appointment with Mackensie Smith to go over her employment contract. Annabel was there when she arrived.

"I hope I'm not interrupting anything important," Jayla said.

Smith laughed. "We're discussing whether to spend money sprucing up our kitchen. I suppose that's important."

"Yes, I would say that it is," Jayla said.

"How are you, Jayla?" Annabel asked.

"Confused would be the best way to describe it."

"You mentioned that you have an employment contract you wanted me to take a look at," Mac said.

She pulled it from her briefcase and handed it to him.

"I'd better be going," Annabel said. "I don't like to be late opening the gallery."

"I'd love to stop by and see it one day," Jayla said. "My father had a few pieces of pre-Columbian art, although he primarily collected artifacts from the Sepik

River region, tribal masks, smoking apparatus, head-dresses, bamboo musical instruments."

"Maybe you should start collecting those things, too, Annie," Mac told his wife. "You could set up a corner of your shop featuring items from PNG."

"I'm having enough trouble keeping up with the market for pre-Columbian art," she said, "but it's an intriguing suggestion."

"If you ever decide to do it," Jayla said, "I'll be happy to help."

"And you'll be the first person I'll turn to," Annabel said. "Please stop by the gallery one day soon."

"I'll make a point of it."

Annabel left the office and Mac read Jayla's employment contract.

"Well," she said when he'd finished, "will Renewal own the rights to anything I do with my father's research?"

"They could certainly make a case for it," Mac replied. "I'd like to give it some more thought. Leave this with me?"

"Sure."

"Have you heard from your father's assistant, Mr. Waksit?"

"No. Knowing that he's in the United States prompted me to consider working with my employer, Renewal Pharmaceuticals, to further develop my father's research. If Eugene stole the notes from the lab—and I don't know for certain that he did—he's probably already trying to interest a pharmaceutical company in buying Dad's discoveries."

"He'd have a tough time selling that information, Jayla," Smith said. "As far as I know from speaking with your attorney in PNG, there's nothing in writing to confirm that he has legal rights to the research. By the way, Mr. Taylor told me during our most recent conversation that the police in PNG have arrested someone in connection with the murder of that fellow who oversaw your father's acreage."

She was about to respond when Brixton knocked and entered Smith's office. "Sorry," he said.

"Come in, Robert," Smith said. "Jayla and I were just discussing her father's murder and the death of the man who tended his plot of land."

"Walter Tagobe," Jayla said.

"They've arrested someone in his murder," Smith said. "It seems that this man got drunk in a bar and bragged about killing him. He's an Australian, works for an outfit called Alard Associates."

"Whoa," Brixton said, sitting forward. "Alard Associates? That's a private security firm that hires out to any government."

"Did this man admit to having killed Walter?" Jayla asked.

"He claims he did it in self-defense," Mac said.

"Ever hear of a lobbyist named Morrison?" Brixton asked.

"I've read about him," Smith said.

Brixton said, "Morrison is evidently friends with the guy who runs Alard Associates. Morrison represents big pharmaceutical companies, you know, shoveling cash under the table to politicians in return for voting his way. Anyway, Jayla's father was involved in developing a new medicine, right?"

"A pain medication," Jayla said.

"A pain medication," Brixton repeated. "Okay. Morrison is a friend of the guy who runs Alard Associates. The guy who killed your father's helper works for Alard Associates. If your father had hit on a new and better pain medication, that's got to create plenty of sweat in the pharmaceutical industry. Am I right?"

Smith looked at Jayla before responding. "Go on Robert," he said.

"Look," Brixton said, "I don't know anything for sure, but it just seems to me that your father's murder is somehow wrapped up with these other people. Want some juicy insider D.C. gossip?"

Smith and Jayla stared at him blankly.

"This lobbyist for Big Pharma, Eric Morrison, has a U.S. senator in his pocket. Senator Gillespie? Ring a bell?"

"Of course," Smith said.

"So," Brixton said, "Senator Gillespie is a champion in Congress of the pharmaceutical industry. Morrison does lots of favors for the senator besides funding his campaigns with money from his clients, including arranging an abortion for a young gal back in Georgia whom the senator got in the family way, as the saying goes."

"That's shocking," Jayla said.

"Welcome to Washington, D.C.," Brixton said. "Anyway, this Alard Associates, according to my very reliable source, hires out to whoever pays the most, which naturally includes the government."

"And?" Smith said.

"And," Brixton said, leaning forward as though he'd just solved the world's greatest mystery, "if the guy who killed the native, Toby—"

"Tagobe," Jayla corrected.

"Right, Tagobe," Brixton said. "The guy who killed Tagobe might also be the one who torched your father's land, Jayla. And maybe he was also the one who killed your father. And maybe he did it because he was told to do it by his employer, Alard Associates. *And . . .*"

They waited for him to complete his thought.

"And maybe our lobbyist friend, Morrison, put him up to it on behalf of one of his clients, a pharmaceutical company."

Everyone fell silent.

"Plays for me," Brixton said proudly.

Mac started to say something but was interrupted by Mrs. Warden, who'd knocked before entering. "Mr. Brixton," she said, "you have a call from a Mr. Eric Morrison."

Brixton looked from Mac to Jayla before saying, "This

should be interesting. Don't go away. I'll be back to give you a play-by-play."

Brixton took the call in his office.

"Brixton here."

"I'm returning your call," Morrison said.

"I appreciate that, Mr. Morrison." He injected pleasantness into his voice.

"What's this all about?" Morrison asked brusquely.

"Well," Brixton said, "to cut to the chase, I'm investigating a situation involving Senator Ronald Gillespie. You know who he is, of course."

"Of course I know who he is."

"A very important senator, chairs important committees including one that oversees the pharmaceutical industry."

"So?"

"So, Mr. Morrison, I'm wondering why you would pay an abortionist to cover up for this important senator."

"You have one hell of a nerve suggesting that."

"Hey, I'm not shooting in the dark. I have plenty of proof that this happened. What I'm doing is giving you a chance to tell your side of it."

"You say you have proof. What proof?"

Brixton forced a chuckle. "You didn't think that you could pull off something like this without other people getting wind of it, did you?"

"Is there any other reason that you called, Mr. Brixton?"

Brixton decided to go for broke. The scenario he'd painted in Smith's office for Mac and Jayla had been another what-if exercise. But as long as he had Morrison on the phone . . ."

"Mr. Morrison, what about the murder of Dr. King on Papua New Guinea and the guy who was hired by Alard Associates to burn his crops—*and*, maybe kill the doctor? Ring a bell?"

The silence on the other end of the line said that Brixton's statement had hit home.

"You there Mr. Morrison?"

"Yes, I'm here." He was breathing heavily. "I know nothing about what you're talking about."

"Did one of your pharmaceutical clients suggest that you arrange to get rid of the doctor's crops—*and* the doctor himself?"

"You keep spouting these kinds of lies and you'll be on the hot end of a slander suit."

"It won't be the first time. Look, Mr. Morrison, Dr. King had a daughter who would like some closure on her father's murder. I'm not looking to get you in trouble. I know that you're a successful and respected lobbyist in town. How about we find time to sit down, someplace private and quiet, and talk it over? I'll make myself available anytime you say."

Morrison's response was to slam down his phone.

Brixton held his phone away from him as though it might be contagious. "Touchy, huh?" he said as he hung up and rejoined Mac Smith and Jayla King in Smith's office.

"I'm sure you have a compelling tale to tell us," Mac said.

Brixton replayed his conversation with Morrison.

"You realize, Robert, that you've gone out on a limb with those kinds of accusations," Smith said.

"Just trying to stir the pot," Brixton countered. He turned to Jayla. "You have a problem with what I've done?"

"No," she said. "I *would* like closure about my father's murder."

"Which you deserve," said Mac.

"Hear anything about where your father's assistant, Whatsit, is it?" Brixton asked.

"No," Jayla said, deciding not to correct him.

"I'd be wary of him," Brixton offered. "If he stole your father's research he might be capable of other things that aren't very nice."

25

Waksit brooded in his room at the Embassy Inn on Sixteenth Street. Morrison's quick dismissal of him had stung. He was angry; the lobbyist hadn't given him ample time to make his case, had brushed him off like he was some crackpot trying to sell magazine subscriptions or prime land in the Australian desert.

What had especially upset him was Morrison's question about King's daughter. Not that raising her name had come as a surprise. He'd known from the moment that he'd removed King's research results from the lab with the intent to sell it to the highest bidder that Jayla could be a stumbling block. Her father's attorney, that pompous ass Taylor, had questioned his claim that he'd been verbally bequeathed the research by Dr. King, who'd left everything in his will to his stuck-up daughter aside from a measly $5,000 for his loyal assistant.

What had she ever done to deserve anything? *He* was the one who had worked side by side with her precious daddy while she was off having fun at college. *He* was the loyal assistant who gave those pathetic creatures who visited the clinic the medicine to make their pain go away. *He* scrubbed the lab every day, not her, made sure there were plenty of plants from the Sepik acreage for

King to concoct his medicine. *He* deserved the results of the search, not her.

He'd spent part of the day following his dinner with Morrison driving his rented car past Jayla's apartment building in Foggy Bottom, and cruising in front of Renewal Pharmaceutical's headquarters in Bethesda. He didn't have a specific goal in mind, nor did he expect to run into her at either location. But he was compelled to see where she lived and worked.

It occurred to him that she might have already approached her bosses at Renewal about using her father's work as the basis for their own development of an improved pain medication. But what did she know? Okay, so maybe King talked to her about his work, but he, Eugene Waksit, had possession of King's research logs and results, and that gave him an advantage over her. He had the goods; she had only her filial relationship. She'd been away at college in Australia while he had worked at King's side in both the lab and the clinic. The fact that she'd gone on to receive her doctorate in molecular biology meant nothing.

Tired of driving, he parked in a garage and, carrying his briefcase with him, settled in an outdoor café on the same street as Jayla's apartment building. The gray sky threatened rain, but it was a warm day with a gentle breeze that kept the humidity from being oppressive. He ordered a grilled cheese sandwich and a beer. While watching the passing parade he became introspective, and his anger swelled. He viewed the passing crowd with disdain, smug young men and women full of themselves, probably without an ounce of brains to share between them. Morrison was a prime example. Waksit had traveled all the way from Papua New Guinea to offer the lobbyist a once-in-a-lifetime opportunity, but he was too stupid to appreciate it. Waksit had been certain that Morrison would welcome the opportunity with open arms. That he didn't, not only told Waksit that the man was dumb, it posed a dilemma. Because Morrison represented a number of leading pharmaceutical companies, he was the ideal person to point Waksit in the right direction. Now, without the lobbyist's collaboration, Waksit was faced with having to choose a pharmaceutical firm to approach, a shot in the dark.

As he pondered the situation, the notion of contacting Jayla and suggesting that they form some sort of partnership came and went. He didn't need her. He had the research, not her. He had intimate knowledge of its potentials. That was his road to riches.

He paid for lunch and headed back toward the parking garage. His car was brought to the exit and he got behind the wheel and began to ease into traffic. Jayla, who'd just returned from having run errands following her meeting with Mac Smith, saw him from the opposite side of the broad avenue.

"Eugene?" she shouted.

Her words were drowned out by a passing bus, which stopped, cutting off her view. When it moved on, Waksit and the car were gone.

"He's here in Washington," she muttered as she dodged traffic and stood in front of the garage.

Was it really him?

If it was, why would he be parking on her street? Surely, if he'd wanted to see her he would have called. Had he gone to her apartment building and rung her unit? What was he doing in Washington? The attorney Taylor had said that the Papua New Guinea police had been tracing his steps. Not that he was a suspect in her father's death, but he was obviously a so-called person of interest.

Despite the warmth of the day, a chill stabbed her as she hurried to her building where she asked the doorman if anyone had been looking for her.

"No, Ms. King, no one's been here."

She went to the apartment and checked her answering machine. No call from Waksit. She looked down at the street in search of him, a wasted exercise she knew. She'd just seen him—if it was him—drive away. She checked her watch. Two o'clock. She considered calling the attorney in PNG but held that urge in check. Instead, she dialed Mac Smith's office number.

"Hello," Smith said in his usual cheery voice. "This is a nice surprise."

"Mac," she said, "I think I just saw Eugene Waksit, my father's assistant."

"Here? In D.C.? He would have called, wouldn't he?"

"Yes, I would have thought so."

"You sound upset, Jayla."

"I suppose I am. There's no reason for me to be but—"

"Why don't you join us at the apartment? It's a slow day here, and Annabel is on her way from the gallery. We can talk about the situation with Waksit and maybe make dinner plans."

"I don't want to intrude."

"You won't be. I think Robert and Flo will be joining us. I'll be here this afternoon going over a contractor's estimate to redo the kitchen. Maybe you can add some PNG design touches to the project."

"I'm afraid that design isn't one of my strong suits, Mac, but I'd love to catch up with everyone. Five?"

"Sounds perfect."

As Jayla caught up on paperwork and bill paying—and pondered Waksit's presence in Washington—Eric Morrison stood on the deck of his Aquariva yacht awaiting the arrival of Senator Ronald Gillespie. His call to the senator's office had been met with "The senator isn't available at the moment."

"You tell the senator," Morrison replied, "that this is damned important, more important than anything else he's doing at the moment."

Gillespie came on the line a minute later.

"What's so damn urgent that I had to pull myself out of a meeting?" he growled.

"I'll give it to you straight, Senator. I got a call from a private investigator here in D.C. who knows all about— all about the thing that happened in Georgia."

"What thing?"

"Not on the phone," Morrison said, "but you know damn well what I'm talking about."

Gillespie fell silent.

"This is serious, Senator," Morrison said. "He knows everything."

"Who is he?"

"His name is Brixton, Robert Brixton."

"Never heard of him."

"Well, he knows about you. Look, I'm in your corner and have been for a long time. If what he knows becomes public you've got one big mess on your hands, personally and politically."

"Can't you take care of it?"

"Not without talking to you first," Morrison said. "I suggest that you break away from your meeting and meet me at the dock. I'll be on my boat. Be there in an hour."

Morrison hung up and worked to control his shaking. He'd never spoken to Gillespie in that way, had never spoken to any member of Congress with such forcefulness. But the situation demanded it. The investigator Brixton not only seemed to know the intimate details of the young woman's abortion, he'd mentioned George Alard and the murder of Dr. Preston King and the destruction of his acreage. It sounded to Morrison that Brixton was not only digging into Senator Gillespie's ill-advised tryst with a teenage girl, he was also building a case against the lobbyist.

He brushed off queries about why he was leaving the office and drove to the harbor in Snoots Bay. He kept reminding himself to calm down as he loosened ropes tethering the yacht to the dock and checked the fuel level, constantly looking to the parking lot for Gillespie's arrival. He wondered whether the senator would show. If he didn't—well, he was not about to take the fall for Gillespie if it came down to that.

He reread the report his assistant had written about Brixton.

"Jesus," he muttered. Brixton sounded like a foul ball, the proverbial loose cannon. Who was he working for? What political organizations back in Georgia had hired him to dig up dirt on Gillespie—dirt on *him*?

He was about to give up on Gillespie when the red Mercedes convertible came into view. Gillespie parked, got out, and walked with purpose to the boat.

"I thought you might not show," Morrison said.

"You took me away from some very important legislative matters," Gillespie said angrily. "This had better be worth my walkin' out of that meeting."

"Your meeting was not as important as this," Morrison said. "Come on, let's get out on the water where the media whores can't snoop on us."

Morrison didn't take the craft far out into the river. He found a spot along the shore and anchored.

"You say that this private investigator knows about what happened with that little lady back home?" Gillespie said.

"That's right."

"Where'd he get his information?"

"I don't know, but it has to be from your political enemies in Georgia."

"And what's he intend to do with this information?"

Morrison shrugged.

"What's this bum into, blackmail? Is that what his game is, blackmail?"

That possibility hadn't crossed Morrison's mind. "Maybe," he said. "He didn't say what he was after other than information."

"Got to be money. Why else would he get involved?"

"As I said before, Ron, he has to be acting on behalf of your political foes back in Georgia."

"You got anything to drink on this boat?" Gillespie asked.

Morrison pulled a half-consumed bottle of Kentucky bourbon from a cabinet and poured a glass for Gillespie. "Sorry, no ice," he said.

Gillespie ignored him and downed the drink. He smacked his lips and looked out over the river.

"I paid that little girl and her folks plenty to keep their mouths shut."

Morrison didn't correct him. *He'd* been the one who'd paid the girl's family, and picked up the tab for the abortion.

"What's important," Morrison said, "is that you decide what to do next. This private investigator might just be blowing smoke, but I don't think so. He's trouble, Ron, and he's not simply going to fade away. Whoever's paying him has his sights trained on you and your reelection. If this gets around with the voters you'll—"

"You think I don't know the ramifications?" Gillespie said. "Not only won't it go over well with the voters, it'll play havoc with my marriage."

Your marriage is a farce anyway was Morrison's unstated thought.

"What do you know about this Brixton character?" Gillespie asked as Morrison poured more bourbon into his glass.

"I had someone run a background check on him. He's a real foul ball, troublemaker, ex-cop, been in a couple of high-profile cases though. He rents office space from an attorney, Mackensie Smith."

"Mac Smith," Gillespie muttered. "He was a big-time lawyer in town. Last I heard he went to work teaching law at some university."

"GW. He's back in private practice again," Morrison said.

"And this Brixton is a licensed private eye?"

"Yes."

"Got to be a lowlife."

"My read exactly," said Morrison, wondering where the conversation was heading.

"So," Gillespie said, "what are you goin' to do about it?"

"I—"

"I am up to my neck at the moment negotiating with my colleagues on the other side of the aisle about the new legislation I've proposed that will make your Big Pharma clients millions. Be a damn shame for you and your clients if I get sidetracked by this nonsense over some stupid slut and a money-grubbing private eye."

His words hung over Morrison like a cloud of gnats.

Gillespie's threats weren't finished.

"I had a very pleasant dinner last night with someone you know," he said.

"Who was that?"

"An interesting fella, Roger Rockland."

Morrison's "Oh?" didn't represent the impact the name had on him.

Rockland was vice president of operations for the largest and most influential member of Morrison's prime client, the Pharmaceutical Association of America, the man who'd set the stage for Morrison going to Alard Associates to destroy Dr. Preston King's acreage in Papua New Guinea.

"We had dinner at Bobby Van's," Gillespie continued. "Roger says that you and he like to get together for a drink there now and then."

The senator's casual use of Rockland's first name unsettled Morrison. What was he getting at?

"I suppose I shouldn't be tellin' tales outta school, but hell, Eric, I like you and always have. Anyway, Roger was tellin' me that he and his company—it sure is a big pharmaceutical company, isn't it?—that he and his company might be in the market for some new representation."

"Representation? You mean—?"

A smug smile crossed the senator's craggy face. "You know, maybe time for a change of lobbying groups."

Gillespie waited for what he'd said to register.

"Why would they want to do that?" Morrison said, annoyed at his hesitancy in asking the question.

Gillespie shrugged. "You know how it is, Eric," he said. "Sometimes people get stale, get lazy, lose their edge, become complacent."

"Why would Roger be telling *you* this?" Morrison asked.

"As long as I've brought it up, I might as well be candid about it, Eric. Roger talked about what a new lobbying firm for PAA might be willing to do for me."

Morrison started to ask what Gillespie meant but the senator anticipated the question.

"Don't get me wrong, Eric. I've always been appreciative of everything you and your firm have done for this United States senator, damned appreciative. But some of your competitors would give their eyeteeth to have PAA as a client."

Morrison tried to put his thoughts in order before responding. While Gillespie was supported handsomely by PAA for voting its way on legislation impacting the pharmaceutical industry, he wasn't in a position to decide which lobbying firm should represent the trade association.

The senator spoke again, filling the leaden silence.

"You see, Eric, I'm like any politician. I don't get paid a hell of a lot as a U.S. senator." He held up his hand. "Not that I'm complaining. It has been my privilege to represent the good people of Georgia, and I wouldn't trade a day of it. But I also know that a politician's life span is limited, has to come to an end someday." His laugh was forced. "I'm lookin' forward to returning to the private sector, and so's my lovely wife, Rebecca. Frankly, she's not happy being a United States senator's wife, would like to see me use my talents and contacts to make a better living, have more of the finer things in life. Can't blame her, can you?"

"No, I suppose not."

"The point is that some of the other lobbying firms in town might set me up real nice when I leave the Senate, and I'd be a big fool to turn my back on that, now wouldn't I?"

"Of course."

Morrison started to elaborate but the senator's hand again went up.

"So I'm faced with a nasty situation," he said. "It's nasty because I believe in loyalty. My friends know that about me. Ronald Gillespie is loyal, always loyal."

"I've always appreciated that about you, Ron," said Morrison.

"And I wouldn't want to be—well, how shall I put it?—wouldn't want to be disloyal to Eric Morrison."

Morrison could only nod.

"I'm also someone who doesn't like to blow his own horn."

Another nod, completely dishonest, from the lobbyist.

"But I know that I carry considerable clout where the pharmaceutical industry is concerned. Without me watching out for Big Pharma's interests in Congress, there's not a hell of a lot a lobbyist can do for PAA. Am I right?"

"I've always known that, Ron."

This time it was a hearty laugh from Gillespie. "So, my friend," he said, slapping Morrison on the back, "as long as you take care of me, those competitors of yours don't stand a snowball's chance in hell of me using my weight to bring in one of your competitors. Do I make myself clear?"

"You certainly do, Ron. I also assure you that when you decide to pack it in as a senator, you'll always have a job with Morrison Associates."

"I much appreciate that, Eric, I truly do. But right now we've got a nasty situation on our hands with this Brixton character."

There were many things that Morrison wanted to say at that moment, but more than anything he wanted to get away from the senator from Georgia. He took some comfort in knowing that what he knew about Ronald Gillespie could bring down the senator. But that would be counterproductive, at least at that juncture.

He simply said, "I'll take care of it."

Later that night, after a few drinks with his wife and salads for dinner, he went to his home office, pulled out a phone number that he'd sworn never to use again, and dialed it.

"Alard Associates," the man answered.

Jayla was about to leave her apartment and head for the Watergate when Nate Cousins called. "Catching you at a bad time?" he asked.

"I was just going out," she said.

"Hopefully not for a date with someone else."

"As a matter of fact I'm going to see friends, Mac and Annabel Smith."

"My loss. I was hoping we could get together."

"I'd like that but—"

"You've mentioned the Smiths before. They're lawyers, right?"

"Yes, although Annabel no longer practices. She owns a gallery in Georgetown. Mac left his teaching job at George Washington and is in private practice again. They're terrific people. You'd like them and I know they'd like you."

"Is that an invitation to join you tonight?"

"I wouldn't be that presumptuous, Nate, but I can call and ask."

"Don't want to put you to any trouble."

"No trouble at all. Hold on. I'll call them on my cell."

Annabel said they'd be delighted to meet Cousins, and

Jayla relayed that to him. He said that he was still in the office but would leave in a half hour and meet her there.

Because Cousins would be driving, Jayla would have a way of getting home. She took a cab to the Smiths' and joined Brixton and Flo on the terrace where Annabel had set out a cheese platter to go with drinks. Jayla took her first sip of Chablis, sat back, closed her eyes, and sighed.

"I should get a picture of you," Flo said. "You look so relaxed."

Jayla's eyes came open. "It's the first relaxing moment I've had all day," she said.

"Tell us about this fellow who's joining us," Annabel said.

"He used to be VP of public relations at Renewal where I work, but he left to open his own agency. Renewal is his biggest client."

"Is your relationship with him—serious?" Annabel asked. "Hope I'm not getting too personal."

Jayla laughed. "Not at all," she said. "Nate and I are at that stage where we're finding out who we are and whether we like what we've learned about each other. At the moment, I like what I've learned very much." She decided to not repeat what he'd said about having fallen in love.

"He's a PR guy?" Brixton said.

"Yes."

"You trust him?"

The others looked quizzically at Brixton.

"I just mean that I've known a few PR guys and—"

"Your drink needs refreshing," Annabel said, taking Brixton's glass and disappearing into the kitchen.

Brixton changed the subject. "What's new with the investigation into your father's death?" he asked her.

"Robert, maybe she'd like to relax with her wine before you start cross-examining her," Flo said.

"That's okay, Flo." Jayla looked at Brixton. "Nothing that I know of."

Mac, who'd just joined them, said, "I thought you'd

want to see this e-mail I received an hour ago from your attorney in PNG." He handed the printout to her.

"What's it say?" Brixton asked.

Jayla read aloud.

Dear Mackensie. Greetings from Papua New Guinea. Hope all is well with you. I thought you'd be interested in the latest developments regarding the murder of Dr. King's trusted assistant, Mr. Tagobe. The gentleman who'd been accused of having killed him, Mr. Paul Underwood, has himself died. As I told you the last time we spoke, the authorities in Wewak had taken him in for questioning in Tagobe's death, which as you know, he claimed had been a matter of self-defense. Although I'm not privy to all the details, it seems that the authorities here in Port Moresby have confirmed that Underwood worked for an organization called Alard Associates, and was in Port Moresby the night Dr. King was killed. Based upon that he was taken to the Bomana prison in Port Moresby for further questioning. Unfortunately, before questioning could commence, Underwood was found dead in his cell, the apparent victim of suicide by hanging. As you may or may not know, corruption runs rampant among our police force and prison guards, and from what I've been told it was unlikely that Underwood would have taken his life in this way. An inquiry is under way. I'll let you know of any future developments. My best to Jayla. Elgin Taylor.

"That's three," Brixton muttered.

"Three?" Flo said.

"Three dead," Brixton said, "Dr. King, his native assistant, and now the guy who probably killed that assistant." He grunted. "What about this Whatsit character who worked with your father?"

Smith said, "Jayla called earlier to say that she saw Waksit here in D.C."

"Is that good or bad?" Flo asked.

"I don't know," Jayla said. "I can't imagine him coming here without getting in touch with me."

"You don't know why he's here?" Annabel asked.

"No, I don't, unless he's trying to interest a pharmaceutical company in my father's research. He claims that Dad left his lab results to him, which I don't believe for a second. Mr. Taylor doesn't buy it, either."

"You're your father's legal heir," Smith said.

"I know, but Eugene told the attorney that my father had verbally promised him the research before he died."

"That could carry a little weight," Smith said, "especially if he had any witnesses. But it pales when compared to a notarized piece of paper. Speaking of that, I went over your employment contract with Renewal Pharmaceuticals. It isn't exactly cut-and-dried, but it seems to me that if you turn over your father's research to your employer for further development they, not you, would have a legitimate claim on it based upon the way the contract is worded."

"I was afraid you'd come to that conclusion," Jayla said.

"Unless, of course, you can negotiate a new contract with them that specifically excludes your father's work," Smith said. "Think they'd be amenable to that?"

"I'd like to think so, but no. I have a feeling that Walt Milkin—he's the top guy at Renewal—would balk. He's asked me about it a few times. Evidently my father's efforts weren't as unknown in scientific circles as I'd assumed."

"You obviously can't offer it to another pharmaceutical company while employed at Renewal," Smith counseled. "You'd have to resign first."

"Which I don't want to do," said Jayla. "I like working there."

"Maybe you and Waksit could team up," Brixton suggested.

Jayla emphatically shook her head. "That's out of the question."

"I suspect that Robert wasn't serious," Smith said, looking at Brixton over raised bushy eyebrows.

"Just thought I'd toss it into the conversation," Brixton said, grinning.

"The last time I was here you got on the phone with the lobbyist," Jayla said to Brixton. "What was his name?"

"Eric Morrison."

"You thought he might be involved in some way with what happened to my father and Walter Tagobe."

"I took a shotgun approach," Brixton said, "fling out everything I'm thinking and see what gets a reaction."

"You raised the question of my father's murder."

"That's right, I did."

"And he denied any involvement in it."

"Right again. I also reminded him that he'd paid for a girl's abortion back in Georgia on behalf of Senator Ronald Gillespie."

"Which he also denied, of course," Annabel commented.

"You're following up this for Will Sayers," Mac said.

"He's paying me," said Brixton.

Smith continued, "So you're following two trails, the senator's involvement in the girl's pregnancy, and Jayla's father's murder."

"I'm being paid to run down the senator," Brixton said. "Jayla's father's murder is off the meter, which doesn't mean I'm not interested."

"You don't have to do this for me," Jayla said.

"I know that," Brixton replied, "but once something grabs me I have trouble letting go."

"Amen to that," Flo said, pleasantly.

"So Waksit is here in D.C.," Brixton continued.

"Yes, I'm sure it was him," Jayla said. "I only caught a glimpse but—"

"And he hasn't called you?" asked Annabel.

"No. He was coming out of a parking garage near my apartment building. The doorman said no one had been there asking for me."

"Want me to find him?" Brixton asked bluntly.

Another round of looks at him.

"I'm curious, that's all," Brixton explained. "I've got a bad feeling about him."

Now all eyes went to Jayla.

"I'm not sure I want to find him," she said.

"Up to you," Brixton said. "Just thought I'd ask."

They were interrupted by a call from the doorman announcing the arrival of a guest. "Send him up," Annabel said. Minutes later Nate Cousins was at the door holding a bouquet of flowers. Annabel welcomed him as he handed the flowers to her.

"How lovely," she said.

"Lovely that you welcome me," Cousins said.

Jayla came to Cousins and he kissed her cheek. She led him to the terrace where hands were shaken and Smith delivered him a single-malt scotch.

"Jayla tells us that you have your own public relations agency," Flo said.

"I haven't had it very long," Cousins said. He explained how he'd once worked at Renewal Pharmaceuticals but had left to open his own shop, with Renewal his prized account. "That's how Jayla and I met."

The conversation shifted to a lively discussion about where to go for dinner. Brixton, as expected, nixed ethnic restaurants, and Flo expressed a yen for seafood. Mac ultimately acted as arbitrator and suggested the Occidental Grill & Seafood, which provided an acceptable compromise. He called, made a reservation, and the six of them set out for dinner at one of Washington's iconic restaurants, the one-hundred-year-old gathering place of politicians, celebrities, and athletes whose photographs would look down on them as they ate.

"Too expensive," Brixton muttered in Flo's ear.

"We don't go there every day," she said.

"What's wrong with Martin's Tavern?"

"Relax and enjoy it, Robert. Think of yourself as a Washington mover and shaker."

His response was to growl and to keep his displeasure to himself for the rest of the evening.

Eugene Waksit hadn't been thinking about dinner as the Smith entourage headed for Pennsylvania Avenue. He was in his hotel room planning his next move to try and interest a pharmaceutical company in Dr. Preston King's research.

He'd made an overture that afternoon to two smaller firms and was met with similar responses: they weren't interested in developing pain medications. One woman he spoke with asked how it was that he was attempting to sell the research developed by King. "I'd heard about his lab experience using native plants from Papua New Guinea, but from what I'd learned his work was primitive and shoddy at best."

"I disagree," Waksit replied angrily.

"Besides," said the woman, "he had a daughter who works at Renewal in Bethesda. Are you saying that the doctor left his research to you and not to his daughter?"

Waksit stumbled through an explanation, which led the woman to thank him for the call and hang up in his ear.

Waksit's frustration and resulting anger stayed with him, and he tried to bring himself under control with a couple of drinks at a nearby bar before returning to his room. Now, having achieved a calmer state, he surveyed everything that had been contained in his briefcase.

Along with King's research results were the cash, the AmEx credit card, notes he'd made before leaving PNG, and the switchblade knife. There were other miscellaneous items in the briefcase, including a leather key case containing a variety of keys—the one for his apartment in Port Moresby, car keys for the Range Rover Dr. King had leased and loaned him, and a few assorted keys whose function he was unsure of. As he turned one of those unidentified keys over in his fingers its origin struck him. On Jayla's last visit to Port Moresby, after she'd begun working and living in Washington, she'd wanted her father to have a key to her D.C. apartment for use whenever he found time to visit her there. King was busy seeing patients in the clinic and had asked Waksit to run to a locksmith and have a copy made for him. But Waksit had two copies made, one of which he'd kept— the key in his hand.

He'd also been privy to e-mail correspondence between Jayla and her father, and had noted her father's password on the pad of paper, which allowed him to log into the doctor's account. He knew that his intrusion into their private communications would be viewed harshly by King, and he limited it to whenever the doctor was away from the house. There wasn't a lot of e-mail between them, and Waksit found the scant exchanges boring and sappy.

He put everything back into the briefcase except the key and a slip of paper on which he'd written Jayla's address, slid the case under the bed and covered it with a towel, splashed cold water on his face, and left the room. Having returned his rental car earlier he hailed a cab and gave the driver the number of Jayla's building in Foggy Bottom. He wasn't sure why he was going there. It was probably a matter of taking an action rather than holing up in a hotel room and wallowing in indecision over what to do next. The notion of contacting Jayla and suggesting that they join forces in taking her father's research to a new level evaporated from his mental list of possibilities as quickly as it surfaced.

His relationship with Jayla had always been cordial— his few romantic overtures to her had been deftly sidestepped—and there had never been any overt hostility. But he'd always sensed her disdain for him, nothing overt, just an unstated attitude that said that she was superior to him, that she was her father's daughter and he was just a hired hand. He often imagined her criticizing him to her father, taking advantage of being connected by blood and urging King to get rid of him. He'd once been accused by a college professor of being paranoid, and had researched paranoia, coming to the conclusion that his suspicions about people were valid. A friend had once quipped that being paranoid doesn't necessarily mean that people aren't following you, or trashing you behind your back.

He had the driver let him off across the street from Jayla's building. He stood there in the dark, his eyes focused on the entrance, which was visible between parked cars. The lobby was brightly lighted; the doorman sat at his appointed position, behind a podium. Waksit looked left and right before crossing the wide street, drew a breath, and entered the lobby.

"Can I help you, sir?" the doorman asked.

"I was just wondering if Ms. King was in," Waksit said.

"No," the doorman said. "I saw her leave earlier in the evening."

"I guess I missed her," Waksit said, shaking his head at his misfortune. "Thank you."

He walked to the end of the block before crossing to where he'd originally stood, shrouded in darkness, his view of the lobby unimpeded. When the doorman disappeared from the podium, Waksit crossed the street again, stopping behind one of the parked vehicles, a small panel truck a car length removed from the front entrance but still allowing Waksit to see the doorman when he returned. After a few minutes, a silver SUV pulled up and double-parked in front of the building. Waksit stepped behind the panel truck and watched as the doorman came from the building and greeted the SUV's occupants, obviously tenants in the building. The man driving the SUV came around to the back and activated the tailgate, which slowly opened. The woman, presumably the man's wife, also exited the vehicle and joined her husband and the doorman. The SUV was filled with packages. The doorman and the husband each removed two large, heavy cartons and followed the woman into the building.

Waksit moved enough to have a wider view of the lobby. The two men and the wife got in the elevator and the doors closed.

Waksit's fear of what he was about to do paralyzed him, but only for a moment. He quickly entered the building, located the stairwell, opened the door and stepped through it. He looked back through its small meshed window and saw no one. He knew that Jayla's apartment was on the second floor, and he slowly, quietly ascended the stairs. He cracked opened the stairwell door on the second level and surveyed the hallway. He was alone. He checked numbers on doors until reaching her unit, took another look around, and inserted the key in the lock. The door opened and he tiptoed inside, gently closing the door to avoid making noise.

He stood in the small foyer and took in his surroundings. Jayla had left two lamps burning, one on a table in the living room, the second on a pass-through from the kitchen to a small dining area. She'd left a radio on; strains of classical music came from it. He went to the window and looked out at the street. He didn't know where she had gone, or what time she'd be home, and that realization stabbed his gut. The last thing he wanted was to be discovered there when she returned.

Her desk was near the window, and he sat at it. Her computer was off. He located the on-off switch and turned it on. When the prompt came asking for her password, he froze. Seconds later her homepage filled the screen, a colorful scene from the Papua New Guinea jungle. *The fool; she didn't use a password at home.* He moved the mouse to guide the cursor to her e-mail icon, activated it, and was rewarded with a list of e-mail messages in her Inbox.

There were only three new messages received that day. The first was from someone named Cousins. Waksit read it. Cousins, whoever he was, had written that he enjoyed the last time they were together, and hoped that they could do it again soon. He also wrote that he was also willing to have another discussion with Jayla about her father's research, and what she might want to do with it.

"Do with it?" Waksit said aloud. "I have the research."

The second e-mail was from a dress shop in Georgetown informing Jayla that new models from the California designer had arrived: "I know some of them would be perfect for you," she concluded.

It was the third e-mail that startled him. It was a copy sent to Jayla of an e-mail Preston King's attorney in PNG, Elgin Taylor, had sent to someone named Mackensie Smith. It was only an hour old. He read it slowly, and then a second time.

> **Dear Mackensie. I hope that all is well with you. I write only to inform you that Dr. Preston King's former assistant, Eugene Waksit, is now actively being sought in the King murder, and the PNG authorities are seeking the help of U.S. authorities in locating him. It is my understanding that he is not considered an active suspect in the murder, but authorities wish to question him further. I have a suspicion that their interest in him goes beyond simply wanting to ask more questions. I thought you would like to know. All my best, Elgin.**

Waksit reacted as though the e-mail had physically assaulted him. He hunched over in the chair, his arms wrapped tightly about him, and emitted a low, slow moan. He snapped out of that response and willed himself to think. What to do? Maybe he should present himself to the local authorities. Surely that would work in his favor. A man who was suspected of murder surely wouldn't do such a thing.

But would they believe him?

A sense of urgency took over. He needed to find a pharmaceutical company that would pay him for King's research, no questions asked, no queries about King's daughter, just cash on the barrelhead. There had to be someone who would leap at the opportunity to build upon what King had created in his lab, someone out there with the brains to see its potential and pay handsomely for it.

But what if he was arrested before he could find that person and make the deal? If that were to happen everything he dreamed of would be in jeopardy.

He pondered what to do next. He'd better leave before she or someone else arrived. But before he got up from the desk his eyes went to its long horizontal drawer. He opened it. Along with assorted pens, pencils, and other office items was a manila envelope. He removed it from the drawer, opened its clasp, and pulled from it the 8×10 color crime scene photographs taken of the lifeless body of Dr. Preston King. His eyes widened as he shuffled through the prints, and a sense of revulsion coupled with fascination filled him. His hands shook as he replaced the prints in the envelope, held it beneath his arm, and went to the apartment door, opened it, and peered into the corridor. No one. He left the apartment and went down the stairs to the main floor where he surveyed the lobby through the small window. The doorman and the husband and wife were bringing in the last of the cartons. Waksit waited until the three of them had disappeared into the elevator before opening the door and crossing the lobby to the street where he waved down a taxi. He went to his room at the Embassy Inn, packed his bag including the crime scene photos, and placed a call.

"Nikki? It's Eugene Waksit."

"Oh, hello, Eugene."

"How was your conference?"

"Fine. Lots of speeches. How are you? Making progress with the pharmaceutical companies?"

He forced a laugh. "Couldn't be better, although they sure do hang on to their money. I'm close to a deal with a big one but the wheels grind slow. Look, I'm calling to ask a favor."

Waksit couldn't see Nikki wince, nor did he know that the first thing she'd done upon returning from her conference was to open the window wide in her guest room and air out the odor of Cuba Black cologne.

"What is it, Eugene?"

"I need a place to stay for a few days."

"I don't know, I—"

"Just a couple of days, Nikki, until all the red tape with the pharmaceutical company is resolved. I'd really appreciate it. I loved seeing you again and—well, you'd be doing me a big favor and I'll do whatever I can to be a good houseguest and pay you back, in spades!"

"A few days?" she asked.

"Two, three at the most."

"All right."

"Great. You're a doll. I'll be there within the hour. A nice dinner out? My treat."

27

Despite the cost of the dinner at the Occidental— Brixton's rib-eye steak was $48—even he appeared to enjoy himself. Flo's dress shop was doing better than anyone had anticipated, which Brixton both applauded publicly while silently suffering the discomfort of not being the primary breadwinner in their relationship, at least for the moment.

"How's your steak?" Mac asked.

"How could it be anything but good?" Brixton replied. "At these prices they should have served the whole cow."

"There are so many good restaurants in Washington," Annabel said.

"And expensive," her husband added.

"It wasn't always that way," Annabel continued. "People from out of town used to joke about how dismal the restaurant scene was here."

"Plenty of ethnic restaurants," said Cousins.

"It's such an ethnically diverse city," Annabel said.

"I usually try and avoid Chinese restaurants," Brixton said. "I like Chinese food but there's not one of them that knows how to make a decent martini."

"Martinis aren't a Chinese drink," Flo said.

"Still, they ought to know how to make one for their customers," Brixton countered, sipping his.

While the banter skipped happily from subject to subject, Cousins sensed that the others at the table were scrutinizing him, but that was to be expected. He was viewed as Jayla's beau, which pleased him; he felt an inner pride at sitting next to the beautiful young woman whom he'd accompanied that evening.

"What was it like playing in the minor leagues?" Flo asked. She was an inveterate baseball fan and an avid booster of D.C.'s Nationals.

"Lots of fun," Cousins answered. "No money, of course, but exciting. Every young guy on the team had visions of making it to the big show even though the chances of that were pretty low except for a select few. But I enjoyed it. I learned a lot about competing and teamwork." He turned to Brixton. "You enjoy baseball, Robert?" Jayla had warned him not to call Brixton Bobby.

"Sometimes," Brixton said. "Flo's the baseball nut in our house."

"I like the pace of it," Flo said. "Football and basketball are too fast."

"I get bored watching it on TV," Brixton said.

"Speaking of TV," Annabel said, "did any of you watch . . . ?"

And so the conversation turned to TV sitcoms, then morphed into a discussion of the gridlock in Congress, and . . .

"Time to go," Brixton announced when everyone had been served after-dinner drinks, compliments of the house.

"Busy day tomorrow, Robert?" Cousins asked.

"Yeah, it looks that way." He didn't mention that it would start with the shrink, Dr. Fowler. He hadn't told anyone, even Mac and Annabel, that he was seeing a therapist. Flo was the only person in his life who knew, and he preferred that it remain that way.

Mac and Annabel took the first cab that passed, and Brixton and Flo took the second. Cousins had driven from the Watergate with Jayla, and they got in his car and set out for her apartment.

"Great people," Cousins commented as he drove. "Thanks for including me."

"They certainly are," Jayla concurred. "Flo's the one who introduced me to the Smiths. Mac has been like a second father to me. He's been in touch with my attorney in PNG."

"What's new on that front?" he asked.

"Mac showed me an e-mail he received today from my attorney. The man who was accused of killing my father's helper, Walter Tagobe, was found dead in his jail cell. He supposedly committed suicide."

"That's interesting."

"That same man was reportedly in Port Moresby the night my father was stabbed to death. It's possible that he was the killer."

Cousins backed into a parking spot.

"You've been through a lot," he said as he turned off the ignition.

"Three people dead," Jayla said. "Robert Brixton commented on that before you arrived. Oh, and I saw Eugene Waksit here in D.C."

"You did?" He came around and opened the door for her. "Where?"

"Coming out of that parking garage up the street. I only caught sight of him for a few seconds. A bus blocked my view. When it moved he was gone."

"And he didn't try and contact you?"

"Not yet. Knowing he's here gives me the creeps."

They entered her building.

"Hello Ms. King," the night doorman said. "Did you have a pleasant evening?"

"Yes, very pleasant. Has anyone been here looking for me?"

"Not since I came on my shift. Can't account for earlier."

"Thanks. Have a good night."

She and Cousins got on the elevator and rode to her floor. He'd briefly seen her apartment when he'd picked her up for a previous dinner. Now, as she turned on the lights, he had a better sense of the space. What immediately struck him was how neat everything was. It put his housekeeping to shame.

She went to her answering machine and checked for messages. There were a few, nothing important. But as she clicked off the machine, she raised her head. Cousins came up beside her and put his arm around her.

She audibly sniffed the air.

"What's wrong?" he asked.

"That odor," she said.

"What odor?"

"You don't smell it?"

He, too, inhaled. "Sweet-smelling," he said.

"It's Eugene."

Cousins glanced around the apartment.

"He's been here," Jayla said. "It's that cheap cologne he always wears."

"You're sure?"

"Unless someone else wears that particular cologne. He's been here, Nate, in my apartment."

"How could he have gotten up here without the doorman knowing?"

"I don't know. Robert Brixton offered to try and find him."

"Find Waksit?

"Yes. Why would he come without me here? How did he get in?"

Cousins plopped in a chair by the desk. "Maybe he's looking for whatever of your father's research is in your possession."

"The material Dad left me is in my safe deposit box."

"Good thing."

Jayla looked at her desk. The computer mouse was not where she usually left it. "It's been moved," she whispered. "*He* must have used it."

"Your computer? How could he? Does he have your password?"

"I don't have a password at home. I'm the only one who uses this computer."

"You'd better add a password to your computer, but changing your lock is at the top of your priority list."

She turned on the computer and went through the requisite prompts until reaching her e-mail site. A few clicks of the mouse brought her to the most recent message.

Dear Mackensie. I hope that all is well with you. I write only to inform you that Dr. Preston King's former assistant, Eugene Waksit, is now actively being sought in the King murder, and the PNG authorities are seeking the help of U.S. authorities in locating him. It is my understanding that he is not considered an active suspect in the murder, but authorities wish to question him further. I have a suspicion that their interest in him goes beyond simply wanting to ask more questions. I thought you would like to know. All my best, Elgin.

Cousins read the message over her shoulder.

"What are you going to do?" he asked.

"I don't know," she said, absently opening desk drawers in search of something else amiss. "The pictures!" she said.

"What pictures?"

"Of the crime scene in my father's lab. Pictures of him! They're gone."

She got up from the computer and walked around the living room in search of other evidence of her space having been violated.

"Any other signs of him?" Cousins asked as he joined her.

Jayla shook her head. "I don't think so. Should I call the police?"

"Based upon smelling a cologne and a few missing photos? They won't do anything. If he's here in D.C. he has to be staying in a hotel. You say that Robert offered to find him for you?"

"Yes."

"Well, he'd be the right one to do that. He's a trained investigator."

"I suppose you're right," said Jayla.

Cousins followed her to the kitchen where she stood motionless, as though not remembering why she'd gone there.

"How about some coffee?" Cousins suggested.

"All right."

She turned on the Keurig coffeemaker, leaned against the counter, and began to cry. Cousins put his arms around her and pulled her close.

"I can't believe that all this is happening," she said into his chest.

"It'll get resolved soon, Jayla. I know it's easy to say but you just have to be strong."

"I thought I was," she said, disengaging from his embrace. "I just want to go to bed and pull the covers over my head."

"Then why don't you?"

He turned off the coffeemaker and urged her in the direction of the bedroom. They stood in the dark at the foot of the bed, saying nothing, Jayla's emotional fatigue almost palpable. She sat on the edge of the bed, then stretched out and let out a sigh. Cousins joined her, both on their backs, his hand reaching for hers. He was conflicted. He'd wanted to be in bed with her since the first moment they'd met, and had hoped when leaving the Smiths that it would happen that night.

It had.

But they were both fully clothed. He considered initiating lovemaking but stifled the urge. This was not the time to take their relationship to the sexual level.

There was something strangely satisfying lying there with her, hearing her soft breathing and smelling the remnants of her subtle perfume. He felt very much the protector, and liked the feeling.

"Are you awake?" he asked.

"Yes," she said, her voice indicating it was only partially true.

"You have to do something about Waksit," he said.

"I know. Maybe I should take Robert up on his offer to find him."

"But what will you do if he does?"

"I don't know. Talk to him. Find out why he's here. Ask him—"

"Ask him whether he murdered your father?"

He felt the nod of her head.

"Jayla, you have to do something with your father's research before *he* does."

She turned on her side and faced him. "What do you suggest?"

"I was thinking that maybe you should give it to me. I know a lot of people in the pharmaceutical industry and could at least narrow down possibilities. You have enough on your plate and—"

"I thought I'd take it out of the safe deposit box and give it to Mac Smith."

"Why would you do that?"

"Because—because I trust him. He's been a good friend and confidant."

Cousins fell silent.

"Do you agree?" she asked.

"Well," he said, "he's obviously a nice man and a good lawyer, but he really doesn't know anything about pharmaceuticals. I'm not a scientist but I do have a sense of what's happening in the industry. All I'm suggesting is that I might be able to point you in the right direction."

She was more awake now. "I'm so confused," she said.

"And I don't blame you." He paused. "You aren't concerned, are you, that I'd share your father's research with anybody at Renewal?"

"No, of course not."

"How about this?" he said. "I'll take a look at it and come up with some suggestions. Then I'll deliver it personally to Mac for safekeeping."

She turned on her back again and said dreamily, "I'm so tired."

"Then you should rest."

He got up, straightened his clothing, leaned over, and kissed her forehead. "I'll leave," he said. "You get dressed for bed and have a good night's sleep. I'll swing by at eight thirty in the morning and we can go to the bank, be there when it opens, and I'll take the research. Trust me, Jayla. I only want to help you fulfill your father's goal of creating a better pain med. He deserves whatever we can do to make that happen."

"All right," she said. "Thank you, Nate."

"Come double lock your door behind me."

"Of course."

"I love you, Jayla," he said, and left.

28

R obert Brixton sat in the tan leather armchair across from Dr. Fowler.

"So, Robert, how are things going with you?"

Brixton's shoulders went up and down. "Could be better," he said.

"Oh? A problem?"

"Business is slow. I've talked to a couple of potential clients but nothing's come out of it, at least not yet. In the meantime I'm . . ."

Fowler's raised eyebrows encouraged Brixton to elaborate.

"My friend, Mac Smith—he's the lawyer I've told you about—he's involved with a young woman, a medical researcher, whose father was murdered. I've sort of gotten involved." Brixton snorted. "Not that I'm making any money from it but—well, I've become obsessed with it."

"Do you often become obsessed with things, Robert?" Fowler asked.

"Sometimes, when it's important to me."

"And how is Flo?" Fowler asked.

"She's terrific. I brought her flowers and—"

"What was the occasion?"

"No occasion. I just felt like doing it. I bought some for my secretary, too, Mrs. Warden."

"Just because you wanted to."

"Yeah. That seem strange to you?"

Fowler laughed and held up his hand. "No, no, to the contrary, Robert. I'm sure that they both appreciated the gesture."

"They seemed to. How much longer you figure I should see you like this?"

"That's entirely up to you. If you think that nothing is being accomplished by coming here, you'll stop coming."

Brixton was impressed with the shrink's attitude. He'd expected him to come up with reasons to keep the sessions going and the fees coming in.

"Have you had any success with coming to grips with the death of your daughter?" Fowler asked.

Brixton said nothing for a few seconds. Then, he said, "I have, sort of. I figure that she'd want me to keep living my life the best way I know how."

Fowler sat silently, suppressing a smile. It was what he'd told Brixton in an earlier session, and what he wanted to hear from him.

They talked about other aspects of Brixton's life, including his relationship with Flo.

"We talked last night about maybe getting married," Brixton said.

"And?"

"And what?"

"Did you come to a decision?"

"No. Flo's gun-shy when it comes to making that commitment with me. I can be a jerk sometimes, you know, a pain in the ass. I don't bend easy."

"Bringing her flowers on the spur of the moment says something about your ability to, well, to bend."

"It felt good."

"Which is all that matters. Afraid our time is up, Robert."

"It goes fast."

"That's a good sign. See you again, or do you feel we've accomplished all that we can?"

"I wouldn't mind coming again," Brixton said.

"Good. Make an appointment with my receptionist. Enjoy the rest of your day."

29

If anyone needed a shrink that morning it was the lobbyist Eric Morrison, preferably a psychiatrist who could administer some sort of potent calming fluid.

He'd made an appointment to see George Alard, head of Alard Associates, at three that afternoon. That was reason enough for his general feeling of dread as he climbed out of bed and made a cup of coffee into which he added a shot of bourbon, followed by two breath mints.

"Busy day?" his wife, Peggy Sue, asked as she padded into the kitchen.

"Huh?" Morrison said, not turning from the window through which he gazed out over their large property.

"I asked if you have a busy day in store," she said.

He faced her. "Yeah, a busy day, a *very* busy day."

It had also been a busy night in bed for him. No matter how hard he'd tried he was unable to get the phone call from Robert Brixton out of his thoughts. The private investigator was there with him no matter which side he lay on. He tried what mind tricks he knew, including counting sheep, which he'd abandoned after only a dozen of the furry creatures had cleared the fence.

He hoped his constant twisting and turning wouldn't wake Peggy Sue, and considered giving up and spending the rest of the night in his office chair. But sleep eventually overtook his heightened anxiety and he quickly got out of bed at the sound of the alarm clock and headed for the kitchen.

Once away from his wife, he verbalized some of his thoughts, speaking in hushed tones to the coffeemaker, or to the birds happily gorging themselves at a large feeder on the deck. "Son of a bitch" was said frequently, along with "Who the hell do you think you are?" and "I'll bury you."

But then another target of his anger replaced Brixton, Senator Ronald Gillespie, whose face filled his mental screen. "Damned old fool," he mumbled. "If you'd kept your zipper up none of this would be happening."

But Gillespie hadn't kept his zipper up, and here he, Eric Morrison, was once again in the position of bailing out the esteemed senator from Georgia by using the services of George Alard, who would undoubtedly do anything for a buck—*like himself* quickly crossed his mind and was summarily dismissed.

Brixton had mentioned during his phone call the burning of Dr. King's acreage on Papua New Guinea, and had even insinuated that whoever Alard had commissioned to do the deed might also have killed the PNG physician. As much as Morrison wanted to dismiss Brixton as a money-grubbing troublemaker without teeth, the investigator obviously knew quite a bit about Gillespie's extracurricular sexual activities. Too, Brixton was aware of Morrison's involvement with the King fiasco. In other words, he couldn't blithely dismiss the investigator's message. Both involved him, Eric Morrison, powerful, upstanding Washington, D.C., lobbyist with a family to feed and a lifestyle to support.

* * *

Die!" he'd muttered to the imaginary Brixton just before Peggy Sue had arrived in the kitchen. "Have a heart attack and die!"

"Who are you talking to?"

"Oh, no one, I'm just—I was talking to myself."

She laughed. "I hope you're not going insane, Eric."

He laughed. "Insane? Me? No. I just have a lot on my mind, that's all. I'd better get a move on."

She stopped him as he was leaving. "Are you okay?" she asked.

"Yeah, sure."

"You've been really uptight lately, wound tighter than—what's wound tight?"

"A spring," he said.

"A spring."

"No, I'm fine, sweetheart, just overloaded with work. Time for us to get on a ship someplace and enjoy a few weeks away together."

"I'd love that."

"Then start planning. You're good at that. See ya."

As she watched him go up the stairs to the bedroom level of their spacious home her creased face mirrored her concern. He *had* been acting strangely lately, walking around as though tethered to a weighty rock that threatened to drag him into some abyss. She was aware that he was busy, that he worked hard at the lobbying firm he'd launched after working in government, but knew virtually nothing of his day-to-day activities. It was time for them to get away on a vacation, and she pulled out their phone book, found the number for their travel agent, and left it open to that page as she, too, started her day under hot water of a different sort.

Morrison was dressed in his usual business attire by the time Peggy Sue emerged from her bathroom and had dressed in gardening clothes. They kissed in the driveway before Morrison climbed into his Jaguar and headed for his office on K Street, where D.C. lobbying groups of any worth were located. He gave a curt hello to others as he passed through the outer offices and settled in his corner space whose floor-to-ceiling windows afforded him a splendid view of the city. His secretary brought him coffee and the day's paper, along with a list of phone messages to be returned. He'd managed to calm his jangled nerves during the drive from home, but the sight of one name on the list brought back his angst.

Paula Silver.

What the hell did *she* want?

Why was she calling him?

They'd broken off their fling more than a year ago. As far as Morrison was concerned he'd treated her decently, showed her a good time on his dime, and even gave her cash the night he'd ended the affair. He'd enjoyed their tryst. Paula was good-looking in a crude, sexy sort of way, and was hot in bed. But he considered her a mental lightweight and had soon grown tired of their inane conversations, made worse by her drinking.

He ignored the call until ten minutes later when she called again.

"Tell her you're not here?" his secretary asked, sensing his discomfort.

"No, I'll take it," he growled.

"Paula?"

"That's right, it's me."

"How've you been?"

"I've been better."

"Oh? Sorry to hear that."

"You can make it better," she said, slowly, as though unsure whether the words would come out as intended.

"What does that mean?"

"I'm writing a book," she said.

"You're writing a—what kind of book?"

"About us."

"Oh, Jesus," he said, pushing back in his red leather executive chair and rubbing his eyes with his free hand.

"Did you hear me?"

Morrison came forward and glanced at his door to be sure that no one was about to interrupt.

"Yeah, I heard you, Paula. A book about us? That's ridiculous."

"No it isn't. It'll be about you and me, and how you used me the way you use everybody, especially politicians like Senator Gillespie, and others, too. I know how you pay off congressmen and senators to get them to vote the way you want them to vote. I know everything, Eric, *everything,* and I'm going to tell it in my book."

He drew a breath before saying in measured tones, "Look, Paula, listen to me. You may think you want to write a book, but believe me when I say that it'll never happen. What do you plan to do, tell the world that we slept together? Big deal." It occurred to him that the conversation might be taped and was sorry he'd acknowledged their intimacy. "And if you think you can get away with telling tales out of school about Ron—about Senator Gillespie, you'll be laughed out of town. He's a popular U.S. senator, for Christ's sake. Have you lost your mind?"

He heard her take a sip of something and was sure it wasn't iced tea.

Her laugh was pointed, harsh. "You think you're such a big shot with your fancy offices and credit cards and hobnobbing with the rich and famous. Well, Mr. Big Shot, I have friends, too, who know all about you and your dirty deals."

He started to say something but a knock on his door diverted his attention. His secretary poked her head in but he waved her away.

"You listening, Mr. Big Shot?" Paula said. He didn't respond. "I'm working with a researcher who has the goods on you and how you paid for Gillespie's abortion for that young girl, and how you and your precious buddy Howie pay everybody off."

"A researcher?" Morrison said.

"That's right, a researcher, and he knows plenty."

"Who is this *researcher*?"

"You don't know him, Eric, but you will plenty soon."

"There's no researcher working with you on your stupid book," Morrison said.

She snorted. "No? You're wrong. If you must know, his name is Brixton, Robert Brixton, and we've already started working together."

Morrison swallowed hard, which was heard on Paula's end.

"What do you want, Paula?"

"I want money so I can get out of this town. I figure that since you're used to paying off people to get your way, people like Senator Gillespie, you'll come up with something for me, you know, for old times' sake."

"That's a threat, Paula?"

This time her laugh was smug. "Call it whatever you want. You have my number and know the dump I work in. Get back to me in a couple of days, Eric. Bye-bye." She delivered her final words in a syrupy southern accent.

Morrison slammed down the phone. "Bitch!" he muttered, and said it twice more. He checked his watch. A few minutes past eleven. His meeting with Alard was at three. He was aware that his hands shook and he clasped them together. It was like what they called a "perfect storm" hitting him, and it all centered on this private investigator Brixton. How did *he* hook up with Paula Silver and convince her to talk about Gillespie and his teenage lover? When Brixton had called he'd also referred to the Dr. Preston King episode on Papua New Guinea. How was he involved in *that*? And there was the obnoxious guy from PNG, Eugene Waksit, who worked as King's assistant and was trying to peddle the doctor's research, if there was anything to peddle in the first place. He'd brushed Waksit off, but maybe King's assistant knew something that he hadn't shared with Morrison. Was Brixton also involved in some way with Waksit? If so, the guy sure got around.

It all added up to problems on myriad fronts, and each one involved Robert Brixton. The question for Morrison as he sat at his desk and chewed on a thumbnail was what to do about it. As much as he didn't want to deal with the services offered by George Alard, his three o'clock meeting with him was suddenly appealing.

30

After Brixton left the psychologist's office he took a call on his cell phone from Will Sayers.

"What's up?" Brixton asked.

"Lots," Sayers said. "Thought you might be interested in getting together this morning."

"Sounds okay, only I was going to spend some time digging into Alard Associates. I've learned that one of its people—an operative I guess he's called—was found hanging in his cell in Papua New Guinea. Seems he'd been in Port Moresby the night Dr. King was killed. This is the same guy who not only got rid of the doctor's plot of land, he also killed the doc's native helper."

"Sounds like a sterling fellow," Sayers said. "Good timing that you called, Robert. I was going to bring you up to date on some snooping of my own that I've done into Alard Associates."

"It's a deal. You show me yours, I'll show you mine. By the way, have you figured out yet how to use that new coffeemaker? If you're still pouring instant coffee I'm suddenly unavailable."

"Only the best for you, Bobby."

Brixton growled into the phone.

"Sorry, Robert, I lost my head. See you within the hour."

Sayers was watching TV when Brixton arrived. The president was in the midst of a news conference at which he'd responded to a question about a private security firm working under contract in Afghanistan to protect embassy workers. Two members of that firm had been accused of gunning down an Afghanistan family of six, and the Afghan government was calling for their indictment.

"I have instructed the Justice Department to look into this allegation," the president said, "and I expect their findings to be available within three months."

"Three months!" Sayers blurted, angrily turning off the TV. "Hell, take three years while you're at it. Just another inquiry that'll go nowhere. These private security firms get away with murder every day. There's no oversight, no military rules of engagement for them. They're a bunch of macho cowboys who can't make it in a normal job and head overseas where they can shoot off their mouths and guns and get away with it no matter how many innocent people they kill."

When Will Sayers was angry his voice boomed, and his face turned crimson. At such times Brixton feared that the big journalist would have a heart attack and drop dead in front of him.

"I could use a cup of coffee," Brixton said.

Sayers pointed to the kitchen.

Brixton brewed a cup and brought it to where Sayers had settled behind his desk.

"Well, here I am," Brixton said. "What do you have on Alard Associates?"

Sayers opened a file folder and withdrew some papers. "Let's see," he said, adjusting half-glasses on his nose, "it seems that Alard Associates is a specialty outfit that hires out to larger private security firms for work those larger firms don't want to be bothered with—or linked with."

Brixton sipped his coffee, smacked his lips, and said, "Good coffee. I'm proud of you, Will."

"Did you come here this morning to talk about coffee, or shall we go further into what I've learned about Mr. Alard and his *business*?"

"Don't get your hackles up, Will. By all means let's stick with the reason I'm here, which was not for a free cup of coffee. Okay, so Alard does jobs the bigger firms turn down. That rings to me of nasty kinds of work, wet jobs, illegal jobs. Am I right?"

"Yes, you are right. Not that anyone has ever been able to pin anything on them. The group's namesake, George Alard, is evidently a careful type, doesn't take on assignments unless he's confident that nothing can be traced back to him."

Brixton pondered what Sayers had said before asking, "Do all these jobs involve overseas assignments?"

"For the most part but not every one. I have a good source who used to do contract work for Alard. He's a good ol' boy from your favorite city, Savannah, who came back from Afghanistan after a couple of tours with Special Forces with a chestful of medals for his sharp-shooting skills, and a metal plate in his shaved head. He couldn't find a job he liked back in the States so he signed up with a big security firm protecting our embassy people in Baghdad. He's a hothead whose temper got him in trouble, so the firm got rid of him by sending him to Alard. The bigger firm has eight hundred security types in Iraq. Alard Associates employs maybe a hundred, mostly discards from the bigger firms. Anyway, my source tells me that he and some of the others have taken on assignments here in the States including—ready for this, Robert?"

"Shoot."

"An apt word to use. My source was hired to assassinate a state politician in Georgia."

"Hired through Alard Associates?"

"Yes, but that was never proved. My friend refused to

reveal to the authorities who put him up to it, although he's been a lot more forthcoming with me."

"He killed this politician?"

"No. Fortunately the plot was thwarted before the trigger was pulled."

"What about your source?"

"He came out of it relatively unscathed. The prosecutor, who rumor has it benefited substantially from an anonymous donor to his reelection campaign, decided to drop the charges for lack of evidence against my source. He walked free."

"And I suppose he's now running for governor."

Sayers laughed heartily. "Not that bad, Robert, although he is doing quite well heading up a company that provides ghost tours of Savannah for tourists. It is, as you know, considered America's most haunted city."

"So I remember. After I left the police force and put out my shingle, I hired a receptionist whose husband ran one of those ghost tours."

"Did you ever take one?"

"Me? No. I don't believe it ghosts. You?"

"I'm open-minded. Have you had further discussions with Paula Silver about Senator Gillespie and the lobbyist Eric Morrison's role in not burdening the senator with an illegitimate child?"

"I plan to call her today, or maybe swing by the restaurant where she works. I'm not sure there's anything else she can tell me. It's not like she was directly involved. What she knows comes from pillow talk with Morrison."

"Still . . ."

"I'll take another stab at her."

"I wouldn't put it that way around Lady Flo."

Brixton stayed another twenty minutes during which Sayers brought him further up to date about his research into Senator Gillespie and the illegitimate child he'd fathered, and the role that Morrison had played in arranging the abortion.

"Let me know if you learn anything new from Ms.

Silver," the journalist said as he walked Brixton to the
door.

"You'll be the first to know," Brixton said. But then he
added, "Unless you want to ante up another fee for me, I'll
be taking on some new clients who pay my going rate."

"I wish I had more to give you," Sayers said.

"It's okay, Will. Seeing a hypocrite like Gillespie exposed for what he really is will make it all worthwhile.
Besides, I got to have dinner with a former Hollywood
star. See ya."

At noon, Eric Morrison and two associates left their
offices on K Street for a lunch date with an executive
of a major American medical equipment manufacturer
whose firm was the backbone of the association representing that industry. The executive, Karl Simone, was
looking to change lobbying agencies; Morrison Associates had come highly recommended. Ordinarily, Morrison would have been at the top of his conversational
game when wooing a potential new client. But on this
day every synapse in his body was close to firing off, and
he dreaded having to make happy talk for two hours.

They met at Del Campo on I Street, N.W., which had
become one of D.C.'s in restaurants and whose prices reflected that status. The possible client had suggested it to
Morrison when he called and Morrison didn't debate it.
If a steak for a king's ransom made him happy, so be it.
It was deductible as a business expense—Uncle Sam would
eventually pay for it—and a new client would generate
some welcome additional monthly cash in the coffers,
which lately had been diminished, partially due to the
money paid to George Alard to torch Dr. King's land.
Morrison had personally pocketed the bonus paid by
the pharmaceutical company's VP rather than run it
through the agency. *"I'm entitled for sticking my neck
out,"* was his self-justification, something that he'd become especially good at in recent days.

His associates were aware that their boss was in a foul mood, and took the lead at lunch, presenting the usual dog-and-pony show of success stories for clients, letters of praise from elected officials thanking them for helping structure sensible and useful legislation in their industries, and copies of personal notes from House members and senators, which, the prospective client was informed, indicated the close personal ties the lobbying agency had forged with movers and shakers on the Hill.

Morrison chimed in occasionally, extolling his friendships with elected men and women who could do the client's association the most good. He casually dropped into the conversation family events that he and his wife had attended—weddings, birthday parties, fishing expeditions, and private plane jaunts to exotic vacation spots—a well-rehearsed pitch that appeared to impress the young man seated at the head of the table.

But while Morrison managed to join the conversation, his mind was far from where they sat at Del Campo.

Paula Silver's threatening phone call reverberated in his head, and her injection of a PI named Robert Brixton into yet another project with which Morrison had been involved was, at best, unnerving, if not downright scary.

His phone call to George Alard to set up another meeting had been impetuous, almost an act of desperation. Now, an hour from his seeing him, he seriously questioned the wisdom of getting together.

What would he ask Alard to do, try and convince this Brixton character to back off? Do the same with Paula Silver? To what extent would Alard go to accomplish that? Have one of his mercenaries threaten them?

Threaten them?

With what? Physical harm?

No, that was out of the question. He'd made it clear when arranging for the destruction of Dr. King's acreage that there was to be no rough stuff, no bloodshed. That it had ended up with the doctor stabbed to death was unfortunate, but he, Eric Morrison, had had nothing to do with that.

As he listened to his colleagues wax poetic to the manufacturer's VP about what Morrison Associates could do for him, Morrison came up with a revelation. This was all about money. That had to be it. Arranging for Dr. King's acreage to be destroyed didn't involve money, at least not the payment of it to persuade the doctor to drop his research.

But Paula Silver had made it plain during her call that she wanted money. That had to be Brixton's motivation, too. They were both lowlifes, greedy hustlers who'd do anything for a buck. Gillespie had said the same thing. The question was, how much would it take to buy them off?

Paula would probably be content with a small amount, enough to move away from D.C. and establish her life in another city—$10,000? $20,000? Everything about her was cheap, he thought while nursing his second drink during the lunch.

But what about Brixton?

The background check that Morrison had arranged for, as cursory as it was, painted a picture of the private investigator as being unstable, maybe even a psychopath. He'd been in plenty of trouble, which meant to Morrison that he was in all likelihood perpetually broke, maybe a gambler. How much would it take to buy *him* off? More than Paula, but how *much* more?

Whatever the amount it would be within Morrison's ability to pay. He knew that. The agency maintained an off-the-books slush fund with money collected from clients that had been established for just such purposes. Too, Senator Ronald Gillespie owed him big-time. The senator was loaded with money; surely he wouldn't hesitate to spend some of it to buy off enemies like Paula and Brixton.

"Do you agree, Eric?" one of his colleagues asked.

"What?" Morrison said, snapping back to reality. "Oh sure, right, couldn't agree more. You're spot-on."

The other associate said, "Eric has an especially close relationship with Senator Gillespie from Georgia. Isn't that right, Eric?"

"Oh, yes, Ron Gillespie and I go back a long way. He's a real champion of the PAA, goes to the mat for us every day. He'll do the same for you, Karl, and your group, provided we're on board to fight for you."

"It's all in the close personal relationships we've developed," an associate told Simone. "It takes time and money to forge those relationships and . . ."

And so it went for the duration of the lunch. Simone seemed duly impressed, and after he'd left the table the consensus was that they'd "hit a home run," "hit it out of the park," and other sports metaphors they were fond of using.

"I think we've got ourselves a new client," an associate said. When Morrison didn't respond he said, "You agree, Eric?"

"Yeah, definitely a home run. Look, I have to run to another appointment. You guys handle the bill, okay? I'll see you back at the office."

His two colleagues watched their agency's namesake walk from the table and disappear into a crowd at the front of the restaurant.

"What's with him lately?" one asked.

"Maybe his wife's giving him a hard time," offered the other.

"Or a girlfriend."

"He doesn't shack up with that movie actress anymore, does he?"

"No, that's over. He had me run a background check on a private investigator named Brixton."

"Why?"

The answer was a shrug.

"Let's get back. We promised Simone a written proposal. Time to get to work."

31

Jayla had awoken at three that morning. Her first thought was that she was fully dressed and had to fight through the mental haze of a sudden awakening to remember why. A few seconds later her time spent with Nate Cousins came into focus and she smiled. Leaving her to fall asleep the way he had, without pressing for anything beyond being supportive and caring, said something good and positive about him.

But then the memory of Eugene Waksit's heavy cologne hit her hard.

She sat up and looked around the bedroom, whose only light came from streetlamps outside the window. A moment of panic set in. She got out of bed and cautiously entered the living room, standing motionless in the silence, her eyes taking in every corner. He'd been there, had violated her space, her life. Anger replaced anxiety.

She checked that the door was securely locked. It was. But the locked door hadn't prevented Waksit from entering and using her computer. She considered wedging a chair up against the door but dismissed that idea.

The lock would have to be changed.

Thoughts came and went as she continued to survey the apartment.

She wondered why Cousins hadn't stayed the night with her, knowing that Waksit had been there. But there had been no reason for him to stay to protect her. Protect her from what? Waksit was gone.

She started to get undressed but stopped after removing her teal V-neck sweater. She patrolled the apartment again, looking into closets and behind chairs and the couch. "Stop it!" she said aloud. "Get a grip on yourself!"

She got out of her street clothes, wrapped herself in a powder-blue terrycloth bathrobe, turned on the living room TV, and stared blankly at the screen on which a paid commercial program played, a toothy young man selling a device that promised to peel vegetables like vegetables had never been peeled before. As his voice droned on, every other sound that came from outside—a car's horn or the screech of tires—or from within the building caused her to stiffen.

She eventually dozed off sitting up. When she awoke the commercial show had been replaced by a movie featuring zombies. She turned off the set, and after another check of the door's lock she shed the robe in the bathroom and stood under a hot shower, unable to shake the image of the woman in the shower being slashed to death in the film *Psycho*. Dressed, she passed the time until Cousins arrived, nibbling halfheartedly on a bagel and sipping tea that quickly became cold.

Cousins arrived at eight thirty and they drove to the bank where she retrieved her father's research material and packets of seeds from the safe deposit box. After rejoining him in the car they drove to Renewal Pharmaceuticals to drop her off for work.

"I'll take a look at this as soon as I get to the office," he told her as he pulled up in front of the pharmaceutical company's building.

Her creased face spoke volumes.

"Hey," he said, taking her hand in his, "get that frown off your pretty face."

She forced a smile. "Sorry," she said. "I didn't get much sleep."

She placed her hand on the thick envelope resting on the console between them. "This means so much," she said. "Even if nothing ever comes of it it's what my father left to me."

"I understand how important it is to you, Jayla, but you have nothing to worry about. I'll see if I can come up with an idea about what to do with it. As I said, once I've reviewed it I'll get it to Mr. Smith."

"I'd rather you give it back to me," Jayla said.

"Sure, if it makes you feel better. What are you going to do about Waksit?"

"I'd like to do nothing and just see him disappear."

"You can't do nothing, Jayla. He broke into your apartment and—"

"He had a key."

"Get the lock changed."

"I intend to today."

"What about that private detective, Brixton? He might be able to help."

"I'll call Mac Smith and see what he suggests."

"Good idea," he said.

She drew a deep breath and kissed his cheek. "I'd better get inside. You'll call me after you've looked at it?"

"Count on it."

She got out of the car and walked to the front entrance, turning halfway there and waving at Cousins, who'd just begun to pull away. He returned the gesture and disappeared into traffic.

Until that moment she'd felt comfortable turning over her father's research to him. But as he drove away a sinking feeling settled in on her. She'd shared the research with no one, and now wondered if she'd become too trusting of him. She was second-guessing her decision as she entered the building, swiped her employee card in the slot, and walked through the door in the direction of the lab to which she was assigned.

Once settled in her cubicle she looked up locksmiths and arranged to meet a technician at her apartment at three that afternoon. After informing the lab's supervisor that she would have to leave at two on personal business she called Mac and explained what had transpired the previous evening.

"No sign of forced entry?" he said.

"No. Eugene must have a key he took from my father."

"I don't blame you for being concerned," Smith said.

"I'm having the lock changed at three," she said. "I was wondering, Mac, whether Mr. Brixton might be able to find where Eugene is in Washington."

"It's probably a long shot, but I'll ask him. Where can I reach you?"

She gave him the number at Renewal and he promised to get back to her as soon as he'd made contact with Brixton.

After speaking with Jayla, Smith tried Brixton's cell phone.

"Robert, it's Mac Smith. I received a call a few minutes ago from Jayla. That fellow, Waksit, who worked for her father, has evidently broken into her apartment. Jayla wonders if you would try and locate Waksit for her."

"There's got to be a thousand hotels in D.C., Mac."

"I told her that it would be a long shot."

"Try 'impossible.'"

"Just thought I'd ask. I'd like to help her. She's liable to be in danger."

"Has she mentioned anybody here in D.C. who Waksit might have gotten in touch with, you know, somebody from back home?"

"Not that I recall."

"Does that place they're from have an embassy here?"

"Papua New Guinea? I assume so, at least a consulate or trade mission. Want me to check?"

"If you don't mind."

Smith made the return call twenty minutes later and caught Brixton as he munched on a donut and sipped coffee at a Dunkin' Donuts.

"The Papua New Guinea embassy is on Massachusetts Avenue," Smith said. "Here's the phone numbers."

Brixton noted them on a napkin.

"Jayla told me that she's meeting a locksmith at her apartment at three this afternoon."

"I'll swing by," Brixton said.

"I'm sure she'd appreciate that. Oh, by the way, I've decided to take on that client we talked about. I hope you can clear your schedule to work on the case with me."

"'Clear my schedule'? What schedule? I'm yours, Mac."

When Brixton reached Jayla's apartment the locksmith was there. While the technician plied his trade at the door, Brixton enjoyed a cup of tea with Jayla in her kitchen. He told her that Smith had mentioned Waksit having entered her apartment, and they discussed the potential ramifications.

"Mac wants me to try and find Waksit," Brixton told her.

"I'd almost rather not know where he is," she said.

"That's up to you."

"Do you think you can find him?"

"Probably not but I'm willing to give it a try."

Brixton remained at the apartment after the locksmith had left. He enjoyed being with Jayla, appreciated her beauty, warmth, and intelligence. When it was time to leave he promised to do what he could to locate Waksit.

"Is there someone in D.C. he might have contacted?" he asked.

"There was a girl he dated in Australia. After college she went to work in New York City, but Eugene once said that he'd heard from her and that she'd moved to Washington to work at—ah, at the embassy, I think.

Dorence was her name. Her first name was something like Mickey or Vickie."

"Did you ever meet her?"

"No."

"How about we call the embassy and see if she's there?"

"You want to call the embassy?" she said.

"Might be better if you did, you know, say you're from—what is it, PNG?—and just say you're looking to catch up with an old friend named Mickey Dorence."

"And what if she's there and comes on the line?"

"You can hang up, or tell her that you're looking for Waksit. If he's been in touch with her she might acknowledge it."

She grimaced.

"Want me to make the call?"

"Would you?"

"Sure."

He removed the napkin on which he'd written the embassy phone number and dialed it from the kitchen extension.

"The Embassy of Papua New Guinea," a woman answered.

"Would you please connect me with Ms. Mickey Dorence."

"I'm sorry but we have no one here by that name. There is a Ms. Dorence but—"

"And?"

"Her name is Nikki. She works in our visa office."

"Right, sorry, I made a mistake on her first name," Brixton said. "Nikki. That's right. Please connect me with her."

A man came on the line.

"I'm calling for Nikki Dorence," Brixton said.

"Sorry, but Ms. Dorence is away for the day."

"Oh, my bad luck. Thanks."

"I can leave her a message and—"

Brixton clicked off the phone.

"She's not there, but you were right. She does work at the embassy. Let's find her home phone and—"

"Do we have to do it now?"

"No, of course not. I'll do it later. You told Mac that Waksit had accessed your e-mail. Anything interesting on it?"

"I'll show you."

She brought up the copy of the message that her PNG attorney had sent to Mac Smith. After reading it Brixton said, "If Waksit saw this when he was in your apartment it must have spooked him and sent him into hiding—either that or caused him to contact the authorities and make himself available to them for questioning. Of course, if he had anything to do with your father's murder it's unlikely that he'd do that, at least voluntarily."

"He also took a group of crime scene photos taken at my father's lab," Jayla said. "They were in this drawer." She tried to not cry. "What do you suggest I do?" she asked.

"You have any pictures of Waksit?"

"Yes, I think I do."

She dragged a green leather photo album from where it shared space with books on a bookcase and flipped the pages until reaching what she was looking for. "Here he is," she said, handing the book to Brixton.

The photo was of Waksit posing with Jayla's father. Waksit had his arm around the physician and a big smile on his face.

"Looks like they got along pretty good," Brixton commented.

"Eugene could be charming," she said. "I don't think that my father ever looked beyond that charm."

"Good-looking dude," Brixton said. "Mind if I take this?"

Jayla carefully removed the picture and handed it to Brixton.

"I'll swing by this Nikki Dorence's place on my way back to the office and see if Mr. Waksit is sitting in front sunning himself. Probably not, but sometimes you get lucky."

"I appreciate you doing this, Robert."

"Hey, what's a friend for? Besides, Mac Smith wants this resolved. Whatever Mackensie wants, Mackensie gets."

She laughed. "You sound like that song about Lola from *Damn Yankees*."

"Yeah, I guess it did come out that way. You know, because the police back in PNG want to talk to Waksit again, I might be able to get the local PD to lend a hand in finding him. I still have friends there."

"Whatever you think is best."

On his way out he asked about Nate Cousins. During Brixton's visit and the locksmith's arrival Jayla had pushed aside thoughts of having given Cousins her father's research results.

"He's fine," she said, her face creased.

"Nice guy. Say hello for me."

Eric Morrison's three o'clock meeting with George Alard of Alard Associates had not gone smoothly.

"How can I again be of service to you?" Alard asked after Morrison had been seated in the sparsely furnished office.

"I don't know where to begin," Morrison replied.

"Try starting at the beginning," Alard said through a slit of a smile, which annoyed the lobbyist, whose pique level was already high.

"There's a man, a private investigator here in Washington, who is threatening me."

Alard raised his eyebrows.

"His name's Brixton, Robert Brixton. He's a lowlife, been in lots of trouble."

"What sort of trouble?"

"He had his PI license pulled, shot a senator's son, a whole lot of things."

"And you say he's threatening you?"

"Yes. He's a loose cannon. Oh, and there's a woman, Paula Silver, a former B-movie actress—actress? Ha!—try bitch. She says she's writing a book about me and her—we had a short affair—and a situation I got involved with concerning a leading U.S. senator—oh, and the project you handled for me in Papua New Guinea—she wants money from me and—"

"Is there anyone else threatening you?" Alard asked.

"Isn't that enough?"

Alard shrugged his small shoulders and examined the fingernails on his right hand. He looked up at Morrison and said, "Is this Brixton fellow threatening you physically?"

"No, but you never know about scum like this. I wouldn't put anything past him. He knows a few things about me that are better left secret." Thinking his statement might be misconstrued, he quickly added, "Not that I've done anything wrong but I know things about other people, important people, that are better kept—well, kept a secret."

Alard prefaced his next comment with an editorial sigh. "I'm sorry to hear about your troubles, Mr. Morrison, but I don't see how I can be of help."

"You don't? Listen, I know that you can do damn near anything you want if the price is right. What I want you to do is get these losers off my back. Chances are they're just looking for a payoff. I know that Paula is. She'll probably get lost for ten grand. Brixton, he won't come that cheap, maybe twice that."

"I don't understand, Mr. Morrison," Alard said. "If all it will take is money why don't you simply pay them yourself? My second bit of advice is that once you pay someone off, as you put it, it won't be the end of them. They'll come back for more."

Morrison felt his anxiety, coupled with rage, rise.

"Look," he said, "I have a reputation here in D.C., which I'm sure you know. Pay them off myself? Getting my hands dirty by meeting with these two and handing over cash won't do that reputation any good. I want it to come from a third party."

Alard started to say something, but Morrison interrupted. "That's what you do, isn't it, do what other people don't want to do? I mean, paying somebody off isn't beneath you, right?" He forced a laugh to soften what he said. "Look, let's face it, you didn't hesitate to burn the doctor's plot of land in Papua New Guinea or arrange to steal his research. I never asked how the doc died. I have my own theory about that but what you did is your business."

Alard grunted. Had he spoken what he was thinking his words would not have pleased Morrison.

"So all I want from you, or the people who work for you, is to buy off these two clowns and make sure they understand that if they make any more trouble they'll have to—well, you know what I mean. Scare 'em off. Don't get me wrong. No rough stuff, maybe just some harsh words that'll get their attention and make them think twice about threatening me again. How much do you want for your *service*?"

"I'll have to give this some thought, Mr. Morrison."

"You want to *think* about it? What's to think about? If it's money there's no problem. Just tell me your fee and you'll get it."

"I don't rush into things, Mr. Morrison," Alard said. "I'm sure that you can appreciate that."

"Yeah, sure, I'm cautious, too, only I don't want to see this situation drag on. There's no telling what this Brixton might do, go to the press with his claims, who knows? There's a lot at stake, Alard, including the reputation of a leading U.S. senator."

Morrison calling Alard by his last name nettled him but he didn't say it. Instead, he said, "I might be able to help, Mr. Morrison. I take it that it is this Mr. Brixton who you are most concerned about."

"That's right. Paula Silver, she's a drunk with a big

mouth. Writing a book? That'll be the day. A few bucks and she'll leave town. But Brixton's a different story. I don't care what you have to do to shut him up, get him the hell out of my hair. By the way, you'll also be doing the country a favor, a big favor. Brixton is out to take down this senator, which would be a tragedy."

A tragedy for you? Alard mused.

"Here's what I suggest, Mr. Morrison." Alard picked up a slip of paper, wrote on it, and handed it to Morrison.

"What's this?"

"A secure number for you to call to inform me when and where you and Brixton will be meeting."

"Why. Whose number is it?"

"Do you have a problem with this, Mr. Morrison?"

"No, no problem, it's just that—"

"I suggest that you arrange to meet with this Brixton fellow as soon as possible, perhaps tomorrow night, say at eleven o'clock."

"Meet with him? I want nothing to do with him."

"Be that as it may, Mr. Morrison, it is the way I wish to proceed, assuming of course that you still want my services."

"I—I just want Brixton to go away."

"Which is the outcome I'm offering."

"Okay. So you want me to get ahold of Brixton and arrange to meet him tomorrow. Where?"

Alard wrote on a second sheet of paper and handed it to Morrison. "It's a secluded area along the river in southwest D.C., Gravelly Point, a few miles north of Reagan Airport. It runs parallel to the George Washington Memorial Parkway on the Mount Vernon Trail."

"Why there?"

"Because it is sufficiently secluded, Mr. Morrison, unless you would prefer to meet Mr. Brixton on the stage at the Kennedy Center."

"I don't need your sarcasm, Alard."

"Then you will meet him there and perhaps find out more about what he knows about you and this senator and anything else you're concerned about."

"That's it? We just talk?"

"Talk, and offer him the twenty thousand dollars you will have with you."

"I don't get it," said Morrison. "Where do you come in?"

"I will arrange for someone to be there in the event Mr. Brixton balks, makes trouble for you. Hopefully, the money will smoothly change hands and your troubles with this gentleman will be over, assuming, of course, that you are correct in judging him as someone who can easily be bought off."

"I'm guessing but—"

"Hopefully your guess is a good one. Should Mr. Brixton take the money but not agree to let up on his threats to you, my colleague who will be there—discreetly I assure you—will step in and make Mr. Brixton see the wisdom of getting out of your life and—and out of the life of this unnamed senator."

"Who is he?" Morrison asked.

"A trusted aide. It isn't necessary to know his name. Mr. Smith, or Mr. Jones, whatever you're comfortable with."

"What will he say to Brixton? Do to him?"

Alard shook his head and waved a hand in frustration. "Mr. Morrison," he said, "I do not have time to take you by the hand and lead you through this. You're free to simply meet with Brixton without my operative, give him the money, and hope that he sees the wisdom of bowing out. If he doesn't—well, that's your problem."

"But this operative of yours. What can he possibly do to make that point?"

Alard smiled in response. "Mr. Morrison," he said, "you may be a successful lobbyist here in Washington, D.C., but you are also a very naïve man."

"What about *your* fee?"

Alard cracked a rare smile. "Mr. Morrison, you and I have done business before. You've proved that you're an honorable man who pays his debts. My fee will be ten thousand. You can pay me after we've concluded our business with Mr. Brixton."

"Glad you see it that way. Look, Alard, I don't want any funny business, okay? Frankly, I wasn't happy the way the last project worked out. You never got the doctor's research results but insisted I had to pay the entire fee. Don't get me wrong, I know that you and your people work in the shadows and don't mind getting your hands dirty. But I think that you owe me. As far as I know you also—well, took care of the doctor—which, I remind you, I specifically forbid. Whatever you and your so-called operative did to the doctor is our little secret. Right? Just so we understand each other."

Morrison had been tempted to thank Alard for his not wanting his fee up front but decided not to bother. He intensely disliked the man and wasn't in the mood to thank him for anything.

"I still don't like having to call this bozo and arrange a meeting with him. I'd rather stay out of it, completely out of it."

"Do you expect *me* to call him?" Alard said. "He won't respond to me. When you place the call say that you wish to cooperate with him. Tell him that you wish to give him a sizable gratuity. Offer to share with him the information he is seeking about this senator. Tell him anything that will entice him to meet with you."

Morrison pouted, his mouth moving silently as though chewing on what to say next. Finally he said, "All right, Alard. I'll call and see if he'll meet with me."

"And if he does agree, call the number I've given you and inform us. You know where the meeting will take place."

"Gravelly Point," Morrison muttered. "Yeah, I'll find it."

"Eleven o'clock." Alard checked his watch. "I have another appointment," he said. "Are we going forward with what I have suggested or—?"

"Yeah, yeah, okay, Alard. You're calling the shots. I just hope it works out better than the last time we got together."

After Morrison had left, Alard called someone in MPD's firearms registration section who'd been of help to Alard in the past.

"I need to know about a concealed weapon permit issued to a private detective, Robert Brixton," Alard said.

His MPD contact checked his computer files and came back on the line within minutes. "I've got it here," he said. "Robert Brixton. He carries a Swiss-made Sig Sauer P226 pistol, nine millimeter, with a heavy double-action trigger. You need the serial number?"

"No, that won't be necessary," Alard said. "Thank you. Payment will be sent the usual way."

While Morrison met with Alard, Brixton drove to where Nikki Dorence lived, parked across the street, and casually eyed the entrance to her apartment building. He didn't expect to see anything or anyone of interest, certainly not Eugene Waksit, but the act of being there gave him a certain satisfaction.

Waksit sat inside the apartment, unaware that a private investigator was outside. The photos of Dr. King dead on the floor of his lab were lined up on a coffee table. Waksit had looked at them whenever he was alone, fixated on the doctor's face and the pool of blood in which he lay. Nikki was at work and wouldn't be home until later in the evening, something about a dinner and meeting to attend. His agitation level was elevated, and he moved the heel of his left and right foot up and down in rapid succession. He was befuddled, couldn't decide what his next move was.

He'd been close to picking up the phone and calling

Eric Morrison again in the hope of convincing him that the research he possessed would be extremely valuable to one of Morrison's pharmaceutical clients. But each time he reached for the phone he pulled back. He wasn't sure that he could deal with another harsh rejection.

He also pondered calling Jayla King. But what would he say? That he had her father's research results and was willing to partner with her in seeking a company to further develop it? He tried to conjure what her view of him might be at that moment, and the picture he painted wasn't positive.

And there was the message he'd read on Jayla's computer about the authorities in Papua New Guinea wanting to question him again about Dr. King's murder. That posed another decision to be made. Should he contact the PNG police and submit to their stupid questions? No, he couldn't do that. Chances were they'd make him a scapegoat in order to boast at having solved the crime. He also considered contacting the PNG attorney with whom he'd spoken about having been verbally deeded the results of King's research. He ruled that out, too. The attorney, whom he'd met on occasion when he'd visited King, was a pompous ass who was probably in cahoots with the local police.

Finally, after giving himself a pep talk, he pulled himself together to a degree and called the office of Eric Morrison.

"I'm sorry," the woman who answered said, "but Mr. Morrison isn't available at the moment. I'll be happy to take a message for him."

"No, that's okay. No, tell him that Eugene Waksit called again. I have something new and exciting to talk to him about."

He couldn't see the amused expression on the woman's face as she jotted the message on a pink pad. "Is there anything else?" she asked.

"No, I'll—"

"Do you have a number where he can reach you?"

"No. I'll call again."

The woman was truthful when she'd said that Morrison wasn't available.

He'd returned from his meeting with George Alard and secluded himself in his office with orders not to be disturbed. The moment he'd left Alard he'd been swamped with second thoughts about the plan to buy off Brixton. What was most upsetting was having to personally take part in the meeting. He couldn't understand why Alard, or one of his so-called operatives, couldn't just meet with Brixton and hand him the money, paired, of course, with the sternest of warnings to get off Morrison's case and never bother him again.

He justified having agreed to Alard's plan based upon what he considered necessity. Someone like George Alard operated in the shadows; Morrison certainly did not want the sun to shine on what he intended to do about Robert Brixton. Alard did business in a netherworld, a world that Morrison wished he'd never entered. But now that he had, he wanted it over and done with.

He knew one thing for certain. Once Brixton was out of the picture he'd see to it that Senator Ronald Gillespie was made fully aware of the sacrifice he'd made on his behalf. Gillespie owed him big-time and he intended to cash in on that debt.

He drew a deep breath and called Brixton's cell number. Brixton still sat in front of Nikki Dorence's building hoping that Waksit would make an appearance, and was about to leave when the phone sounded.

"Mr. Brixton?"

"Yes."

"This is Eric Morrison. We've spoken before."

"Morrison. Sure. Good hearing from you."

"Is this a good time to talk?"

"I can't think of a better one. What's on your mind?"

"I would like to meet with you," Morrison said, working to keep his voice calm.

"Yeah?"

What was this all about? Brixton mused. *Why would he want to meet?*

"Why?" Brixton asked.

Morrison had decided to not mention the $20,000 payoff he was prepared to offer in return for Brixton dropping queries into his life. When Brixton had called earlier he'd asked about Senator Gillespie and the abortion, as well as about Dr. King's research and plot of land on PNG. He'd wanted information about those events. Offering it stood the best chance of wooing Brixton to a meeting.

"I have information," Morrison said, "about Senator Gillespie."

"I'm listening," Brixton said.

"I don't want to talk on the phone," Morrison said.

Where's this going? Brixton wondered.

"All right," Brixton said. "Lunch? Dinner? My treat— provided the information you have is worth anything."

Morrison hoped that the laugh he forced sounded dismissive and wise. "Oh, no," he said, "It can't be a public place. I'm really sticking my neck out. I'm sure you understand that."

It made sense, Brixton decided.

Morrison read from the note he had. He'd practiced it a few times before making the call to have it sound as though Gravelly Point was a location with which he was intimately knowledgeable.

"Never heard of it," Brixton said.

"It's a favorite spot of mine," Morrison said, "very secluded after dark. Can we meet there at eleven tomorrow night?"

Brixton's antenna went up as he processed the situation. He wasn't concerned that Morrison would be a physical threat. He was a fat-cat lobbyist, probably balding and flabby. Was there something else to worry about? He couldn't come up with one. He'd participated in a number of late night meets with a variety of lowlifes while a detective on the Savannah PD, usually informants looking to cut a deal to get them off the hook. Despite these questions, Brixton saw only an upside to meeting with Morrison. If the lobbyist was about to sell out Gillespie—and why he would do that was irrelevant—Will Sayers would be as happy as the proverbial pig in mud.

"Okay," he said, "eleven o'clock tomorrow night at this Gravelly Point."

"Good," Morrison said. "I'll be carrying a yellow umbrella and wearing a navy blue blazer."

Brixton almost laughed out loud. It was beginning to sound like a scene from a bad Cold War novel.

"I'll be looking for a guy in a blue blazer carrying a yellow umbrella. See ya."

Brixton lingered in front of Nikki Dorence's apartment building for another fifteen minutes before heading home to have dinner with Flo, who announced that sales that day at Flo's Fashions had been the most lucrative since the shop opened. They toasted the news and settled in for a night of domestic bliss—Welsh rarebit and bacon on English muffins, pecan pie à la mode, single-malt scotch, and Netflix.

32

Brixton and Flo started the next day enjoying breakfast on their small balcony. Flo was in good spirits based upon the previous day's sales, and Brixton's mood paralleled hers. He'd spoken with Mac Smith after arriving home last night and the attorney filled him in on the new client that would need Brixton's investigative savvy. Brixton was pleased on two levels. One, he could use the money to pay bills. Two, it would lift his spirits after having Flo carry the financial load for the past few months. Life was good.

"What's on your agenda today?" she asked.

"I see the shrink at ten."

"He's made a difference," she said.

"Think so?"

"I *know* so," she said.

"Today will be the final session with him," Brixton said. "No sense continuing writing checks when there's nothing more he can do."

"Robert!" she said sternly. "We can certainly afford it, and there's more to be gained by continuing to see him."

"Why? You say he's made a difference. There are people who see their shrinks for years, every week, maybe twice a week. A waste of money."

Flo knew better than to debate with him. She had faith that Dr. Fowler would convince Robert to continue seeing him. At least she hoped that would be the case.

"I'll be late tonight," he said, changing the subject.

"Oh? Why?"

"I've got a meeting at eleven o'clock."

"*Eleven o'clock?* Who with, that movie actress?"

"No."

"Then who are you seeing at such an hour?"

Brixton hadn't intended to share with Flo that he was meeting with the lobbyist Morrison but he decided it would head off any questions on her part. He told her of Morrison's phone call and shared some of his interest in him.

"You sure you want to meet this guy at what?—Gravel Point?"

"Gravelly Point. I checked it on a map. It'll be fine. Maybe he'll give me what Will Sayers is looking for."

"And will Sayers pay you for that information?"

"I don't care. The truth about Senator Gillespie needs to come out. If I can I want to help bring that about."

Flo smiled, and finished her coffee, and went to her clothing shop. Brixton drove to his office and spent two hours with Mac Smith and Smith's new client, who needed not only Smith's keen legal mind, Brixton's investigative prowess would also be brought into play. He engaged Mrs. Warden in conversation about her life, something he'd never done before, and learned that she was more interesting than she'd seemed.

After lunch at his desk he drove to Nikki Dorence's apartment building and read a newspaper and a magazine while waiting for Eugene Waksit to show his face. When he didn't, Brixton drove home and took a nap in preparation for his eleven o'clock meeting with Eric Morrison. He'd have waited at the apartment to have dinner with Flo but it was a late night for her at the shop, which was just as well. Anticipation of meeting Morrison had begun to build, and he wondered how forthcoming the lobbyist would actually be. He also wanted to make Will Sayers fully aware of the meeting, and called the corpulent journalist to suggest dinner. Sayers, who never met a meal he didn't like, said that he'd been thinking all day of the lobster rolls at Hank's Oyster Bar on Pennsylvania Avenue—"Not the one in Dupont Circle," he clarified—and that's where they met. Sayers became positively excited that Morrison had called Brixton and was ready to pass along some dirt on Senator Gillespie.

"Did he say anything specific?" Sayers asked over dessert.

"No, just that he was willing to share information with me."

"Any idea what prompted him to do this, Robert?"

"No, but I figure the senator did something to tee him off. I also let him know the first time we talked that I'm aware of his part in what happened to the doctor in Papua New Guinea."

"Don't get sidetracked by that, Robert. I need evidence of the abortion that Morrison arranged for Senator Gillespie."

"Yeah, I know," said Brixton, "but I'm also interested in getting to the truth about Jayla King's father."

"Smitten with her, are you?"

"No, Will. I just want to right a wrong."

The check had been placed in front of Brixton, but he slid it in Sayers's direction.

"Fair enough," Sayers said.

"That's the way I see it," Brixton said. "I'll call you tomorrow with what I come up with."

"Call tonight at any time. I won't be able to wait until tomorrow."

Brixton was early for the meeting with Morrison and decided to go to the appointed place and scope it out in advance. He had no difficulty finding a place to park close to Gravelly Point. He remained in his car for a half hour taking in his surroundings. There were few people strolling on the Mount Vernon Trail at that time of night even though the sky was clear, and a full moon cast flattering light over plantings, mostly tall bushes that formed barriers between the parking lot and the public spaces, and benches that had been occupied earlier. He kept a lookout for a man in a blue blazer carrying a yellow umbrella, smiling and shaking his head at the silliness of it all. But while the method of identifying Morrison seemed silly, the stakes weren't. If things went the way he hoped they would he'd walk away with some sort of proof that Ronald Gillespie, senior senator from Georgia, had gotten a teenager pregnant and arranged for her to have an abortion.

At a quarter to eleven he got out of the car and went to a bench that was nestled in bushes, secluded from others, but affording him a view of the surrounding area. At a few minutes before eleven he heard a car come to a stop in the parking lot behind him. Although he didn't expect to have to use it, he used his elbow to assure that his Sig Sauer P226 was where it should be, secured in its holster in his armpit. A man emerged through a break in the bushes and looked nervously around. He wore a blue blazer, and carried both a yellow umbrella and a briefcase.

"Morrison?" Brixton said.

Eric Morrison turned in Brixton's direction. "Yes," he said, and approached the bench.

Brixton didn't bother to stand to greet the lobbyist. He patted the space next to him. "Sit down," he said.

Morrison looked as though he wasn't sure whether to do what Brixton had suggested.

"Have a seat," Brixton repeated.

Morrison sat, gingerly, and perched on the edge of the bench.

"Let's not string this out," Brixton said. "You know that I know about Senator Gillespie, and the role you played in arranging and paying for an abortion for a teenage girl back in Georgia. I'm not looking to get you in trouble, Mr. Morrison, but the senator is another story. Voters back in Georgia have a right to know what he's really all about."

Morrison stared into the dark perimeter of the mini-park and said nothing.

Brixton said, "You give me evidence about the abortion and I'll pass it along to the interested parties. I'll keep you out of it best I can."

"This is very difficult for me, Mr. Brixton."

"Yeah, I'm sure it is. What's your biggest problem, Morrison, that you might lose your senator buddy in congress? He pretty much does your bidding, doesn't he, votes the way your Big Pharma clients want him to in return for hefty donations to his campaigns?"

"But what you don't understand is—"

A man who'd been lurking in the parking lot approached, stopping at a spot directly behind the bench where the two men sat, the bushes shielding him from their sight. He silently took a step into the narrow opening created between two of the shrubs.

"Get to it, Morrison," Brixton said, losing patience.

Morrison opened his briefcase and showed Brixton the $20,000 it contained. "It's for you," he said. "Twenty thousand dollars. I'm sure you can use it. I mean, I'm sure you can put it to good use. What's to be gained by bringing down a United States senator? I mean, what's in it for you?"

Morrison closed the briefcase. As he did, the large man behind them reached through the gap in the bushes and brought a spring-loaded lead-weighted sac across the back of Brixton's neck. He went forward, off the bench, facedown on the gravel.

Morrison leaped to his feet.

"Why did you do that?" he said as the man pulled open Brixton's jacket, pulled the Sig Sauer from its holster, and pointed it at Brixton's prone body.

"Don't shoot him!" Morrison yelled.

The man turned to face the lobbyist. He raised the pis-

tol and pulled the trigger twice. Both shots blew apart
Morrison's heart. He was dead before he hit the ground,
the tip of the yellow umbrella piercing the moist soil and
standing vertical like a colorful graveyard monument.
The man grabbed the case from Morrison's limp hand
and was gone.

33

Flo Combes was in the midst of a deep sleep when the ringing phone jarred her awake. She glanced at the digital alarm clock next to the phone: 12:44.

"Hello?"

"Hey, babe, it's me."

"Robert? Is something wrong? Why are you calling? Where are you?"

"Yeah, I'd say something's wrong." He was thick-tongued.

Now fully awake, she sat up. "What is it?"

"It's like this, Flo. I'm in the ER at GW University Hospital being coddled by a cute young nurse and a not so cute young doctor."

"What happened? Are you all right?"

"Aside from a head that feels like a truck ran over it, I'm okay. I even have company, two uniformed members of the city's finest making sure I don't get up and—" He groaned. "It hurts whenever I move my head. Somebody cold-cocked me tonight."

"Are you well enough to be released?" Flo asked.

"As far as I'm concerned I'm good to go now. The cops are another story."

"The cops? What are you talking about?"

"It's like this, Flo. They say that I shot that sleazy lob-byist Morrison tonight."

She gulped.

"He's dead. The guy who whacked me over the head took my gun and shot him, two bullets square in the chest. The guy took the money, too, the twenty thou Morrison wanted me to take in return for getting off his case about Senator Gillespie."

"He tried to bribe you?"

"Yeah. He should have known better, huh?"

Flo heard Brixton speaking with others but couldn't make out what was being said. He came back on the line. "Look," he said, "they insist that I spend the night here in the hospital, you know, test for concussion, cover their asses. I'll have plenty of company with my friends in blue."

"I'll be there as soon as I can."

"No need for—"

The click in his ear said that she'd hung up.

A few minutes after their conversation ended a famil-iar face arrived at the ER, Superintendent of Detectives Zeke Borgeldt.

"Things must be slow at the PD," Brixton said to Borgeldt from the gurney, "for the heavy artillery to show up."

"I had nothing else to do," Borgeldt said. "How are you feeling?"

"I feel wonderful aside from a pounding headache and these little pieces of gravel in my face. You know what happened, right? You've been filled in."

"Yes, but I'd like to hear it from you. What were you doing in Gravelly Point at eleven o'clock at night with one of our top lobbyists?"

"Getting a payoff."

"A payoff? What the hell are you talking about?"

"I know, I know," Brixton said, "it sounds crazy but that's what happened." He explained how he'd been in touch with Eric Morrison regarding Senator Ronald

Gillespie and the young girl he'd gotten pregnant back in Georgia, and how Morrison had called to arrange for them to meet. "Hey," Brixton said, "I didn't pick Gravelly Point, *he* did. I thought he'd be giving me evidence about the senator's extracurricular activities. Instead he offers me twenty thousand bucks to get off his back."

"You took the money?" Borgeldt asked.

"*'Took the money'*? Hell no."

"There was no money at the scene."

"I'm sure there wasn't. Whoever hit me on the back of the head must have taken it."

"You think that was his motive, robbery?"

"No. He wasn't some punk who just happened to be passing by at eleven o'clock in Gravelly Point. It had to be someone who knew we were meeting, and also knew that Morrison had twenty grand with him."

"You see who hit you?"

"No. I didn't completely black out when he hit me from behind, but he put me out for a minute or two. When I woke up there was one dead lobbyist. My weapon was lying on the ground minus two rounds."

Borgeldt let out an exasperated stream of air and pulled up a chair to the side of the gurney.

"I know what you're thinking, Zeke," Brixton said. "Here we go again, another mess for you to deal with and I'm at the center of it."

"There was the senator's son you killed after he and his female friend blew up the outdoor café a few years ago."

"And blew up my daughter in the bargain. I came out clean on that one, Zeke, and I'm clean on this one. Whoever did it grabbed my gun and used it to shoot Morrison, probably figuring that I'd take the rap. My gun. My bullets. Nice try, but it doesn't wash."

"I believe you, Brixton," said Borgeldt. "I just wish you lived and worked someplace else. You're nothing but trouble."

"Tell that to the yahoos who make trouble for me, Zeke."

"The press is already gathering downstairs. A TV remote truck pulled up when I arrived. Morrison was hardly an anonymous shooting victim. He was a well-known lobbyist with powerful connections."

"He was a sleazebag, Zeke, but I didn't want to see him dead. Somebody did, though, somebody who—"

Flo Combes and Mackensie Smith walked in accompanied by a uniformed police officer who'd been screening visitors at the ER entrance. Flo immediately came to the gurney and kissed Brixton.

"It's okay, honey," Brixton said. "I'm fine." He saw Mac and said, "Hey, what are you doing here?"

"I called him," Flo said.

"Hell of a time at night to call somebody," Brixton said.

"Actually, I was awake," Smith said. "I was engrossed in a novel when Flo called." He shook hands with Borgeldt, with whom he'd been friends for years, and said, "Ms. Combes gave me a rundown of what happened tonight but I'm sure you have more details."

The superintendent gave Smith a fast recap of what had transpired. When he was finished, Smith said to Brixton, "Does that pretty much sum things up, Robert?"

Brixton sat up and moaned. "Yeah," he said. "That's what happened."

Smith beckoned for Borgeldt to accompany him out of the patient bay.

"What's Robert's legal status?" Smith asked as they stood alone in the hallway.

"Right now he's a material witness to the murder of Eric Morrison," the detective replied. "I believe his story. Somebody knocked him out, took his gun, and shot Morrison. What I don't get is the story about Morrison offering him twenty thousand dollars to end some sort of investigation he was undertaking involving Senator Gillespie."

"I know about that," Smith said, "although the twenty-thousand-dollar bribe to Robert is news to me."

"Tell me what you know," said Borgeldt.

After receiving an assurance that their conversation would remain confidential, Smith recounted what he knew about the allegation that Gillespie had gotten an underage girl pregnant in Georgia, and that Morrison had financed her abortion. He also said that Morrison might also have been involved in an illegal act in Papua New Guinea in which a doctor who'd been researching a natural painkiller was murdered, and his research stolen. "And," he ended with, "there seems to be an involvement of some sort by a group called Alard Associates."

Borgeldt didn't respond except to say, "That's a hell of a story." But Smith sensed that his mention of Alard Associates had triggered an unstated response.

"Robert's been digging into that story for Will Sayers, the editor of the Savannah newspaper here in D.C.," Smith said.

"You'll be representing Brixton?" Borgeldt asked.

"I suppose so, although he's not being charged with anything, at least not at this point."

"He is the pivotal witness to what went down tonight," Borgeldt said. "I'll be speaking with Morrison's widow tomorrow to see whether she has any clue as to why her husband was meeting with Brixton and carrying twenty thousand dollars in cash."

"I'd be interested in what you come up with," Smith said. "Actually, I'd like to be there."

Borgeldt looked at him quizzically. "Because you're representing Brixton?"

"That's as good a reason as any. Look, Zeke, the last thing I want to do is get in your hair. You've got a major investigation to conduct, and far be it from me to get in the way. But there might be more to this than simply what happened tonight."

"You'll inform me of these other things?"

"Count on it," said Smith.

They were interrupted by the young emergency room physician, who announced that Brixton was about to be taken to his room for overnight observation. "He'll be kept awake for a period of time to make sure that he has full brain function," the doctor said.

Flo might have made a sarcastic comment were it not a serious situation.

Smith stayed with Brixton and Flo until he was settled in his hospital bed.

"Take you home?" Smith asked her.

"Thanks, Mac, but I'm going to stay."

She walked with him into the hallway where a uniformed police officer sat in a chair just outside the room. Smith informed her that Brixton would not be charged with Morrison's murder but would have to maintain a low profile. "Keep him on a short leash," he advised.

She managed a laugh. "If I can find one strong enough," she said as she kissed Smith on the cheek and watched him walk from the area.

Jayla King and Will Sayers learned of Brixton's hospitalization and involvement in the shooting almost simultaneously. Both had turned on their TV sets at the about the same time the following morning and saw the "Breaking News" report that one of D.C.'s leading lobbyists, Eric Morrison, had been shot to death in Gravelly Point. The anchor went on to say: "The details of the shooting are murky at this early stage but sources tell us that Morrison was shot twice in the chest by a weapon belonging to Washington private investigator Robert Brixton. We're told that Brixton had arranged to meet Morrison at Gravelly Point for reasons yet unknown. These same sources also tell us that Brixton has claimed that he was offered a twenty-thousand-dollar bribe by Morrison to drop an investigation, was knocked unconscious by an unidentified person or persons, and his weapon was taken from him and used in the killing. Brixton, you may recall, had been involved in another high-profile case, the shooting of former senator Walter

Skaggs's son Paul following a terrorist bombing in an outdoor café that took the life of Brixton's daughter. He was exonerated in that shooting. Mr. Brixton was admitted to George Washington University Hospital and remains there under observation. More on this breaking story as details come in."

Sayers's first call was to Brixton's apartment where he was greeted by Brixton's voice on the answering machine. He tried Flo's shop and was again connected with a machine. Frustrated, he tried Mackensie Smith's number and was pleased to hear a live human voice. "Will Sayers here," he said. "Hope I'm not waking you."

"I've been up for hours," Smith said. "You've heard, of course."

"Hard to miss it. How's Robert?"

"He's all right. I just got off the phone with a doctor at the hospital. They're releasing him in a few hours."

"Did the TV talking heads get it right?"

"Pretty much."

"He was meeting Morrison for me," Sayers said.

"So he said."

"I have to talk to him."

"I imagine he'll be up for it later today."

"I'll call him. But before I get off, did Robert mention Alard Associates?"

"Not last night as I recall, but I remember the conversation about them at our apartment. Why?"

"Nothing, Mac, just free-associating. Hope to see you soon."

Mac had no sooner hung up when Jayla King's call sounded.

"I just heard about Mr. Brixton," she said.

"Quite a story," Smith said.

"Is he all right? Is he in trouble?"

"He got a pretty good blow to the head, and some gravel in his cheek from his fall. Other than that—and of course his involvement in the shooting—he'll be fine."

"He didn't—he didn't shoot that man, did he?"

"No. Whoever attacked Robert took his weapon and used it to kill him."

"I recognize the name of the man who was shot. Morrison. Mr. Brixton talked about him regarding my father's murder."

"Yes, he did."

"The last time I spoke with him was here at the apartment when I was having the lock changed. He said that he was going to see if he could find Eugene Waksit for me." She told Mac about finding the name of one of Waksit's former girlfriends who now worked at the PNG embassy. "I think he intends to contact her."

"I don't know anything about that, Jayla, but I'll ask him when I see him, which I hope will be later today. He's being released from the hospital and will recuperate at home. I'll tell him you called and asked after him."

"Please do."

"How about you, Jayla? Are things all right? No more unannounced visits from Mr. Waksit?"

"No, thank goodness. Is there anything I can do for Robert and Flo? I almost consider them family along with you and Annabel."

"The feeling is mutual, Jayla. No, I'm sure that they have everything they need. Please stay in touch."

Smith had the TV on in the background during their conversation. The Morrison shooting was the lead story on every cable news channel, and Smith tired of the constant repeat of the same information, all wrapped in breathless "Breaking News." He turned off the set as Annabel came into the room.

"Robert certainly has a knack for being at the center of controversy," she said.

Her husband couldn't help but agree. "At least this time he didn't lose a member of his family. Will Sayers called. So did Jayla King. They saw it on TV. Robert was meeting with Morrison for a story that Sayers is doing."

"I imagine Zeke and his people have their hands full trying to find who shot Morrison with Robert's gun."

"He's interviewing Morrison's widow at noon. I'm going with him. He didn't balk when I asked to be there. After all, I am representing Robert, who's considered a material witness."

Smith sat back and rubbed his eyes.

"You're thinking?" Annabel said.

"There's more to this than what happened last night, Annie, and I shared that with Zeke. In a way, Zeke wants to question me as much as he does Morrison's widow. When I mentioned Alard Associates he reacted, didn't say anything, but it rang a bell with him."

"Does Robert know you're going with Zeke?"

"No. I'll tell him when I go to see him this afternoon after he gets home from the hospital. Maybe I'll have information that he'll find useful. On a more pragmatic note I want to see him back in action as soon as possible. My new client will keep him busy once he starts working for him." Smith's laugh was sardonic. "I know one thing, Annie. With Robert 'Don't call me Bobby' Brixton around we can always count on some excitement in our lives."

34

As Smith and Superintendent Borgeldt prepared to interview Peggy Sue Morrison, Jayla King arrived at Renewal Pharmaceuticals for another day of lab work. She'd called Nate Cousins before leaving her apartment but didn't reach him. She later tried his office and was told that he was away at meetings and wouldn't return until that afternoon.

She was eager to hear his reaction to the materials that her father had left her. She hadn't heard from him since turning over the items and wondered why. Since they'd started seeing each other socially he'd been quick to keep in touch; the sudden lack of contact concerned her, even though she knew that was unreasonable. He had other things on his mind besides calling her. He was busy. His PR agency was growing. He was chasing new business. He'd call soon.

The call she'd been waiting for came as she was about to head for lunch in the company cafeteria. Most of the gossip that morning at Renewal revolved around Eric Morrison's murder. Although Jayla knew more about it than the others, thanks to Mac Smith, she didn't add her knowledge to the conversations.

"Hi," Cousins said.

"Hi. How are you?"

"I'm okay, swamped with work but okay. I saw on the news that the guy I met at the Smiths' apartment was involved in the shooting of Eric Morrison."

"He didn't shoot anybody, Nate. Someone hit him and—"

"Yeah, I know. He claims that somebody knocked him out and used his gun to kill Morrison. The whole pharmaceutical industry is in shock. Morrison was the top lobbyist for Big Pharma. Did you ever meet him?"

"No."

"He was a powerhouse in Congress, had the ear of every House member and senator whose vote impacts the industry."

She recalled Brixton's cynical view of Morrison and lobbyists in general but thought better of bringing it up.

"Have you had a chance to go over my father's research?" she asked.

He hesitated.

"Nate?"

"Yeah, sorry. I was distracted by something on my computer. I did peruse it but need to spend more time with it. Hope you don't mind."

"No, not at all. I just feel—I feel funny not having it."

"I can understand that. I'll carve out time later today to take a better look. Up for dinner tonight?"

"Yes, that would be fine, only I've been going out a lot lately. How about ordering something in at my apartment?"

"Sure. Whatever you say."

"Will you have had a chance to go over it again before we get together?"

"No promises, but I'll try. I've got a series of meetings today, including one with our boss, Walt Milkin."

"Stop by the lab?"

"If I can. Have to run. If not, see you at seven."

* * *

The TV newscasts also informed Eugene Waksit that Eric Morrison had been shot to death.

The news stunned him. While Morrison had blown him off, Waksit hung on to the belief that he could eventually convince the noted lobbyist to work with him.

Nikki Dorence also watched the TV reports as she prepared to leave for work at the embassy. As the reports played out on the screen, Waksit told her of his connection to the slain lobbyist, which he'd done before—too many times.

"I can't believe this," Waksit said. "We were going to be partners. Murdered? Shot by this private eye? What a tragedy."

Nikki's thought was that the real tragedy for Waksit was that he had lost a potential business partner, not that a man had been brutally murdered. But her less than sanguine view of her houseguest wasn't based on his reaction to a lobbyist's murder. She'd decided that he had to leave—and soon. Having another person sleeping in her apartment was annoying enough. She liked her privacy. But the longer he was there the more the traits that had turned her off during the period when they'd dated back in Australia were now magnified. She wasn't trained in psychology but had decided that he had a passive-aggressive personality, cloyingly sweet one moment, grumpy and indifferent the next. And there was his ego, outsized and fed by his grandiose talk of making millions from the medical research he'd been given by Dr. Preston King. Added to those negative personality traits was her conclusion that he was an inveterate liar, to say nothing of being pathologically cheap. She'd never been particularly fond of Eugene Waksit, but her feelings had now progressed to active dislike.

"What will you do now that your future partner is dead?" she asked before leaving for work.

"I have to figure that out. Maybe one of his partners will want to hook up with me."

"Do you know his partners?" she asked, not particularly successful in keeping sarcasm from her voice.

"Not personally, but I'll give them a call. They'll want to hear from me. I'm sure that Eric filled them in on everything. I'll wait a few days out of respect for him. We were close."

"Eugene, I hate to bring this up at the same time that you've lost your good friend and future partner, but when will you be leaving?"

"Soon. Soon."

There were many angry things she was on the verge of saying. Instead, she grabbed her purse from a chair, left the apartment, and slammed the door behind her.

Waksit, too, was angry. He seethed as he went to the window and watched her leave the building and wave down a taxi. "Stuck-up bitch!" he muttered.

He poured a second cup of coffee in the kitchen and carried it into Nikki's bedroom where he went through her dresser drawers. He did the same with her night table and searched the closet shelves for anything of value. Empty-handed, he returned to the living room and sprawled in a chair, his mind racing as he attempted to sort out his options.

He could book another hotel room, preferably one outside the city. He had money and a credit card, although he hated to use it.

It occurred to him that what he'd seen on Jayla's computer about authorities back in PNG wanting to question him precluded returning there, or to Australia. Maybe his best move was to leave the United States and travel to a country where no one would think to look for him, Thailand, an Arab nation, maybe even Korea. But that meant giving up on turning Dr. King's research findings into gold. He wasn't ready to do that yet. There had to be a way. Morrison's death complicated things, of course, but maybe he'd been foolish putting all his hopes in the shortsighted lobbyist.

Maybe Jayla was the way to go. Her father's work

was worthless to her without his notes, and he had them. Surely she would want to see her father's work carried on by a large, reputable pharmaceutical company, and he, Eugene Waksit, could make that happen.

But could he simply call her out of the blue? How would she respond? Why did she dislike him so? He'd always been courteous with her, and he felt that her father viewed him as the son he'd never had. Did she consider him a suspect in her father's murder, or a so-called person of interest? How could she? Such a dreadful thought would never cross her mind; she knew him better than that. He had her phone number at Renewal Pharmaceuticals and at home. Maybe she'd enjoy going out for lunch or dinner. He'd suggest it when he called—*if* he called. He had to plan what he would say and how he would say it, the way he'd written a script of sorts before his cold call to Morrison.

The images on the TV screen changed as fast as his thoughts. He'd mentioned Morrison's partners to Nikki, assuming that Morrison had partners. Maybe that was the direction to take, call his agency and ask to speak with the one in charge now that Morrison was dead.

Who was the attorney, Mackensie Smith, who was mentioned on the e-mail he'd read on Jayla's computer? Why was the PNG attorney Elgin Taylor, King's buddy, writing to this Smith character about the authorities wanting to speak again with him concerning King's murder? The question resurrected Waksit's concern that they were looking for him. Staying with Nikki Dorence was ideal; who would think to look for him here? But she wanted him gone. "Bitch!"

He'd have to find another place to stay. Would Jayla let him crash at her apartment for a few days? He knew nothing about her living arrangements. Maybe she lived with a boyfriend. Had she married? He saw no evidence of either.

He poured what was left of a bottle of vodka into his empty coffee cup and downed it. It burned his throat and caused him to gag. He didn't want to leave Nikki's apartment but knew he'd have to. Charming her into allowing him to stay longer had its limits. He decided against staying in Washington itself, in the District, and booked a room at a Days Inn in Silver Spring, Maryland. He'd become convinced that people were watching him, judging him, waiters and shopkeepers, cops walking the beat and everyday passersby.

Check-in was at three. It was now a little after nine. He decided to linger until after lunch. Nikki had bought an assortment of cold cuts and a loaf of artisan bread. No sense wasting a free lunch.

Mac Smith met up with Detective Zeke Borgeldt at police headquarters on Indiana Avenue and rode with him in the backseat of an unmarked squad car driven by a uniformed officer to Eric Morrison's house in Chevy Chase. Borgeldt had phoned Peggy Sue Morrison and arranged for a convenient time to interview her.

"Tell me more about Morrison arranging for an abortion on behalf of Senator Gillespie," Borgeldt said as they crossed the line separating the District from Maryland.

"You've met Will Sayers, the D.C. editor for the *Savannah News*," Smith said.

"At your place."

"Right. Sayers is chasing down the Gillespie story and hired Robert to help dig up facts about it. There's a former movie actress named Paula Silver who also knows some of the details. She was Morrison's mistress for a time."

"Jesus," Borgeldt said, "this sounds like some cheap novel."

"It does have that ring to it, doesn't it?" Smith said through a laugh.

"So Brixton tells Morrison that he's on that story and arranges to meet him to gather more information."

"Right you are," said Smith. "You heard from Brixton about the twenty grand that Morrison offered him."

"To keep quiet about the abortion."

"Right. But there's another angle to this."

"Don't tell me," Borgeldt said. "The abortion never happened and the baby is being raised by this former actress Paula Silver."

"*You* should write cheap novels, Zeke."

"I may do that when I retire. What's this other angle?"

Smith gave him a capsule account of the murder of Dr. King in Papua New Guinea, the torching of his research site, and the theft of the research results from his laboratory.

After digesting what Smith had said, Borgeldt asked, "Are you saying that Morrison had something to do with that, too?"

"It's possible, at least based upon what Brixton and his journalist friend Will Sayers have conjured up."

"You put any faith in what Brixton 'conjures up,' Mac?"

"Yes, I do. I know that Robert can be a loose cannon at times, a hardhead about many things, but I trust his instincts. If I didn't, I wouldn't have brought him back to D.C. and set him up in an office next to mine."

"If you say so," Borgeldt muttered.

There were half a dozen cars parked on the street in front of the Morrison home as they approached.

"I told Mrs. Morrison when I called that I wanted to interview her without others present," Borgeldt said, not sounding happy at the sight of the cars.

"I'm sure she'll honor that," Smith said. "Probably family and neighbors surrounding her to help cope with the grief. She might balk at me being there."

"I already told her that I would have another person with me," Borgeldt said.

The driver stayed with the car as Smith and Borgeldt walked up to the front door. Borgeldt rang. They were greeted in seconds by Peggy Sue Morrison, whose face mirrored the tears she'd shed.

"Superintendent of Detectives Borgeldt," Zeke said, extending his badge. "This is Mackensie Smith. He's an attorney who's involved with the investigation."

"Yes, please come in," she said, stepping back to allow them to enter. Voices could be heard from elsewhere in the large, impressive house.

"Friends and some family members are here," Peggy Sue said, "but I told them that you would be coming and that I'd have to excuse myself."

"We'll try not to take too much of your time," Borgeldt said. "Sorry for your loss."

That prompted another flow of tears as she led them into the large living room where others had gathered.

"These are the gentlemen I told you about," Peggy Sue announced through a voice that cracked. "You'll have to excuse me."

Smith and Borgeldt followed her from that room, down a hallway, and into a handsomely furnished and decorated library that obviously also served as a home office, a man's refuge judging by the masculine surroundings.

Peggy Sue confirmed it. "This is where Eric worked when he was home," she said. "He was always working."

"I suppose being a top lobbyist demands lots of work," Borgeldt said.

"It certainly did for Eric," she said. "Oh, I'm sorry. Let me get you some coffee or tea."

"Nothing for us thanks," Borgeldt said, his eyes taking in the room.

After an awkward silence, Borgeldt and Smith were invited to take seats in matching chairs; Peggy Sue pulled the chair out from behind the desk and faced them. "I hope this won't be too difficult," she said, her hands folded in her lap. "I know you have a job to do, and I hope you find who killed my husband."

"We're doing our best," Borgeldt said.

Peggy Sue turned to Smith. "You're an attorney involved in the investigation, Mr. Smith?"

"Yes," Smith replied. "I represent Robert Brixton, who—"

"The man who shot Eric."

"No, ma'am," Smith said. "Robert didn't shoot your husband. Someone knocked him out and used his weapon to shoot Mr. Morrison."

Her expression didn't say that she bought that scenario, nor did it indicate that she dismissed it. She sat silently as Borgeldt pulled out a pad and pen and said, "It's obvious to us, Mrs. Morrison, that whoever killed your husband knew that he was meeting Mr. Brixton at eleven o'clock at Gravelly Point, and that your husband would be carrying twenty thousand dollars on his person."

"That's ridiculous," Peggy Sue snapped. "Why would Eric be meeting some private detective in such a godforsaken place in the middle of the night with twenty thousand dollars? It's absurd."

"I understand your confusion over the details of what happened," Borgeldt said, "but right now we need to know of anyone who might have threatened your husband recently, someone with a grudge against him."

"Eric? Threatened? Someone with a grudge against him? He was the nicest, most easygoing man in the world. Yes, he worked hard, and I suppose he might have rubbed some people the wrong way. But enough to want to kill him? That can't be."

Borgeldt ignored her evaluation of her husband's relationships and said, "What about the day he was murdered? Do you have any idea of his schedule that day, appointments he'd made, someone who would know about his meeting with Robert Brixton that night?"

"No. I have no idea."

"He didn't mention anyone?" Smith asked.

"No. He was unusually high-strung the past few days, as though he had the weight of the world on his shoulders. Eric was—well, he was dedicated to his job and respected the importance of it." She sniffled and used a Kleenex to wipe away the tears. "He told me just a day or two ago that it was time for us to get away, maybe on a cruise somewhere. I've been looking into cruise lines." She cried more openly now and Smith and Borgeldt waited patiently until she brought herself under control.

"Did your husband keep an appointment book here at the house?" Smith asked.

She seemed surprised at the question. "Yes, of course. Eric was meticulous about his schedule. He kept an appointment book here and at the office."

"Some of my detectives will be at his office later today," Borgeldt said. "Could we see the appointment book he maintained at home?"

"I suppose so," she said, getting up and going behind the desk where she picked up a leather-bound book and handed it to Borgeldt. Smith leaned closer to share a look with the detective. They opened it to the date that Morrison had been killed. Among other entries was "Brixton 11 Gravelly Point."

Borgeldt turned the page back to the previous day. One entry captured the immediate attention of both men: "3-Alard."

"Do you know what this means?" Smith asked, handing her the book and pointing to the entry.

She shook her head.

"Do you know someone named Alard?" Borgeldt asked.

"No. It must be someone in government that Eric worked with. He was so proud of what he was able to accomplish with elected officials. My goodness, they lead such busy lives and can't possibly keep up with everything going on in the world and the votes they must make. Eric took a lot of pride in educating them about his clients, especially the pharmaceutical companies he represented."

"I'm sure that's true," Smith said. "You're sure you don't know anyone named Alard?"

"No, it's not a familiar name."

Two loud voices from the living room captured her attention.

"Is there anything else you need from me?" Peggy Sue asked.

"I'll want to take this book with me," Borgeldt said.

"I suppose that's all right," she said. "Is there anything else you want from me? I have family and friends here and—"

"No, ma'am," Borgeldt said, "but I'm sure we'll have more questions at a future date. Thank you for your courtesy today."

"I just want to see Eric's murderer behind bars where he belongs." As an afterthought, she added, "You're sure that this Brixton man, this private investigator, had nothing to do with it?"

"Positive," Smith said through a reassuring smile.

"I heard on the TV that he's an unsavory sort," she said.

Smith said, "He's a very good private investigator, Mrs. Morrison, and an upstanding individual."

Once in the car Borgeldt said, "You call Brixton an upstanding individual, Mac?"

"I sure do."

"He always seems to create trouble," Borgeldt said.

As they returned to the District, Smith thumbed through the pages in Morrison's appointment book. "Look at this," he said.

Borgeldt took the book and looked at what had captured Smith's interest. "Looks like he had another meeting with Alard, days earlier."

Smith went through a mental calculation. "If I'm not mistaken this meeting with Alard precedes the murder of Dr. King in Papua New Guinea and the theft of his research."

"I wouldn't know about that," said Borgeldt as Smith noted the date and time on the back of a business card. He continued flipping through the pages until another entry stopped him. It was a notation that Morrison was scheduled to have dinner with Waksit.

"Interesting," Smith said.

"What is?"

Mac pointed out the entry. "Waksit worked for that doctor who was murdered on Papua New Guinea. Annabel and I are friends with the doctor's daughter, Jayla King. Waksit claims that the doctor willed him the results of his research into finding a better pain medication."

"Did he? Will him the research?"

"Jayla finds it hard to believe. I wonder if Waksit was meeting with Morrison to try and sell the research."

"You'd have to ask him."

"I hope I have the opportunity someday. Let's talk about Alard," Smith said. "When I raised his name the last time we were together I had the feeling that it struck a nerve."

Borgeldt, who'd been looking out the window, turned to Smith and said, "You seem to know about him, Mac."

Smith explained how Brixton had learned about Alard through Will Sayers and had shared what he knew. He finished by saying, "Alard evidently met with Morrison the day before he was shot and killed, at least according to what Morrison had written in his appointment book."

Borgeldt finished the thought. "As a result of that meeting Alard probably knew where and when Brixton and Morrison would be meeting."

Smith picked up the thread: "And Alard possibly knew that Morrison would be carrying thousands of dollars to buy off Robert." Smith's brief laugh was an editorial comment. "Fat chance buying off Robert Brixton," he said.

"The Justice Department is investigating Alard Associates," Borgeldt said matter-of-factly.

"Oh?"

"Hired hands," Borgeldt replied, "sort of a quasi–employment agency that takes on jobs too dirty for decent folks. They started in Iraq and Afghanistan but were split off from a larger independent contractor. Justice has evidence that Alard and the people he represents have been involved in assassination attempts here in the States and overseas."

"Nice folks," said Smith. "How far has Justice gotten in its investigation?"

"I'll know more this afternoon. I have a meeting at Justice at five. I'll bring to the meeting the possible connection between Alard Associates and Morrison's murder. This is all between us, of course."

"Of course. Thanks for sharing it with me."

"You've shared plenty with me in the past, Mac. Tit for tat as they say. What's on your schedule for the rest of the day?"

"I'll check in on how Robert is doing, and I have a meeting with a new client. I hope Robert gets back on his feet soon. I need him on this one."

Smith retrieved his car from where he'd parked at police headquarters and drove to his office where Brixton's receptionist, Mrs. Warden, asked after Brixton.

"I'm just about to call and find out," Smith said as he settled behind his desk and picked up the phone. His first call was to the hospital and he learned that Brixton had been released earlier that day. He tried Brixton's number at the apartment and reached his answering machine. "Robert must be resting and is letting the machine take his calls," he told Mrs. Warden. "I'm sure he's fine."

35

Brixton was fine aside from his head still aching, and one cheek looking as though it had been sandblasted. He'd assured Flo, who'd brought him home from the hospital, that he would take it easy for the rest of the day. He hadn't been lying when he'd made that pledge to her. He intended to camp in front of the TV and let time heal his wounds.

But after she left for Flo's Fashions in Georgetown, he found himself pacing the apartment. A TV remote truck was parked on the street in front of the building, and a couple of print reporters milled around, drinking coffee and looking bored.

He rapidly flipped through the TV channels, pausing at newscasts in which the Morrison murder had slid from the lead story to third place behind a trip the president had taken to the Middle East, and a terrorist attack in Iraq that had taken the lives of four Americans. In one of the reports on the Morrison murder Superintendent of Detectives Zeke Borgeldt held an impromptu and brief press conference. At its conclusion a reporter asked about Brixton's role in the shooting.

"Mr. Brixton has not been charged in this incident," Borgeldt replied. "He was attacked by the individual who shot Mr. Morrison and who used Mr. Brixton's handgun in the shooting."

Borgeldt's statement buoyed Brixton's spirits, but not for long. Along with being restless he was hungry and considered going to a local bar for a sandwich and beer. But he wasn't eager to have anyone see his face with its little red dots and wonder whether he had a communicable disease. But there was always a drive-in. The few media types outside the building wouldn't pose a problem. He knew from a previous experience when the media had hounded him—dozens of them had camped outside the building after his daughter had been killed in the outdoor café bombing and he'd shot a senator's son who'd been with the terrorist bomber—that he could evade them by driving away from his underground parking spot that came with the apartment lease. After pondering how angry Flo would be if he went back on his word about staying put (he had it all figured out—she'd never know he'd left as long as he returned before she did; the answering machine would take her calls and she would assume he was sleeping), he slipped on a sport jacket over his black T-shirt, took a final peek at whoever lay in wait for him on the street, and left the apartment, ignoring the ringing phone as he got into the elevator and rode it down to the parking level where he got into his recently purchased used white Subaru, drove from the garage, and gunned it in a direction away from the media.

He pulled into a drive-through line at a McDonald's and ordered a Big Mac, fries, and a vanilla shake, which he consumed while parked at a mini-mall. His hunger sated, and after depositing the wrappers and cup in a refuse can—Brixton was meticulous about keeping the interior of his car clean—he drove to Nikki Dorence's apartment building.

Jayla King's problem with Eugene Waksit had dominated his thinking while eating lunch and he thought that another pass at spotting Waksit would be a productive

way to spend the next hour. He knew that he should
check in with Mac Smith and Will Sayers but preferred,
at least for that moment, to be alone.

He'd taken magazines with him when leaving the apartment and browsed them while simultaneously keeping
an eye on the entrance to Nikki Dorence's building from
where he'd parked across the street. He hadn't been there
for more than twenty minutes when a man emerged.
Brixton narrowed his eyes and took in the man, then
looked at the photo that Jayla had given him. No question about it. It was Eugene Waksit.

Waksit had his carry-on suitcase and briefcase with
him as he went to the curb and looked for a taxi. Brixton felt adrenaline flow as he started his car and waited
for a cab to show up. It did a few minutes later. Waksit
got in the back and the taxi drove off. Brixton executed
an illegal U-turn and fell in behind. He surmised that
Waksit was going to the airport considering he had luggage with him, but the direction the cab took ruled that
out, either that or the driver had no idea where he was
going. Brixton followed the cab as it made its way up
Georgia Avenue past Howard University and the Walter
Reed Medical Center, and crossed into Maryland. Once
in Silver Spring it navigated local traffic until pulling up in
front of a Days Inn on Thirteenth Street.

Brixton found a parking space that afforded him a
view of the hotel and watched as Waksit got out of the
taxi, paid the driver, and disappeared into the building.
Brixton's mind went into gear and he considered his possibilities. He could sit there and wait for Waksit to
emerge, but that could take hours. He could go into the
hotel and linger in the lobby, which was no better than
sitting in the car.

He decided that there was nothing to be gained by
staying. He didn't have a reason for confronting Waksit,
although he wished he did. He didn't like the guy based
upon what Jayla had said about him, and there was the
possibility that he'd murdered her father and stolen his

research. The e-mail on Jayla's computer indicated that officials back in Papua New Guinea wanted to question Waksit in the King murder; the Washington PD would be interested in where to find him. Jayla, too, would want to be informed of his whereabouts. A call to Mac Smith would accomplish both needs.

"Hi, Mac, it's Robert."

"Hello soldier. Feeling better?"

"A little."

"I left a message for you but I assumed you were resting."

"Not exactly. I'm sitting in my car in Silver Spring."

"Oh? Why?" The hint of exasperation in Smith's voice summed up what he was thinking.

"I got antsy hanging around the apartment so I took a ride, got me some fast food, and picked up where I left off the other day, looking for Jayla's old pal from PNG, Mr. Eugene Waksit."

"You found him?"

"Yeah, I did. He was staying with a friend from PNG but he left there and checked in to the Days Inn on Thirteenth Street in Silver Spring. I thought you might want to let Jayla know, and Zeke Borgeldt, too. The cops back in PNG will be interested in talking with him."

"How did you locate him?" Smith asked.

"A trade secret, Mac."

"Superior investigatory technique?"

"Exactly. Do me a favor. Flo assumes I'm resting at home. I want to get back before she returns from the shop. I never left the apartment. Right?"

"Right, Robert."

"I'll see you in the morning."

"Take your time."

"I did. Overnight in that lousy hospital bed was all the time I needed. Ciao!"

36

Smith had been huddled with his new clients when Brixton called. He took the call in his outer office, after which he returned to the meeting, which lasted another two hours. He spent part of the time assuring his clients, four gray-suited titans-of-industry types, that his private investigator would join them in subsequent meetings. When the meeting finally broke up Smith picked up the phone and called Zeke Borgeldt.

"I'm calling to pay back what you shared with me," Smith told the superintendent of detectives.

"You're an honorable man, Mackensie Smith. I'm listening."

He told Borgeldt of Brixton's call informing him that the investigator had traced Eugene Waksit to a Days Inn on Thirteenth Street in Silver Spring, Maryland.

"Why should that interest me?" Borgeldt asked.

"The authorities back in Papua New Guinea are looking to question Waksit about the murder of a physician there, the one I told you about."

"I haven't seen any queries from New Guinea," Borgeldt said, "but that doesn't mean one hasn't come through. Those kinds of requests tend to get lost in the shuffle."

"Well," said Smith, "if you do run across it you know where to find the person of interest."

"Thanks, Mac. I'll check it out."

Smith's next call was to Jayla King at Renewal Pharmaceuticals.

"Sorry, but she's just left," Smith was told.

"Thanks. I'll try her at home."

He didn't have any better luck reaching her there. He considered leaving a message about Brixton having located Waksit but decided it would be better to tell her in person. He busied himself with myriad legal matters that had been piling up until he took a break at six and called Annabel at her gallery in Georgetown, where she was in the process of ending her day. He told her of Brixton's call.

"Does Jayla know?" Annabel asked.

"No. I didn't want to leave it on her machine. I'll call later after she gets home. What are we doing for dinner?"

"Anything simple that's in the freezer. I'm beat. How's Robert?"

He laughed as he told her how Brixton had left the apartment without Flo's knowledge, and that it was to remain a secret. "Hopefully he got home before she did," he said.

Another call came in and Mac signed off with, "Whatever strikes your fancy in the freezer is fine with me. See you in a few hours."

The other caller was journalist Will Sayers.

"Have you been in touch with Brixton?" Sayers asked.

"As a matter of fact I have," Smith said.

"How's he doing?"

"He's doing fine," said Smith. "What's new with you?"

"I've left messages on his infernal answering machine."

"He must be sleeping."

"Yeah, I suppose that's it. Have you heard anything new about the Morrison murder?"

Smith didn't mention that he'd accompanied Borgeldt to interview Morrison's widow.

"I've been thinking about it all day, Mac," Sayers said. "Whoever shot Morrison didn't need to if robbery was the motive."

"I don't follow," Smith said.

"Morrison had twenty grand to give Robert as a bribe to stop digging into Senator Gillespie's past."

"I know. According to Robert that's precisely what Morrison intended."

"But why was Morrison shot? And why would the shooter take Robert's gun and use it for the murder? If whoever planned it thought that by using Robert's gun he would take the rap for it he's an idiot. But I keep coming back to the reason that Morrison was gunned down. Somebody wanted him dead."

"Why?" Smith asked.

"Because he knew something that the shooter, or whoever sent him, didn't want known. Morrison was behind the murder of that doctor in PNG. He—"

"That's supposition on your part," Smith said, unsure of how much to share with the journalist.

"And Robert's suppositions have always been pretty damn good, Mac. The thug who killed that native who tended King's plot of land worked for Alard Associates. You know about them."

"Yes. I also know that the same thug committed suicide, hanged himself."

"Whoa. Where did you hear that?"

"From my contact in PNG."

"I need to get ahold of Robert," Sayers said.

"I'm sure he'll wake up and return your call, Will. When I talk to him I'll pass along that you want to speak with him."

"Thanks. Before I get off let me give you a heads-up. I'm going with a story about Morrison and his involvement with Senator Gillespie and the abortion in Georgia."

"You have enough hard evidence to avoid a lawsuit?" Smith asked.

"Yeah, I think so. If not you'll be the first lawyer I'll call. Thanks again."

Don't do me any favors, Smith said to himself.

Smith arrived home a little after seven, fifteen minutes after Annabel. She pulled out two frozen pieces of salmon and the makings of a salad while he mixed drinks to enjoy on the balcony. He recounted the highlights of his day—the interview of Peggy Sue Morrison, the discovery of Morrison's appointment book that mentioned *two* meetings with Alard, and expanded on Brixton's tracking of Eugene Waksit and his plea that Flo not know he'd left the apartment.

Annabel laughed. "Tough guy Robert Brixton is afraid that Flo will find out that he left. Nice to see that he's afraid of *somebody*."

"I promised him that we'd keep his secret."

"My lips are sealed."

Mac stood. "I forgot," he said. "I have to let Jayla know that Robert found Waksit. Be right back."

Jayla answered on the first ring.

"It's Mac Smith," he said. "Hope I'm not disturbing your dinner."

"Not at all," she said. "I'm waiting for a guest to arrive. You met him, Nate Cousins."

"Yes, of course. Give him our best. Jayla, I received a call earlier today from Robert Brixton. He's located Eugene Waksit."

Her silence said volumes.

"He found him at a Days Inn in Silver Spring, Maryland."

"How? I mean, how did he discover where he was?"

Smith's easy laugh diffused the palpable tension on her end. "Annabel and I often ask how Robert does anything. Suffice it to say he succeeded."

"Did he go to that woman's house?" she asked.

"What woman?"

"Nikki Dorence. She works here at the PNG embassy. Eugene dated her for a short time back in Australia."

"I don't have an answer to that Jayla. I just thought that you'd want to know."

"Thank you, Mac," she said, her voice reflecting her anxiety.

"I also informed the D.C. police where he was. They may want to contact him regarding the interest the PNG police have in questioning him about your dad's murder."

Smith heard a buzzer on her end.

"Have to run," she said. "Nate is here. Thanks again."

"Stay in touch," Mac said, "and be safe."

He rejoined Annabel on the balcony. "I told Jayla about Robert finding Waksit."

"Do you think she's in any danger?" Annabel asked.

"I don't know. I'm glad that she had her locks changed. Waksit seems to want to establish some sort of link to her. Entering her apartment the way he did doesn't bode well, and there's the big question of whether he played a part in her father's murder."

Annabel wrapped her arms about herself. "How terrifying to have someone like that hovering over you." She came forward in her chair and grabbed his hand. "Mac, shouldn't the police know about him?"

"They already do," he said. "I called Zeke this afternoon and told him."

"Will they pick up him up? You'd mentioned that the police back in Papua New Guinea want to question him about the murder."

"Zeke hadn't heard anything about it but he's checking on it."

They enjoyed the salmon and a salad, and returned to the balcony for coffee and after-dinner drinks.

"I'm really worried about Jayla," Annabel said.

"Hopefully the police will make contact with him—provided he *stays* at that motel—and it'll be resolved. When I called Jayla she was entertaining that young fellow, Nate Cousins."

"A budding romance in the offing?"

"Maybe. I liked him."

"So did I."

While the Smiths settled in for a quiet night of reading, Jayla King and Nate Cousins sat on her small balcony awaiting the delivery of their dinner from an Italian restaurant a few blocks away—manicotti, salads, and crunchy Italian bread—accompanied by a red wine that Cousins had brought. Jayla had set the table with her best pale yellow linen tablecloth and silverware her father had given her that once belonged to her mother. Two slender white candles cast a warm glow over everything.

They toasted each other.

"Mr. Brixton found Eugene," Jayla said.

"What? He did? Where is he?"

"At a Days Inn in Silver Spring."

"Did he talk to him?"

"No, I don't think so."

"How did he find him?"

"I don't know. Mac Smith called me earlier. I was on the phone with him when you arrived."

"That's—well, that's incredible. I'd promised that I'd look for him but—well, I really didn't know how to do it. Mr. Brixton must be a good investigator."

"I told him about a woman here in Washington who used to date Eugene. She works for the PNG embassy. I know that Mr. Brixton was going to look for Eugene there in case he was staying with her. Maybe he was."

Cousins sat back and frowned. "What are you going to do?" he asked.

"I don't know what to do."

"The police ought to arrest him."

"For what?"

"For breaking into your apartment for openers."

"He had a key, Nate. Mr. Brixton said the police wouldn't be interested. I've changed the lock."

"He has your father's research."

"I know. He claims my father willed it to him, which is a lie."

"But you have another copy."

"Not the actual results, not the charts and day-by-day notations. Mine is more of a letter to me. But you already know that. Have you finished reading it and decided what I should do with it?"

"I've been swamped, Jayla, running from one meeting to another. I need another day or two."

His response didn't please her but she let it go, asking instead, "How was your meeting with Walt Milkin?"

His dismissive laugh didn't strike her as genuine.

"Just another meeting," he said. "You know how Walt likes to pontificate."

Cousins's meeting with the CEO of Renewal Pharmaceuticals that afternoon had started off pleasant, but soon turned tense.

"How are things?" Cousins asked after settling in a chair across the desk from Milkin. The briefcase he'd brought with him that contained Jayla's father's letter to her in which he laid out his research results in narrative form sat at his feet.

"Things could be better," Milkin said, touching his white mane with his fingertips as though to assure that it was still there. His tan testified to having been on a brief vacation in the Bahamas. "The government is sticking its nose into our business like never before."

"I've been reading those guidelines from the FDA," Cousins said. "It seems to me that their proposed changes in law will only further delay the introduction of new drugs to the marketplace."

"You're damn right, Nate. The way I see it we have to introduce drugs that are not only easier to formulate, but that stem from natural ingredients without the potential of side effects."

"You're right, Walt. How can I help? I might be able to place an op-ed piece by you in some newspapers and—"

"I think it's time we had a candid conversation, Nate."

Cousins didn't like Milkin's tone. "All right," he said.

"You were going to locate this guy who worked closely with Dr. King in PNG, Eugene Waksit."

Cousins started to respond but Milkin cut him off.

"To lay it on the line, Nate, we need a new and profitable drug here at Renewal, one that will stand out because of its uniqueness, a departure from the usual run of pain relievers. As you know I've been privy to industry talk about what King was working on when he died. Obviously, what he came up with is of interest to me. The problem is that we don't have any hard evidence of the efficacy of the drug he was developing using homegrown plant life. If we had documentation of his work up until his demise, we could take it a step further, refine it, stand the pharmaceutical industry on its ear."

"I understand all that," said Cousins, "but as you've heard from others in the industry his work was primitive, probably poorly documented, hardly the sort of research that would please a major pharma or the FDA."

"Since when are you a scientist?" Milkin asked.

"I'm not. It's just that—"

"What about your relationship with King's daughter, Jayla? That was supposed to lead us to Waksit and to King's research."

Cousins hoped that his growing pique wasn't evident in what he said, or in his body language. He shifted in his chair, crossing one leg over the other and reversing them. He didn't agree with Milkin that his relationship with Jayla King had been solely for the purpose of wheedling out of her the results of her father's work. Yes, he'd approached her with that in mind, but their relationship had rapidly developed into something far more meaningful.

At the same time he respected Milkin's business needs:

he headed a company that depended upon developing breakthrough drugs potentially worth billions, and had his stockholders to answer to. Too, Cousins's livelihood depended upon executives like Walt Milkin. At their last meeting Milkin had tossed into the conversation that Cousins's agency contract with Renewal was up for review. If he'd meant it to be a veiled threat, he'd succeeded.

Milkin raised the agency review again.

"I'll be seeing Jayla, Ms. King, tonight," he told the CEO. "I'll urge her to share with you whatever her father left her regarding his research. There's a private investigator looking for Mr. Waksit. Ms. King certainly knows more about that than I do. That's all I can do, Walt. I'll give it my best."

"Yes, I'm sure you will, Nate. Let me add this. If you deliver this information, I'll see to it that not only will your agency contract be renewed, there'll be a nice bonus in it for you."

"I appreciate that," Cousins said, picking up his briefcase. He shook Milkin's hand and left the office, stopped in the hallway, and reflected on what had just occurred.

The briefcase contained everything that Jayla had entrusted him with. There was a moment when he'd considered handing it to Milkin, thus becoming the knight in shining armor, the fair-haired boy who'd delivered the goods.

But something had kept him from doing it. It wasn't that he'd decided to never share it with Milkin. But he knew that once he did his relationship with Jayla was finished.

The food arrived. Cousins paid the delivery boy and tipped him generously. Jayla put the food into serving dishes and they sat at her small dining room table in front of the sliding glass doors to her balcony. They said little as they ate, commenting on the food, and discussing the latest political gossip reported by the media. Jayla had put a jazz CD on her stereo, a recording by the guitarist Gene Bertoncini with strings, the lush sounds providing a peaceful background to what they were saying—and thinking.

"I know you're disappointed in me for not having come up with ideas about your father's research," Cousins said.

"Disappointed? No, Nate, not at all. Mac Smith reviewed my employment contract with Renewal."

"I'm glad he did. I raised it with you as a possible problem if you turned over your father's work to them."

"I remember. After you suggested that I review the contract I gave it to Mac."

"And?"

"He feels that it's pretty much ironclad. If Renewal is given the research, I lose it. Just that simple."

He finished the last of his manicotti. "It's best you know that," he said. "The problem is that Waksit is probably negotiating with a pharmaceutical company as we speak. He may not have the legal right to your father's work but legalities never stood in the way of guys like him, or some pharmaceutical companies for that matter. It's a cutthroat business, Jayla."

She fell silent.

"Are you worried about Waksit?" he asked.

"Of course."

"Do you want me to call him?"

"No, no, that wouldn't help anything. I was thinking that maybe Mr. Brixton should contact him, or Mac Smith. Probably Mac Smith. Having a call from a lawyer might bring him to his senses."

"He hasn't tried to make contact with you aside from coming into your apartment?"

She shook her head. "Maybe *I* should call him," she said.

"Absolutely not! Look, Jayla, the best approach is for you to try and cut a deal with Walt Milkin."

"What sort of deal?"

"Some sort of bonus if you turn over your father's research to him. I know that Renewal isn't in the top tier of pharmas, but a bird in hand, as they say. I'm sure that Mac Smith would be happy to represent you in forging an agreement that would benefit both you and Renewal. Let's face it, Jayla, there's always the possibility that what your father came up with in his lab doesn't work."

Her eyes flared. "It *did* work," she said. "He said it did."

"I know, I know," Cousins said, "but he was working with a small patient population and without classic double-blind procedures. Just a thought, Jayla, something for you to chew on."

"I'll chew on it," she said angrily. "Nate, I'd like to have my father's materials back."

"Sure. Give me another day to digest what's there and I'll deliver it to you." His eyes went across the room to his briefcase but he said nothing about it.

When the night commenced it was assumed by both Jayla and Nate that it would end with them in bed making love. But while there wasn't an overt sense of tension, it was present nonetheless, wafting in the air. He helped clear the table, rinsed dishes as she handed them to him, and wadded up the containers the meal had come in and deposited them in the trash.

"I suppose I'd better go," he said.

He picked up his briefcase and left.

Eugene Waksit sat in a rented car across the street from Jayla's building and saw Cousins leave the building, get in his car, and drive away. Waksit fell in behind and followed Cousins to where he pulled into the underground garage at his apartment building.

He returned to Jayla's building, drew a deep breath, removed his cell phone from his pocket, and pressed the key activating a stored number.

"Jayla?" he said when she answered. "It's me, Eugene, a blast from the past."

37

B rixton and Flo spent a quiet night at home, although it hadn't started out as domestic bliss.

He'd been sitting in front of the TV watching a newscast when she walked through the door after a day at Flo's Fashions. He got up from his chair and kissed her.

"I found that guy Waksit," Brixton said.

"Who?"

"Eugene Waksit, the guy who used to work with Jayla King's father in Papua New Guinea, the one she's afraid of."

"How did you manage that?"

He explained how he'd sat outside the apartment building where Waksit's former girlfriend from PNG lived and spotted him leaving. "He took a cab to Silver Spring," he elaborated. "I followed him. He's staying at a Days Inn there. I called Mac Smith and told him. He said he'd let Jayla know."

"You're incorrigible," she said, smiling and shaking her head.

"Difficult but adorable," he said.

* * *

When Brixton had arrived home late that afternoon he'd returned a few calls including three from Will Sayers.

"How are you?" Sayers asked in his usual direct way.

"Couldn't be better. How are you?"

"Couldn't be better. Nice of you to return my calls."

"I just got out of the hospital. Remember? I've been recuperating."

"You sound all right."

"Why have you been calling, Will?"

"To tell you that I filed a story this afternoon with my esteemed newspaper back in Savannah."

"Good for you." The pulsating headache that had plagued Brixton on and off all day was on again.

"It's the Gillespie abortion story," Sayers said, "including Morrison's role in it."

"That's pretty gutsy, isn't it?"

"Not really. I've managed to obtain some hard information from a friendly source in Georgia that adds weight to the story. Besides, Morrison is dead. Dead men can't sue."

"What about Morrison's wife?"

"The piece doesn't defame her, unless you want to consider her an idiot for marrying the likes of Eric Morrison."

"And the senator?"

"Oh. Gillespie will huff and puff and claim media bias, but I have the goods. Yes indeed, I do have the goods on him. I contacted his office to let them know that the article will be running, and in search of a comment from the senator. His press aide, whose name escapes me for good reason, declined."

"Congratulations."

"Thank you. I humbly accept your offer of a celebratory drink."

"I didn't make an offer."

"I'm patient. Speaking of Morrison, what do you hear

from your friend, the blond former movie actress, Ms. Silver?"

"Nothing."

"I take it that Lady Flo is within earshot."

"I have to go. I have a headache."

"Don't let me get in the way of your recovery. By the way, I will want to do a feature on your involvement in Morrison's murder. You were, after all, a treasured member of Savannah's law enforcement agency."

"And maybe I'll sue for defamation. I'm not dead yet. I'll buy you that drink when I'm feeling up to it."

Will Sayers's call to the Senate offices of Ronald Gillespie had its intended effect. The press aide who'd taken the call immediately called his boss out of a meeting to deliver the bad news.

"What's the damn article say?" Gillespie demanded.

"I don't know, sir."

"Why didn't you get ahold of it?"

"I asked to see it but the guy refused, laughed off my request. All he said was that he had evidence that you had—"

"I had *what*?"

"Well, sir, the journalist said that he had evidence that you had gotten a young lady pregnant back in Georgia and that the lobbyist, Eric Morrison, had paid for an abortion on your behalf, sir."

"You get back to this whore who calls himself a journalist and tell him that I'll sue him and the rag he writes for. I'll bury the bastards. You hear me? Give him that message."

"Ah, sir, maybe it would carry more weight if you made that call. I have the number and—"

With that, Gillespie, his face crimson, stormed from the conference room, went to his office, and slammed the door with a bang. The meeting he'd been called from was with a lobbying group in competition with Morrison Associates that was pushing hard to land the Pharmaceutical Association of America account. Gillespie had promised them that he would personally lend his weight with PAA to see that the Morrison agency was dropped and the new group hired.

Morrison's death had not been viewed with sadness by the senior senator from Georgia. Morrison had turned out to be a magnet for trouble, something Gillespie had seen coming and had grappled with ever since the private investigator Robert Brixton had entered the picture. As far as Gillespie was concerned Morrison was weak, someone who would fold under pressure. What was he doing meeting Brixton in the middle of the night and carrying $20,000? What had he told Brixton before he was shot? And who shot him? Why? What had he left behind that would link him to the abortion? He'd put too much faith in Morrison to handle things. Brixton was the one who should have died. He was still out there digging into what was none of his business. And what about this reporter, Sayers? He was friends with Brixton; they'd worked together to put together the newspaper article that was due to run.

While all these questions and ruminations dominated his thoughts, a different problem that had nothing to do with Morrison or Brixton loomed large.

Rebecca!

He knew that he could ride out any political fallout from whatever this journalist had written about an unfortunate situation that happened years ago. The public shared his negative view of the media. Whatever was alleged in the article could be turned back on his political opponents in Georgia. He, United States Senator Ronald Gillespie, had been a champion of his home state, had been responsible for millions of federal dollars funneled to state projects. He was beloved back home, a tried-and-true son of the Old South who shared the electorate's distrust of big government and weak-kneed liberal values.

Rebecca!

Their May-September marriage was shaky to begin with. She'd recently expressed her doubts about having married a senior citizen who seemed more interested in his political fortunes than in her. He wasn't sure how to deal with this once the article appeared and the media wolves started harassing her for comment. Maybe it was time to get away. The new lobbying group assured him that they were willing and able to satisfy him in whatever way they could. Let them pick up the tab for a week in the Italy, or Paris. Rebecca had a love affair with gay ol' Paree even though she'd never been there. That was the answer. Get out of town.

The people he'd been meeting with had returned to their offices on K Street. He reached for his phone and dialed the number there. They wanted his help in landing the PAA account?

It was time to start paying.

While the other players in this distinctly Washington game took care of their business, Jayla King paced her apartment, the phone in her hand.

"Eugene?" she said, incredulous.

"It's me all right," he said, forcing gaiety into his voice. "How in the world are you, Jayla?"

"Eugene, I—I'm surprised that you called."

"Yeah, I know, I've been a bad boy being here in Washington and never getting together. The truth is that I've been busy day and night, meeting people, getting to know my way around. But hey, enough about me. How is Jayla King?"

She didn't know how to respond.

"Caught you at a bad time?" he asked, thinking of the young man he'd seen through the window and whom he'd followed. He continued to look through the window at her pacing the living room from his parked car across the street.

"No, not at all. I'm just—well, shocked. I knew you were in Washington and wondered why you hadn't made contact."

"Like I said I've been crazy busy. Boy, this city is nothing like being in PNG, huh? Everybody's running around and making deals and doing their thing. How about you? Still with that pharmaceutical company? What's its name?"

"Renewal Pharmaceuticals."

"Right. Renewal. Coming up with some super-drug that'll cure every disease known to man?"

Her mind raced. She was talking with the man who stole her father's research and who possibly took his life. This was a man who had violated her space by entering her apartment without an invitation. This was the man—"

"I'm serious, Jayla. I think we should get together, maybe have dinner together, some nice place you go to a lot, something fancy to celebrate reconnecting. My treat. I owe you that."

"Eugene," she said, "this is all terribly sudden and I'm not sure what I want to do. I know that—well, you took my father's research papers from his lab."

"Hey, wait a minute, Jayla. I didn't take anything that didn't belong to me. Your father always said that when he died he wanted me to have those papers."

She started to argue but decided it was pointless, at least at that juncture and considering the circumstances.

"Eugene," she said, "how about we talk again sometime tomorrow, or the next day? I have a busy schedule at work and you sound busy, too."

"Why do I get the feeling that you're putting me off, Jayla?"

"No, I'm not. I'll call you. What's your number at the Days Inn in Silver Spring?"

There was silence on the other end.

"I'll call you at your hotel and—"

"How do you know where I am?" he asked.

"I—that's where you are, isn't it?"

His tone changed from upbeat to serious, all business.

"We have to meet, Jayla, about your father's research. We have an obligation to carry on his work. We can do it together, the way it should be done."

"I'll call you," she said. "What's your number at Days Inn?"

"*I'll* call *you*," he said brusquely. "Tomorrow."

The line went dead in her ear.

Shaken, she went to the door and checked that the new lock was securely fastened. She then went to the window and lowered the blinds.

Waksit cursed that she'd cut off his view and drove away.

Jayla pondered what to do. Finally, she dialed Nate Cousins at home and told him of Waksit's call. "I'm scared," she said.

"I'll be there within the hour."

38

At seven o'clock the following morning two plain-clothes detectives and a uniformed police officer from the Washington PD drove to Silver Spring and pulled up in front of the Days Inn on Thirteenth Street. Zeke Borgeldt had called the commander of the Silver Spring Third District station to alert him that some of his officers would be entering that department's domain in order to locate and detain a material witness in a murder that had taken place in Papua New Guinea. Borgeldt was given the go-ahead with the commander's added comment, "Papua New Guinea? That's on the other side of the world. Good luck."

The officers had been briefed by Borgeldt before heading for Silver Spring. Eugene Waksit wasn't a suspect in the murder investigation, but the authorities there wanted to further question him as part of their ongoing investigation. The officers were to inform Waksit of that interest and "suggest" that he accompany them to headquarters where a Skype setup could be arranged for long-distance questioning. The officers found their assignment to be unusual but didn't question it. One of the detectives had a favorite restaurant in Silver Spring where he claimed the pancakes were the best in the area.

They could stop in there for breakfast if Waksit declined to accompany them back to headquarters.

The uniformed cop waited in the marked patrol car while the detectives entered the hotel, went to the front desk, and presented their identification.

"We're here to speak with a guest of the hotel," he said.

The desk clerk, a fresh-faced young man, immediately got off the stool on which he was sitting and said, "Yes, sir. Who is the guest?"

"His name is Eugene Waksit. He checked in yesterday. He's from Papua New Guinea."

"Where is that?"

"It doesn't matter. What room is he in?"

"I'll look it up for you right now, sir."

It took only a few seconds for the clerk to have an answer for them. "He checked out last night," he said apologetically.

"A quick stay, huh?" one of the detectives said. "He only checked in yesterday."

"I wasn't here when he left," the clerk said. "I work days. Maybe he had a family emergency. One of the night clerks left a note that he'd complained about having to pay for only a few hours here, but the policy is—"

"Was he alone?"

"Ah, I believe so. I mean, the record indicates that he checked in alone. But sometimes . . ." His smile was boyish.

"Do you know where he went after checking out?"

The clerk shook his head. "No, sir."

"He didn't make a reservation at another Days Inn in the area?"

He checked his computer screen. "No, sir. If he did we have no record of it."

They thanked him, and twenty minutes later enjoyed banana pancakes and bacon.

* * *

Cops from the District weren't the only ones interested in Eugene Waksit that morning.

Jayla and Nate Cousins sat at her breakfast table after a sleepless night.

"You should call the police," he insisted, something he'd been urging since arriving.

"And tell them what, that an old friend from home who worked for my father wants to get together while he's here in Washington?"

"It's harassment, Jayla. He's stalking you."

She shook her head to clear it.

"Look," Cousins pressed, "he stole your father's research and must be here in D.C. trying to sell it. I've told you how interested Walt Milkin is in seeing what your father developed. Others will be interested, too. But more than that, Jayla, chances are he killed your father, *murdered* him for God's sake."

"He wants us to have dinner to discuss working together to find an outlet for Dad's work."

Cousins slapped his hand on the table, causing their cups to rattle in their saucers. "Wake up, Jayla!" he said. "Waksit is a bad guy who's already killed once and won't hesitate to kill again. Go to dinner with him? You'll be lucky to come away from it alive."

"I think I should call Mac Smith," she said. She wanted to defuse Cousins's frustration but her suggestion only fueled it.

"What can *he* do?" Cousins asked, struggling to moderate his tone. "He's a lawyer, not a cop."

"He works with Robert Brixton."

"So what? Brixton's not a cop."

"He was. He's also been a friend. He's the one who found where Eugene is staying. When Mac called he said that he'd told his friend at the police department, a chief of detectives, where they could find Eugene. Maybe they'll go and question him."

"That's great, but in the meantime he's made contact with you, knows where you live, even had the nerve to enter your apartment without your permission. He's dangerous, Jayla. You have to accept that."

She dialed Mac Smith's number at the Watergate.

"Mac, it's Jayla King. Hope I'm not calling too early."

"We've been up for an hour. How are you?"

"Not good, Mac. I'm at my apartment with Nate Cousins. Eugene Waksit called me last night."

"Oh?"

"It came out of the blue. He—he wants to get together with me."

"Why?"

"To talk about my father's research. He seems to think that we can work together to find a pharmaceutical company that would be interested in it."

Mac hesitated before saying, "Jayla, I certainly don't want to be telling you what to do, but it's my sense that you're better off staying away from Mr. Waksit. There's something that I've neglected to mention to you. I had the opportunity to go through Eric Morrison's appointment book. He's the lobbyist who was recently killed. It seems that Morrison met with Waksit before his death."

Mac said, "I think it's best that you avoid Waksit. There's no telling how he might fit into the Morrison murder."

What he said made sense to her. At the same time she knew that she couldn't simply turn off her thoughts about Waksit and what she was desperate to know about the role he might have played in her father's death.

"I know you're right, Mac, and I appreciate the advice."

"You say that Cousins is with you."

"Yes. I called him after I heard from Eugene. He came right over."

"I'm glad that he's there for you. Just let Annabel and me know if there's anything we can do."

"I will. I really appreciate it. How is Mr. Brixton?"

Smith laughed. "Robert is fine. It'll take more than a hit on his hard head to put him out of commission."

"What did he have to say?" Cousins asked after she got off the phone.

"He thinks I should stay away from Eugene."

"What I've been saying to you all along."

"I know, Nate, I know." She checked the wall clock. "I have to get ready for work. Thank you for being here for me. I never should have called. I guess I panicked."

"And for good reason. I have to get to the office, too. Promise me you'll call if you hear from him again."

She walked him to the door where he embraced and kissed her.

"I love you, Jayla," he said.

Her words expressing the same sentiment almost came out but didn't. She locked the door behind him, drew a breath, and headed for the shower.

39

When Smith got off the phone with Jayla he called Brixton.

"How are you feeling?" he asked.

"Pretty good, Mac. Nothing like a good night's sleep. What's up?"

"I'd like to get together this morning to go over what came out of the meeting with our new client."

Our new client. Among many things Brixton admired about the attorney was his lack of ego. *Our* new client. Typical of the way Mackensie Smith saw things.

"Sounds like a plan to me," Brixton said. "Eleven?"

"Earlier? I just got off the phone with Jayla King. Our friend Mr. Waksit called her last night. She's shaken. I have some thoughts about that to run by you, too."

"I have an appointment at ten, Mac. I can cancel it but—"

"No need for that. Eleven will be fine."

Brixton realized that at some point he should share with Smith that he was seeing a shrink. He knew, but didn't necessarily agree, that being embarrassed at seeking help from a psychologist was uncalled for, yet he suffered discomfort with the concept. He had a ten o'clock appointment with Dr. Fowler and, as had often been the case, he looked forward to it. Maybe it was Flo's satisfaction that he was seeing Fowler that influenced his positive attitude. But the *why* really didn't matter. That he enjoyed the forty-five-minute sessions with the psychologist was good enough.

The wounds on his cheek had faded to some extent; he no longer looked like a character from a Wes Craven horror film, and his headache had abated, just an occasional pulsation in his temple to remind him what had caused it.

"Don't forget your appointment with Dr. Fowler," Flo reminded him as she prepared to leave the apartment for Flo's Fashions.

"I'll be there," he assured her.

She was no sooner out the door than Will Sayers called.

"Well, what do you think?" he asked Brixton.

"About what?"

"About the piece on Senator Gillespie. I e-mailed it to you."

"I haven't looked at my computer in days."

"The original Neanderthal," Sayers said. "Get with it, Robert. I'll wait while you pull it up."

Brixton booted up the computer and brought the article up on the screen. He quickly scanned it, his eyes immediately going to his name. Sayers had devoted two paragraphs to Brixton's meeting with Morrison and how Brixton had aided in researching the piece.

"You should have left me out of it," Brixton said.

"Credit where credit is due, Robert. Now, let's discuss when we can get together—and I pray it won't be long—for me to interview you about your involvement in this sordid mess. It deserves an article all its own."

"I'd just as soon that you didn't do that, Will."

"You don't want me to have to depend upon what others have written, do you? The article will be done with or without your input, and I'd much prefer to include your view of things."

"I have to run, Will. Congratulations on the article. The fur will really fly when the senator reads it."

"I'd pay anything to be there when he does."

Brixton went to the underground garage and checked whether any media had staked it out. The coast was clear, and he drove to his appointment with Dr. John Bradford Fowler.

"I see that I have a celebrity with me this morning," Fowler said.

"Don't believe everything you read about me," Brixton said.

"You're all right, Robert? That was quite a traumatic experience you went through."

"I'm feeling fine, only I debated coming here this morning."

"I can certainly understand that," Fowler said. "If you'd prefer to cut this session short we can—"

"No, no, I don't mean that. It's just that I have a busy day ahead of me, which I suppose is good. I'm not much for sitting around."

"Yes," said Fowler, "being active is good for anyone. So, tell me how this latest incident in your busy life has impacted your relationship with Ms. Combes?"

"Impacts it?" Brixton said with raised eyebrows. "Why would it?"

"I was just curious whether being involved in another high-profile incident, like the one in which you lost your daughter, influences your relationship with her—with others, too, friends, colleagues, everyday interactions."

"It doesn't help, I guess. When Janet was blown up in that terrorist bombing it really changed me, and not for the better. Flo will testify to that. And this latest mess just sours me all the more about Washington and the big shots who run it. We really should pack up and leave."

"That doesn't sound like a man of action," Fowler said, "turning and running rather than making it work for you."

Brixton elaborated on his role in exposing Senator

Gillespie's sexual escapade in Georgia, and how he had tracked down Eugene Waksit on Jayla King's behalf.

"Is this Waksit fellow a danger to Ms. King?"

"I think he is. He might have murdered her father back in Papua New Guinea."

"It sounds more like a police matter than something that you should take on."

"My friend Mac Smith, the lawyer, has told the cops where to find Waksit. I'm finished with it, the same way I'm finished with anything to do with that sleazeball Senator Gillespie and the lobbyist who paid for the abortion. Mac Smith has a new, high-paying client and I'll be working on it with him. It'll be nice to get back to normal."

"So things are working out?"

"Yeah, but look, Dr. Fowler, maybe it's time we end these sessions. Not that they haven't been helpful, but like I said it's time for me to get back to normal."

Fowler smiled. "I think that you're probably right, Robert. I consider it a privilege having met you, and know that if you ever feel the need to talk with me again I'll always be available. Please give my best to Ms. Combes."

Brixton paid for the session and drove to his office where Mrs. Warden handed him a batch of phone slips. "Some of these people from the media can be so rude," she said.

"That must be the first thing they teach you in journalism school, Mrs. Warden, how to be rude. Sorry you had to put up with them."

He surveyed the pile of papers on his desk and would have liked to attack it, but it was time to meet with Mac Smith, who was dealing with his own stack of correspondence in need of attention.

Smith asked when Brixton entered his office, "No lingering fallout from your concussion?"

"No, I'm fine. I just came from—well, I just saw a doctor."

"That's good. The effects of a concussion can linger. Best to follow up on it."

"He's a head doctor."

"A neurologist?"

"A shrink."

"A psychiatrist?"

"A psychologist. I've been seeing him for a few weeks now, you know, to help me get over my daughter being killed the way she was. He's a nice guy. You'd like him."

"And he's helped you?"

Brixton nodded.

"That's all that counts. Let me fill you in on the situation with Jayla King. Zeke Borgeldt sent a couple of detectives to the Days Inn in Silver Spring to convince Waksit to contact the authorities back in PNG."

"Good," Brixton said.

"But he'd checked out last night."

"Checked out? He'd just checked in."

"I know. The question is why did he leave, and where did he go?"

"Something or somebody spooked him."

"He called Jayla last night."

"Maybe there's your answer. You told her where he was?"

"Yes."

"Maybe she let slip to him that she knew."

"I'll ask her."

"So he's still lurking around."

"Seems that way."

"Will Sayers's piece on Senator Gillespie ran today in *Savannah*."

Brixton sat at Smith's computer and brought up the article.

"That's a tough piece of reporting," Smith said after he'd read it over Brixton's shoulder. "I see that he mentioned Alard Associates toward the end."

Brixton looked up. "I stopped reading when I got to my name," he said as he finished the piece.

"Alard! Dr. King! Senator Gillespie!" Brixton rattled off. "Morrison was involved with all of them."

"And Eugene Waksit," Smith said. "His name was also in Morrison's appointment book. They evidently had dinner together."

"It's a shame Morrison is dead," Brixton said. "I'd love to get him one-on-one for questions. Are Zeke and his people continuing to look for him?"

"Probably not," Smith replied. "The police in PNG aren't labeling Waksit a suspect in the King murder. I have a feeling that Zeke checked out of the Days Inn in Silver Spring as a favor to me. I'm sure they have more pressing things to do."

"Jayla must be freaked out by all of this," Brixton offered.

It was one o'clock when Smith and Brixton concluded their meeting. Smith handed Brixton a check as an advance on the project and ordered in lunch, which Brixton declined. "Not hungry," he said. "I've got a lot of paperwork to catch up on. Glad to be on board with this new client, Mac. Thanks for the advance. It'll be put to good use."

He was in the midst of sorting papers into piles when Mrs. Warden informed him that Paula Silver was on the line.

"Is she? Well, I—okay, might as well take it."

"Hello Paula. I've meant to call you but—"

"You heard what happened to Eric."

"*Heard* what happened? Hey, I was there, or don't you read the papers or watch TV?"

"I talked to him before he died." She had trouble getting the words out.

"Did you? So did I. That's how we ended up meeting."

"The bastard! He was going to pay me to not write about him in my book but—" She cried.

"I'm sorry it ended this way for you. Are you still going ahead with the book?"

"You said you'd help me."

"Yeah, but—"

"I want the world to know what a lousy guy he was. It'll be a bestseller, probably be a movie, too."

How many times had people said that? Brixton wondered. He knew nothing about books and writing and publishing, but he'd heard his share of people claiming to have a bestseller when all they had was their inflated egos and a mundane story to tell.

"I'm sure you're right, Paula, but I'm really busy now and—"

"You, too," she said angrily.

"Huh?"

"Just walk away when somebody needs help."

Her words stung. He didn't have any obligation to her. At the same time he'd lied to find out what she knew about Morrison and Gillespie. Conning people to achieve a goal was a staple in a detective's bag of tricks, and Brixton had often used it without feeling guilty. But there was something about Paula that struck a nerve with him, a vulnerability that she wore on her sleeve. Despite her whiskey-fueled tough talk she was a frightened little girl in grown-up clothes, a victim of the Hollywood myth of glamour and success.

"How about I buy you a drink at the end of the day?"

"All right."

"I'll meet you at—"

"Pick me up. I would like that."

"Okay. I know where you live. Six o'clock?"

"Yes. Six o'clock."

He hung up and hoped that she'd run out of booze. She was already drunk, and he didn't look forward to being with her in that condition. He'd buy a drink, apologize for not shooting straight with her, wish her well, and sever the connection.

A bag of potato chips and two Cokes comprised lunch as Brixton waded through paperwork, and read Mac Smith's long dictated report about the new client and what was expected of him as the investigator in the case.

While his focus was on the work, his thoughts kept shifting between Jayla King, the whereabouts of Eugene Waksit, and Will Sayers's article about the senator from Georgia and what flames it would fan once the D.C. media got ahold of it. He called Flo at her shop to tell her that he was meeting someone for drinks but would swing by about eight. It was her late night at the store; with any luck customers would stop coming in by eight and she could close up earlier than the stated closing hour of nine.

"Who are you having drinks with?" she asked.

"Ah, that actress I told you about, Paula Silver."

"The one who had an affair with the lobbyist."

"Right. She's the one who gave me some information for Will Sayers about Morrison and—"

"You don't need information from her about him any longer, Robert. He's dead."

"I know, but she called and—well, I feel sorry for her."

"I have to go," Flo said, her voice cold. "Enjoy your evening."

He sat back in his desk chair and slowly shook his head. Maybe he shouldn't have made a date for drinks with Paula. Maybe he should have blown her off. But then he decided that he was entitled to have drinks with anyone he wanted. It wasn't as though he had carnal thoughts about Paula Silver. He'd taken advantage of her and the least he could do was buy her a drink to atone. What could be wrong with that?"

There was plenty wrong in the Gillespie household. The senator had told his wife, Rebecca, the previous evening that they needed to take a vacation. Pressures were piling up at the Senate and he had to get away. He'd called their travel agent and had her book a trip for the following day to Aruba.

"Tomorrow?" Rebecca had said. "I can't get ready to leave on a vacation trip tomorrow."

"I really need the break," Gillespie told her, "and it

would do you good to get away, too. I've already made the arrangements and that's that! Our flight leaves tomorrow at three from Reagan. You get yourself packed up and be ready to go. Hell, you don't need more than a couple a' bathing suits and a big floppy hat."

Now, the next morning, the phone rang as Rebecca was trying on outfits to put in her suitcase. The caller was a reporter from the *Washington Post*.

"Mrs. Gillespie?"

"Yes?"

"Kerry Brothers from the *Post*. Is your husband there?"

"No. He's at his Senate office gathering up some materials to take on our trip."

"Oh, you're taking a trip. To a nice place I hope."

"Aruba. I—why are you calling?"

"I'm calling about the article in the *Savannah Morning News* about your husband and—"

"What article?"

"I'll read you the headline," the reporter said. "'Teen Abortion Funded by Senator Gillespie.'"

Rebecca, who wore only her bra and panties, fell back on the bed. "What abortion?" she managed. "What in hell are you talking about?"

Brothers read her the first few paragraphs of the Will Sayers article. She listened quietly, breathing rapidly, furiously chewing her cheek.

"I'll try to get ahold of your husband, Mrs. Gillespie, but as long as I have you on the phone maybe you'd like to make a statement."

"I have nothing to say," she said and ended the connection.

She went to Gillespie's home office, turned on the computer, Googled the article, and read it with a combination of disgust and fury. "You bastard!" she screamed loud enough for a passerby to hear on the street. "You rotten, filthy, miserable . . ."

* * *

Will Sayers's exposé of Senator Ronald Gillespie affected another wife, too.

The piece had chronicled Eric Morrison's role in the abortion, how he had arranged for and paid the abortionist on behalf of the senior senator from Georgia. That prompted another phone call, this one to Peggy Sue Morrison, who had just met with the funeral director. She was watching him drive away when a different reporter from the *Post,* a young woman, Nita Evans, called. The reporter read portions of the piece relating to Morrison to Peggy Sue, who remained silent. When she was done reading, Peggy Sue said through clenched teeth, "My husband was a fine and decent man, Ms. Evans. He was a respected member of the lobbying industry, a man loved by everyone he worked with. How dare you slander such a man after he was gunned down by an evil, demented person? How dare you call me on the day I am arranging his funeral and spew such venom? *How dare you?*"

40

Waksit's sudden and unplanned departure from the Days Inn in Silver Spring the previous night had further unraveled him.

Deciding to call Jayla hadn't been easy, and he'd assessed her possible responses, ranging from slamming down the phone to expressing joy at hearing his voice. Neither extreme had occurred. But she had put him off, which to Waksit in his frazzled mind-set represented a cruel rejection. On top of that he'd been forced to flee the Days Inn and find another place to stay, this time a Holiday Inn in Crystal City, close to Reagan National Airport.

He sprawled on the bed and talked to himself, verbalizing his jumbled thoughts to an otherwise empty room, fingertips performing a drum roll against each other, uttering an occasional pained cry from deep inside.

The trip to Washington, D.C., was turning out to be a disaster.

He'd left Port Moresby, Papua New Guinea, with Preston King's research in his briefcase—his ticket to riches and glory. He'd made contact with Eric Morrison, who'd initially treated him shabbily but who he knew would eventually come around and see the wisdom of joining forces. Now Morrison was dead, murdered in some secluded part of the city by a madman. The news reports claimed that the private detective, Robert Brixton, had been exonerated of the killing, but Waksit didn't buy it. This Brixton probably had connections that got him off the hook. That's the way the world worked, especially in places like Washington, D.C., where connections meant everything.

He got off the bed and stood at the window watching planes take off and land. He wished that he was on one of them, abandoning the corrupt city with its fancy architecture and pretty avenues. But he couldn't leave yet, not without accomplishing what he'd come here to do. He spent the next twenty minutes mentally rewriting the unpleasant aspects of his life, something he was good at. He replayed his phone conversation with Jayla and decided that she hadn't put him off. She was just surprised to hear from him. That was it. And she was probably pleased to receive the call. After all, they went back a long way together, and had in common the work her father had done in his lab. They would make an unbeatable team if they joined forces and sold that work to the highest bidder.

But his rosy interpretations were interrupted by darker thoughts. Who was the young man he'd seen with her when he'd sat in his car and peered through her window? He decreed that it didn't matter. Waksit believed that Jayla had always found him attractive and had often flirted with him. He wouldn't have minded a roll in the sack but he'd been too smart to allow his hormones to get in the way of his close relationship with her father. Now that the father was out of the picture he would rekindle her romantic interest in him. That was the key. He would woo her before jumping into a business relationship and make her realize that he had her best interests at heart.

He checked his watch. It was a few minutes past

eleven. He opened his briefcase and took out some cash. He was about to close the case when he saw the Italian stiletto switchblade that he'd purchased upon arriving at Dulles Airport. It was tucked in a sleeve within the briefcase and he'd forgotten that it was there. He considered for a moment taking it with him, decided not to, then changed his mind and slipped the knife into his pocket. Washington was a dangerous city; he would no longer venture out into it unarmed.

He drove his rental car to Jayla's apartment building, parked in the same spot as the previous night, and looked up at her window. The blinds were open. Jayla was speaking into a phone while walking back and forth in her living room. *Who was she talking to?* Maybe that guy he'd followed the other night.

But then Nate Cousins came into view, causing Waksit to grimace and curse under his breath. *Who was this guy?*

Cousins and Jayla had gone out for dinner and returned to her apartment after it had been agreed that Cousins would spend the night. Jayla had gone to work at Renewal that day but left early. Sleep had been elusive the previous night and she'd had trouble keeping her eyes open. The nap refreshed her, enough so that she felt up to dinner with Cousins at Pearl Dive Oyster Palace on Fourteenth Street Street, N.W.

Once back in the apartment Jayla had returned a call from a colleague at Renewal who wanted to discuss the next day's work. The call completed, Cousins came to where she stood in the middle of the room and embraced her. Anger welled up in Waksit. Then Jayla closed the blinds. Ten minutes later the lights went out.

Waksit returned to the Holiday Inn and stewed about what he'd seen. He came to many conclusions before falling asleep, the final and most compelling one that he had to act quickly.

41

Jayla and Cousins woke the following morning, their naked bodies entwined. He moaned and stretched, causing her to sit up and use the sheet to cover her bare breasts.

"Good morning," he said, rubbing his eyes and joining her against the tufted headboard. "Sleep okay?"

"Yes. It felt good. You?"

"Like a log."

He watched her get up and head for the bathroom, admiring the rear view of her shapely figure. He slipped into his shorts and the pale yellow button-down shirt he'd worn the night before, went to the kitchen, and turned on her coffeemaker. She soon joined him wrapped in her terrycloth robe. She sat at a small table by the window and looked out.

He said as he retrieved two cups from a cabinet, "Hey, Jayla, is something wrong?"

"I just wonder whether I'll ever come to grips with my father's murder, and that his assistant is prowling around Washington trying to sell what he stole from him."

Cousins poured their coffee and joined her. "There's nothing you can do about your father's death, Jayla, and

Mr. Eugene Waksit will eventually leave you alone and go back home with empty hands."

"And get away with my father's murder."

"If, in fact, he did kill your father. You don't know that for certain."

Her eyes became moist, and he took her hand in his. "You've been through a lot," he said, "but the important thing is that you move ahead."

"I want to, Nate, but I feel as though I've stepped in wet cement and can't move in any direction."

He smiled and gave her hand a squeeze. "Drink your coffee. After we shower we'll grab breakfast out. I've got a busy day ahead, and I'm sure you do, too."

She remained at the table while he showered, her thoughts flitting from one thing to another.

Until receiving that fateful phone call at Flo's Fashions about her father's murder, her life been rich and rewarding. She had a good job in her chosen field, her health was good, she had many friends, and the future looked even brighter. But now . . .

"Your turn," Cousins said as he emerged from the bathroom and went into the bedroom to put on a change of clothes he'd brought with him. He heard the shower and pictured her in it. No question about it. He'd fallen head over heels in love with Jayla King. He was relieved that she hadn't asked about her father's research. He knew he had to make a decision regarding Walt Milkin's interest in it, a decision now complicated by his feelings for her.

Milkin's ham-handed references to Cousins's agency contract with Renewal being up for review had put Cousins on notice. Unless he delivered to Milkin what Jayla possessed of her father's research—and including whatever the elusive Waksit could contribute to it—the Cousins public relations agency faced the possibility of losing its major source of income.

"You look lovely," Cousins said when Jayla emerged

from the bedroom wearing the dress she'd bought at Flo's Fashions. "That looks great on you."

"Thank you. Nate, I was thinking about my father's research. Have you finished with it?"

"I know, I know," he said, "I've been dragging my feet. I'll devote part of the day going over it again and return it to you the next time we're together—which, I hope, is soon."

She didn't raise the issue again as they had breakfast in a neighborhood café.

"Will I see you tonight?" she asked.

"Absolutely, but it'll have to be later. I'm having dinner with a possible new client. I'll call you if it isn't too late."

"That sounds fine. I—I enjoyed being together last night."

Jayla got to work the minute she entered the lab at Renewal Pharmaceuticals and immersed herself in the team's new round of experiments. But as had been the case for days, she had trouble concentrating on the task.

While Jayla worked in the lab, Brixton continued hibernating in his office wading through reams of paperwork given to Mac Smith by their new clients. Judging from what he read he'd be busy for a year, which translated into a welcome steady income. He took a break at four, left the office, and went for a walk to clear from his head all the details contained in the material. He thought of his six o'clock date—if you could call it that—with Paula Silver. Maybe it wasn't smart to have agreed to meet her for a drink. It obviously had annoyed Flo, and he'd learned early in their on-again, off-again relationship that it was prudent to avoid such situations. Too, he wasn't in the mood for a conversation with the former actress after she'd had a snootful of booze. Judging from their telephone conversation she'd gotten an early start on her imbibing. Hopefully he could limit it to one drink, cut ties with her, wish her well—which he'd sincerely mean—and escape.

When he walked back into his office Mrs. Warden said that Mr. Sayers was on the line.

"I know," Brixton said when he picked up the phone in his office, "Senator Ronald Gillespie has sent a firing squad after you."

"No such luck," Sayers said. "If he did I'd have a great follow-up piece. The local press has picked up on it, calling Gillespie's wife and Eric Morrison's wife in search of pithy quotes. One of my primary sources tells me that the senator is fleeing Washington for some sunny island *without* his Mrs."

"You're nothing but a home wrecker," Brixton said.

"The truth shall always prevail. And how are you. Robert?"

"I'm pretty damn good. Mac Smith has landed us a lucrative new client, which means the rent will be paid on time for at least a year, and Flo will be proud of me. Doesn't get better than that."

"And have you communed with the former actress, Ms. Silver, again?"

"As a matter of fact we're having drinks tonight."

"Ah hah! I don't imagine that Lady Flo is overjoyed with that."

"Why should she mind? Flo is a worldly woman. Besides, she trusts me implicitly."

"You're a lucky man, Robert."

"I already figured that out. By the way, now that your piece has run you owe me that other thousand."

"Stop by anytime, my friend. You'll be pleased to know that I now brew *real* coffee."

"There's hope yet."

Eugene Waksit slept late that morning at the Holiday Inn and had to tell the chambermaid to come back to clean the room. He awoke with the same thought he'd had when finally falling asleep, that he had to make his move with Jayla. He cursed himself for having wasted so much time since arriving in Washington. Pursuing the moron Eric Morrison had been a huge mistake. He'd squandered time and energy trying to persuade Morrison that what he possessed would revolutionize the pharmaceutical industry, and he wasn't the least bit surprised, or sad, that the lobbyist had been killed.

He stood in the bathroom and observed himself in the mirror. The trip to Washington had taken a toll on him physically. He'd allowed his hair to grow longer than he liked, and the stubble on his chain testified to having forgotten to shave the previous day. He wanted to look his best when seeing Jayla. There was no doubt in his mind that she'd always wanted to have an affair with him, and it was only his reticence that had kept it from happening. As he stepped into the shower he envisioned her fending off Washington's weak-kneed young men, and thinking of him—wanting to rekindle their relationship. They were kindred spirits, no question about that. They shared a common heritage in Papua New Guinea; that sort of bond couldn't be broken.

Showered and dressed, he took his briefcase with him to a barbershop and had his hair trimmed, and indulged in a shave, enjoying the warm towel the barber draped over his face. Back in his room he applied a liberal dose of Cuba Black cologne and took a final check of his appearance. Satisfied, he left the hotel, got in his rental car, and drove to a street near Renewal Pharmaceuticals where he parked. He'd written on a lined yellow legal pad some of the things he would say when he called. After a few minutes of drawing deep breaths he punched into his cell phone Jayla's work number. A man answered.

"I'm calling for Ms. King," Waksit said.

He heard the man say, "Jayla, it's for you."

"Hello?"

"Hello, Jayla," Waksit said in exaggerated friendliness. "It's Eugene."

She didn't respond immediately. When she did she asked, "Where are you calling from?"

"Right here in Washington, D.C. I told you I'd call again."

"Yes, I—Eugene, you've caught me at a bad time. I'm working and—"

"Of course you are," he said, maintaining his upbeat tone. "You're working to come up with a better pain reliever." He glanced at what he'd written. "But you and I already have a better pain reliever, thanks to your father. It's really important that we get together as soon as possible and put together a plan to sell it."

"Eugene, I—"

"How about this?" he said. "Let's have dinner together, just the two of us. You pick the spot, someplace quiet where we can talk. My treat, Jayla. It'll be my pleasure."

"I'm busy," she said, glancing about the lab to see whether anyone was eavesdropping on the conversation.

"I'm sure you are, Jayla, but never too busy to have dinner with me. We go back together a long way, Jayla." Another glance at the legal pad. "We come from the same roots, you and me. I'll tell you, Jayla, it would be a fitting tribute to your wonderful father if we joined forces, joined hands, and brought the fruits of his groundbreaking work to the world. What do you say? Dinner?"

"No," she said firmly. "I'm busy tonight."

His voice changed; it took on a harder edge. "Busy with what, that guy you're seeing?"

"What guy? How do you know who I'm seeing?"

"I know a lot of things, Jayla. Most of all I know that you owe your father this, and I'm the one who can make it work. He left me his research and—"

"No, he did not!" she said loudly, causing co-workers in the lab to look at her. "You stole his research and you won't get away with it."

He softened his tone. "Jayla, listen to me," he said, working to control his trembling. "We have to work together. It's only right. Look, I don't need you. I mean, I've had some real serious talks with big names in the pharmaceutical industry. I can sell the research to any one of them like that." He snapped his fingers. "But I'm willing to share the spoils with you. That's fair, isn't it? I don't have to but you're his daughter and—"

The sound of the phone on her end being slammed down reverberated in his ear. He stared at the dead cell phone and swore under his breath. His hands shook, and he worked his mouth as though chewing on something unpleasant.

Jayla, too, shook as she leaned against a lab table.

"You okay?" a colleague asked.

"Yes, I'm okay," she said.

"What was *that* all about?" another co-worker asked.

"Excuse me," Jayla said and walked from the room. She went to the ladies' room, where she leaned on a sink and wept. She remained there until another woman came in and asked if she could do anything.

"No, thank you," Jayla said, managing a smile.

"Why don't you go home?" the woman, who knew about Jayla's father's murder, said. "You still have a lot to get over."

"I'll be fine," Jayla said. "Just a meltdown. Happens now and again."

She splashed cold water on her face, reapplied lipstick, thanked the woman again, and returned to her lab. "Nothing to worry about," she told her co-workers through a smile. "Back to work."

She remained working in the lab after the others had left, focusing on the experiment she was working on. At six her cell phone sounded. It was Flo Combes calling from her Georgetown shop.

"Hope I'm not interrupting an important medical breakthrough," Flo said.

"It should only be so," Jayla replied.

"Have plans for tonight?"

"No. Nate is—you met him. Nate Cousins—Nate is having dinner with a potential client."

"Hope he lands him. This is my late night at the shop and I thought you might like to swing by and take a look at a new delivery I just received. My designer in California has come up with some really beautiful designs. I usually have dinner delivered when I'm here late. How about joining me? There's this little Chinese restaurant that makes wonderful hot-and-sour soup, General Tso's chicken, and moo goo gai pan. It's been a slow day and I'd enjoy the company."

"I'd love it," said Jayla.

"Great. I'll hold off ordering until you get here. I have their menu. And, I have a bottle of lovely Chardonnay in the fridge."

"You certainly know how to tempt someone."

"That's what Robert says."

"Will he be joining us?"

"No," Flo said. "He's out on a date with a beautiful former movie actress."

Jayla wasn't sure how to respond.

"Strictly business," Flo said. "He'll probably swing by later. See you at seven?"

"I'll be there," Jayla said.

Cousins called as Jayla was tidying up the lab and she told him where she'd be. She left the building, said good night to the night security guard, got in her car, and pulled out of the employee parking lot. As she headed for Georgetown, she didn't see Waksit, who'd been parked on the street and who fell in behind her.

CHAPTER

42

The moment Paula Silver opened the door for Brixton he knew that she'd continued drinking after their phone conversation. She was drunk, hopelessly so. She looked at him through watery eyes and smiled; lipstick that had been applied haphazardly gave her a clownish appearance. She wore a white blouse mostly unbuttoned; there was no bra to contain her bosom. Her yellow skirt was stained, and looked to him to be on backward.

"Hi," Brixton said.

She seemed flustered, didn't know whether to return the greeting and invite him in, or slam the door in his face. She finally said, "Come on in."

Her apartment mirrored her personal disarray. Clothing was strewn on a sofa and chairs. Two watercolors of bucolic scenes hung crookedly on a wall. A bottle of whiskey sat on a coffee table along with a pile of newspapers and magazines. Brixton noticed two large suitcases near a door leading to the bedroom.

Paula walked on unsteady legs to the kitchen. She returned with a plate on which she'd piled crackers, some of them broken into small pieces.

"Sit down," she slurred, pointing to the couch that was covered with her clothing.

"Are we going out?" Brixton asked.

"Out? Oh, for a drink and dinner. Have a drink here." She picked up the almost empty bottle of bourbon from the coffee table and handed it to Brixton. She stumbled into him and he kept her from falling.

"Look," he said, "maybe we should do this another time, get together when you're—when you're feeling better."

"I feel fine," she said, and pressed her lips to his.

He gently disengaged.

"We're writing a book together," she said as though talking to an unseen person. "That'll serve him right, the bastard."

"Morrison?"

"You bet your ass," she said. "We'll make a fortune. How about *that*?"

She took the bottle from him and tried to pour what was left into a glass that already contained bourbon, but she missed and the whiskey went on the carpet. She giggled and fell into the clothes on the couch. "What are you standing there for?" she said. "Come here."

Brixton faced a dilemma.

On the one hand he wanted to escape, to leave the apartment and the drunken former B-movie actress. But he wondered if leaving her in this condition was responsible. In her present state she was capable of hurting herself. Maybe she'll pass out, he thought, fall asleep and wake up in the morning with a world-class hangover. It wouldn't be the first time he'd seen drunks end up that way. At the same time he didn't want to hang out long enough to see it happen.

She stretched her arms out and again invited him to join her on the pile of clothing.

"I have to go," he said.

"Hey, what's going on?" she said. "We're writing a book together. Come on, let's get started." She tried to stand but her legs wouldn't cooperate.

Brixton went to her and took her hand. "How about you go to bed, Paula? We'll get together another time."

Her expression hardened. She struggled to get up, finally made it with help from him, and staggered in the direction of the kitchen. Brixton saw her start to topple and made a move to grab her, but he was too late. She crashed to the floor, her head making solid contact with the door jamb. Brixton looked down and saw blood seep from a long gash on the side of her head.

"Paula," he said. "Wake up."

She was out cold.

Now, there wasn't a decision to be made. He called 911 on his cell and told the dispatcher of the situation.

"Somebody will be there shortly," the woman said.

Ten minutes later two EMTs and a uniformed police officer arrived. While the EMTs positioned her on a gurney, the office took a statement from Brixton, and it quickly became obvious to him that the cop suspected foul play.

"She's drunk, fell, and hit her head on the door jamb," Brixton said.

The officer inspected the door jamb. There was no sign of blood.

"You don't always start bleeding right away," Brixton said.

"You'll have to come with me," the officer said.

"Why? I didn't do anything."

The cop's hard look told Brixton that there wasn't any sense in arguing with him.

"I didn't say you did, sir, but the hospital will need information from you about your wife."

"My wife? She's not my wife. She's a friend, a former movie actress."

The cop's sober expression perked up. "She was in the movies?"

"Yeah."

The EMTs rolled the gurney out the door.

"Let's go, sir," the officer said.

Brixton sighed. "Mind if I make a call first?"

"No, it's okay."

He called Flo at the shop.

"I'm in a situation here with Paula Silver and—"

"A situation? What sort of situation?"

Brixton tried to explain but did a poor job of it.

"You're at her apartment? She's drunk? You're going to the hospital with her?"

"That's about it," he said. "I'll be more specific when I see you."

"Jayla King's coming to the shop for dinner."

"That's nice. I'll see you there."

The ER at the hospital was busy, but Paula was seen quickly. By this time she'd awakened and babbled incoherently. Brixton explained to the physician what had occurred.

"That's a nasty gash on her head," the doctor said.

"Yeah, well, she fell pretty hard against the door jamb."

Brixton wasn't sure whether the physician believed it or not, but at this juncture he didn't care.

"Will you be our contact?" Brixton was asked.

"She doesn't have anybody here in D.C. that I know of," he said. "I suppose you can call me." He gave his contact information and was told by the cop that he could go. As he was leaving the ER a young man intercepted him. "Aren't you Robert Brixton?" he said.

"Who are you?" Brixton asked.

"Joel Gibbons, *Washington Post*. You brought that lady in."

"That's right. You see—"

"Who is she?"

She's—she's a very nice lady who's had some hard knocks in her life. I'm sure she'll be glad to talk to you. Have a nice night."

The reporter threw a few questions at him but Brixton ignored them and walked away. *That's all I need,* he thought, *to be in the paper again.*

He hailed a taxi to take him to where he'd parked his car near Paula's apartment. Once there he called Flo. "I just left the hospital," he said. "They've admitted her. I gave the hospital my number as her contact."

"And you're all right?" Flo asked.

"Yeah, I'm fine."

"Jayla is here. We're ordering in Chinese. Do you want me to order something for you?"

"I'll nibble on whatever you two order."

Flo ignored the comment. Brixton was big on nibbling other people's food. She'd order what she knew he liked, ribs and shrimp fried rice.

As he drove to Flo's Fashions he came to the realization that the incident with Paula Silver had shaken him. He pulled up in front of a restaurant that he and Flo often frequented, went inside, sat at the bar, and ordered a martini. Flo had Jayla to keep her company and would probably, hopefully, be busy with customers. She wouldn't miss him for the half hour it took to enjoy a quiet drink.

Waksit had seen Jayla park in an outdoor lot a block away from Flo's Fashions, walk to the shop, and go in. He circled the block once before finding a metered space across from the store where he sat, his attention focused on the door in which an OPEN sign hung. He reasoned that she was shopping and would soon emerge. A meter maid approached. Waksit got out and fed his meter. She passed, and he debated what to do. He felt exposed standing by his car—he didn't want Jayla to see him—and got back behind the wheel.

A half hour passed. Waksit was tense; he opened the briefcase on the passenger seat and confirmed, for the fourth time, that it contained Dr. King's research findings. Another ten minutes passed. During the time he'd been there only two people had entered the shop, a man and woman. They didn't stay long and came out empty-handed.

What was Jayla doing in there? When would she exit the store?

A car pulled up in front of the shop. The driver, a young Asian man, activated the emergency lights on the vehicle, got out, and disappeared inside the store carrying two brown bags. He emerged seconds later, hopped in his car, and drove away.

Waksit waited for Jayla to reappear until he could no longer sit idly by. He got out of his car, briefcase in hand, and crossed the street, standing to the side of Flo's Fashions' front window. He leaned forward to look inside and saw no one.

Where was Jayla? Where was the store's owner?

Waksit couldn't see where Jayla and Flo sat at a small table in the rear of the shop. Flo had laid out disposable plates, utensils, and paper napkins.

"Are you sure I can't pay my share for dinner?" Jayla asked.

"Absolutely not," Flo replied, opening the white food containers and inserting serving spoons in them. "Eat up and enjoy before another customer comes in. I love it when the shop is busy, but I also appreciate when it's quiet. After we eat I'll show you the new arrivals. You'll love them."

Flo had told Jayla of Robert's call and the situation he'd found himself in. She couldn't help but laugh. "Leave it to Robert to find himself in another mess. He seems drawn to trouble like a moth to a summer candle. I could kill him sometimes but—"

Her thought was interrupted by the chime announcing that a customer had come through the door. "Excuse me," she said, getting up from the table and skirting the portable room divider that separated the front of the shop from the back rooms.

"Welcome," Flo said to Waksit, who stood just inside the door. She flashed a smile. "Can I help you with something, or just browsing?" She noticed the briefcase he carried; probably on his way home from work. She also took note that he appeared to be nervous, his eyes darting left and right.

"I'm here to see Jayla," he said.

Flo hadn't expected that reply.

"Oh, you're a friend of Jayla's," she said. "She's—"

Waksit locked the door behind him.

"Excuse me," Flo said, "but—"

Waksit also turned the OPEN sign around so that CLOSED appeared in the door.

"What are you doing?" Flo demanded, taking steps toward him.

"I want to see Jayla," Waksit said.

Jayla had heard the exchange and appeared from behind the room divider.

"Eugene!" she said.

Not immediately connecting the name to Jayla's father's assistant, Flo went to push past him to reverse the sign and unlock the door, but Waksit stopped her. He withdrew the switchblade from his pocket and pushed the button, causing the blade to snap open, the stainless steel glittering in the shop's lighting. Flo gasped and stepped back, but Waksit was too quick. Dropping the briefcase to the floor, he grabbed her arm, turned her so that her back was to him, and held the tip of the knife to her neck.

Waksit pressed the knife under Flo's chin and pushed her toward the rear of the shop; Jayla moved with them. Flo could feel Waksit's hot breath on her neck.

"Sit down at the computer," he instructed Jayla. "Bring up the Word menu."

When she had, he began dictating: "I, Jayla King, daughter of Dr. Preston King, do hereby swear that whatever research my father did to find a more effective painkiller is now the property of his loyal assistant, Mr. Eugene Waksit, and I have no claim on it whatsoever and forever." Jayla thought he was finished, but he added: "Dr. King left all his research results to me, Eugene Waksit, his loyal assistant."

"Print it!" he commanded.

Suddenly, he turned his attention to a noise from in front of the shop; a car had stopped suddenly and screeched to a halt.

The letter came out of the printer. Jayla removed it from the tray, signed it, and handed it to Waksit. "You have what you want, Eugene," she said. "Please go and leave us alone. There's nothing further to be gained by staying here."

"Oh, I'm going to leave all right—after I'm sure you won't go to the police."

After paying his tab, Brixton had driven to Georgetown where he found a metered spot two cars removed from where Waksit had parked. After feeding the meter he crossed the street and turned the handle on the door. It was locked. Then he saw the CLOSED sign. It was too early for Flo to have closed the shop and gone home. Besides, she wouldn't have done that without having called him. He peered through the glass in the door. He saw no one, but the lights were all on. His antenna went up. Something was wrong. He was poised to knock but an instinct told him that it was the wrong thing to do.

Checking that his handgun was under his belt, he circled around behind the building and stood in the alley outside the rear door. He tried the lock. It, too, was locked. He pulled out his cell phone and dialed the number for the shop. He heard it ring inside, but no one picked up. He placed his ear to the door and heard the drone of a male voice, the words muffled.

As Brixton pondered the situation, Nate Cousins, whose dinner with the prospective client had ended early, walked up to the shop's front door and tried it. Locked. Jayla had said that Flo closed at nine. It was just a few minutes past eight. He knocked, loudly.

Inside, Flo and Jayla heard the banging on the door. So did Waksit. His eyes widened and he swung the switchblade back and forth as though to cut away the intrusion.

Brixton also heard the loud knocking. He ran from

the alley to the front of the store where he confronted Nate Cousins. "What are you doing here?" he asked.

"Jayla said she'd be here," said Cousins. "What's going on?"

"Whatever it is it's not good," Brixton said. "Look. You keep banging on the door while I go around back again."

"What do I do if—?"

"Just keep knocking."

The incessant rapping on the door further unnerved Waksit. He was gripped with indecision. He thrust the knife at Flo and Jayla as a warning not to do anything foolish, left the office area, and stood amid the multiple racks of women's clothing. He saw a man through the door's glass panes. While he stood frozen, Flo did what Brixton had hoped she would. She ran to the rear door, followed by Jayla, unbolted it, and flung it open.

"What the hell is going on?" Brixton asked, his Sig Sauer in his hand.

"It's Waksit," Jayla said. "He has a knife."

Brixton entered the shop and paused. Cousins continued to beat on the front door. Brixton moved from the rear section of the store to its main sales area where Waksit stood, the knife in his hand, confused by the pounding on the door.

"Hey, Waksit," Brixton said.

Waksit spun around.

"Drop the knife," Brixton said, his pistol aimed at him.

"Who are you?" Waksit said, dropping the knife to the floor.

"Robert Brixton."

Jayla and Flo reentered the shop.

"Call nine-one-one and get some cops here," Brixton said. "And open the door. All that banging is driving me nuts."

43

THREE MONTHS LATER

W elcome back!"
        Mac and Annabel stood at the door to their apartment in the Watergate, hands outstretched to Jayla King and Nate Cousins, who'd just returned from Papua New Guinea.

"It's good to be back," Jayla said.

She and Cousins had traveled together to Port Moresby where Jayla took care of legal matters with her attorney, Elgin Taylor. Her father's house had been sold; the buyer intended to turn the laboratory into a small apartment for an aging relative. Jayla had wanted to pay one last visit to the Sepik River region where her father had planted and cultivated the native plants used in his quest for a better painkiller. The trip had provided Jayla with closure; she'd taken her father's ashes with them and sprinkled them over the plot of land that had meant so much to him. For Cousins, the Sepik River and its lush, forbidding jungle and primitive natives was an eye-opening experience into a culture that existed for him only in movies and *National Geographic*.

Shortly after they'd arrived at the Watergate, Brixton and Flo showed up. The occasion was a brunch that the Smiths had put together for the returning couple.

"Congratulations," Flo said when she and Brixton joined the others on the balcony, referring to the news that Cousins had proposed marriage and that Jayla had accepted.

"Have you set a date?" Mac asked.

"We haven't had time to even think about dates," Cousins said.

"We have another bit of news to share with you," Jayla said.

All eyes went to her.

"I'm leaving Renewal Pharmaceuticals."

"When did you decide that?" Annabel asked.

"I'd been thinking about it ever since my father died. Walt Milkin—he's CEO of Renewal—made up my mind for me. He's a very intelligent man, no question about that. But when he threatened to cancel the contract with Nate's PR agency unless Nate delivered my father's work to him, I decided that he's not a very *nice* man." She turned to Brixton. "But you *are* a very nice man," she said, coming to where he sat and kissing his cheek.

"Robert doesn't handle compliments well," Flo quipped.

"That's because I'm not used to getting them from one unnamed lady."

"Oh, poor baby," Flo said, planting a kiss where Jayla had. "I agree with Jayla. You *are* a very nice man—most of the time."

"You saved our lives," Jayla said.

"Nothing to it," Brixton said in his best modest voice. "Waksit wasn't about to kill anybody. He was a pussy-cat."

"Speaking of Mr. Waksit," Mac said, "I spoke with his attorney today here in Washington, an old friend. I also spoke yesterday with Jayla's attorney, Elgin Taylor, in Port Moresby. He told me of your visit to him, Jayla, and how impressed he was with your demeanor while dealing with so many unpleasant events."

"I spread my father's ashes, the way he would have wanted me to."

"So he said. He also told me that it's the opinion of the local police investigating your father's murder that the fellow who torched and bulldozed your dad's property in Sepik, and who killed your father's native helper, Mr. Tagobe, also killed your dad. His name was Underwood, Paul Underwood if I have it right. Underwood allegedly hanged himself in his cell where he was being held in the Tagobe murder. The police don't necessarily buy that he took his own life, but they don't have solid evidence to the contrary. It's their belief that he was killed by whoever he was working for to keep him quiet."

"Alard Associates," Brixton said.

"Evidently so," Mac said. "Speaking of Alard Associates, the Justice Department, working in conjunction with the local police, has brought criminal charges against Alard Associates and its namesake, George Alard. He was taken into custody yesterday. They're charging him in the Morrison murder. The hit man who knocked out Robert and used his gun to kill Morrison has been apprehended and confessed, and has implicated Alard as the person who ordered the hit."

The conversation shifted subjects as Annabel and Mac laid out the brunch spread—salmon with capers and onion, bagels, cold cuts, with cups of lobster bisque as a starter. It was over dessert that Eugene Waksit was again mentioned.

"You said earlier that you'd spoken with Eugene's attorney here in D.C.," Jayla said to Mac.

"That's right. He's been charged with attempted murder, physical assault, and a variety of other things connected with having held you and Flo at knifepoint."

"He's sick," Jalya said.

"That gives him a pass," Brixton said. "We're too quick to label bad people as sick. Dr. Fowler says that—"

"Who?" Annabel asked.

"Just a friend of mine," Brixton quickly said. "He agrees with me. Besides, the people back in Papua New Guinea don't know for sure that this Underwood character killed your father. "It still might have been Waksit."

"He admitted that he stole my father's research," Jayla said, "but he swears he didn't commit murder."

"That's right," Mac said. "According to his attorney Waksit claims that he came into your father's lab minutes after he'd been stabbed to death, and that his arrival scared off the killer before he could steal anything. Waksit also says that he tried to help your father but that he died almost immediately."

"A nice story," Brixton said.

"One that I tend to believe," said Jayla. "I don't carry any grief for Eugene, but I don't think he's a murderer."

"What about what he almost did to you and Flo?" Brixton asked.

"I think he panicked," Jayla said, "that's all. I don't think he intended to do us any harm. All he wanted was that ridiculous letter he had me type. My father never willed him the research. That was his fantasy, part of his mental illness."

"If you say so," Brixton said.

"What about your father's research?" Annabel asked. "Now that you're leaving your present job will you be taking it with you to wherever you land a new one?"

Jayla looked to Cousins to respond.

"I've just signed up a new pharmaceutical client that's interested in what Jayla's father managed to come up with in his lab. I've discussed with them carrying that research to its next level, and I think they'll agree to that, along with hiring Jayla to spearhead the research."

"I've already spoken with Mac about drafting an employment agreement giving me a fair share of the profits from whatever commercially viable painkiller comes out of it," Jayla said. "It may not amount to anything but it will be exciting to be furthering what my dad had accomplished before he died."

Because it was Washington, D.C., talk eventually turned to politics.

"What do you think of the news about Senator Gillespie?" Flo asked.

"No surprise," Brixton said. "His run for reelection was dead in the water before it ever started."

"I mean about him joining that K Street lobbying group," Flo added.

"At least it wasn't Morrison's," Mac said.

"Business as usual in our nation's capital," Brixton grumbled.

"Robert should go to work for the Chamber of Commerce," Flo said, and they all laughed.

An hour later, after everyone had left, Mac and Annabel enjoyed an hour of solitude on their balcony.

"Robert's been seeing a psychologist," Mac said casually.

"Really? It doesn't seem to have changed him. He's still as cynical as ever."

"No, I see some subtle changes in him. I hope he continues seeing whoever it is. He's been through a lot the past couple of years. I think seeing a shrink is a good decision."

Annabel agreed, then said, "I'm pleased for Jayla and Nate. They make a nice couple." She laughed. "Do you think that if Robert continues to see this psychologist he'll pop the question to Flo?"

"They make a nice couple, too," was Mac's answer. "So do we."

Are you and Flo still talking about getting married?" Dr. John Bradford Fowler asked Brixton weeks later when Brixton sat in his office.

"Yeah, now and then," Brixton said. "Do you think we should?"

Fowler laughed. "That's not for me to say, Robert. It's just that you've been saying especially nice things about her lately."

"Like I said, I've been thinking about it."

"Life is short, Robert," Fowler said.

They spent the rest of the session discussing Brixton's feelings about marrying Flo and about marriage in general. When time was up, Brixton made another appointment before leaving, stopped at a florist and bought bouquets for Flo and Mrs. Warden, delivered Flo's flowers to Flo's Fashions, and went to his office, where he handed the other bouquet to Mrs. Warden.

"That is so sweet," she said, getting up from her desk chair and kissing his cheek.

"Yeah, well, life is short, Mrs. Warden. We have to remember that."

Read on for a preview of

MARGARET TRUMAN'S

ALLIED IN DANGER

▸ DONALD BAIN ◂

Available in February 2018
from Tom Doherty Associates

A FORGE HARDCOVER

1

Robert Brixton and his paramour, Flo Combes, stood with Mac and Annabel Smith in a suite at Washington's iconic Willard Hotel. Brixton had decided that "paramour" was a classy way to refer to Flo rather than "girlfriend" or "sweetie" or "partner." He was too old to have a girlfriend, he felt, and "partner" sounded like they ran a business together. But "paramour" had a nice ring to it, sort of literary. Of course, marrying Flo would solve the question of how to explain their relationship but he wasn't ready for that, nor was Flo sure she wanted to legally commit to the occasionally volatile, mule-headed Brixton. He wasn't known as Robert "Don't Call Me Bobby" Brixton for nothing.

Their attention was focused on the strikingly beautiful woman who'd been encouraged to take center stage by one of a dozen "suits" at the gathering, attorneys of the international law firm of Cale, Watson and Warnowski. Walter Cale waited until conversation had ebbed before saying, "I propose this toast to Elizabeth Sims, our newest partner." He glanced at a note in his hand and added, "Take a look at our other partners and you'll agree that she adds a needed dose of beauty to the firm."

There was laughter. "Here's to Elizabeth—although if

you get to know her well enough she might allow you to call her Liz."

"To Liz," the gathered said in unison as glasses were raised. "To Lizzie," a man who'd had too much to drink slurred.

"Thank you so much," Elizabeth said, lifting her champagne flute.

"She's beautiful," Annabel commented.

"And obviously smart," her husband, Mac, said. "There aren't many female full partners in firms this size."

"It's the law firms that are getting smart offering partnerships to women," Annabel quipped. "They've been missing out on a lot of talent. How is your friend David Portland?" she asked Brixton. "We haven't seen him in a while."

"David's in London," Brixton said. "They call him back frequently to report to his boss. That's why he keeps his flat there. He'll be returning in a few days."

David Portland was a member of the security staff at the British Embassy to the United States on Massachusetts Avenue, N.W., along Washington's famed Embassy Row. He also happened to be the ex-husband of Elizabeth Sims, the attorney at the center of attention that evening.

"Do they find it awkward living in the same city?" Annabel asked.

Brixton chuckled. "No," he said, "David's pretty cool about it. They talk from time to time but not often. He says she wasn't thrilled when he took the job at the embassy and moved here, but they're grown-ups, live busy separate lives, the way it should be. He called me from London. I'll pick him up at the airport."

"It was tragic what happened to his son," Annabel said.

"David's never gotten over it," Brixton said. "Not that you ever do. He told me that he's come up with new information about what happened to Trevor."

"The boy's death goes back a long way, doesn't it?" Smith said.

"Not that long," Brixton said, "maybe two years. David has never been able to let go of it. I understand where he's coming from."

Brixton's empathy was fueled by having lost an adult child of his own, a daughter who was slaughtered in a terrorist bombing in an outdoor café not far from the State Department, where he'd been employed at the time.

"Trevor was Elizabeth's stepson?" Annabel said.

"Right," Brixton said. "David's wife Trevor's birth mother died when he was a little kid, and his grandmother raised him until she died, too, from cancer. He was eight or nine at the time. That's when David met Elizabeth. He'd been bringing up Trevor best he could, considering that his work had him constantly traveling. When he met and married Elizabeth in London she took over the job as Trevor's surrogate mom and continued even after their divorce. David says she was terrific at it."

"How long were they married?" Flo asked.

"A couple of years," Brixton replied. "David is—well, he's tough to get along with at times."

Flo's laugh was wicked. Brixton gave her a stern look. She raised her hand, still laughing. "I didn't say anything," she said, still laughing.

They were interrupted by a tall, angular man with the look of an Ivy League professor. Despite the Harris Tweed jacket with brown leather elbow patches, pale blue button-down shirt, regimental tie, and highly polished ankle-high brown boots, Brixton knew that he didn't spend his days in a classroom. He was Cameron Chambers, a retired Washington, D.C., cop who headed up the law firm's investigative unit and who'd recruited Brixton to augment his full-time staff on an as-needed basis. Brixton had been one of two private detectives in the city who'd signed on as contract employees, available when Chambers needed help on an investigation for a client.

He apologized for breaking into the conversation and said to Brixton, "Spare me a few minutes, Robert?"

Brixton followed him to an unpopulated corner of the lavish suite. "What's up?" he asked.

Chambers looked across the room to where Elizabeth chatted happily with other attorneys. "She's a knockout, isn't she?" he said.

"No argument from me."

"I understand that you're friends with her ex," Chambers said.

"We know each other."

"You stay in contact with him now that he lives here in D.C.?"

"We're friends, only we don't get to spend much time together," Brixton said. "Why?"

"His reputation is—well, let's just say that he has a penchant for making trouble."

Chambers's pinched-nose way of speaking grated on Brixton. Chambers had never been a cop who'd dirtied his hands working cases, had never walked the mean streets of Washington's less genteel neighborhoods. A Maryland native, he'd gone off to college at Dartmouth, where he received a degree in sociology. Upon returning home he was pursued to help flesh out a growing intelligence unit within the Washington PD and eagerly accepted the job. He went on to get his Master's Degree in psychology from Georgetown University under MPD's tuition assistance program, and after six years was tapped to run the intelligence unit, which he did until his retirement. Although not a lawyer, he had the self-assuredness of one, a man without any doubts about his views and conclusions. He'd been married twice and had two sons by his first wife, one of whom lived in Los Angeles, the other in Boston. His second marriage fell apart after a brief run.

"Making trouble?" Brixton said. "What sort of trouble?"

"I've done some checking on him, Robert. He wasn't

a stranger to getting into scrapes around the globe, personal *and* legal."

Brixton laughed away the comment. "You're talking past tense," he said. "David *was* on the wild side when he was working as a security pro for hire, but those days are behind him. You don't get hired by the British Embassy unless your background check comes up clean."

"That may be true, Robert, but my sources tell me that he enjoys sticking his nose in where it doesn't belong."

"I don't follow," Brixton said, although he thought he knew where Chambers was going with it.

While Portland hadn't been specific when he'd called, he did say that he'd been doing some "nosing around" into XCAL Oil, the company for whom Trevor's geological surveying firm had been working in Africa at the time of his death. XCAL was Cale, Watson and Warnowski's biggest client, generating almost half of the firm's sizable income. And Elizabeth Sims, who'd gone back to using her maiden name following her divorce from Portland, was the lead attorney on the XCAL account. A small world indeed.

"I received a call from London," Chambers said. "It seems that Mr. Portland has been asking questions concerning XCAL's possible involvement with his son's unfortunate demise."

Portland had shared what had happened to his son with Brixton over many dinners, lunches, and drinks. After receiving a degree from West Virginia University in geological surveying, the young man had gone to work for Sealcom, a geological survey company working in the Niger Delta under contract with XCAL.

"All I'm suggesting, Robert, is that if you hear anything along the lines of what I've just alluded to you let me know," Chambers said.

"Sure," Brixton said, anxious for the conversation to be over.

"That would be helpful, Robert, very helpful. I see

that your glass is empty. Mustn't ever allow that to happen, must we?" He slapped Brixton on the back and walked away.

Brixton watched Chambers move gracefully through the crowd in the direction of Elizabeth Sims. Chambers was a smooth operator, no doubt about that. Washington, D.C., teemed with smooth operators and Brixton tried to avoid them whenever possible.

"What do you say we get out of here?" Flo said after Brixton had rejoined her and Annabel.

Annabel's husband, Mac, had drifted away to speak with an attorney for CW&W whom he knew from practicing law in Washington. Smith, like Brixton and Portland, had also lost a child, a son, who'd perished along with his mother in a crash on the Beltway years before he'd met Annabel. That event, and the relatively light sentence the drunk driver of the other car received, had shaken Mac's faith in the law, at least as a practitioner. He closed his office and became professor of law at George Washington University, where he stayed until recently when he again put out his shingle and reentered the combative world of trial advocacy. Annabel, too, had been an attorney when she and Mac met but had abandoned her matrimonial law practice to open a successful pre-Columbian art gallery in Georgetown.

"I thought you'd never ask," Brixton said to Flo.

"You two run along," Annabel said. "I have a feeling that Mac is in for a long conversation."

Flo, who mirrored Brixton's disdain for stuffy D.C. cocktail parties—Washington parties of any sort for that matter, especially those populated by lawyers and politicians—happily took Brixton's arm as they headed for the door. He considered seeking out Chambers to say good night but decided to not bother despite knowing that it would have been politically correct. The retainer with the law firm's head of investigations would pay plenty of bills.

They did stop to congratulate Elizabeth, who graciously

accepted their good wishes. She, of course, was aware that Brixton and her former husband were friends, and her infrequent conversations with Brixton were always with that knowledge and the restraints it placed on what was said.

Once back in their apartment on Capitol Hill, Brixton and Flo fortified the party's finger food with bowls of pasta and a salad.

"I get the feeling that you don't particularly like Mr. Chambers," Flo commented after they'd changed into pajamas and sat in front of the television, their meals on folding TV tables.

"He's a type," Brixton muttered.

"Everyone's a type," she said.

"Right, but there's good types and bad types."

"And he's a bad type?"

"Maybe he falls somewhere in between," was Brixton's response. He filled her in on the conversation he'd had with Chambers at the party.

"I'm glad you didn't get into an argument with him," Flo said, speaking from experience. Brixton's fuse was notoriously short, especially when it came to someone like Cameron Chambers. "It was good of Mac to set you up with him," she added. "We can use the money."

"Yeah, I know, it's a good deal getting paid to be on tap in case they want something from me. With any luck they won't."

As they carried their empty plates to the kitchen Brixton said, "David's due back in town in a few days." He recounted what Portland had said during his phone call from London.

Flo winced as she filled the dishwasher. "Your friendship with David puts you in an awkward position with Chambers," she said.

"Chambers is just blowing smoke," Brixton replied. "David's been around, working all those security jobs in every corner of the globe. So maybe he got into a few hassles along the way. Hell, so have I."

He didn't add that he knew of a few assignments that Portland had undertaken over the years as a soldier of fortune that resulted in his taking of a life in order to save his own. He ended his defense of Portland with, "David's a straight shooter."

"Like you," Flo said.

He put his arm around her. "I accept the compliment," he said. "You know, I kept wondering while we were at the party with all those high-paid lawyers whether the rumors are true about the law firm."

"What rumors?"

"About them helping launder money that some Nigerian scam artists raise over the Internet from suckers who buy their pitch."

"Where did you hear that?" she asked.

"From one of Mac's clients whose father got scammed by the Nigerians. Mac's trying to come up with a legal path for the son to take, but there's not much he can do. Enough about that. Let's catch a movie."

They returned to the couch and debated which film to watch. After coming to a consensus they ordered their choice with a few clicks of the remote. As the opening credits crawled down the screen they settled back for another evening of domestic bliss, Robert "Don't Call Me Bobby" Brixton and his paramour, Flo Combes.

2

Brixton drove to Dulles Airport to meet David Portland's flight from London.

They'd first met a year ago when Portland arrived in D.C. as part of a security detail for an Arab potentate who was to meet with the American president in an attempt to salvage a long-standing rift between their countries. Brixton had watched a press conference with the two leaders on television and came to the conclusion that with all the empty talk of human rights and an equitable justice system, the only thing that mattered was oil. We needed it; the Arabs had it. Business as usual. End of any cozy fireside chat.

Portland had bailed out of the assignment when the Arab leader left Washington. The money was good and the assignment easy, and he could have continued working for the security firm that had the contract to keep the potentate and his sizable entourage safe. But he'd had enough of the hypocritical robed dictator and his circle of so-called advisors, and eagerly jumped ship.

Timing had been right. Portland had been accepted into a government-sponsored program that brought British security professionals to the United States for an intensive hands-on two-week CIA-sponsored boot camp at which they were immersed in the latest anti-terrorist techniques. The camp was held at the Pentagon's training grounds in Virginia, and participants were housed in a nearby hotel.

Brixton and Portland had met in a D.C. bar the second night of Portland's training. Both men were alone. Brixton was in a foul mood. Portland's outlook wasn't any brighter.

"You from here?" Portland asked.

"Not originally. I'm from New York. Where are you from?"

"London."

"Never been there."

"You should visit someday," Portland said. "London has its charms, or so the tourist guidebooks say."

They drank before Portland asked what Brixton did for a living.

"I'm a private investigator," Brixton said. "You?"

"Security," Portland said. "I hire out to security companies around the world."

"Sounds a little like what I do," said Brixton. "Hiring out, I mean."

By the time they were on their second drinks they'd bonded, at least professionally. It was when Portland mentioned that he'd had a son who'd been murdered in Nigeria that Brixton shelved his previous reluctance to prolong the conversation.

"I lost a daughter to a terrorist attack here in D.C.," he said.

"How dreadful."

"You ever find out who killed your son?" Brixton asked.

"Depends on who you talk to. My son Trevor was in the Niger Delta with a geological survey company doing work for XCAL Oil. He could have gone elsewhere with a different company, but he chose Nigeria. Turned out to be a bad choice."

"How did you find out?" Brixton asked.

Portland snorted. "I received a call from the CEO of the security firm hired to protect workers at XCAL. The guy is a pompous type, the kind of chap who keeps clearing his throat while he talks. He told me that Trevor had been killed, his body discovered by someone from SureSafe."

"The security firm?"

"That's right. He said that Trevor had been killed by rebels. He called them 'savages,' which I suppose they are if they slaughtered a peaceful young man just doing his job. Trevor was an easy target for those rebels who are fighting XCAL's rape of their land, sucking out the oil and raking in millions in profits while the native population starves. What a bloody evil world."

"Must have been a tough call to take," Brixton offered.

"Like a knife to the gut."

"I didn't learn about my kid's murder from a phone call," Brixton said. "I was there with her when some young Muslim woman blew herself up and killed a dozen other people, including Janet."

"How did you—?"

"Avoid getting killed, too? I'd walked out of the café just before it happened and tried to get Janet to come with me. I had a feeling, you know, a hunch that something wasn't right. Janet stayed behind for a moment." Brixton swallowed hard. "I wish it had been me." He downed what was left in his glass.

"At least you know what *really* happened to your daughter," Portland said.

"You don't buy that your son was killed by rebels?"

"I had to buy it," said Portland. "I had no information to counter it." He paused. "But I've never fully accepted it."

They were silent.

"Another drink?" Portland asked.

"No. You have dinner plans?"

"No. You? You have a missus?"

Brixton managed a laugh. "I have what they call a 'significant other.' What yahoo came up with *that* term? At the moment we're on the outs. She's gone back to New York."

"Sorry."

"It happens. Yeah, let's grab dinner. You can tell me what the CIA is teaching you about fighting terrorists."

"So far nothing I didn't already know," Portland said. "Dinner sounds good."

Their friendship was cemented that night over drinks and food, and lots of talk about their parallel experiences. Both worked in risky businesses that put their lives on the line, and often resulted in wondering when the next check would arrive. Both had lost a precious child under barbaric circumstances. And both were divorced men.

Brixton's ex-wife, Marylee, had come into his life when he was a uniformed cop in Washington years earlier, and had delivered two daughters during their brief fling as a married couple. Portland's former wife, Elizabeth, who had almost single-handedly raised his son, Trevor, as his stepmother despite her abbreviated marriage to Portland, was now a top lawyer at a prestigious Washington law firm with offices around the world. Ironically, she was the lead attorney for the firm's biggest client, XCAL, the same multinational oil company that had employed the security firm whose CEO had broken the news of Trevor's death to his father.

Lots in common.